GW00691891

Rose Edmunds gained a degree in mathematics at the University of Sussex and a doctorate from Cardiff University, before qualifying as a chartered accountant and embarking on a successful career in professional services. She worked for Arthur Andersen and Grant Thornton, before being headhunted to join Deloitte as a partner. In 2007, after 20 years in the business, she decided to jump off the corporate hamster wheel and focus all her energy on writing commercial thrillers. Rose lives in Brighton with her husband, David.

To Ros

Hope you enjoy this!

NEVER SAY SORRY

Rose Edmunds
Haywards Heath
21/06/12

Rose Edmunds

Book Guild Publishing
Sussex, England

First published in Great Britain in 2012 by
The Book Guild Ltd
Pavilion View
19 New Road
Brighton, BN1 1UF

Copyright © Rose Edmunds 2012

The right of Rose Edmunds to be identified as the author of
this work has been asserted by her in accordance with the
Copyright, Designs and Patents Act 1988.

All rights reserved. No part of this publication may be
reproduced, transmitted, or stored in a retrieval system, in any
form or by any means, without permission in writing from the
publisher, nor be otherwise circulated in any form of binding or
cover other than that in which it is published and without a
similar condition being imposed on the subsequent purchaser.

All characters in this publication are fictitious and any resemblance
to real people, alive or dead, is purely coincidental.

Typesetting in Baskerville by
Keyboard Services, Luton, Bedfordshire

Printed in Great Britain by
CPI Group (UK) Ltd, Croydon, CR0 4YY

A catalogue record for this book is available from
The British Library

ISBN 978 1 84624 652 4

To David and Peter

1

Hugo stood, mesmerised by the gun pointing towards him, deciding whether to stay put or run. Cold sweat dripped from his brow. It didn't much matter – either way he'd had it.

Imminent death brought a stark mental clarity. He was unemployed, had maxed out his credit cards and been written off as a crazed drug addict. Yet all these trivial problems were soluble given time – unlike this new crisis. For Hugo, time had run out.

He cast around wildly for an escape – the car parked 50 yards away might as well have been on the other side of the world. Even if he reached it, the keys wouldn't be in the ignition.

Claudia caught his eye – an understanding flashed between them. One gun couldn't shoot in two places at the same time – if they fled in opposite directions, one of them might make it out of range.

Hugo had it badly wrong. Overcoming the weakness in his legs, he bolted, zigzagging to confuse their assailant. A volley of shots rang out, but Claudia stood still, screaming horribly – the last sound Hugo would ever hear.

He'd got that wrong as well. He heard the final gunshot. And as the thick black velvet enveloped him, he realised how pointless it had all been.

2

Bill Gordon looked back with nostalgia to the days of manual typewriters, fuggy newsrooms and long liquid lunches at El Vino in Fleet Street. Even after twenty years, he still felt uneasy amid the flickering TV screens and ornamental pot plants of the *Daily Globe*'s Canary Wharf headquarters.

That was not the worst of it. The sterile offices were merely the outward sign of a puritanical contagion which saw lunchtime drinking demonised, smokers banished and expense accounts trimmed. All in all, the world had become a miserable place.

Yet in this joyless wilderness, one pleasure remained. Bill could still torment his staff – and he did, without mercy.

Most of them were too scared to complain, but Claudia Knight had different reasons for keeping quiet. She and Bill played a private game and they both understood the rules. If she protested, the whole dynamics of the game would shift – and not in her favour.

The newsroom was laid out in a 'hub and spoke' design, with editors presiding over the hub and lesser mortals along the spokes. According to Globe Media's expensive management consultants, this layout had many logistical advantages. One of the advantages they had not foreseen was the opportunity it gave Claudia to assess Bill's mood as he approached. That morning, as he marched purposefully towards her, she reckoned she was in for nothing more damaging than some good-humoured repartee.

'Aren't you a bit hot and sweaty in those things?' was his opening gambit, as he eyed her purple leather leggings.

'Well, I'm not taking them off,' she retorted. 'Anyway, leather's a natural fabric – it breathes.'

'But suppose I asked you to interview the CEO of a major corporation – how would he feel about you showing up looking like that?'

'You never know,' said Claudia with a winning smile. 'It might make his day. Anyway, why lay into me? I'm better dressed than almost anyone else in this place.'

At least she tried to look different, dreadlocks and all – the others were plain scruffy. And her trump card was a navy suit hanging in the locker room.

'That's debatable,' he said. 'But no matter, because I'm sending you somewhere where your clothes won't be out of place at all.'

Claudia raised her eyebrows as he paused for effect.

'Oh yes?'

'I'm assigning you to cover a naked speed-dating event.'

Bill's chortling segued into the spasm of a smoker's cough as the rest of the team applauded.

'Great – a real exposé,' Claudia said, folding her arms in a mock defiant pose.

She waited for the hoots of derision to die down before continuing.

'So – now you've literally made me the butt of everyone's jokes, are you going to tell me what I'm really doing?'

Claudia's conviction that it was a wind-up wavered as she spotted a hint of hesitation in the veteran newsman's eyes. Whatever he had in mind, she wasn't likely to enjoy it.

'It's next Friday,' he said, scratching the back of his neck. 'And it actually is a speed-dating event, but don't worry – you'll be able to keep those hideous clothes on.' He grinned, exposing a mouthful of brown teeth.

'Doesn't sound like a cool story to me. There must be hundreds of speed-dating events in London, every night.'

'This one's different. It's an attempt at the world record for the largest speed-dating event ever in one venue – more than three thousand people. You'll be there – a part of this historic event, soaking up the drama, the atmosphere, telling the story.'

'OK, you can cut out the hard sell. It still sounds crap.'

'It's what you make it, sweetie. Find the killer angle that'll set your story apart from everyone else's. And don't worry, I've already registered you to participate.'

'Oh – you mean you've got me a press pass?'

'No – I've registered you to participate.'

Claudia groaned. It might have been fun to wander around, charge up a few drinks, natter to a few people. Participation put a whole different complexion on the assignment.

'What – you mean I have to chat up a load of guys?'

'Is that so difficult? Since when were you such a shrinking violet?'

'Suppose I've other plans?'

'Cancel them.'

Claudia frowned.

'Cheer up, Goldilocks – you might even pull.' He winked at her and smiled lasciviously. She winked back, although the leathery old relic would have run a mile if she'd really tried to hit on him.

'You could always come with me,' she said.

'I wouldn't want to cramp your style.'

If she kicked up a fuss and refused to go, she'd only provoke a snide comment about feisty Jamaican women. Why hand him the opportunity on a plate?

'It's fine – I'll go,' she said nonchalantly.

'You mean you're happy about it?' Bill didn't even try to conceal his surprise.

4

'I said it was fine, didn't I?'

'So I'm not about to get an earful about how this isn't real news, or any pious claptrap about how you became a journalist to alert people to important issues?'

'No – we've done that one to death now.'

'We did it to death at your interview, Goldilocks. Not that it would have mattered what you said, seeing as we were down on our Caribbean quota for the month.'

He'd managed to get his dig in anyway. He let the comment hang there, waiting for a response. Well, she wouldn't give him the satisfaction.

'Any particular angle you're looking for?' she asked instead.

'No, but I'm sure you'll come up with something.'

'I'm sure I will too.' She kept her face poker straight, leaving Bill under no illusions – he would not succeed in riling her today. Apparently accepting defeat, he retreated to the hub.

'You should report him to HR, love,' advised one of the secretaries when he was safely out of the way. 'The man's a sexist, racist pig and you shouldn't let him get away with it.'

'No way,' said Claudia. 'Bill's no racist, no sexist either – he's playing a game.'

The secretary looked at Claudia, puzzled. She didn't get it at all.

3

Brad Hillman, global CEO of BEP Pharmaceuticals, sat
in his pristine but soulless office in New Jersey trawling
through the morning's snail mail. The letter marked
'Addressee only' in spidery handwriting stood out from
the junk mail shots and circulars. He studied the envelope
– the return address was a Mr G. Hubbard, London,
England.

Dear Mr Hillman,
Although it is unlikely you will recognise my name, I
was employed by your company in R & D (oncology)
from 1978 to 1990, when I retired and moved back
to England.
For the last couple of years of my employment I
reported to Edgar Morrison, who I understand is still
in situ as global head of R & D.
I have held my silence for the past twenty years
about a matter of major public interest in which
Morrison is implicated, and this has weighed on my
conscience. Now I am eighty years old and awaiting
heart surgery, I consider it is high time this shameful
episode was exposed. Since the attendant publicity is
bound to have an adverse effect on BEP's image, I
thought it fair to give you advance warning, so you
may take the appropriate action. The details are as
follows:
In the mid eighties, a group of Brazilians carried
out a study into the effectiveness of loucura (an

evergreen shrub which grows exclusively in the Amazon basin) on cancer patients. Early results indicated a surprising success rate.

Following this, Morrison, then in post at Princeton University, was sponsored by BEP to carry out tests on the effects of loucuramine, believed to be the active chemical component of loucura, on tumours in rats. This study concluded that while loucuramine did indeed have the potential to shrink such tumours, the dosage necessary to achieve this result was liable to cause fatal internal bleeding. The earlier work of the Brazilian team was dismissed on the grounds that the methods used fell short of the standards required of modern medical trials. The references for the relevant academic papers are attached.

Upon completion of the study, Morrison was appointed as head of R & D in oncology by BEP, before being subsequently promoted to his current position. Since his paper was regarded as the leading authority on the subject, all research into loucura and its active components was abandoned.

I have in my possession conclusive documentary evidence that:

1. Morrison's appointment at BEP was contingent on the results of his study.
2. His study was flawed.
3. A further study by the Brazilian team, which rectified the deficiencies of their first study, was suppressed by Morrison and BEP.
4. Morrison believed loucura to be an effective cancer cure.

In summary, both Morrison and BEP acted in this matter for pure financial gain and with no regard for scientific integrity. As a direct result of their actions, millions of people have had their lives truncated.

Should you wish to discuss these allegations with me further, before I proceed to air the evidence in the public domain, I should be delighted to assist.

Yours sincerely,

George Hubbard

Brad laid the letter on his desk and sighed. In his five years as CEO, they must have averaged several of these loony accusations every week, many of them relating to events long before his time. Generally they ignored them, but experience had taught Brad that allegations about specific employees were best dealt with face to face. He buzzed his secretary and asked if Morrison could come over. With luck, he'd be able to knock this one on the head in a few minutes.

Superficially, Morrison was as chipper as ever – smug, even. And why shouldn't he be? The guy was on the home straight to retirement after a long and distinguished career. He strode confidently into Brad's office – shiny shoes, shiny head.

But Brad hadn't risen to the dizzy heights of CEO without having a nose for impending trouble. Some nuance of Morrison's body language suggested more than the normal apprehension of a man called into his boss's office at short notice.

'Thanks for coming, Edgar,' Brad began. 'Nothing for you to worry about.'

Somehow, he didn't think Morrison was reassured.

'I've received this letter from some nutcase – thought you should take a look as it mentions you.'

'I've seen it already,' Morrison said. 'The bastard sent me a blind copy.'

'Is this guy for real?'

'In the sense that he used to work here – unfortunately, yes.'

'And in other senses?'

'It's all lies. The man's a nutter – always was.'

'You know him well?'

'I did, yes. We collaborated on research projects when we were both on the faculty at Princeton – before he left and came here.'

'So he joined us before you did?'

'Yes.'

'And in your opinion Hubbard wrote this letter?'

'Without a doubt. I'd recognise his handwriting anywhere.'

'But why?'

Now Morrison was suddenly more expansive – this part of his story he had off pat.

'It all goes back to when I was hired. He claimed he'd been promised the top job in oncology, but I came in from outside over his head. Afterwards, he made a real nuisance of himself, claiming I'd been hired under false pretences. In the end, we had to retire him early.'

It struck Brad as a classic case of sour grapes. Yet two aspects puzzled him – why rake over it again twenty years later, and why was Morrison jittery?

'So there's nothing in what he claims?'

'Less than nothing,' Morrison replied, waving his hand in a dismissive gesture. 'My research showed that loucuramine killed the rats – end of story. The results were published in a reputable journal – if the study had been flawed, surely someone in the scientific community would have spotted it by now. Plus, as far as I'm aware, there was no further study by the Brazilians. The conclusions of the tests came as no surprise to anyone – you know as well as I do, there is no simple remedy for cancer.'

'That's not what Hubbard says here,' said Brad, pointing at the letter.

'The results were unambiguous.'

Morrison's veneer of bravado had slipped a little now. He shuffled uneasily in his seat. What could the problem be, Brad wondered?

'Is something bothering you, Edgar?'

'No,' Morrison replied. 'Except you do appear to be taking this quite seriously.'

'Why wouldn't I take a veiled blackmail threat seriously?'

'Because it's the ravings of a lunatic. And these accusations are hardly new – take a look on the internet if you don't believe me. People have been speculating about a loucura conspiracy ever since my paper was published.'

'What evidence can this man Hubbard have?' asked Brad, subtly shifting his line of questioning.

'None – because none of it's true, as I told you already. Isn't that enough?'

'Yes,' Brad replied. 'It's enough.'

It wasn't, of course, but the look in Morrison's eyes told him it was all he was getting.

'In any case,' said Morrison, in a final feeble attempt at rationalisation, 'surely the media wouldn't be concerned now about events from twenty years ago?'

'Oh, I'm not sure about that. Kennedy was assassinated nearly fifty years ago, but you can't tell me folks wouldn't be mad keen to read all about it if the truth came out.'

Brad was goading Morrison now, hoping he might prompt a full disclosure. But his needling had the opposite effect.

'This is quite different,' Morrison protested. 'It's a crazy conspiracy theory. Hell, if there was a magic cure for cancer, I'd have been out of a job years ago.'

'Why yes,' agreed Brad. 'And so it follows you have a vested interest in the matter.'

He smiled, showing Morrison he was kidding him. Morrison gave a wintry smile back.

'Well, since you're clear there's no basis to this, we'll just ignore it and see how it plays out. Thanks for your time, Edgar – end of meeting.'

Some of the usual swagger was missing from Morrison's step as he left the office. The discussion had also unsettled Brad – it wasn't so much Morrison's lying, but the fact that he had no idea what Morrison was lying about. He simply had to learn more.

To do this, Brad needed some help, and not the kind available within the squeaky clean confines of BEP headquarters. He picked up the telephone and dialled a familiar number.

Morrison sweated as he left Hillman's office. Hubbard's letter had wrong-footed him and he hadn't had time to figure out the moves before his boss had summoned him. Even so, how had he mismanaged the meeting so badly? Now Hillman was suspicious and that was dangerous, more dangerous even than Hubbard's threats.

Morrison attended church with his wife every Sunday, but he wasn't religious. Even so, he now prayed to the Lord for a solution. Surely God, if he existed, wouldn't obstruct an attempt to atone for past wrongs? But Morrison's prayers went unanswered.

At lunchtime he went driving – nowhere in particular. A way forward might come to him if he didn't concentrate too hard on his problem. It was no use, though – he could think of nothing else. When the lunch hour was up, he returned to his office, glum and defeated.

4

By Friday, after days of relentless joshing from Bill and the team, Claudia was impatient to have the speed dating over and done with.

At lunchtime, Bill pulled on his well-worn leather jacket. Thank God, he was going out – perhaps she'd have a couple of hours in peace. But at the last minute, he doubled back as though he'd forgotten something vital, and made for Claudia's workstation. She cringed – if he mentioned tonight's shindig once more, she would be tempted to strangle him with her bare hands.

'I'm off now – won't be back this afternoon,' he began. 'Can you do me a favour?'

Claudia hung back. Experience had taught her never to accede to Bill's requests in advance of the facts.

'Depends what it is.'

'It'll take your mind off the trauma of tonight.'

'What?'

'Can you call this fruit and nut case – says one of the big pharmaceutical companies concealed a natural treatment for cancer. I expect it'll be a waste of time...'

But somebody had to check it out. He handed her a piece of paper with the name and number.

'I spoke to him briefly, but I'm due to meet an important contact so I told him someone would call him back.'

'And I got the short straw,' moaned Claudia.

Bill was downright lazy at times. 'Meeting an important contact' was a euphemism for spending the afternoon with a crony in a pub – not one of the synthetic bars nearby created by bankers for bankers, but a proper watering hole. There was no reason why he couldn't have dealt with the caller himself.

'You never know, there might be something in it,' he said. 'Report back tomorrow.'

Claudia opened her mouth to plead immense pressure of work, but it was too late. Bill had already scuttled off.

It was a quiet afternoon for news. Forget the big scoops and holding the front page – the toughest challenge in journalism is filling newspapers when little of consequence is happening in the world. And the main function of trainee reporters is to churn out the necessary drivel. Claudia re-hashed some turgid press releases into stories as she ate her cheese sandwich.

Nine months working with Bill had made her cynical. If he'd judged there was any truth in the cancer story, he'd have kept it for himself. She glanced at the piece of paper. George Hubbard – it even sounded a numpty name. What a waste of her time. Almost as bad as the speed dating – no coincidence that the event was sponsored by one of the *Globe*'s major advertisers.

There was always a tiny chance this crank call might be genuine, but the omens weren't promising. A quick Google session yielded dozens of cancer cure conspiracy theories. The substances involved differed, but the basic premise was the same – a miracle cancer remedy was being kept back by big pharma and wicked governments for financial reasons. The theories were eloquently argued but so were the medical profession's rebuttals. On balance, Claudia sided with the medics. With a heavy heart, she turned a fresh page in her notebook and dialled the number.

Hubbard had an old man's voice, his gentle Scottish accent combining oddly with a mid-Atlantic twang.

'Mr Hubbard, my editor tells me you have a story for us.'

13

'Not any old story, my dear, but the journalistic scoop of the century.'

I'll be the judge of that, Claudia thought, and I'm not 'your dear' or anyone else's.

'Tell me more,' she said tersely.

'As I told your editor, my former employer suppressed a cure for cancer.'

Whistleblowers were sometimes vindictive, deluded people with old scores to settle. By the sound of him, Hubbard's scores must be ancient.

'Who did you say you worked for?'

'I didn't, but it was a global pharmaceutical company.'

'Which one?'

'I'm not prepared to disclose that at the moment.'

Claudia didn't press him – if Hubbard was his real name, she could probably find out.

'When did you leave there?'

'I retired in 1990.'

'And your role?'

'I was in the R & D team – oncology, or cancer in simple terms.'

I know – I'm not a moron, Claudia wanted to say.

'This happened while you were working there?' she asked.

'Yes.'

'That's quite a long time ago.'

'Look,' he cut in, irritated by the clear insinuation that old news didn't sell. 'If you're not interested I'll speak to another paper – I thought the *Globe* had a strong track record exposing corruption in big business. In any case, the person involved is now very senior in the company.'

'No, no, we're interested,' said Claudia, trying to sound as if she was. Following up leads that led nowhere, from sources who were fruitcakes, went with the territory. If you assumed at the outset they were all rubbish, sooner or later a mega scoop would slip from your grasp. 'No – please go on.'

'As I say, the company concealed a cancer cure.'

'Which you believe was effective?'

'You're quick to catch on.'

Claudia ignored Hubbard's sarcasm.

'So what was this cure?'

'I'm not prepared to say any more unless we meet.'

'Can you prove any of your allegations?'

If not, an interview would be a waste of time. She rather hoped he'd say no – Hubbard's condescending style grated majorly on her nerves and she'd have been glad of an excuse to avoid further contact.

'I have documents.'

Claudia vacillated – yet she knew Bill would insist she followed through to the bitter end.

'When?'

'Tuesday – come to my house at ten o'clock.'

She scribbled down an address in Highgate.

'Oh, and bring someone with authority to negotiate a financial agreement,' he added, as an afterthought.

This startled Claudia – she'd presumed that Hubbard had acted out of pure altruism. It annoyed her as well. She resented the suggestion, however well-founded, that she lacked the clout to broker a deal. And she couldn't help wondering whether the delay in meeting with her meant he was trying to sell the story to someone else and she was merely a back up.

'How much are we talking?'

'Bidding opens at a hundred thousand pounds.'

The *Telegraph* had paid more than that for the low-down on MPs' expenses – if this was authentic, the *Globe* would cough up.

'You show me what you've got,' she said, feigning great confidence, 'and I'll decide what it's worth.'

Bluffing was easy when the stakes were low.

'I should warn you,' said Hubbard, confirming her suspicions, 'that there are others in the running for this information.'

'Didn't you say we had first refusal?'

'I said nothing of the sort – the story goes to the highest bidder.'

She hung up, depleted by the interaction, and grabbed a coffee to kick-start her brain. Common sense said Hubbard was a crackpot. How could a cancer drug be kept quiet for more than twenty years? Why had he taken so long to come forward? And what proof could he possibly supply after all this time?

She googled Hubbard.

A selection of academic papers from the seventies popped up on screen – papers with long, clumsy titles, written while Hubbard had been at Princeton. But by 1978, he'd dropped off the radar.

OK – time for some lateral thinking.

Many of Hubbard's research papers had been co-authored with an Edgar Morrison. She googled Morrison. Success! Morrison was still very much in the public domain – global head of R & D at BEP, no less. Surely he must be the senior person Hubbard had mentioned. With an irrational surge of excitement, Claudia allowed herself to wonder fleetingly whether there might be some substance to this after all.

5

Hugo Fleming's boss glared at him as he rose to leave at six o'clock. You weren't supposed to have a life in the corporate finance department of the Big 4 accountancy firm of Pearson Malone.

'I hope I'm going to have your comments on that draft offer announcement by first thing Monday morning as you promised,' Stephanie said.

'Nearly finished,' Hugo lied. 'I'm taking it home to put the finishing touches to it.'

He pointed to the laptop bag slung over his shoulder.

'You're lucky to be working on Project Acorn. Don't mess it up.'

'Don't worry – I won't. Have a great weekend!'

Stephanie Clark wore pastel suits and matching shoes – ill-judged female business attire from the early eighties. A blonde helmet of hair sat stiffly on her head. In spite of his cheery farewell, Hugo didn't consider her capable of having a great weekend, or any kind of weekend at all, judging by the number of e-mails she habitually sent.

Stephanie and Hugo were never destined to be soulmates, but that shouldn't have mattered. He'd only planned on staying in her group for a year before joining one of the large investment banks. But ten months in, and with the economy in poor shape, it didn't look as if the investment banks would be hiring people like Hugo any time soon. His short-termist strategy with Stephanie had been another error of judgement. She'd already pulled his promotion from Assistant Manager to Manager once, and was poised to do it again.

Only Project Acorn could save Hugo's bacon. Christian Temple, Stephanie's boss, had told her firmly in Hugo's presence that it wasn't fair if a chap missed out on promotion because he hadn't enough scope to show his mettle – Hugo had to be given the chance to prove his worth. As a result of this intervention, Hugo's future now rested on his success in advising IDD, an AIM quoted company, on a friendly takeover bid from the pharmaceutical giant BEP.

Denise, the group secretary, held open the lift doors for Hugo. He always pretended not to notice her obvious attraction to him. Although she was hot, the office grapevine told him she was a high maintenance babe.

'Anything lined up for the weekend, Hugo?'

Hugo paused. He'd foolishly agreed to go to a stupid speed-dating event for a bet with his flatmate, Charlie Lewis, but he'd no wish to be outed as a sad loser, especially to Denise.

'Oh, nothing much,' he said. 'A few drinks with friends.'

He shrank from asking her the same question in case – shock, horror – she suggested they got together.

'Why's Stephanie always telling you not to mess up?' she asked.

'Because she derives a sadistic pleasure from trying to psych me out.'

'Ground floor,' announced a disembodied electronic voice. Eager to escape, Hugo darted through the doors as soon as they opened.

Hugo paid no heed to Stephanie's blatant attempts to destabilise him. The client loved him, he was on top of the work and there was no reason why the transaction shouldn't proceed to a successful completion. In fact, as he strolled out of the office into the warm evening sunshine, it was hard to see what could possibly go wrong.

6

In the middle of the keynote plenary session at the European Hedge Fund Convention, Marcus Cunningham's mobile blared out the theme tune to *Mission Impossible*. He beat a hasty retreat, ignoring the supercilious glares of the other delegates. In the real world, Marcus enjoyed a certain status as the head honcho at Umbra Capital Partners – in the hedge fund world he was a minnow.

'Ah, the elusive Mr Cunningham,' said the caller. 'George Hubbard here.'

Marcus recognised Hubbard's name from the several voicemails he'd left during the conference – he was certain he'd never heard it before.

'You didn't respond to my messages,' said Hubbard. 'That's extremely poor manners.'

'Apologies – I've been terribly busy the last few days.'

Truth be told, Marcus had procrastinated. In his first message, Hubbard said he'd recognised Marcus going back thirty years from a rare picture in the press. This was disturbing. It had been a long time since an unpretentious Mark Coates from a Croydon grammar school had reinvented himself as suave old Etonian, Marcus Cunningham. How could anyone have recognised him after all this time? And how come this Hubbard had his mobile number? His secretary was under strict instructions not to give it out to the world at large.

'Changed your name, eh? Well, you always did have big ideas about yourself.'

Ignoring the jibe, Marcus asked him, 'Forgive me, but where do I know you from?'

'You're Mark Coates – went to school with my son Roger, in Croydon.'

'You must be confusing me with someone else.' Marcus had absolutely no recollection of a Roger Hubbard.

'Oh, I'm sure I'm not, Mr Cunningham, or perhaps I should say Mr Coates. I've a very reliable memory for a face.'

Even assuming this tenuous connection, why was Hubbard contacting him now?

'So what can I do for you?' asked Marcus, neither confirming nor denying his identity. A strange anxiety had inexplicably gained a foothold in his mind and he was keen to quell it

'I understand your hedge fund specialises in pharmaceutical stocks.'

'Yes, that is one of our niches,' Marcus agreed. 'Are you a potential investor?'

The old man didn't sound as though he'd have the minimum £250,000 to shell out, but you never knew. Hubbard snorted at the suggestion.

'Good heavens, no! I have some valuable data that could make you a lot of money.'

This rang alarm bells – unworldly old men like Hubbard didn't usually understand the value of information let alone trade it.

'What?'

'Proof of a huge scandal about one of the giants in the pharma industry – am I right in thinking that might be useful to you?'

Indeed it would, if it were true. But Marcus was wary.

'How did you come by your knowledge?'

'I used to work for the company – we emigrated to the US, if you recall.'

Marcus recalled nothing, which unsettled him more than anything else.

'You must have retired...'

'Twenty years ago,' said Hubbard.

'And this is about something which happened then?' asked Marcus in a voice loaded with scepticism.

'Naturally, but the person involved is still high up in the organisation.'

Potential for blackmail at the very least.

'What happened?'

'They blocked an incredibly potent organic remedy for cancer.'

Perhaps so, but they'd never have left a trail. Instinct suggested the man was either a madman or a fraud, maybe both. Yet something caused Marcus to waver, and he played for time.

'Tell me about it.'

'That's all you get, unless you purchase the documents. Are you willing to buy? I'm already sounding out the press, but I guess you might pay more.'

Marcus knew better than to talk money until he'd checked his facts – he'd heard disquieting rumours of law enforcement sting operations in recent weeks. His people would thoroughly verify Hubbard's bona fides before any negotiations took place.

'We should have further discussions,' he replied carefully. 'I'm in Switzerland on business at present, but I can do Monday lunchtime if that works for you.'

'Can you come to my house in Highgate?'

'Highgate's rather out of my way, I'm afraid,' said Marcus. 'I work in Mayfair – just off Curzon Street.'

'I know where you are,' snapped Hubbard. 'Your secretary sent me your card.'

Which at least explained how Hubbard had his mobile number.

'So could you come over to my neck of the woods?'

'I guess so.'

Intuition told Marcus it would be safer to meet Hubbard in a public place, away from his offices.

'Excellent. There's a pub called the Audley in Mount Street – I'll see you there at one – I'll be sitting outside if it's not raining. Obviously, you'll have no difficulty in recognising me.'

'Obviously,' Hubbard agreed.

After Hubbard rang off, Marcus put out a call to Richard, his key researcher.

'Richard, dig up all you can on George Hubbard – he used to work for one of the pharma big boys about twenty years ago.'

'Any more info?'

'He says the company squashed a treatment for cancer.'

'Leave it with me.'

If anyone could flesh out Hubbard's back story, Richard could. Marcus Cunningham hadn't made his name by skimping on due diligence.

7

If it hadn't been for the bet with Charlie, Hugo wouldn't even have been at the speed-dating event. Life turns on such trivialities.

Charlie was supposed to be there as well, but he'd texted Hugo at 5.30.

'stuck in meeting till 18 – u r on yr own'
  'bet off?' Hugo had texted back.
  'bet is u get girl into bed – don't need me there. If u don't go u owe me £100!'

Oh well, thought Hugo – in for a penny, in for £100. Eighty or so girls to choose from in three hours; if he couldn't pull one of them, he was losing his touch – it would be a breeze.

The venue, an anonymous concrete hotel in a godforsaken corner of West London, could at best be described as uninspiring. But no more so than the disappointing collection of women who'd gathered for the big event. Hugo very nearly turned tail and fled as soon as he'd stuck his nose round the door, but a bet was a bet and surely there must be one girl in there who was worth the effort.

As he progressed round the tables, Hugo began to question this assumption – it seemed that each girl was uglier and had less charisma than the last. Until, that is, he came to the final rotation, when his spirits soared.

Claudia sat queen of all she surveyed – arms folded, feet

up on the table. And what a pair of legs – beautifully toned, showcased in a pair of purple leather leggings with vertiginous gold sandals. His eyes moved to the top half of her body – there weren't many girls who had the bravado to carry off a gold plunge-neck top without looking tarty, but Claudia had chutzpah which defied you to find fault with any aspect of her appearance. Her face was no less stunning than her body – what exquisite bone structure. She could have been a model – perhaps she was. And the dreadlocked hair was amazing. One thing was sure – she didn't belong in a dive like this.

She smiled at him. That instant was sheer perfection.

'Sit down, honey – don't be shy. I'm Claudia.'

Hugo wasn't shy, but he was extremely drunk. Guinness World Records' rules had all the men moving round every three minutes. Even if you went to the toilet, an official had to sit in your seat to fill in. There would have been chaos if people had been allowed to wander off to the bar, so they served refreshments at the tables. In the inevitable confusion, Hugo had downed a large number of un-identifiable drinks intended for others, and they hadn't mixed together at all well. Now Claudia's beauty made for an even headier cocktail.

Obediently, Hugo sat – he could barely move his mouth. What should he say?

'I don't really do black girls,' he blurted out.

The words had come unbidden to his lips and he knew instantly he'd made a terrible mistake, but he couldn't take them back. Claudia rewarded him with a corrosive stare.

'Glad we got that out of the way early on,' she replied, her voice acidic. The smile had disappeared like the sun behind clouds.

'All I was saying...'

But she had no intention of helping Hugo salvage the situation.

'I know exactly what you're saying. You're telling me you're a racist.'

'No, no, I'm not – definitely not, or not in the way you think...'

She removed her feet from the table and leaned forward.

'What would a little prick like you understand about what I think?'

Hugo floundered. She was itching for a fight and he was in no state to retaliate.

'Um, no, I'm not sure ... all I meant was...'

She jabbed her forefinger at him.

'Oh, I get what you meant. So tell me, Hugo,' she said peering at his name badge, and pronouncing his name with disdain, 'what do you do when you're not being a xenophobic bigot?'

'I'm in corporate finance.'

Hugo vainly hoped the conversation would now move onto less controversial ground.

'That figures, although I guess even your sort don't wear red braces any more.'

'Actually, the red braces always were a bit of a cliché.'

'Well, now you know how it feels.'

She leant forward aggressively, her tits practically falling out of her top.

'How what feels?'

'To be regarded as a cartoon character, a stereotype.'

'I didn't say that. I didn't mean...'

'People like you never do.'

Now who's stereotyping, he thought, but in his drunken state he was totally unable to translate the brain activity into speech.

'So what do you do?'

'Me? I'm a reporter for the *Daily Globe*.'

'What do you report?'

'News, dumbo – what else?'

'What sort of news?'

'I expose the injustices and inequalities in our society – people like you.'

'Now hang on a mo,' said Hugo, 'you here tonight in a professional capacity?' As he slurred over the word professional, her lips tightened in a cruel smile. She was out to get the better of him, and he knew instinctively that he didn't stand a chance. He stood up abruptly, almost knocking over the table.

'I'm out of here,' he said, with rising panic.

Claudia glanced at her watch.

'One minute ten seconds left – you go now and you spoil the whole record attempt.'

'I don't give a shit about the record – couldn't care less about you. Just don't print anything, all right, I'm warning you – or else!'

Hugo swayed, gripped the table for support and then sat down again. Claudia glared at him fiercely, her arms still folded.

'Or else what?'

'I'll get my lawyers on you.'

She rolled her eyes and whooped with derision.

'Your lawyers? That's a joke. Still, it's all I'd expect from a colonial prick like you.'

Her game was transparent now – to goad him into walking away and ruining the record attempt. Hugo folded his arms, mirroring Claudia's body language.

'Well, I'm not going to argue and I'm not having you say I effed up the record attempt – I'll stay here, but I'm not saying a word.'

Claudia shrugged.

'Suit yourself.'

The remaining thirty seconds felt as if they would never end. At last, the bell rang.

'Right – I'm off,' he said, moving decisively towards the exit.

Without realising it, he'd been holding his breath. Now, as his lungs refilled, his head started to function again. What a psycho the girl was – and what a narrow escape he'd had.

Out in the fresh air, Hugo tottered unsteadily for a moment before regaining his balance. He lit a cigarette and walked towards a taxi rank on the corner.

8

Marcus fancied himself as a good judge of character. He sized up Julia Fraser, *Sunday Globe* Female Entrepreneur of the Year and founder of IDD, even as she walked towards him for their first meeting.

Julia was quite a looker, and knew it. Accustomed to men reacting to her in a certain way, she would take it badly if they didn't. This was a weakness Marcus might play on. Otherwise, she seemed invulnerable – a woman in complete control.

She strutted towards his table in the bar – skinny jeans, boots, long cardigan, loose hair, pretending not to notice all the guys eyeing her up. Her outfit gave the illusion of having been put together effortlessly, but Marcus knew nothing looked so chic by chance.

Julia's confident air reminded Marcus of his first ex-wife, Susan. The marriage had been a disaster, but Marcus still had a grudging admiration for her brass neck. Other wives clung pathetically onto their rich husbands, but Susan had discarded Marcus like an item of unwanted clothing, claiming he was 'emotionally absent'. The court agreed – he'd scarred her for life – and awarded her a huge financial settlement in compensation. Not content with her own success, she had then befriended his second wife, Olivia, and encouraged her to follow suit, coaching her through the whole process. Unsurprisingly, Olivia's polished performance had yielded an even larger award.

Now the two women were the best of chums, lunching, shopping and holidaying together at his expense while

Marcus was left on his own – poorer and warier.

'Marcus Cunningham, I presume,' Julia smiled and extended her hand. Her handshake was firm for a woman, but nevertheless hinted at a warmth which both Susan and Olivia had conspicuously lacked. Marcus smiled back.

She hadn't told him in advance what was on her agenda, but Marcus had been to some trouble to find out. He had no wish to be ambushed by a woman, particularly one who 'happened' to be in Geneva at the same time as him. Her mission was quite simple, he'd discovered. Umbra had built up a seven percent stake in IDD in the past few months, and Julia wondered why. Well, fair enough, they could talk – although he would be careful to skate round a number of important issues.

For a woman who believed she was in control, there was a lot that Julia Fraser didn't know. For starters, she had no clue that Marcus, along with a select few others, was well aware of the secret BEP takeover bid, or that his broker pal held a further three percent stake on his behalf. With an effective ten percent holding, Umbra had the means to make life difficult for BEP if they so desired.

As matters stood, Marcus didn't intend to make life difficult for anyone. The deal being mooted was for more than double the current IDD share price, and that was enough for him. The fact was, IDD investors were losing heart – the company had developed cutting-edge technology, but who knew whether it was of any commercial use? According to Marcus's source, BEP would use the software to fine-tune the formulae of their blockbuster drugs and extend the life of their patents. Marcus was sceptical, but if BEP were misguided enough to piss away £100 million on a speculative acquisition it was their problem, not his.

'Pleased to meet you, Julia – and if I may say so, you're even prettier in the flesh than in your photographs.'

The pictures he'd seen of Julia had been sympathetically

airbrushed publicity shots, but now it seemed she'd been airbrushed in life as well.

'Why you smooth-talking charmer,' she replied with a smile, sitting herself down opposite Marcus. He beckoned to the waiter.

'Will you have a glass of wine?'

'Yes please, but only a very tiny one – it does tend to go to my head.'

'If you drank more, you might find you handled it more easily,' observed Marcus, after ordering a bottle of Chablis.

'Maybe I don't want to,' came her crisp reply.

'Well in that case, there'll be all the more for me. Now, you asked to see me – so what can I do for you?'

'I'll come straight to the point. My board have expressed some concerns about the position you've been building up in our shares. There are so many hedge funds nowadays who are activist shareholders – we wondered whether Umbra may be one of them?'

'Why do you ask?' said Marcus, poker-faced. 'Is the company in play?'

He watched her closely – if all the hype about her ethical standards was true, she wouldn't breathe a word about the takeover ahead of it being announced. As he'd predicted, she skilfully ducked the question, while avoiding a lie.

'It's simply that we'd be interested to know what your intentions are – that's if you're happy to tell me.'

Marcus opened his arms, as if to indicate his own honesty.

'Perfectly happy,' he said.

Julia stood to gain more on the sale of IDD than anyone – she still had a twenty-five percent shareholding, even though the company was now publicly listed. She would net the best part of £20 million post tax – more if she had a sharp accountant. What would someone like her do with that kind of money? Did she have anyone to help her spend it?

'So what are your intentions?' asked Julia, bringing Marcus abruptly back to earth.

'We've bought into IDD as part of a portfolio of technology based companies which should show us a superior return over the next few years. These are meant to be passive investments for the medium term, where we're satisfied with the integrity and quality of the existing management teams, and the intrinsic value of the business proposition.'

He sounded idiotic – like a talking advertisement – but strangely, Julia's charm had thrown him off his stride, forcing him to take refuge in this stream of jargon. But Julia wasn't impressed. Predictably enough, she was keen to pin him down on the specifics.

'How exactly do you envisage IDD will generate that return?'

'The technology you've developed is revolutionary,' replied Marcus. 'So far, no one has exploited its clear commercial potential, but before long I would wager someone will.'

'If you can see such definite potential,' said Julia, homing in with ruthless logic on the key issue, 'wouldn't you wish to be actively involved?'

'We're a small organisation. We have too many of these investments to take an active role in all of them. Our view is that the quality of the existing management team should ensure the value of our stake is maximised.'

They chatted round this for a few more minutes. At the end, Julia appeared both satisfied and relieved.

'Well, thank you for your frankness,' she said, as if she'd bargained for much less.

Marcus topped up his own wine glass and offered some more to Julia. Was there more to this woman than met the eye? He had caught her staring past him to her reflection in the mirror behind – vanity might well be the one flaw in this paragon of virtue. These days Marcus preferred women who showed their imperfections early on – the ones who seemed ideal in the beginning always turned out the worst in the end.

'OK, perhaps a tiny bit.'

Marcus filled her glass more than halfway, but not so full she wouldn't drink it.

'While you're here,' he said, 'could I possibly tap your brains about something?'

Julia smiled, unsuspectingly.

'Tap away,' she said.

'What I'd like to know,' Marcus began, 'is whether in principle it would be possible for there to be an organic miracle cure for cancer?'

9

Hugo savoured the view from the Windows Bar at the Hilton, as he glugged his second beer and summoned the waiter for a third. He'd sobered up appreciably in transit from the speed dating, and considered that lucidity at this stage on a Friday night might set a dangerous precedent.

Charlie's client meeting had conveniently wrapped up in time for some drinks. Did tax specialists really have late meetings on a Friday night, Hugo wondered? More likely, Charlie's non-attendance at the dating resulted from remote-control interference from his lawyer girl-friend, Marianne, currently attending a conference in San Francisco.

Charlie sympathised as Hugo outlined his shambles of an evening. But, sympathetic or not, he'd won his bet and Hugo knew he couldn't afford to pay.

'So this Claudia girl, you say she was a stunner?'

'Irr-rrelevant,' slurred Hugo. 'You wanna go home with psycho bitch black woman?'

'Sounds as if she didn't fancy going home with you.'

'Irr-rrelevant.'

'Though you wouldn't have minded shagging her?'

Hugo took a large slurp of his beer and belched loudly. He was struggling to explain to Charlie exactly what was so repulsive about the girl.

'Nightmare,' said Hugo. 'Total psycho.'

'Why do you say that?' asked Charlie – he was considerably more sober than Hugo, although rapidly catching up.

'Whass right? Shwass rude to me.'

Charlie laughed. 'Sounds to me as if you were scared of her.'

Hugo sat up as straight as he could.

'No way.'

'Yes you were.'

'Was not,' Hugo repeated. 'Called me names, called me colonial prick.' He stammered over the words.

'Colonial brick?' said Charlie, puzzled.

'I said prick, not brick,' shouted Hugo, so loudly that people at the adjoining tables tut-tutted.

'Scared or not, the end result's the same – you owe me a hundred pounds.' He rubbed his fingers together. 'Come on – hand over the money.'

Hugo patted his pockets.

'No cash – I'll owe it to you.'

'OK,' said Charlie. 'You can buy the drinks, as a payment on account.' He clicked his fingers to summon the waiter, who went off to prepare the bill.

Hugo tried two cards in the machine before the third was accepted. Charlie chuckled at rat-arsed Hugo muddling up his PIN numbers. Hugo played along with the fiction, but drunk as he was, brutal reality still intruded. He'd been living on the expectation of future earnings for too long. Now, not to put too fine a point on it, he was up financial shit creek without a paddle.

The cab driver was disinclined to take two drunks to Balham – and who could blame him? Hugo was verging on comatose. But silver-tongued Charlie talked the cabbie round and before long, the taxi drew up outside their flat.

Hugo rushed out – he knew he was about to puke. He could have puked on the pavement, but he headed indoors. Even then, he could have dashed to the bathroom – but no. With all logic temporarily suspended, he made a beeline for his bed and lay down.

For a few deluded seconds he believed he might recover.

When he fixed his gaze on the light fitting, the nausea receded. But try as he might, his eyes wandered and the room spun round like a carousel. He tried again – for God's sake, how difficult was it to focus on an object and keep focused?

Extraordinarily difficult – impossible, in fact.

One more time – perhaps if he locked onto the chest of drawers instead of the light fitting? No, big mistake – the chest was far too large. How about the knobs on the drawers? Maybe not. No – definitely not.

The battle was lost. Accepting the inevitable, he leaned over the side of the bed, vomited, and passed out.

Claudia unzipped the laptop bag. She'd found it all too easy to walk away with it at the end of the evening, and the temptation had proved irresistible. She would return it to Hugo in due course, but not until she'd had a thorough nose around.

A Pearson Malone business card confirmed the bag's ownership: 'Hugo Fleming BA ACA – Assistant Manager – Corporate Finance'.

Assistant Manager was a meaningless job title, especially as Hugo appeared incapable of either assisting anyone or managing anything. Still, he had a degree and had passed his accountancy exams, so he couldn't be quite as dim-witted as he'd seemed.

Now for the bag's contents.

The Pearson Malone computer would be impenetrable to an amateur hacker, but the stack of papers underneath the laptop was a different matter.

It was some kind of offer document – the company names replaced by blobs to preserve secrecy. But with a bit of googling, and the other details still visible, it didn't take Claudia long to work it out.

This was one hell of a high-profile transaction. Julia Fraser, *Sunday Globe* Female Entrepreneur of the Year, was selling out – to none other than BEP, the drug company Hubbard claimed to have the dirt on. Now how was that for a twist of fate? From Hugo's handwritten notes, she gathered he was advising IDD.

She confirmed the share prices online and quickly gauged that she'd earn a fortune if she bought the shares and the takeover went through. But Claudia wasn't tempted by the money – she was more taken with the story.

Julia Fraser, 'the ethical entrepreneur', would run from the deal like a rabbit if what Hubbard claimed was true. Now that was interesting in itself. And even without the moral angle, she could give the *Globe*'s business editor a heads-up on the takeover. But even as she began to evaluate all the different angles, a guilty conscience stopped her in her tracks.

How would she feel if she'd carelessly left the bag somewhere after a few drinks? Wouldn't she hope whoever found it would act like a decent human being? Besides, she'd already been mean to Hugo and so arguably he'd suffered enough at her hands. It went totally against the journalistic grain, maybe even against common sense, but she resolved there and then not to use the information.

Perhaps illogically, she felt that this decision somehow justified some further snooping, and explored the side compartments of the bag. Out came a bank statement, addressed to Hugo's home. Balham Grove – not too bad an address, especially if Hugo owned his flat. Claudia scarcely paused before giving in to her curiosity.

She gasped out loud at what she saw. Shockingly, even with a very healthy inflow of funds each month, the account was perpetually and substantially overdrawn. Claudia was always careful with money, mainly because she didn't have much. Hugo, it seemed, was the exact opposite. The flurry of direct debits to credit card providers confirmed he was financing a lifestyle way beyond his means. And him an accountant as well.

Claudia replaced the papers and stashed the bag in her wardrobe – she'd give it back to Hugo sometime over the weekend. Although her prying didn't weigh on her conscience, she did now regret jumping down Hugo's throat – he'd been the one tasty looking dude she'd seen all night. Thanks to her, he probably never would do black girls now.

However, she did have a fantastic idea for her story – racism at a multicultural dating event! Hugo had made what she now believed to be a perfectly innocuous comment, but it had come at the end of a tedious evening. And without a doubt she had picked up a distinct whiff of prejudice from some of the other guys who'd been there.

Claudia's fingers flew over the keyboard of her own laptop as she pulled her evidence together. Pausing only to do some online research on the Race Relations Act, she re-read what she'd written and re-hashed the bits which sounded whiny. The evening had been a washout, but she had her unique angle all the same, exactly as Bill had suggested.

She lay in bed mulling over Hubbard's story. It was most probably crap, but wasn't there a chance, however remote, that this was the mega scoop which would make her name? Holding on to that cheerful but improbable concept, she drifted off to sleep.

10

Brad Hillman met Wayne Hardy, his private security consultant, in a diner out of town, where no one would recognise them and BEP's in-house security would have no reason to look.

Wayne was a big ugly brute, a straight-talking Vietnam veteran turned CIA agent, turned consultant. He'd seen more of the seamier side of life in each of his jobs than most men did in a lifetime. He lacked the necessary civilised veneer to fit into the wholesome environment of BEP, but his less than orthodox techniques made him a top-notch investigator.

Wayne ordered the giant T-bone with fries and onion rings. Brad, let off the leash for the night by Jill, his calorie-control-freak wife, ordered the same.

'Are you drinking beer?' asked Brad.

'If you are.'

Brad dithered before yielding to temptation. He'd put on thirty pounds in the last six months, even though Jill forced him to eat salad with lo-cal dressing every night at home.

'Why not – it's Friday night. Anyway, it's useless to drink diet soda with all this food.'

'So what did you manage to unearth on George Hubbard?' asked Brad, once the waitress was out of earshot.

'He's genuine all right – a Brit who used to work in oncology research and went back to his roots when he retired.'

'That much tallies with our personnel records – what else?'

'We searched for his documentary evidence, as he calls it. Found a file labelled BEP in his house, but it was empty.'

'Well, unless he's an idiot he's not going to leave it lying around,' said Brad.

'Oh, you'd be surprised at how careless people are.'

'I took a peek at Morrison's paper on loucuramine,' Brad went on. 'There's no evidence of defective work or falsified results. As Morrison said, the chemical was proven to be toxic to rats. There's no doubt the work the Brazilians did was flawed, and no trace of any study they did afterwards. So although it sure was convenient for everyone when those clinical tests went the way they did, that should be an end to it.'

'It's not an end to it, though, is it? I guess you're worried about the press.'

Brad didn't look particularly worried – he tucked into his steak with gusto.

'Not really – our PR people can sort that. Hardly a day goes by without someone flinging mud at us, but not much of it sticks. No – what vexes me is Edgar Morrison. He's as antsy as hell and I'd like to know why. I'm sure he's hiding something from me.'

'I'll tell you this for free – when one of your own people is holding out on you, it never amounts to good news,' said Wayne, wiping his mouth with his napkin.

'My thinking exactly,' agreed Brad. 'So, I'm asking you to watch him, Wayne, watch him carefully. If he visits the bathroom, I need to be told about it. We have to find out what he's keeping from us.'

11

'Are you OK to speak now?'

Morrison was panting after haring out of his house to find a payphone.

'Why the secrecy – why ask me to call back from a payphone?'

'Your landline and cell phone may not be secure, and what we have to discuss is top secret.'

He looked around him – paranoia fed on itself, but no one was around. And this line wasn't bugged, for sure.

'So what's it all about?' asked Morrison, fearing the worst.

'Has a man called George Hubbard been in touch with you?'

Morrison's mood darkened. He faltered, unsure of what to say. He couldn't deny it, yet admitting it didn't seem like the smartest move either.

'Yes, yes, he has.'

'I guessed he'd have tried to blackmail BEP first. Is there any truth in what he says?'

'No, none at all – Hubbard's a lunatic.'

'I agree with you.'

Morrison almost dropped the receiver in surprise. Unquestioning acceptance of his statement was the last reaction he'd expected. Encouraged, he said, 'Hubbard's threatening to go to the press – did you know?'

'Yes I did, and it can't be allowed to happen. There's too much resting on the IDD takeover – it's essential for the deal to go through, but it'll be difficult if Hubbard goes to the media.'

Morrison needed the transaction to go through as well, for different reasons, but he'd spotted an inconsistency. If the caller truly believed the allegations had no substance, why should the deal be affected? And more to the point, how had the caller known what Hubbard was up to? Still, there was no merit in arguing with someone who so unmistakeably shared his own objectives.

'Yes – it will be difficult,' he agreed.

'So, I thought you should know – I intend to make sure Hubbard doesn't talk.'

'What, you mean buy him off, or something? He's a difficult bugger – I'm not sure he's for sale.'

'Oh everyone's for sale, Mr Morrison, it's just a question of the price – which brings me neatly on to what I'm about to ask you for.'

'I don't have much money.'

'On a million bucks a year? Pull the other one! Anyway, I don't mean money. You have a more valuable commodity – influence. I hear some senior people in BEP are questioning the commercial rationale for the transaction.'

As far as Morrison knew, this wasn't true. If it was, it would be equally disastrous for him. But he was keen to avoid appearing ignorant.

'I'll ensure it isn't a problem, if that's what you mean,' he said.

'Excellent,' said the caller, and hung up.

Morrison couldn't believe his luck. Or maybe luck didn't come into it –was it possible that the Good Lord, if a little belatedly, had answered his prayers?

12

Hugo tentatively opened one eye and instantly regretted it. The room had stopped spinning, but his suffering had barely begun.

Shafts of sunlight stabbed at his temples as the sound of a pneumatic drill in the road sent shockwaves of pain through the rest of body. Surges of nausea washed over him during the brief interludes of silence. All in all, he wished he'd died during the night.

He endeavoured to recollect what he had drunk. It hardly mattered. Whatever it was, he'd overdone it big time – he hadn't even been able to undress. A raging thirst overcame him – water – water!

Hugo sat up slowly, and dragged himself out of bed, narrowly missing the pool of vomit on the floor. In the bathroom, he peered at himself in the mirror. A red-eyed deranged stranger peered back.

He knocked back two glasses of water and reached in the cupboard for some Alka-Seltzer. The packet was empty, but he dislodged a bottle of TCP, which smashed on contact with the unforgiving floor. Nauseated by the antiseptic smell, he steadied himself against the wall, deftly sidestepped the broken glass and shuffled back to his room, before collapsing again on the bed, suddenly anxious for no reason he could pinpoint.

Gradually, and in no particular order, fragments of the previous evening drifted back to Hugo – a tray of drinks being placed in front of him, the bowl of nuts on the table at Windows, some dreadlocked black girl shouting at him, going home in the taxi, moving round from one table to another, the room spinning, leaving the office with the laptop bag slung over his shoulder. Oh God – no! Hugo sat up with a jolt, desperately scanning the room. His free-floating anxiety had found a home – the laptop bag was missing.

Willing himself not to panic, he hauled himself out of bed. He searched the hallway, the lounge, the kitchen, even the bathroom. Each time he latched onto a new possibility, his hopes were raised and then cruelly dashed. Could it possibly be in Charlie's room? Gingerly, he opened the door – Charlie's still sleeping shape was plainly visible under the duvet, but there was no bag. Hugo's computer was gone, and along with it the confidential papers on Project Acorn.

The future panned out like a horror movie – confessing to Stephanie, his promotion cancelled, getting fired, being unemployable, the banks foreclosing... he was finished. In the hallway, he slumped on the floor, with his head in his hands. Somehow, he'd taken a wrong turning in life from which there was no way back. For the first time in longer than he could remember, he wept.

The speed-dating record had failed on a technicality. Claudia found it fitting, even pleasing, that the event should have been rendered so utterly pointless. All the same, she e-mailed her racism story off to Bill, and breezed into the office at around 10.30.

'What time do you call this?' said Bill. He bore no visible signs of the previous day's bender, but then he never did – an ability to bounce back was key to his survival. Claudia wished her own constitution were so robust. As it was, the entirely reasonable amount of vodka she'd drunk the night before had left her with a niggling headache and sour stomach.

'I was working late last night, thanks to you.'

She rummaged around in her bag for a paracetamol.

'You might as well have not bothered.'

'Why – because they didn't get the record?'

'No – because we can't run with the rubbish you wrote.'

'Why not?'

'Point number one – One Stop Dating spends a fucking fortune with us on advertising, so we can't slag them off.'

'That's not the...' Claudia began, but Bill choked her off. 'And point number two, you've completely missed the angle on this.'

'What?'

'You've been scooped, babe.'

He slammed a print out from The *Sun*'s website onto her desk.

'Scooped? You must be joking.'

But he wasn't. A rival dating agency had planted participants who'd been paid to break the rules and sabotage the attempt. Who'd have imagined it was worth the hassle?

'Jeez – how did they get hold of that?'

'Search me, but you were nowhere near it were you?'

Claudia shook her head.

'No – all we get is this anti-racist claptrap. Some white boy gave you the brush off, did he?'

'That wasn't the reason,' said Claudia, rather too defensively.

'Ah, so he really got under your skin, if you'll forgive the pun.'

No he hadn't got under her skin, and she wouldn't forgive the pun, but the image of Hugo kept bursting randomly into her mind. He was, she'd decided, despite his very obvious deficiencies, amazingly sexy.

'OK, OK – I'll do a rewrite.'

'By the way?' asked Bill. 'How are you getting on with that pharma story?'

'Meeting the dude on Tuesday and I'm doing my homework, like you're always telling me.'

'Terrific.'

He didn't sound too interested. But despite her gung-ho response to Hubbard, Claudia was worried.

'But he's after cash and I'm not too sure how to play the financial negotiations.'

'Look,' said Bill, swiftly dismissing her concerns. 'There's no way Hubbard has any documents worth paying for. If you've done your job right, you should be pretty definite about that before you even sit down with him. So don't worry – there won't be any financial negotiations.'

'In that case, what's the purpose of the meeting?'

'To close the bloody thing off.'

'How can you be so sure there's no meat to this?'

'I've a nose for these things.'

'But...'

'End of discussion,' said Bill. 'You've got work to do, remember?'

It was futile to challenge Bill once he'd made up his mind. Downcast by their unsatisfactory conversation, she set to the task of revising her piece on the speed-dating event.

13

Physically, Hugo slowly recovered. Charlie helped him tidy up his room, and cooked him bacon, eggs and fried bread. This saturated fat extravaganza miraculously settled Hugo's stomach, but his morale was harder to restore. He was overwhelmed by a fatalistic despondency, and Charlie's incessant bonhomie only added to his gloom.

'Look on the bright side,' said Charlie. 'If you'd brought your bag home, you might have puked all over the keyboard. Imagine that – you'd have had a devil of a job cleaning it.'

Hugo did not find much solace in this line of reasoning. Skint as he was, he'd gladly have paid for a specialist cleaning service.

'Why don't you think back to when you last had the bag?' Charlie suggested.

In theory, this was sound advice, but in practice it was useless. Hugo's memory of the evening was at best fragmentary. Vast chunks of it remained inaccessible, like data on a broken computer hard drive.

'I had it when I left the office – I can't remember anything about it after that. Was it with me when I arrived at the Hilton?'

'I don't know – perhaps you left it in the cloakroom?'

Hugo rallied at this. Now Charlie mentioned it, he could almost see the supercilious concierge handing him a ticket – which, logically, he must still have somewhere. Seized with excitement, he searched everywhere from his suit pockets to the compartments in his wallet. He extracted many scruffy bits of paper, all of which proved to be irrelevant.

'Did you lose the ticket, or leave it on the table?' Charlie said. 'Why don't you call them and ask?'

Two minutes later the hope which had blazed so strongly flickered and died.

'They say no items were left in the cloakroom last night.'

'Did you have it in the taxi?'

'I'm really not sure,' Hugo confessed. 'I'll try the lost property office.'

Another abortive phone call.

'Bloody useless. The cabbies hand in stuff at a police station, and then it goes to the lost property office. Apparently it can take up to five working days to arrive. Fat lot of good that is – Stephanie will have had my balls on a plate by then.'

'Did you leave it in the cloakroom at the speed dating?'

An image emerged from the recesses of Hugo's mind.

'No – I didn't leave it there because I was worried it might be stolen, so I carried it round with me.'

'Well, there you are, it's obvious – all that circulating round. It stands to reason you must have left it there. Let's hope someone's handed it in.'

Hugo called the event organisers. The woman who answered the phone had clearly dealt with dozens of similar calls that morning – her script was well-rehearsed.

'We did a thorough sweep round at the end of the evening, and you'd be amazed at some of the items people left behind. But we didn't have a single laptop case. I'm very sorry, I do hope you find it.'

Hugo hoped so too, only he'd run out of places to look.

Sunday evening, Wayne called Brad at his home.

'So – what do you have for me?'

'Morrison is a model citizen. He's devoted to his wife, children and grandchildren, attends church every Sunday, and enjoys mowing the lawn even though he retains a gardener. He has no criminal record, not even so much as a parking violation. He's a non-smoker who seldom drinks liquor. You've checked out his personnel record yourself.'

'He's a model employee as well, unless you're going to tell me any different.'

'There's one observation we made,' said Wayne. 'Over the last couple of days, our loyal employee has been making calls from payphones.'

'You heard what he said?'

'Nope.'

'Well, it's not good enough, Wayne – I'm disappointed in you.'

Brad had a certain gravitas as CEO – Wayne never quite knew whether he was serious or not, especially over the telephone.

'We tried, but he won't make the calls if there's anyone hanging around, and he never uses the same payphone twice. He's not street smart, but my gut feeling is someone's been giving him advice. Fact is, why would the guy use payphones all the time?'

There was only one reason.

'Can you tell who he's been speaking to?'

'Already been down that road. And the good news is I have some friends in law enforcement who were able to help.'

'What's the bad news?'

'Two of the three calls were placed to a pay-as-you-go cell phone, registered in the UK, and untraceable.'

'The UK,' Brad reflected. 'That's where this George Hubbard is. Is Morrison trying to cut a deal with him?'

'He might be.'

'And the third call?'

'To a residential line in San Paulo – a Vincente Ferreira. He's a middle ranking official in the Ministry of the Environment.'

'Interesting,' said Brad.

'Even more interesting, when we examined Morrison's office line, we found he'd called Senor Ferreira in the office several times before all this Hubbard business blew up.'

'He'd been calling Brazil? That's where the team were based who did the work on loucura.'

'Yes,' said Wayne, 'it was.'

'There has to be a connection. What is it?'

'I don't know yet, but I plan to keep watching Morrison until I get to the truth.'

'Great stuff, and how's Hubbard doing?'

'Still no trace of any papers, but according to his telephone records, he's been talking to the *Daily Globe*, a London newspaper, and Umbra Capital, a hedge fund specialising in pharmaceutical stocks. We'll keep at it, but I must say, Hubbard leads a very uneventful life.'

'Let's hope it stays that way,' he said.

Brad couldn't put his finger on why, but he didn't like the sound of the hedge fund.

14

Claudia set to work without delay. After a perfunctory rewrite of the speed-dating piece, she turned her attention to Tuesday's meeting.

Morrison's academic papers had dried up around the late eighties, around the time he'd joined BEP. If Hubbard had retired twenty years ago, they hadn't overlapped at BEP for long.

For \$32.50 Claudia downloaded Morrison's final research paper. Having only a GCSE in chemistry, she worried it might be tough going. But the abstract was cogent enough. A chemical called loucuramine shrank cancerous tumours in rats, but it also caused fatal internal bleeding.

The paper referred to previous work done by a team in Brazil headed up by a Cristiano Rodrigues at the Rio De Janeiro State University. The Rodrigues study was not available online, but Claudia e-mailed the journal and asked for a copy – it would be in Portuguese, but she'd figure out how to deal with that problem later.

Meanwhile, she googled loucuramine and came up with a whole host of conspiracy theories. Some implied that the results of the Morrison study had been falsified. Others queried why the tests on loucuramine had been conducted at all given that the original Brazilian work had used infusions of loucura tree bark, reputed to be an ancient remedy for any number of ailments.

Something so well-documented on the internet surely must be a hoax, Claudia decided. And much as it pained her to admit it, in the cold light of day all the evidence pointed to Bill being right.

But she wasn't quite done yet – if nothing else, Bill had taught her to be thorough. She tried to call Morrison and Rodrigues, but no reply. Then she remembered it was Saturday – no surprise she'd drawn a blank. She would try again on Monday.

Most of the rest of Claudia's weekend disappeared in a blur. Bill sent her out to cover a motorway pile-up and she returned home in the early hours of Sunday morning. Exhausted, she slept until mid afternoon.

Sunday evening, she remembered Hugo. She hadn't meant to leave him to sweat for the whole weekend, and now guilt prompted her into action. She began to dial the mobile number on Hugo's business card. Then she had a better idea. Hugo lived in Balham, about a quarter of an hour's walk from her house. He was almost certain to be in on a Sunday evening – she would deliver the bag in person and surprise him.

A virtual clone of Hugo answered the door, with the same strong jawline and foppishly highlighted hair. Perhaps they were brothers.

'Can I help you?' he asked warily. He sounded like Hugo as well.

'Is Hugo in?' she asked.

'He's in the shower.' He looked her up and down, as men did, but at the same time seemed puzzled.

'I've brought a present for him.'

When she revealed the laptop bag, the brother was transformed.

'Oh, wow, the bag. He'll be so relieved. Where on earth did you find it?'

'He left it at the speed-dating thingy.'

Comprehension dawned.

'You must be that girl, Claudia,' he said.

'I am that girl,' she agreed, smiling.

So she'd made enough of an impression on Hugo for him tell Charlie about her, and remember her name.

'I'm Charlie, Hugo's flatmate.'

'Oh,' said Claudia. 'You could be brothers.'

'People always say that. Why don't you come in and wait for him – I know he'd like to say thanks.'

He took Claudia into the lounge. Two leather sofas faced each other either side of the fireplace, with brown and turquoise cushions. A selection of carefully chosen *objets d'art* picked up the same colours. Rented furnished, Claudia concluded – no way would these two lads choose this tasteful decor. The overall effect was spoiled by a giant television screen, placed for optimal viewing rather than appearance.

She removed a pizza box and some newspapers from one of the sofas – the *Telegraph*, not the *Globe* – and sat down. Charlie was in the hallway, trying to rouse Hugo from the bathroom.

'It's that weird girl,' he said, not caring whether Claudia heard him, 'the one you were telling me about.'

Claudia dreaded to imagine what Hugo might have said to Charlie. She couldn't quite catch Hugo's mumbled reply from the bathroom, but his tone didn't sound very complimentary.

'She's brought your bag,' Charlie added.

'Fantastic,' she heard Hugo shout, abruptly changing his tune. 'Tell her I'll be out in a mo.'

Hugo emerged from the bathroom wearing a bath towel and two days worth of stubble. His wet hair was slicked back. Half-naked, he was even more hunky than she remembered.

'Hello Hugo.' She held out the bag as a kind of peace

offering. 'I guess you didn't mean to leave me this to look after.'

'God no! Did I really leave it there?'

''Fraid so – you went off in a bit of a huff, if you recall.'

'I don't recall much,' said Hugo, shamefaced. 'I was actually quite drunk.'

So there was a chance he might not remember how insufferable she'd been.

'Mind you,' he added, shattering her hopes, 'you were pretty obnoxious.'

'Yes, well,' said Claudia.

'Aren't you sorry for the way you behaved?'

In Hugo's world, she figured an apology was customary.

'No – I make it a rule never to say sorry – it shows weakness. But I brought your bag, so I reckon we're quits.'

'How did you know where to find me?'

'There was some stuff in there with your address on.'

'You should have handed it in.'

'Didn't trust them,' said Claudia, unable to meet Hugo's eye.

'Well, thanks for bringing it back. I can't tell you what a relief it is.'

Hugo swiftly inspected the bag's contents.

'It's all here.' He sounded mildly surprised.

'For sure,' said Claudia. 'What did you expect?'

She stood up.

'Well, that's my good deed done for the day.'

'You're not leaving are you?'

'Well, I came to bring your bag – I've brought it, so I'm off. What else did you have in mind?'

Claudia fluttered her eyelashes and looked decorously at the floor, flirting outrageously. It was now or never to grab his attention.

'The least I can do is take you out for a drink and a bite to eat – unless you're in a tearing hurry.'

He had taken the bait. Claudia pretended to demur, but not for long.

'No, I'm in no hurry at all,' she said. 'I'd love to.'

'Fine. Wait there a mo, while I get dressed and shave.'

That had been easy.

As soon as he'd left, Charlie came back – to suss her out, she reckoned.

'Hugo tells me you're a journalist.'

Hugo had said a lot, in the circumstances.

'Yes, I'm a reporter for the *Daily Globe*.'

'That sounds exciting.'

'Not so exciting as all that,' said Claudia nonchalantly. 'It's often quite tedious – the same as any job, I suppose. What do you do?'

'I work for the same firm as Hugo – Corporate Tax Manager.'

Claudia knew she was meant to be impressed by this, but saw no reason to inflate an already over-stuffed ego.

'Well, you'll understand what I mean about tedious,' she said and then, changing the subject, 'Why don't you and Hugo read the *Globe*?' She gestured towards all the discarded *Telegraph*s.

'Don't take this the wrong way, but isn't it aimed at left-wing intellectuals?'

He spoke as though the *Globe* was a subversive propaganda machine which might at any time undermine civilised society.

'And you're not left wing or intellectual?' Claudia suggested.

'I suppose we can't be, can we?'

'How long have you known Hugo?'

'Twelve years,' Charlie replied. 'We were at Winchester together.'

'The school, not the prison, I guess.'

Charlie laughed.

'Not much difference, really. Except you don't get parole at school.'

'I went to a state school.'

'You've done well then, getting into journalism.'

'Not everyone who goes to state school ends up flipping burgers, you know.'

Charlie's polite mask slipped almost imperceptibly, but he recovered it fast.

'I didn't mean that,' he said. 'It's just I'm aware it's hugely competitive.'

Claudia smiled, now he'd paid her a compliment.

'It is,' she agreed. 'And I'm hugely talented.'

Both were relieved when Hugo returned, rescuing them from their stilted dialogue. She caught Charlie grimacing at Hugo – rather you than me mate, his expression suggested. Hugo either didn't notice or ignored him.

'OK, let's go,' he said.

15

The Avalon had once been the George before gentrification transformed it into a metropolitan gastro pub. It was still Hugo's preferred local, though.

They sat in the garden and Hugo ordered a bottle of New Zealand Sauvignon Blanc. He offered Claudia a cigarette, before lighting one himself.

'All guys like you smoke,' she remarked, refusing the offer.

'You keep saying "guys like me",' said Hugo. 'I don't understand what you mean.'

'Yes you do. Public school types.'

'Colonial pricks, maybe?'

She had the grace to smile. Surely such a stunner with an unbelievably sexy mouth couldn't be totally unbearable? On reflection, the hair was far too out there, but Hugo was prepared to overlook this for now. Mainly, he hoped for some meaningful communication without being assailed by a barrage of insults. And then – well, who could say?

'Does it bug you that I'm a public school boy?'

'Only if it bugs you that I'm black.'

'Why would it?'

'Because you don't do black girls?'

'I didn't mean it like that. All I really meant was I didn't really know any.'

'You do now,' she replied briskly.

'And I guess you haven't come across too many public school boys?'

'You're quite wrong there,' she said. 'I've met lots of guys like you.'

Hugo made a real effort not to rise to the bait, but failed.

'I'll have you know all sorts of people go to public school,' he said, bristling.

'Surely you can't argue Winchester represents a microcosm of society.'

'Did I say it was? Although not everyone there is loaded. In fact, because my father's with the diplomatic service, the government paid most of my school fees. If you went to a state school, the government paid for your education as well, so we're not all that different.'

'That's the biggest load of bollocks I've heard in ages,' said Claudia. 'But for now I'll buy it.'

'Were you really there as a reporter on Friday?' asked Hugo.

'Yes, of course – surely you don't imagine I would have gone otherwise?'

'Certainly not – and me neither,' Hugo added hastily, terrified she might think he was some saddo who habitually went speed dating. 'I was only there because of the bet with Charlie.'

She giggled as Hugo described his fuzzy memories of the odd assortment of girls he had encountered during the evening.

'Believe me, the men were no better.'

'Shame we got off on the wrong foot,' said Hugo. 'You were the most beautiful girl by a mile.'

'And you were the tastiest guy.'

After a few mouthfuls of the wine, Hugo was already mellow. His two-day marathon hangover from Friday had at long last abated, he had his bag back and he was sitting outside on a perfect summer's evening with a gorgeous girl who unmistakeably fancied him. He listened intently as she described being scooped and Bill's outright rejection of her proposed story.

'You weren't planning to print my name I hope,' he said. 'How ghastly to be immortalised in print as a racist jackass.'

'No, definitely not.' Claudia seemed amused by his anxiety.

'Do you mind if I ask where you come from originally?'

'Near Croydon,' she replied with a sardonic smile.

'No, I mean where are your family roots?'

'My parents were born in London as well – both my grandfathers came over from Jamaica fifty odd years ago.'

'Ah, I see. And you're proud of your roots?

'Yes – of course. Aren't you?'

Hugo was itching to ask why she sounded the way she did when she'd never been anywhere near the Caribbean, but not at the risk of offending her again.

'Do you enjoy your job?' he said, moving onto safer territory, 'or do you always get the crappy stuff to do?'

He topped up Claudia's wine glass.

'It's OK most of the time. You take the rough with the smooth. Do you enjoy yours?'

Hugo paused. Unaccountably, the glib assurances he often gave people didn't seem adequate for Claudia.

'I don't know,' he said truthfully. 'It's not something I had a burning desire to do, but it pays quite well and I didn't have a better game plan. Some of the deals are fun, though . . .'

'Like Project Acorn.'

Hugo tensed.

'You've been reading the papers in my bag.'

She flashed him a guilty little smile.

'Well, I am a journalist – I'm nosy.'

That was no excuse, and she knew it.

'It's a price sensitive transaction,' said Hugo, panicking. 'It hasn't been announced yet. I hope to God you're not intending to write about that.'

'Lucky for you the draft was anonymised.'

Hugo relaxed, then reverted to panic stations as she delivered the killer blow.

'Though they didn't do a very thorough job, did they? It took me all of about ten minutes to work out it's Miss Perfect Julia Fraser's company selling out.'

'Shh,' said Hugo, looking around uneasily.

The waiter came to take the food orders. Hugo ordered hurriedly, distracted by this latest revelation.

'Please,' he said, 'I beg you – don't print anything about it.'

'Don't worry – not my cup of tea.'

'Thank goodness.'

'Though the business editor would be quite intrigued,' she went on, twisting the knife a second time.

'No, no,' said Hugo. 'You mustn't – I'll get into terrible trouble.'

'Hugo – I'm pulling your leg. I won't say a word – promise. Though you should be more careful – next time you might not be so lucky.'

Hugo caught Claudia's ironic smile. It occurred to him she'd read his bank statements as well, but he pushed the suspicion away. Jeez, he didn't even care to read them himself.

'To even things out a bit,' said Claudia, 'I'll give you a piece of information which might be useful for your Project Acorn. Suppose some bad press came out about BEP – what would happen to your transaction?'

Hugo sat up at this, reflecting on how much effort they'd put in trying to convince Julia Fraser that BEP was an ethical organisation – a subject she cared passionately about.

'It would depend, but it's no secret that Julia would be seriously concerned.'

'And since she and her staff own more than forty percent of the company, they can probably stop the takeover.'

'My, you have been doing your homework,' said Hugo. 'So what's so awful about BEP?'

Claudia told him all she knew about George Hubbard and loucura.

'Could it be true?' asked Hugo when she'd finished. Frankly, he considered it unlikely.

'Not sure – I'm trying to find out. But in the meantime, I'd appreciate it if you didn't mention the story to anyone – it's highly confidential.'

'Just like Project Acorn,' said Hugo, calmer now one confidence had been traded for another.

His thoughts turned to Julia – his favourite client of all time. She always saw him as a mature professional rather than the village idiot of Stephanie's perception. And she was so beautiful as well – not along the Claudia 'in your face' lines, but delicate and serene. Was he under some sort of obligation to tell her what might be brewing? She'd be devastated if a huge scandal emerged after she'd sold out. On the other hand, there were plenty of reasons to keep quiet. Claudia had told him it was hush-hush, and in addition his promotion most likely depended on bringing Project Acorn to a successful completion. Did the rationale for remaining silent over-ride his duty to his client? The answer seemed far from easy. Ethical issues were never comfortable if you had a conscience.

'What are you thinking?' asked Claudia, taking his hand.

'About moral dilemmas.'

'That's a weighty subject for a Sunday evening. You're a more serious dude than I imagined.'

Hugo drained the last of the wine from his glass – dusk was gathering and they had switched on the lights in the garden. Time to go home and finish the work for Stephanie – then an early night. Or...

'I'm thinking something else as well.' He hardly dared

to ask her – she was bound to say no. Don't ask, don't get, a cheeky internal voice told him.

'What?'

She was leaning forward, her chin cupped in her hand – eager, maybe?

'If we go home now, is it too late to win Charlie's bet?' Claudia leaned forward and whispered in his ear.

'Well, why don't you grab the bill and we'll go and see.'

Which was easier said than done – all of Hugo's cards were rejected. He grew more and more red-faced as the waiter tried one after another in his machine. But the exercise was futile – his money had fallen into a banking abyss, debited from his current account but not yet credited to his cards.

'I'm so sorry,' Hugo said. 'I can't imagine what the problem is.'

'I can,' said Claudia. 'I read your bank statements.'

Hugo started to protest but she cut him short.

'I'm a journalist – I'm hard-wired to be inquisitive.'

This was no justification, but if Hugo made a fuss, she wouldn't come home with him. Besides, Claudia was reaching into her bag for her own card.

'Have it on the *Globe*. We've been chatting about a story. The expenses in journalism aren't what they were, but I'm sure I can wangle this one on the paper.'

After the waiter had left, she said, 'So, can we still go back to yours, or has your ego been too badly bruised?'

'Assuming you still want to, my ego will survive.'

'Now remember – you don't do black girls.'

Hugo kissed her full on the lips, all thoughts of Julia and the moral dilemma erased from his mind.

'I do now,' he said.

When Hugo woke, Claudia had already left, leaving him

a note scribbled on one of the pages of her reporter's notebook.

'Thanks for last night – gone back home to get changed. Take care C x'

He wished she'd woken him, if only because he was now running late. And sickeningly, he'd made no progress towards finishing the work for Stephanie – a plausible excuse was required, and fast.

His best suit lay crumpled beyond redemption after the excesses of Friday night, but his second best was still in reasonable shape. He sniffed the armpits of a shirt draped over his chair and decided it too was wearable.

What did Claudia's note mean, Hugo wondered as he carried out his perfunctory morning routine in the bathroom. There was no contact number, no mention of seeing him again – had it been a one-night stand?

Not if he had anything to do with it. She'd been great fun, but there was more to it than that. They'd met in a random way, but they already had this uncanny connection through BEP. He would simply have to see her again, if only to hear how her story had panned out. It was, Hugo reflected, as if there was a higher power controlling events. He dashed out of the house, filled for once with enthusiasm for the new week.

16

Stephanie began her Monday drained and dispirited. Who would be mad enough to give birth to twins at 43? Answer – someone who'd prioritised promotion to partnership before children and nearly ended up with neither.

Now the boys were two and the time for partnership had long been and gone. She was stuck as a director for the rest of her career – on a salary too high to lose but not enough to compensate for all she'd sacrificed.

The sight of Hugo rushing past her office in the hope she wouldn't notice his late arrival did nothing to improve Stephanie's mood. The boy was a wastrel and a hedonist and she simultaneously despised and envied him for it. What was wrong with young men these days? In previous generations, at twenty-five they would have been marching off to war, or already married. Now, they drifted – and Hugo drifted more aimlessly than any of them.

She made a point of stopping by his desk as she headed for the coffee machine.

'You look dreadful, Hugo – what on earth have you been up to?'

He smiled. He knew it cut no ice with her, but to her annoyance he always did it anyway.

'Actually, I've been very ill.'

'Hangover was it?'

'I believe it may have been some kind of virus.'

There was that smile again – he was lying.

'I suppose this means you haven't done the work I gave you.'

She was damned if she was going through the social niceties of asking Hugo if he was recovered when his illness was at best self-inflicted, at worst fictional.

'I'll finish it right now,' he said. 'The client isn't coming in till four o'clock.'

Stephanie sighed – Hugo was more than capable of rushing into her office at 3.57, giving her only minutes to skim over what he'd done. Which was why she'd asked for it by Monday morning.

'I need it by midday, absolute latest.'

Hugo smiled at her again.

'No problem,' he said. 'No problem at all. Um, by the way...'

'Yes?'

'There's something you should know.'

Stephanie winced. Hugo's disclosures were seldom helpful.

'Yes? What?'

'Never mind,' said Hugo, shrinking back as he sensed her alarm.

'You might as well go on now you've started.'

'Oh, no – perhaps it's not very important.'

Damn him – he couldn't leave it there.

'Hugo – will you spit it out?!'

'Well, um, the point is, there's an important issue that Julia should be told about this afternoon – something we didn't know before.'

'Yes?'

Most probably something important which Hugo had failed to mention.

'Now, you mustn't repeat it to anyone, because it's a secret,' Hugo warned.

'In which case, we won't be able to tell Julia in any event.'

'We may conclude that it's so important we have to tell Julia, secret or not.'

'Well, come on, cough it up. What on earth is it?'

Hugo was obviously trying to cover up for some mistake or other. He cleared his throat.

'According to a journalist friend of mine, there's a big story brewing about BEP.'

Hugo might be a slacker, and Stephanie had never regarded him as a great brain, but until now she hadn't considered him to be insane.

'You've been speaking to a journalist about this project? You must be crazy – you know how confidential it is!'

'No, no – I haven't discussed Project Acorn. It's just that she happened to mention she was working on this story.'

Despite Hugo's assurances, Stephanie was nervous, and the gender of the journalist had only heightened her apprehension. Hugo would be putty in the hands of a seasoned female reporter who turned on the charm. He might easily have let some vital information slip without realising it.

'What story?'

She tried not to sound sour, not to prejudge. In his own misguided way, Hugo might be trying to be helpful.

'Twenty years ago BEP quashed a natural cure for cancer, because they couldn't patent it and it would lose them money.'

Stephanie did her utmost to stay calm – Hugo was a tad green behind the ears, that's all. She should neither be surprised nor angry if he took everything at face value.

'Hugo – has it occurred to you that journalists sometimes write stories which are untrue?'

Hugo's quizzical face suggested that it hadn't.

'Well, yes,' he said, 'but my friend's meeting her source tomorrow morning to try to get to the truth. The guy's name is George Hubbard and apparently he has documents to prove it.'

'I'll believe it when I see it,' said Stephanie. 'And has it also occurred to you that conspiracy theories against drug companies are ten a penny?'

'But there might be some basis to it – and supposing there was, shouldn't we warn Julia?'

'No.'

'Why not?'

Stephanie tried hard to keep her cool. Wasn't it obvious?

'Hugo, we've spent a lot of time ironing out the teething problems on this deal and you know how hard we've worked to convince her of BEP's integrity.'

'That's exactly where I'm coming from,' countered Hugo. 'If there's any sniff of scandal about BEP, she wouldn't be willing to throw her lot in with them. So shouldn't we keep her in the picture?'

'No, we should not. It would be disastrous if something unsettled her at this late stage – all the more since it might not be true. And you told me it was a secret.'

'Well, it is, but I was kind of weighing up whether our duty to our client might override...'

Hugo's lunacy had to be stamped on once and for all. Stephanie wasn't even prepared to let him finish his sentence.

'Over my dead body,' she said in her firmest tones.

'What – even if my friend gets proof?'

'Especially if your friend gets proof.'

'But we'll look so silly if this comes out of the woodwork later and we knew, but didn't warn her.'

'We'll have to take the risk.'

'But don't we have a moral duty?'

'Hugo, do I have to spell it out in words of one syllable? I've specifically instructed you not to say a word to Julia about this. And that is an end to the matter. Do I make myself plain?'

Hugo opened his mouth to protest, but thought better

of it. 'Midday, Hugo. Don't forget,' said Stephanie as she turned to leave his workstation.

'Don't worry,' he replied. 'I won't.'

17

George Hubbard stood at the pedestrian crossing, waiting for the green man. Marcus spotted him immediately from his seat outside the Audley pub – he could have been a caricature of an elderly boffin. Eighty-year-olds of any type were a rarity in this part of Mayfair – but ones with goatee beards and tweed jackets were unprecedented. The lights changed and the old man stepped out from the kerb.

He never stood a chance.

A black Honda SUV appeared from nowhere and hurtled towards him. Marcus's lips moved to shout a warning, but no words came out. Too late, Hubbard saw the car. He raised his arms in a useless gesture, dropping his briefcase.

The impact was brutal and noisy. It threw Hubbard up with such force that his body hit the windscreen – old bones cracking against glass. For a moment, he hung suspended on the car bonnet, as if held there by some invisible tether. Then he slowly slid off, catching another glancing blow from the bumper, before hitting the ground with a stomach-churning thud. The SUV skidded round the corner and was gone.

Cars manoeuvred round Hubbard's inert form, pedestrians gawped, Marcus held his breath. After an age, someone went to check on Hubbard and called 999. Although there wasn't much point. A crimson trickle ran from his head into the gutter. Marcus exhaled, picked up his glass and drained the rest of his Scotch.

It was time to leave, before the police came asking

questions. He stepped out into the street and, looking nervously around him, began the short walk home.

He lived in a penthouse flat on Berkeley Square – a few minutes' walk from the office and a symbol of his one-dimensional life. It was a place to sleep and he rarely went back there during the day. But then he was rarely so rattled by events as he was now.

Shutting the front door behind him, Marcus slumped onto the lime green S-shaped sofa, his body trembling uncontrollably as he reached for the whisky bottle. He spilled more than ended up in his glass, and more still dribbled down his chin as he attempted to drink. Get a grip man, he told himself – get a grip.

He'd bought the flat lock, stock and barrel two years ago when his second wife Olivia had unilaterally called time on their marriage. The surreal, minimalist decor reflected the tastes of the flat's previous owner, a flamboyant TV executive who'd emigrated to California. Marcus had never felt any necessity to express his own personality through interior design, but now he found these alien furnishings suddenly irritating.

At least he was on his own, without some woman trying to tease out what was wrong. That was the trouble with women – they tried to fuck with your mind as well as your body. In truth, Marcus's mind was usually fairly empty, but women never seemed to accept that – they had an irresistible urge to prise him open and look for whatever pearls they supposed might be hidden inside. Still, Marcus had learnt his lesson now. Since Olivia, only women who respected his need for mental space made it anywhere near his bed.

As the shaking gradually subsided, a more specific concern took its place. Hubbard's death was no accident and Marcus had a transparent motive. If anyone made the connection, he was a prime suspect, presumed guilty until he could prove his innocence, and he'd done himself no favours by his speedy exit from the scene of the crime. Marcus refilled his whisky glass and lit one of his cigars as he mulled over his predicament.

If Hubbard hadn't told his wife about the meeting, Marcus figured he was in the clear – they might try tracing the call to his mobile, but where would that get them? Hubbard was an old acquaintance who'd got in touch again. What was wrong with that? If Hubbard had confided in her ... well, that scenario might be a touch more tricky, but he'd simply tell them Hubbard never showed. Hell – this even had the virtue of being true. And surely no one would really imagine he'd had a hand in Hubbard's killing. His attention drifted instead to what Hubbard's death might mean.

In Geneva he'd asked Julia Fraser of IDD whether a simple treatment for cancer was possible. He'd been more than a little piqued when she'd poked fun at his naivety. Afterwards, though, he'd reflected on the conversation.

It didn't take a genius to discern that a quick-fix cancer cure would be a commercial disaster. At a stroke, all the billions the pharma companies earned from chemo and other next to useless therapies would be wiped out. And they couldn't even patent a natural product. No wonder they all chorused in unison that it was impossible. Marcus had built his fortune on cynicism and, on that basis alone, he figured Hubbard was worth a punt.

Richard, his researcher, had done a sterling job. From the minimal information Marcus had provided, he'd produced a detailed file on loucura. Still, Marcus had kept an open mind – maybe there was some value in it, maybe not. He wasn't a man to get carried away. But now, Hubbard's murder had dramatically shifted the odds.

Hubbard might be dead, but his papers lived on – his briefcase would be returned to the widow. And given the historic connection – also confirmed by Richard's enquiries

– a visit to the grieving widow might be in order. Why, there was every chance of getting hold of those papers without paying out a penny. At the same time, he could suss out what she knew and what she'd said to the police.

Marcus was no stranger to the benefits of forward planning and had already formulated an outline strategy to be executed if Hubbard's contentions were true. The share prices of all the companies most dependent on revenue from cancer treatments would plummet once the news of a simple cancer cure was out there. And he could take advantage of that. He would take short positions, agreeing to sell shares in the future at today's price – shares that he didn't actually own. Once he'd leaked the story to the press and the share prices had nose dived, he'd buy them for a song and sell them at the agreed price, raking in a colossal profit. It was a simple but effective ploy, which might still work even if Hubbard's story turned out to be a hoax – the mere rumour of a cancer cure could be enough to send share prices into a tailspin.

And that was only part of the plan. If IDD sold out to BEP, Umbra would make a respectable return on its investment. But there was no way Julia Fraser would get into bed with bad boys like BEP once she knew the facts. That didn't matter to Marcus – he saw even more lucrative possibilities now. IDD's technology had the capability to synthesise any molecule – including loucura. Synthetic loucura could be effectively quality-controlled and patented. Conclusion – overnight, IDD would be worth a fortune. If only he could dream up of a way to massively increase Umbra's stake...

Encouraged by the prospect of hyper profits, Marcus poured himself a third Scotch and raised his glass to the late George Hubbard.

18

'I got your message to call.'

Morrison glanced around furtively as he telephoned from yet another filling station. He was OK – no one was watching.

'Just to let you know my part of the bargain's done. George Hubbard won't be sharing his secrets with the press.'

'Was he all right about it?'

'He didn't raise any objections.'

That was strange, thought Morrison. In the past Hubbard had always reminded him of a vulture picking over a carcass – he would raise objections purely for the intellectual pleasure of a debate. But perhaps this time he'd simply decided to take the money and run.

'Good. And his proof?'

'Gone. It'll never see the light of day again.'

'Even better.'

'So – all that's left is for you to fulfil your side of the bargain.'

'Easy.' Morrison was filled with a new-found confidence. 'I can deliver on that.'

Before leaving the filling station, he bought himself a coffee and an iced donut – for the first time in days he could relax. Now the threat of Hubbard had retreated, Morrison would salvage his own plans.

19

Julia and Stephanie were both slim and physically well-maintained. There the similarities ended. Julia's relaxed elegance showed up Stephanie's forced and dated style. Her emotional warmth highlighted Stephanie's coldness, and her calm approach rendered Stephanie's Rottweiler aggression ridiculous.

In spite of, or more likely because of, their differences, the two women collaborated well on Project Acorn. Without Stephanie's tenacity, Julia would have backed away from the offer. Without Julia's expertise, Stephanie would have blown the negotiations.

Stephanie had called the meeting to thrash out the draft offer document. Pearson Malone had to sign off on IDD's recommendation for shareholders to accept BEP's offer, but they wouldn't put their name to any statement which didn't stand up to rigorous analysis. At the same time, Julia understandably wished to present the information in the best light so the deal would go ahead. At this stage, there were still some differences of opinion to be reconciled.

Hugo met the noon deadline with one minute to spare. In their pre-meeting Stephanie congratulated him on picking up on all the main areas of concern. Such praise was rare, although he wished she hadn't sounded so surprised about it. Stephanie would now sit in front of Julia, passing off Hugo's profound observations as her own, but this didn't matter to Hugo at all – for the time being she was not on his case.

Stephanie signalled to Hugo to pour out the coffee. With

attitudes stuck somewhere in the eighties, she judged it demeaning for women to serve drinks in business meetings. Hugo always deliberately waited for her to ask him to do it, rather than volunteering. Holding onto these titbits of power made working with Stephanie almost bearable.

Stephanie waved aside the plate of biscuits Hugo offered – Julia took two. She had brought along Neil Burrows, IDD's company secretary and principal bean counter. Neil would soon have a bucketful of beans to count – he stood to net about £2 million post tax from Project Acorn. He also helped himself to two biscuits – one for each million. Hugo took three.

'I was thrilled to hear about that anti-epileptic drug of yours,' observed Stephanie, eager to show her superior insight.

'What anti-epileptic drug?' asked Hugo. He didn't care to appear ignorant, but on the other hand Stephanie often chided him for not asking enough questions.

'Oh, I'm sure I explained it to you last week,' said Stephanie, with a little flick to her hair which gave away her lying.

Julia was more expansive.

'We've recently concluded some tests to establish whether the drug might also be effective to reduce anxiety and all the signs are positive. BEP's buying our technology to reposition their existing drugs, so to have a successful example of the technology being used right now is brilliant timing.'

'Don't they see any value in synthesising improved versions of plant-based molecules?' asked Hugo. 'Doesn't your technology do that as well?'

The loucura situation had been weighing on him all day – surely, if IDD were able to synthesise it, they were better off without BEP. Stephanie immediately spotted where he was going, and tried to head him off with a steely glare.

Hugo ignored her – she couldn't stop him from making intelligent enquiries.

Julia smiled benignly.

'Exactly so, Hugo. The problem has always been how to put it to practical use. Anyway, big pharma has pretty much abandoned research into naturally occurring compounds over the past few years. They have more pressing issues, such as blockbuster drugs coming off the patent and a thin pipeline of new drugs. They're always keen to find new uses for existing drugs, or to change the formulae so they can lengthen the life of their patents – "evergreening", as it's sometimes called.'

'Why have they abandoned the research?' asked Hugo. 'I mean, what about aspirin and penicillin – they came from natural sources, didn't they?'

'That's true,' agreed Julia. 'Although as a line of research, biological molecules haven't generated as much as everybody hoped. It's not a straightforward area for a variety of reasons.'

The toxic gamma rays from Stephanie bored into Hugo – she hated that he'd commandeered the meeting.

'You mean because they can't be patented?' he asked, reflecting on what Claudia had told him. No pharmaceutical company would spend vast sums researching and trialling a drug without exclusivity.

'That's one of the issues, yes. But there are many other problems, such as the technical challenge of determining which molecules are the active components, and then there's the whole bio-piracy arena.'

'Bio-piracy?'

'Yes – many organic medicines originate from remote and underdeveloped countries. The governments of these countries feel strongly that it's wrong for more advanced nations to reap all the profits from their physical resources, so they try to prevent anyone from collecting samples.'

'Going back to the patents for a minute,' said Hugo. 'Isn't it unethical to deny people cheaper generic versions of a drug?'

'You have to understand where the drug companies are coming from,' said Julia. 'They invest a huge amount in research and development, and they need to recoup that.'

'I suppose so,' said Hugo, vaguely dissatisfied by the ethical Julia's pragmatic approach.

He asked himself why Julia would sign away control of this valuable technology by selling out – wouldn't it have been more sensible for her to enter into some sort of joint venture with BEP? IDD would then be free to pursue other uses for the software. But this was a question too far. Stephanie's enthusiasm for the takeover possibly even outstripped Julia's – she wouldn't thank him for querying the rationale at this stage.

Stephanie gave Julia one of her most ingratiating smiles.

'Thank you so much for clarifying all this for Hugo,' she said. 'It's terrific for more junior staff to get a broader perspective on the businesses they're advising.'

In reality, she would have put blinkers on her staff if she could, but you'd never have guessed it from her fluent corporate-speak. And how much had Stephanie herself known about what Julia had told him? She held herself out as an expert in the pharmaceutical sector, but how much was real and how much was hot air? In Pearson Malone everyone was a bullshitter in their own way.

'By the way,' said Stephanie. 'Did you manage to discover any more about the mysterious shareholder who's built up that seven percent stake?'

'Yes, no mystery – it's a firm called Umbra Capital Partners. They're a hedge fund,' Julia replied. 'There's nothing sinister about them at all. I met with the owner of Umbra in Geneva at the weekend to discuss his intentions. Naturally, I wasn't in a position to tell him about the deal at this stage, but I needed to get an impression of whether they planned to be active investors and potentially interfere with Project Acorn.'

'And?' said Stephanie and Hugo in unison.

'They're not. IDD is part of a broad strategic acquisition program.'

'You believed him?' said Stephanie incredulously.

Julia dealt head on with the tacit implication that she was a gullible fool, and apparently without taking offence.

'Yes, I can guess what you're thinking. He's a hedge fund manager, a wheeler-dealer who'd no doubt sell his own auntie given half the chance – but you have to go with your judgement sometimes. On balance, I trust him. I may be wrong, but I doubt it.'

Good for you, thought Hugo, impressed at how efficiently she'd put Stephanie back in her box.

'BEP are after ninety percent acceptance from IDD's shareholders, but these Umbra people only have seven percent, so they couldn't block it anyway,' he pointed out.

'Remember, Hugo, they don't know about the negotiations with BEP yet,' said Julia. 'The offer hasn't been announced. They can always increase their stake later and torpedo the takeover. Though I honestly don't believe that's their intention.'

Hugo squirmed in the uncomfortable realisation that a reporter for a national newspaper was privy to all the details of the deal. His judgement told him that Claudia could be trusted too but, as Julia had reminded him, you never knew. Hopefully, if the worst did happen it would not be traced back to him.

'It's a fair offer,' said Hugo. 'Umbra should be satisfied with such a high return when the takeover's announced.'

'Well yes, you'd suppose so, wouldn't you?' said Julia. 'But it wouldn't take much to turn a friendly takeover into a hostile bid – hence my concern.'

'While we're on this subject, have you asked where Bioinvestments sit with all this?' said Stephanie.

Bioinvestments was a private equity firm with a twenty percent stake in IDD. They had a place on the board and were in an influential position.

'We're safe there as well,' Julia replied. 'They're absolutely desperate for a realisation to get a decent return to their investors. It's a very difficult time for them. They're apparently on an extremely tight deadline.'

All in all, Hugo reflected, there was a huge collective will for this transaction to go ahead – would he really care to be the person to derail it? Perhaps not.

Stephanie and Julia whipped through the formal agenda at a cracking pace. Compromises were negotiated and additional evidence produced. Hugo was instructed to contact the lawyers acting for IDD on a number of minor issues. They touched on a few quirks emerging from BEP's preliminary due diligence and whether the proposed completion timetable would be achievable. Only two items of substance remained – the level of Julia's involvement after the sale, and how IDD's activities would dovetail with the rest of BEP's research and development division. These key areas were to be thrashed out in a meeting with BEP at their R & D headquarters in New Jersey the next week. After that, everyone hoped the offer would be finalised.

'It might be handy if Hugo attends next week,' Julia suggested. 'It'll be a useful learning experience for him, and he can take detailed notes of what's been discussed, since Neil's unable to come.'

'I'd been thinking the same,' said Stephanie.

Once more, Hugo was struck by her capacity for shameless lying.

'That would be excellent,' he said.

He wasn't wild about the idea of note-taking, an activity best left to bean counters like Neil. But the prospect of spending a few days out of the office in Julia's company more than compensated for the tedium of the task in hand. Julia smiled at him broadly – was it possible she looked forward to spending some time with him too?

'Great,' said Stephanie. 'If you could leave us for a moment, Hugo – there's something I'd prefer to discuss with Julia and Neil in private.'

What on earth was it? This smacked of some kind of attempt to undermine Julia's confidence in him, but as he left the room, he heard Julia say, 'What a very intelligent young man Hugo is – I'm so glad he's working on the project.'

'Oh we're glad as well,' said Stephanie with her feigned but practised professional enthusiasm.

'Now what was it you wanted to speak to us about?'

Hugo smiled to himself as he heard Stephanie dissembling. He was going to the US whether she liked it or not.

20

Joyce Hubbard was as alert and light-footed as a bird – more like a retired ballerina than the wife of a research scientist. Only her shapeless tweed skirt and tired sweater detracted from the image – that and the eyes red-rimmed from crying.

'Mrs Hubbard,' Claudia began, wondering what the heck she'd walked into. 'I'm here to see your husband – Claudia Knight from the *Daily Globe*.'

At the mention of her husband, Joyce's eyes filled with tears – she wiped them ineffectually with a well-used handkerchief.

'I'm so sorry dear – I couldn't remember your name so I didn't know how to contact you. I'm afraid George died yesterday.'

Claudia was used to dealing with the unexpected, but nothing could have prepared her for this. Never mind that she wouldn't get her interview – what on earth did you say to someone who'd lost her partner of at least fifty years?

'I'm so sorry, I can't believe it – this is so sudden. I'm so sorry for your loss. What happened?'

She blurted out the last question unintentionally, her curiosity trumping the necessity for bland condolences.

'He was run over,' Joyce said, 'mowed down in the street.'
'Really?'

Claudia's journalistic antennae twitched madly: source for a major story killed out of the blue – coincidence? Not.

'I can hardly take it in myself,' said Joyce.

'Mrs Hubbard, I don't want to intrude on your grief, but I'd still be keen to talk to you about your husband. If now isn't a convenient time...'

Claudia was shocked at her own callousness – obviously it wasn't a convenient time. Joyce hung back, evaluating her visitor.

'You'd better come in,' she said finally.

Claudia thanked the Lord she'd opted to wear the staid navy suit. Silly old Bill was right sometimes, after all.

'Let me organise some tea.' Joyce still assumed the role of the gracious hostess even in her grief, and refused Claudia's offer to help.

While Joyce was in the kitchen Claudia took the opportunity to explore. The room was comfortable, but the furniture and decor were dated and well-worn. Evidently, Hubbard and his wife had outlasted their money – that had to be where the £100K came into the picture. Books lined all four walls – Hubbard's scientific books, none of his wife's. An upright piano stood in one corner of the room, with the music for Chopin's Studies open; a small writing desk occupied the opposite corner, with a Rolodex card holder on top of it. Claudia leafed idly through it, as much out of boredom as nosiness.

Hubbard was no more, but she might still see his papers. The question was – how much had he kept Joyce in the loop?

Claudia heard Joyce returning and rushed back to her seat – it was one thing to pry but quite another to be caught. Joyce placed the tea tray on the desk and poured out two cups with rock steady hands. She was tougher than she looked, Claudia decided.

'Do you know why I'm here?' Claudia asked Joyce gently as she took her tea.

'Yes. You're that journalist.'

'Did he tell you why we were meeting?'

81

In Claudia's experience, husbands either told their wives everything or told them nothing. Which type was Hubbard?

'Oh yes,' Joyce replied. 'It was to do with that dreadful creature Edgar Morrison he used to work with when we were in the US.'

'You mean what happened with loucura?'

Joyce frowned.

'Did George tell you about that?'

'No he didn't,' said Claudia, 'but I worked it out for myself.'

'Well, you're obviously a very clever girl.' Unlike her husband, Joyce sounded as if she meant it.

'Actually, it's my job to work things out.'

Claudia described what she'd found, and Joyce chipped in extra details as necessary. There was no mention of money.

'Had he ever talked to anyone about loucura before, apart from you?' Claudia asked.

'No, I don't believe so. At first he kept quiet so as to hold onto his job, but to no avail – Morrison put George out to pasture all the same. After that, he worried no one would take him seriously.'

He'd said he had proof – was that a bluff? She would return to the matter of the papers – there were other questions to be asked first.

'Do you have any idea why your husband chose to come forward now?'

'He'd given up caring what people thought – he simply wished to do the right thing. You see, it troubled him that he'd kept quiet all these years. He was on the waiting list for heart bypass surgery. Superficially, he was always optimistic, but I'm not sure, deep down, whether he believed he would make it.'

Claudia was now certain Hubbard hadn't mentioned the money to Joyce – he intended it to be a nest egg for his widow.

'What happened yesterday?' she asked gently.

'He was meeting someone in Mayfair to talk about all this.'

'Another journalist?'

'It might have been. He didn't say.'

'Do you have a name?'

'No, I'm afraid not. And whoever it was hasn't come forward.'

'Didn't you think that was odd?'

'Not particularly – it's possible he doesn't realise what happened to George. Maybe he was waiting and waiting, as I waited for George to come home. And then there was the knock at the door, and I knew, I knew something terrible had happened.'

The routine actions of making tea had distracted Joyce from dwelling on her loss. Now, as she relived the events of the previous day she began to sob again. Claudia put her arm around Joyce's bony shoulders.

'What have the police said about the accident?' she asked.

'It was a stolen car – probably kids on a joyride. They found it later, abandoned a few streets away.'

'In Mayfair you said?'

'That's right.'

'Do you know where exactly the meeting was?'

'No, I'm terribly sorry, I don't – just somewhere in Mayfair.'

The police might not regard this as murder, but Claudia had other ideas. Why else should Hubbard die while about to blow the lid off an enormous scandal? Plus Mayfair wasn't noted for joyriders.

'He went out, as happy as Larry, carrying his briefcase.'

'Could I see the briefcase?' asked Claudia, trying to stifle her excitement.

'I don't know what happened to it,' said Joyce. 'I asked the police and they didn't know either.'

Even odder – Hubbard was dead and his briefcase was missing. But Bill had taught Claudia not to jump to conclusions. She would probe a bit more.

'It looked to me as if your husband and Edgar Morrison were thick as thieves at one time. At least, they wrote a lot of academic papers together.'

'Yes, they did a lot of research together about thirty years ago. They were friends as well. Then George joined BEP, and after some years he was in line for the top cancer research job, but he never got it because Edgar cheated to get appointed.'

'What happened?'

'BEP asked George's boss to be involved in a study of this loucura – and the people at the top of the company spelled out in no uncertain terms what they expected the results would be. The boss refused, and so they asked Edgar. When Edgar produced the desired outcome, George's boss was sacked and Edgar was hired in his place. When George tried to protest, they sacked him as well – early retirement, they called it, but you can take it from me that George was fired.'

Joyce was crying again, dabbing at her eyes in a vain attempt to stem the flow of tears.

'Now the world will never find out the truth,' she said.

Claudia gently took Joyce's hand. Her empathy wasn't exactly fake, but at the same time she was still focused on Hubbard's papers. It occurred to her that they might not have been in his briefcase after all.

'It may not be too late,' Claudia said. 'Your husband told me he had written proof of what Edgar did. Do you have any idea where his documents would be?'

'Oh I do,' said Joyce, moving confidently towards the bookcase. 'George was very well-organised.'

She pulled out a box file labelled BEP.

'Can I take a peek?' asked Claudia, hardly daring to hope.

The file sprung open – empty. Somehow, Claudia was not surprised.

'Oh dear,' said Joyce. 'If they're not there, he must have taken them with him – in the briefcase.'

'Surely he would have kept copies?'

'I'm sure he did, but I can't imagine where they are.'

'Do you have a computer?' asked Claudia.

'No – we're not very up to date with things like that,' said Joyce.

Surprising, with Hubbard's scientific background, but entirely consistent with the bulky television and hi-fi equipment in their living room.

What had Hubbard been doing keeping such sensitive information in an indiscreetly labelled file? And why take the original papers across London in a briefcase? These were questions which deserved an answer, but Claudia had pushed Joyce far enough.

'I should leave you in peace,' she said. 'If you do find those papers, will you call me?'

She handed Joyce her card.

'Yes,' said Joyce. 'I will.'

'And if there's anything you need...'

It was a meaningless statement. All Joyce needed was something no one could give – her husband back.

'You don't believe George's death was an accident, do you?' she said.

Claudia had no desire to add to Joyce's misery, but she couldn't tell a lie.

'I don't know. But I'm sure he would have wanted his story told whatever happened.'

'Yes,' Joyce agreed. 'He would.'

'But I can't write a word without proof, my editor wouldn't let me.'

'I wish I could help you – if the briefcase turns up, I'll be in touch.'

Without anything being said, both of them knew that it would never resurface.

As Claudia left, a nondescript man in a grey suit arrived at the Hubbard house. Claudia didn't pay much attention to him, didn't even remember him till much later, but he'd noticed her.

21

'Good God!' said Bill as Claudia walked into the office. 'Have you been for a job interview at a bank or have you actually listened to me for once?'

'Neither. I've been to see Hubbard and I took a tactical decision about what to wear.'

'I didn't even realise you owned a suit.'

'Don't you approve?'

'Well, yes – very nice.'

Claudia had the distinct impression that Bill felt threatened in some way by her Establishment uniform, but she didn't have time to psychoanalyse his insecurities now. She excitedly outlined all the latest developments in the Hubbard saga. But Bill hooted at her theory about Hubbard's murder.

'Oh, come off it. Isn't it more likely the old codger didn't look before he crossed the road? And how would BEP have known he was meeting someone?'

An excellent point, to which Claudia could think of no instant rebuttal.

'His wife said he might be seeing someone from another paper.'

'Quite possible,' said Bill. 'Perhaps they bumped him off so they could get the story for free.'

He winked to show her he was kidding.

'OK, you can joke about it, but you have to ask – where have the documents got to?'

'Maybe they never existed, except in his imagination. Of course, if another paper has them, I suspect we'll find out before long. Anyway, haven't you any other angles to follow up?'

He rather sounded as though he hoped she hadn't.

'Actually, I do,' said Claudia. 'I'm waiting for someone in Brazil to get back to me about a research paper.' She consulted her watch – half past twelve. 'I guess they haven't woken up over there yet. And I've still got to speak to Morrison and Rodrigues.'

'I'd check out the police report on Hubbard's accident as well, just to be sure,' said Bill. 'But don't spend too much time on it – I'm certain this is a damp squib.'

Hello – my source has died in mysterious circumstances, does no one think it's odd apart from me? But it would be a waste of her breath to say any more. The time to argue with Bill was when she'd found some evidence – and she was a long way off that.

Claudia couldn't bring herself to call the one person who she was certain would agree with her. Phoning Hugo would make her look needy – and damn it, she felt needy, he should have rung her yesterday. Where were those fancy public school manners now? Admittedly, she hadn't left him a number, but finding the main switchboard number at the *Globe* must surely be well within even Hugo's limited capabilities. He even had a ready-made excuse to call now – wasn't he burning to hear how her interview with Hubbard went?

There was only one explanation. He hadn't called because he really, really didn't fancy seeing her – which was a bummer. Although her rational self screamed out that Hugo was a prat, for some irrational reason she really, really had the hots for him.

Her indignation simmered away all day. Each time the phone rang she practically jumped off her seat – but each time it was a false alarm. The Brazilian journal hadn't replied to her e-mail, so she rang them. For $30, they would supply a copy of the paper – yes they would accept the credit card. It was odd, the woman remarked in passing, but this was the second request in the past few days for the same paper. Aha – the other journalist, for sure.

By the time Hugo did call, she had all but written him off. A shot of euphoria rushed through her as she recognised his voice.

'You sound surprised to hear from me,' he said, indignant.

'You think I've nothing better to do all day than sit by the phone waiting for you to call? I've been busy – I'd forgotten all about you.'

Who was she kidding?

'The other night was great.'

'Yes – fab.'

'Be nice to meet up again – that is, if you're up for it.'

'Oh yes,' said Claudia, without even pretending to play hard to get. 'There's loads to tell you.'

'What – about Hubbard? How did it go?'

'I'll give you the low-down later – you free tonight?'

'Definitely,' said Hugo. 'Come up to town.'

She wondered whether his enthusiasm was for the story or her – maybe it didn't much matter.

'Would it be OK to go to the Avalon again?' she asked. 'I'm tired.'

Sunday night and the emotional drain of the encounter with Joyce Hubbard had taken their toll. And odds were she wouldn't get much sleep tonight either.

'I planned to take you somewhere nice.'

'You can't afford to take me somewhere nice.'

He didn't disagree.

'Fine – come round to my place at eight, we'll go from there.'

After she put the phone down, a wave of exhaustion engulfed her. Not that this would stop her from seeing Hugo again – she could always catch up with sleep later, but Hugo might not wait.

22

On Tuesday evening, Brad and Wayne met in the fake grandeur of BEP's grounds. Brad had been tempted by another trip to the diner, but Jill was starting to get suspicious. Two unauthorised meals in the space of a few days would be pushing his luck.

'You said there was a development. Did you get some more on what Morrison's playing at?'

'Not much, no,' Wayne admitted, dodging to avoid a jet of water from a misfiring ornamental fountain.

'So why are we here?'

'Because something happened.'

'What?'

'My people tell me George Hubbard died yesterday in a hit-and-run.'

Brad looked at Wayne with calculated astonishment.

'How convenient for Morrison.'

'Convenient for you too,' Wayne replied. His expression gave nothing away – impossible for Brad to tell what was in his mind.

'Do we know whether it was an accident?'

'I don't. Why wouldn't it be an accident?'

The emphasis on 'I' riled Brad – Wayne was a hired hand and he was out of order. Brad couldn't let the comment go, but equally he shouldn't be defensive.

'Hey – remember who you're working for here. And I'm not the one who's been calling furtively from payphones,' said Brad. Keeping the number of calories he consumed from his wife seemed a minor foible by comparison.

'You saying Morrison might have been involved in this?' asked Wayne.

'Who knows? You keep telling me you don't believe in coincidences.'

'You're right – I don't.'

'Well, neither do I.'

'All the same, my guts are telling me you're on the wrong track here.'

There were many reasons for this not to be an accident, as Wayne knew well. If Hubbard really did have proof of a cancer cure conspiracy, and had been shooting his mouth off about it, any number of people would have a motive to eliminate him.

'But Morrison's up to something.'

'Without a doubt,' said Wayne.

'Did you turn up any other info?'

'Not yet. Some more calls from payphones to that same UK cell phone – nothing else.'

'The UK – where Hubbard lives? You guys aren't getting very far with this, are you?'

Brad felt amply justified in turning on the aggression after Wayne's innuendo.

'These projects take time,' said Wayne. 'We've been working on this one less than a week. Patience is a virtue.'

'So they tell me,' said Brad sourly. 'Still no luck with Hubbard's documents either, I suppose?'

'Trust me, we tried. Got one of my men into the house on a pretext – spoke to the widow.'

'Boy, that was quick work.'

Credit where credit was due – Hubbard had only been dead for a day.

'See, we're not always slow,' said Wayne. 'But equally we don't always get results. Either old Ma Hubbard is the best actress in England, or she doesn't have a clue where the papers are. She did say something interesting, though.'

'Yes?'

'Hubbard was due to meet someone the day he was killed. He took a briefcase with him – it was never found.'

'Who was he meeting?'

'The widow wasn't sure – thought it might be a journalist.'

'The briefcase had the papers in it?'

'Seems probable, doesn't it?'

'So who has it now?'

'Who can say?'

'Not the person he was talking to at Globe Media?'

'Nope. We know who she is – a young woman named Claudia Knight. She's still looking for the papers, and was leaving the Hubbard house as our man showed up. According to Ma Hubbard, she isn't going to let the story drop.'

'She might be lying about not having the papers,' Brad said. 'What more effective smokescreen than to make a big play of looking for something you already have?'

Wayne considered this.

'I doubt she's that smart, but we can make certain – put the frighteners on her as well if you think it'll help. Frankly, I'm surprised you're still so het up about all this – didn't your PR team tell you they could easily take care of the problem?'

Brad paused.

'That's right. But whatever's eating Morrison is spelt out in those papers. Now can you get them or not?'

'Sure,' said Wayne. 'Though it may take a little time.'

He looked and sounded confident. But then he would, wouldn't he, Brad reasoned. The guy was a real pro.

23

Charlie was nit-picking – what else would you expect from a tax specialist? They made their money from dissecting other people's logic.

'The bet was you'd get off with someone at the end of the evening, not some other evening. You've lost and you owe me the cash.'

This was the latest in a series of fruitless attempts by Hugo to renegotiate the outcome of their bet. The matter of principle didn't concern him one iota, but the credit card payments were still in transit and another unauthorised overdraft loomed large on the horizon. He simply needed the money to take Claudia out. But no matter what arguments he deployed, Charlie refused to budge.

In the end, Hugo backed off and neatly bypassed the banking system by drawing out £100 from petty cash at the office. They'd take it off his salary at the end of the month, but that was a distant worry.

Claudia showed up on the dot of eight in a clingy electric blue dress.

'Wow,' said Hugo. 'You look amazing.'

So amazing that everyone stared at them as they walked along the street. The men ogled Claudia, as men did, but the women eyed her as well, hoping to find some minute imperfection. They peered at Hugo too, figuring there must be more to him than met the eye if he'd landed this exotic creature. And the men gave Hugo half-envious, half-pitying glances, as though they foresaw the relationship ending in disaster for him.

'So,' he asked Claudia when they were seated, 'what happened with Hubbard?'

'Nothing – he's dead.'

Hugo looked at her, aghast.

'No – how?'

'Hit-and-run yesterday.'

As predicted, Hugo lapped up the all gory details.

'This can't be an accident, it just can't,' he said. 'And that means somebody's taking this loucura business very seriously indeed – BEP, most likely.'

'I completely agree with you – but Bill's being so negative. He says BEP couldn't have known Hubbard was going to the press with the story.'

In fact, Bill had said much more, most of it unrepeatable. To Claudia's shame, the whole news team had enjoyed a good laugh at her expense. But that had only stiffened her resolve.

'Who's he to say what they knew?' countered Hugo.

'Dead right, and then there's the missing briefcase.'

Hugo considered the problem.

'Here's my take on it. The reporter's waiting to interview Hubbard, he sees what happens and in all the commotion, he picks up the briefcase and walks off with it.'

'Funny – that's what Bill said.'

'Well, isn't it what you'd have done, if it had been you?'

From what he'd seen of Claudia so far, she wouldn't respect many boundaries in the stampede to nail a story. She bridled at the very suggestion.

'Certainly not.'

'Let's put it this way,' said Hugo. 'You'd have had a good poke around before handing the briefcase in.'

The stunt she'd pulled with his own bag spoke for itself, and it still rankled that she'd examined his bank statements.

'Possibly,' she agreed grudgingly.

'What do the police make of it all?' Hugo asked, shifting adroitly to less dangerous ground.

'Good question. They say it was kids joyriding in a stolen car – an unfortunate accident. It was bloody Mayfair, for fuck's sake, not Brixton! I tried to tell them Hubbard was on the verge of meeting a journalist with a big story, that his briefcase was taken, but they're not interested – they've made up their minds already.'

'But they haven't found the kids yet?'

'No – they haven't.'

'So where does this leave you?'

'Desperate to learn more. I've got Edgar Morrison's paper and I've ordered the Brazilian paper, which will be a challenge – it's written in Portuguese...'

Hugo paused in the act of putting his wine glass to his mouth.

'Did you say Edgar Morrison?'

'Yes – why?'

'I'm flying over to New Jersey for an all parties meeting on Project Acorn next week. He's going to be there.'

'Really?'

'Yes – I could size him up, ask him a few questions even.'

'That would be brilliant – I'm planning to call him but I doubt I'll get much out of him. Perhaps face to face it'll be easier. But Hugo...'

'What?'

'You should be careful – if BEP had any involvement with Hubbard's death, you might be putting yourself at risk.'

'Well, so are you.'

Claudia flinched, as though this hadn't occurred to her before.

'But it's my job to uncover what's happening.'

'And I have a duty to my client.'

Even if Stephanie had decreed otherwise.

'I'll be very subtle,' he said.

'Well, it would be fab if you could do something.'

She still sounded doubtful, as if she didn't trust him not to balls it up.

'One thing's for sure. If the story's true, Project Acorn is toast,' said Hugo, trying to sound sanguine about the prospect, 'and my promotion as well.'

'What bollocks! Surely they can't pull your promotion because a transaction falls through.'

'Stephanie would latch onto any reason to pull my promotion,' he replied gloomily.

'Seems as if it's either your deal or my story, then.'

Frankly, Hugo was far more worried about his promotion than his safety. He secretly hoped that speaking to Morrison might lay the whole business to rest.

'So when do you go to the US?'

'Next Monday,' said Hugo. 'Julia Fraser specially requested me to be there – what do you think of that?'

'Most impressive.' She didn't sound impressed. Maybe she didn't understand how important Julia was.

'Julia is one of Britain's leading entrepreneurs,' Hugo added.

'I know who she is.' Claudia's voice had a frosty edge.

'She's such a nice person to work with as well. She's one of those rare people who's brilliantly successful in business but also a lovely human being,' Hugo continued, puzzled by Claudia's lack of enthusiasm. 'That's why I owe it to her to establish if there's any truth in this loucura business.'

'I thought you were doing it for me,' she said, choking him off.

'Hey – you sound as if you're jealous of Julia or something,' said Hugo, finally cottoning on to Claudia's displeasure.

'Well, from the pictures I've seen in the press, she is a gorgeous woman.'

'I hadn't really noticed.'

Claudia's disbelief was plain.

'I mean, she's nowhere near in the same league as you,' he added, rather late in the day.

Claudia opened her mouth to shout him down, but Hugo was saved from a barrage of abuse by the waiter arriving with the food.

She did have a point, though. He certainly found Julia attractive, and he knew, as you always know, that the spark was mutual. But Julia would never make a move on Hugo in a million years, and he would never dare to make a move on her. Claudia had the advantage of being here now, if only they could get through the evening without killing each other.

Hugo poured out some more wine and hoped for the best.

24

'I guess you heard the news,' said Brad, before Morrison even had a chance to sit down.

He hadn't shared his decision to eyeball Morrison – Wayne would only have advised against it. But surely if Morrison knew anything, Brad would be able to tell instantly.

'What news is that?'

Either Morrison was a better actor than he'd imagined, or he had no idea.

'George Hubbard died yesterday.'

Morrison blinked as a trace of emotion flashed across his face – was it surprise, shock or something else?

'How? Did his heart finally give out?'

Hubbard had suffered cardiac problems for as long as Morrison could remember.

'Yes, in a sense – after he was hit by a large SUV.'

He studied Morrison's expression intently – stunned first and then quizzical. He really didn't know a thing.

'How did you find out?'

This was a fair question, which Brad was reluctant to answer.

'We made it our business to find out,' he replied, carefully, before adding, 'they say it was an accident.'

'Why do you sound so surprised?' Morrison crossed his legs and uncrossed them again.

'Thought you might have some idea about that.'

Morrison's eyes glinted with hostility.

'What's that supposed to mean?'

'Nothing,' said Brad. 'Only wondered if you might have heard any news.'

'Why should I have heard anything?'

'No particular reason – only wondering, that's all. You can't deny it suits you right down to the ground now Hubbard's out of the way.'

Morrison stood up.

'I don't care for the implications of what you're saying.'

It was time to try a different tack. Brad smiled at him broadly.

'Come on Edgar, where's your sense of humour? I'm kidding you. In fact, the last couple of times we've met up you've been real jumpy. Now, what's going on? You can tell me.'

Brad's avuncular CEO concern only intensified Morrison's hostility.

'If you want to fire me, fire me. Give me a decent pay-off and I won't cause any trouble – I'm within a year of retirement in any case. Is that what your end game is – to have me move over for a younger man?'

'That's not what this is about and you know it, Edgar. I just hate to see one of my people unhappy.'

'Well, in that case, I appreciate your concern. Now, I'm a busy man, so are we done?'

'Not quite,' said Brad. 'On a totally different subject, is there a problem with your cell phone?'

'Why do you ask?'

'Someone happened to mention he saw you using a payphone in recent days.'

'My cell must have gone dead. It's been acting up.'

'You should order a new one.'

'I'll do that,' Morrison replied.

Morrison left Brad's office drenched in sweat. He'd messed up again, and allowed Brad to toy with him, like a cat with a mouse.

So now he knew – they'd been following him. He'd suspected as much and taken extra care, but they were experts. He'd half hoped that his caution was excessive paranoia, but saw now how misguided that hope had been. And it wasn't only Brad who worried him – he was caught up in some wider agenda he didn't understand. Hubbard's death had never been part of the bargain.

The bleak reality struck him like a punch between the eyes – the lifeline he'd been thrown was a noose.

25

In the morning Claudia rushed home to change before work. She would have taken a chance on the blue dress – even at the risk of raising Bill's pulse to dangerous levels – but she'd spilt a glass of wine on it and it reeked.

She lived in a room in a shared house – a trainee journalist's salary wouldn't stretch to a place like Hugo's, and Claudia didn't do debt. Debt kept you chained to the treadmill – much wiser to fit your aspirations to your money than the other way round.

The door to her room gaped open. The lock had always been crap, but there'd been no finesse in picking it – the door had simply been kicked in. Claudia's student housemates had either slept right through it all, or hadn't troubled to investigate.

Inside, the place was a shambles; her clothes had been flung from the wardrobe, the bookcase and the drawers all emptied, the bed taken apart. Even the plants had been tipped out of their pots. Shocked, Claudia gazed for several minutes at the scene of devastation, before beginning to pick through the debris.

A quick check revealed that nothing was missing – iPod, TV and laptop were all present and correct. But stealing valuables hadn't been the aim of this break-in. Someone had been looking for something, and she had a pretty shrewd suspicion of what it might be.

Her mind was a jumble of questions, all crying out to be answered. Who were they anyway – BEP? Who else would be after Hubbard's documents – the other newspaper?

Would a global pharmaceutical company or a rival publication really resort to housebreaking? Besides, how had they known who she was and where she lived? And when they hadn't found what they were after, would they conclude she didn't have it or would they come back again? The questions were as disturbing as they were unanswerable, and Claudia ducked them by launching into practical mode. If she cleaned up, she could pretend this had never happened.

Since there had been no theft, and no serious damage, there was little to be gained from calling the police – instead Claudia rang the landlord and asked him to send someone round to fix the door. Then she telephoned Bill.

'Well, at least nothing was stolen,' he said chirpily.

'I wish it had been,' Claudia replied. 'I could cope with a burglary, but these people are after something I don't have.'

'What?'

'Hubbard's evidence on loucura.'

There was a short silence at the other end of the line.

'Oh come on Goldilocks, get real. You're always moaning about how those dope-heads you live with don't shut the front door – it's probably some opportunist wandered in off the street.'

'Some opportunist – I've been burgled and they've left all my stuff. How bizarre is that?'

'They might have been looking for drugs?'

'Oh yes – I hadn't considered that. I forgot to check my stash of cocaine.'

Bill sighed at the other end of the line.

'Will you stop arguing and get yourself in here as soon as you can, all right?'

For all Bill's scepticism, Claudia was convinced that her theory was correct. And as she continued the salvage operation, a new insight emerged. Assuming Hubbard's killers had trashed her room, it didn't look as if they had Hubbard's briefcase.

In which case, who did?

According to the calculator on the 'Moneyexpert' website, Hugo would clear his debts in fifty-two years if he made the minimum payments each month. And that was assuming he didn't spend anything further on the credit cards, which was patently impossible when debt repayments ate up more than half his monthly pay.

Hugo groaned at this depressing news. He was sick of living hand to mouth, his money languishing for days in the banking ether while he suffered the humiliation of rejected cards. Why, he couldn't even take a girl out without worrying about money. But the debt calculator had only confirmed in hard numbers what Hugo had known for a long time – he was in a humungous financial mess.

If his promotion came through, he could cut up the cards and live without them. But that merely took him back to the grim fifty-year scenario. Would he really be an old man before he was debt free?

The answer had to be no. Such a bleak outlook was for losers, people earning the same for the whole of their miserable lives. He was on an upward career path – even the big ticket job in the investment bank was still within his reach. They had to start hiring again sooner or later.

And if that didn't come off and he was forced to stay at Pearson Malone, Hugo didn't see any reason why, if he applied himself, he shouldn't go all the way to partnership. He was far smarter than Stephanie, who hadn't made the grade, and brighter than Charlie, who was already on the accelerated partner track. Partners' earnings averaged around £800,000 per year. His debts would be a drop in the ocean then – he would eliminate them in six months, max. So in context, his difficulties amounted to no more than a short-term cash flow problem.

This analysis should have cheered Hugo, yet the vision of a prosperous future as an investment banker or a partner in Pearson Malone unaccountably alarmed him. A little voice deep inside him asked whether this was really what his life was about.

The voice was quickly silenced by the sight of Stephanie striding towards him at a pace unimpeded by her stilettos. He hastily flicked the screen back to the IDD spreadsheet he'd been working on.

'How are you getting on with the financial sensitivity analysis?' she asked him.

Hugo jumped. Now he had the IDD spreadsheet open, his lack of progress was all too visible.

'I'm doing fine, thanks – I've had to handle a couple of unscheduled phone calls but it won't take long to finish now I've got cracking.'

'I hope not – I'm due to walk Julia through the numbers this afternoon.'

'No problem,' said Hugo. 'They'll be ready long before then.'

She strutted off, a predator in search of a new victim.

Hugo set to with zero enthusiasm, but was beginning to make some headway when his mobile rang – Claudia. He failed to get a word in edgeways as the story of her burglary spewed out in a continuous torrent.

'This loucura conspiracy must have some truth behind it,' she concluded excitedly. 'And it's a bit scary.'

'Have you been to the police?'

'To say what? My room was trashed but nothing's been stolen – they're going to prioritise that, aren't they?'

'No, to tell them someone's after you.'

'Wouldn't that sound a bit paranoid?'

'You can always stay with me for a bit,' Hugo said, without answering her question.

But she dismissed the suggestion immediately.

'I'm not as scared as that.'

'Well, I'll give you the keys to my flat, just in case.'

Out of the corner of his eye, he saw Stephanie approaching again – this time clearly on the warpath.

'Sorry Claudia, gotta go.'

26

Marcus sat at the gigantic desk in his Mayfair penthouse office, contemplating the view across Green Park as he figured out his next move.

His visit to Joyce Hubbard had been time-consuming, but had yielded no useful facts, apart from confirmation that she'd been unaware of his rendezvous with her husband. Even that information was of doubtful value now – the police hadn't been anywhere near him. Depressingly, it appeared that whoever had the briefcase also possessed the sole copy of Hubbard's proof, and there was no way to uncover who that might be.

At this point, many people would have thrown in the towel, but Marcus was made of sterner stuff. He had moved swiftly on to Plan B, despatching Richard to Rio to negotiate with Rodrigues, the Brazilian who'd headed up the original research. This was at best a speculative move, but what was the price of a trip to Brazil when the upside was so huge? If anyone was in a position to tell them about the work on loucura, it was Rodrigues.

Marcus flicked the ash from his cigar into the wastepaper basket. The harridan who ran Umbra's human resources claimed that smoking in the office was illegal and had read him the riot act several times now. The woman was so ignorant – why had he ever hired her? Any moron could see these rules did not apply to the owner of a company. He'd told her so, and she'd taken his ashtray away. Now her days were numbered, although she didn't know it yet.

For Marcus to implement his plans, he required nothing

less than watertight proof that loucura was a real cancer-busting phenomenon. His instructions to Richard had been explicit – now there was nothing to do except wait. Loucura might be a dead duck, or it might be the goose that laid the golden egg. At this stage, it was impossible to say which.

Meanwhile, he had another little problem – his investment in IDD. He'd been following movements in IDD's shareholdings in minute detail. The price hadn't changed much, but his surreptitious peeks at the shareholder register had revealed some activity by nominee companies. Someone was accumulating a secret stake, and he feared they might try to block his grand scheme. That made him nervous. Once Richard was back from Rio, it was clear to Marcus where his next priority should be.

27

Claudia found Bill in a crabby mood when she finally arrived at the office. Driving rain had prevented him going out for a ciggie and anyone who was within shouting distance was forced to bear the brunt of his ill humour.

'You've taken your time – I don't see why you had to wait for the carpenter to come anyway.'

There was only one way to deal with Bill when he was in unreasonable mode – fight back.

'Oh don't you – well it might have been because I was scared someone might nick my stuff while the door was open.'

'Don't you trust your housemates?'

'I do, but as you said yourself, they're always leaving the front door on the latch – anyone could wander in off the street. I'm here now, aren't I, so what's your problem?'

'My problem is you've done bugger all work this morning and we're running behind. I am sick and tired of having to carry the can for staff who're utterly incapable of organising their personal lives.'

Claudia pointed out that Bill had the advantage of being able to subcontract the organisation of his personal life to Mrs Gordon, before proceeding to attack him for his lack of enthusiasm about her story.

'So do you still say this is all a coincidence, me having been burgled and George Hubbard being massacred in a quiet street in Mayfair?'

In his present frame of mind, Bill was unwilling to enter into any debate.

'Goldilocks – did you not hear what I said? We haven't the time to stand here chatting. Now shut up and get rid of this morning's backlog.'

'But the balance of probabilities...'

'I don't care about probabilities – and you've got a mountain of work to do. So will you button it and get your head down.'

Bill was normally zealous in his pursuit of the big scoop. Why was he so sure this one was a false lead? And if anything, the more circumstantial evidence racked up, the more negative he became – it was a puzzle.

Claudia checked her e-mail again. While she'd been on the Underground Bill had bombarded her inbox with leads to follow, press releases to verify and sources to contact – all entirely worthless activity. Among the crap was an e-mail from Brazil – the paper.

Claudia had barely begun to attack the backlog when her mobile rang. It was Hugo.

'Hang on, hang on a mo,' he said, as though he'd been interrupted. She caught muffled fragments of conversation, including 'riddled with errors' and 'circular cross reference'.

'Sorry,' he said. 'That was my boss, Stephanie.'

'Sounds like you screwed up.'

'Well, it's difficult to concentrate with all this happening. Anyway, I want to ask you something.'

'What?'

'It's our group's summer ball on Saturday at The Dorchester – can you come as my guest?'

'It's a bit short notice. Did your first choice blow you out?'

'No, no – or at least not in the way you think.'

Claudia was still smarting from her encounter with Bill – she hated people treating her as if she was brainless, and Hugo was the second one to do it this morning.

'Hugo, don't bullshit me.'

'Yes, all right, she did blow me out, but at any rate I'd prefer you to come.'

Claudia was reluctant to play second fiddle to some mystery girl.

'I'll think about it,' she said, sulkily.

It wasn't Claudia's sort of party. The very notion of eating a formal dinner surrounded by a huddle of arrogant penguins made her queasy.

'Well, don't take too long,' quipped Hugo, 'otherwise I'll have to ask somebody else.'

'Clearly you've a whole harem of women to choose from.' Not that she had any right to object – she'd only known him a few days.

'It was my sister, OK?'

'Oh yes.' She didn't believe him for an instant.

'Is that a "no"?'

Suddenly and irrationally, the prospect of Hugo asking someone else seemed even more painful than going herself.

'Go on, I'll come.'

'Great,' said Hugo, apparently insensitive to the maelstrom he'd created in her head. 'We'll firm up on the details later.'

He hung up.

Why, oh why, was Claudia letting him run rings round her like this? She controlled men – not the other way around. On a good day, even Bill knew his place. But there was some aspect of Hugo she found completely irresistible.

In her more lucid moments, she wondered what it could be.

Bill was astonished at how quickly Claudia caught up with the day's work.

'I'll say this, Goldilocks. When you put your mind to the job, you're not half bad.'

But her sudden spurt of energy had not been solely to appease Bill – more importantly she'd created a window of opportunity to continue her trawl of the internet.

It was difficult to decide what to make of these cancer conspiracy theories. As she'd discovered earlier, loucura was one of many miracle medicines allegedly denied to the world. There was vitamin C, laetrile, graviola, bicarbonate of soda, to name but a few.

Without a doubt, a simple cancer treatment wouldn't benefit pharmaceutical companies. They were known to keep quiet about harmful side effects of profitable drugs – so why not hold back an effective drug which was unprofitable? Equally, the drug industry's strenuous denials also made sense. Collusion on such a massive scale was unthinkable. The entire medical profession couldn't be so callously commercial – someone would have stepped forward if only out of a personal desire for global renown.

Yet for all that ambiguity, George Hubbard had died and she had been burgled. And Hubbard's papers had now vanished from the face of the earth.

Claudia googled Dr Cristiano Rodrigues, the principal Brazilian researcher. He was still at the Rio De Janeiro State University, only now he was head of his department, and a bigwig in the Brazilian medical community. His failed research into loucura evidently hadn't stalled his meteoric rise.

She was conscious that she still hadn't called Rodrigues or Morrison – fact was she'd been a little scared to since she'd found out about Hubbard's death.

Rodrigues was hardly likely to be implicated in Hubbard's murder. But a telephone call out of the blue might severely piss him off. Instead, she drafted up a polite e-mail enquiry and asked him when it would be convenient to speak.

Morrison was a different proposition and all Claudia's instincts told her he shouldn't be given time to prepare for a discussion. She took a deep breath and dialled the number.

The secretary accepted her pretext without question, but Morrison was more cynical.

'Hubbard gets an obituary in a national newspaper?'

'Why yes – we understand that his work in the field of oncology was groundbreaking.'

'I suggest you revisit your facts, young lady. What particular area of his work did you have in mind?'

'His work into loucura,' said Claudia, massively irritated by the 'young lady'. 'Didn't he work with you on discrediting an earlier Brazilian study?'

There was silence at the other end of the line, and Claudia knew she'd hit on something. It turned out to be a brick wall at the end of the road.

'I'm not permitted to speak to journalists – it's company policy.'

Strange his secretary hadn't been aware of that.

'Not even about an obituary?'

'Especially about an obituary,' Morrison replied.

The line went dead.

28

'What should I do about this journalist from London?' asked Rodrigues. 'She e-mails me – she asks to interview me.'

'So let her.'

'What do I say?'

'The same as you've been saying for the last twenty years. Heavens – you've been practising long enough.'

'It's a worry – why is everyone so interested in loucura these days? Is it possible they know about our strategy?'

'How could they? I told you before, this is all Hubbard's doing.'

'You also tell me Hubbard is dead.'

'He is – but not before he stirred up a hornet's nest. If you're worried, tell her you won't do the interview over the telephone – she'll have to fly out to Rio if she wants to talk.'

'But she might decide to make the trip.'

'There's no way her editor will authorise a visit to Brazil. But if he does, you will ensure that she has a wasted journey.'

'Yet it is a powerful story for a journalist, is it not, this miracle cancer remedy?'

'Only if it can be proved – otherwise it's mere conjecture. As long as you stick to your guns, the proof is under my control, and these people can't go on digging forever.'

'What about afterwards?'

'Afterwards, we'll invent a new story.'

'What will it be?'

'I'll decide. You worry too much – everything will be fine.'

Rodrigues replaced the receiver in its cradle. How he wished he was as self-assured as his new business partner.

29

'You're the finest looking black woman in the room,' quipped Hugo as they took in the elegant surroundings of The Dorchester.

'I'm the only black woman in the room,' said Claudia, beaming – she knew she was the best looking at the party full stop.

He wouldn't have risked his flip comment, but he'd noticed that in the last couple of days, now all her aggression was directed at solving the loucura mystery, she'd become noticeably less prickly. At times, Hugo almost forgot how obnoxious she could be.

'Seriously Claudia,' he added quickly, although he was fairly sure he hadn't caused any offence. 'You look gorgeous.'

And she did. Claudia had confided that her dazzling turquoise dress had cost £12 in New Look's sale. But this didn't stop the partners' fashionista wives peering enviously at it as they quaffed their pre-dinner champagne.

'It's all a waste of money this Armani dress business,' she proclaimed. 'However much dough I had I wouldn't spend a thousand pounds on a dress – I mean, what's the point? They all know who's wearing what and how much it cost, but nobody has a clue where my dress came from. It's a joke. Plus, there's no danger of anyone showing up in the same outfit as me. Who else in here would be brave enough to come to the ball in a twelve-pound dress?'

'Quite honestly, none of them could carry it off as well as you,' said Hugo smoothly. 'It's like a thousand-pound dress on you. Anyway, if you came in sackcloth, they'd all assume that was the new fashion.'

Claudia rewarded him with a winning smile.

'You are a sweet-talking bullshitter, Hugo, but I love it.'

Hugo tensed as he spotted Stephanie in the distance.

'Uh, uh – the wicked witch of the west is coming towards us.'

'What?' Claudia hissed, 'You mean the famous Stephanie?'

'Yes, and that drippy husband of hers is with her.'

Sure enough, Stephanie was headed their way. No surprise there – the nosy cow would be curious to discover who he was with. She wore a floaty peach pink number in a Grecian style, with matching nail varnish, and gold evening bag and sandals. The dress wasn't quite up to Armani standard, but equally it almost certainly wasn't from New Look either. As a nod to the occasion, she sported a glamorous updo, with quite literally not a hair out of place. Hugo stifled an insane but powerful urge to run his hands through it and mess it up.

'Hugo!' she cried, as though they were best buddies. 'Meet my husband, Pod.'

Hugo didn't warm to Pod. For a start, what self-respecting chap would allow himself to be known by such an emasculating nickname? Or bear the brunt of the childcare, even though he was the finance director of an IT company? Pod's handshake was limp and clammy, reinforcing Hugo's negative impressions.

He introduced Claudia.

'Are you an accountant as well?' asked Stephanie.

He could practically see the thought balloon above Claudia's head: 'Hey – do I look like an accountant?'

'No, I'm a reporter for the *Daily Globe*.'

Stephanie stiffened and fixed Hugo with a beady stare.

'Ah yes, your journalist friend.'

She turned to Claudia, in the spirit of polite enquiry.

'I hear from Hugo you're working on a story about a miracle cancer treatment.'

If Hugo had ever doubted it, he was now certain his boss was an out-and-out bitch. This was deliberate stirring – Stephanie knew he'd been asked to keep the story quiet.

There was an awkward little silence, but Claudia's fleeting daggers-drawn scowl was instantly replaced by a social grimace.

Pod, either not noticing or ignoring the potentially poisonous atmosphere said, 'How exciting – and how are you getting on with it?'

'Not great, since you ask. My source died.'

'How very inconvenient for you,' said Stephanie. 'You'll never get to the bottom of it now.'

'Probably not,' Claudia agreed.

'What a shame,' said Stephanie with mock sincerity.

Hugo began to relax – he had got away with it. If he was unlucky, Claudia might have a go at him later in private, but for now it seemed a public scene had been averted. Claudia smiled sweetly, further fuelling his hopes. Then she delivered the punchline.

'Not for you, though. Hugo tells me it would be curtains for Project Acorn if a big scandal about BEP came out.' She gleefully ran her finger across her throat as though to emphasise the danger.

As a retaliatory move, this was a masterstroke. Stephanie glared at Hugo as though he were a dog turd she'd scraped off the bottom of her shoe. Claudia grinned broadly, fully satisfied by the reaction she'd evoked. Hugo wished he could disappear in a puff of smoke – permanently.

'Project Acorn,' hissed Stephanie, her party facade slipping, 'is strictly confidential and price sensitive. I hope you can understand that, even if Hugo doesn't.'

'What's not to understand? I'm a fucking journalist – I make my living out of confidential information.'

Stephanie had kicked off the stirring, but Claudia had added her own explosive ingredients into the mix for good measure. Both women were gunning for Hugo now. And they were a formidable pair.

Stephanie took Hugo aside, leaving Pod to take his chances with Claudia.

'Hugo – you specifically told me you hadn't discussed Project Acorn with your friend. Was that a lie?'

'She may have come across some papers,' Hugo replied, unable to think of a less damning response on the spur of the moment.

'Which you carelessly left lying around, I suppose.'

Thankfully she didn't know quite how carelessly – but doubtless Claudia would be ready to divulge all the embarrassing details if anyone asked.

'Look, I'm so sorry about this...'

'Sorry – you're sorry? Not half as sorry as I am. If it wasn't for Christian giving you the benefit of the doubt, you wouldn't even be on this assignment. And you can kiss your July promotion goodbye. You've been pulled from the list.'

Which at least meant he'd been on the list – he'd never made it that far the last time.

Stephanie peered around her apprehensively – it wasn't the time or place for a reprimand. Christian and his wife Amanda were approaching and, predictably, Stephanie felt the urge to ingratiate herself with them.

'Meet me half an hour earlier than planned at Heathrow on Monday – we'll go into it then,' she said, making it obvious that Hugo's continued presence was an unwelcome distraction. 'And please inform your "friend" that if a word leaks out into the press you are in big, big trouble.'

Reprimand over, Stephanie was magically transformed back into her charming social persona. She extracted Pod from Claudia's clutches and glided off, trailing a cloud of diaphanous material and smiling seraphically.

118

Hugo shuddered. Claudia could not have wreaked more damage if she had attacked him with an ice pick. But the worst was yet to come.

'You lying bastard,' said Claudia, 'you promised you wouldn't tell anyone about the story. How dare you?'

How had he been naive enough to imagine she was beginning to relax with him? One tiny perturbation and she exploded.

'So what – you promised me you wouldn't say a word about Project Acorn.'

'I didn't say anything,' she retorted, not caring who might hear, 'except to Stephanie, who's already in the loop.'

'You're not supposed to know about it. That's the point.'

'So?'

She stuck out her chin defiantly – she knew very well what she'd done.

'So you dropped me in it with my boss. That's way out of order.'

'But you told that stuck-up cow about my story.'

'I only mentioned it in passing, and besides, I can't see it's a huge state secret.'

'Well it is – she could have ruined everything.'

'No – you've ruined everything. My promotion's been pulled because of you.'

'You didn't deserve it in the first place.'

People stared at them, perplexed by the raised voices. She gave a slight shrug, underlining how little she cared. Hugo fancied Stephanie had a triumphant air about her, although she was too far away to be sure.

The dinner gong sounded – thank God. But Claudia had no intention of sitting quietly through four courses and coffee. And she was determined to have her moment of glory before she left.

'You're a complete and utter lying piece of shit. You

119

ask me to keep your secrets but what do you do with mine? You trumpet them around all and sundry. Still, why am I surprised? All you're after from me is the novelty of a quick shag with a bit of black pussy.'

Horrified, Hugo tried in vain to calm her.

'Claudia, I'm sorry – I shouldn't have mentioned loucura to Stephanie, but I was worrying about Julia, and whether or not she had a right to be told. I needed clarification...'

The mention of Julia sent Claudia into fresh paroxysms of rage.

'I knew the sainted Julia was involved in this somewhere. She's obviously a lot more important than keeping your promise to me.'

'Oh, come on Claudia – my promotion was hanging in the balance.'

'Everything is about you, isn't it? Your project, your client, your boss, your promotion. Man, yes, you're desperate for that promotion. How did you pass your accountancy exams when you can't even balance your own books?'

'You shouldn't have read my bank statements – I let it go the other night, but the writing was on the wall then, wasn't it?'

'It certainly was. I should've realised then what a public school twat you are.'

She was back to how she'd been at the speed dating – pouring out resentment against Hugo, not so much as an individual, but as a member of a privileged elite.

'Come on Claudia, let's forget it and go to our table.' Despite the commotion, people were drifting away into the dining room.

'You must be fucking joking!'

Those remaining, including Christian and Amanda, all gawped at them now.

'There's no way I'm sitting at a table for the next two hours with all these stuffed shirts, chatting about "the state of the economy" and worrying about whether I'm using the right knife and fork.'

'Please, you can't leave me on my own, it would be so embarrassing...'

'There you go again – all about you. You don't give a monkey's about me. So why don't I really embarrass you...'

She chucked the remains of her champagne over Hugo's head.

'Goodbye Hugo, you arrogant little prick – I never want to see you again. Ever!'

She stomped off, leaving Hugo to his public humiliation.

He mopped the wine off his hair with a napkin. All in all, you had to hand it to Claudia – she had a flair for the dramatic.

30

On Monday morning, Hugo prised himself out of bed at 6.30. He was cutting it fine, but he always got off on the adrenaline rush of brinkmanship.

Charlie had advised Hugo to pack his suitcase the night before – and he'd been full of wise suggestions about how Hugo might rehabilitate himself with Stephanie. But Hugo wasn't in the mood for any of it – anyway, how long would it take to throw a few garments into a bag? Now, as he endeavoured to assemble a suitable collection of clean and ironed clothes, he wished he'd taken more notice.

His best suit was still screwed up in a ball after the speed-dating evening. Worse, an alarming brown stain had appeared on the trousers of his second-best suit – he couldn't even begin to imagine its source. This left suits three and four, which didn't cut nearly such a dash. He successfully counted out underwear and socks, but the shirt situation was a disaster to be rescued only by the hotel laundry. He surveyed the clothes laid out on the bed with dismay. By no stretch of the imagination was this a suitable travelling wardrobe for an up-and-coming professional hoping to redeem his career. But Hugo had no time to brood. It was now 6.53 – and he was due at Heathrow by 8.00. He threw everything into his bag and strained to zip it up.

Hugo dreaded the discussion with Stephanie, and fretted as he sat on the Tube. The only reason she hadn't bumped him off the US trip was because she would have otherwise had to account for his absence to Julia. In no way did her decision mean she was done with him – and Hugo was sure she would make his life hell in New Jersey. What should have been a pleasant trip had become a nightmare, and all because of that deranged bitch Claudia.

What nastiness had possessed her to sabotage his career? The punishment had been out of all proportion to the crime. Ironically, he'd even been beginning to think she was a nice person – how could he have been so wrong? This was a lesson for the future which Hugo resolved not to forget in a hurry.

By some miracle, Hugo arrived at Heathrow only a few minutes late. Stephanie stood at the meeting place, grim-faced and pacing up and down. She didn't comment on his lateness, nor on his dishevelled appearance – bigger problems preyed on her mind.

'Words fail me, Hugo. I can't begin to tell you how angry and disappointed I am.'

Hugo was prepared for this, and had elected for once to follow Charlie's advice.

'Stephanie, I'm so sorry Claudia found out about the deal – it was careless of me, and it won't happen again. But there's no harm done.'

At this, Stephanie exploded.

'No harm done! How the hell can you say that? Are you a total idiot?'

Charlie's recommendation for defusing the situation – be contrite and stress there's been no loss – had failed spectacularly. Hugo was left wondering what his next move should be.

'Read this,' she said, thrusting the business section of the *Globe* under Hugo's nose.

Hugo gulped. The headline read 'BEP in talks with IDD'.

'No prizes for guessing where they dug up that story,' she said.

Even at his most pessimistic, he hadn't foreseen this – the

betrayal was mind-blowing. Saturday night had been bad enough, but this was beyond belief.

'Yes, um no, I mean...'

'Client confidentiality is of the utmost importance, Hugo. Even an idiot like you should realise that. Yet here you are, entrusted with important price sensitive information and it ends up in the hands of a bloody journalist. I mean, what were you playing at?'

'Um, I don't know – it was a mistake.'

'And a mistake you will never make in my team again – I would look for another job if I were you Hugo, because you're going nowhere in Pearson Malone.'

Whatever Hugo said was unlikely to improve his position – not that Stephanie offered him the opportunity to defend himself. Quite possibly silence was the best option.

'This is the most serious breach of confidentiality I've seen in the whole of my career – what were you doing?'

'I don't know.'

He had no answer ready – his mind was numbed by Claudia's treachery.

'You realise what this means, don't you Hugo?' She glowered at him as she put her hand baggage on the belt at security.

He could take a guess – formal disciplinary action, final warning. She'd already told him to find another job.

'It means IDD will have to make an immediate announcement to the market,' she said, to his surprise.

'Yes – Rule 2.2 of the Takeover Code,' Hugo mumbled. He wasn't at all interested in these technicalities, he was desperate to know what would happen to him – desperate to know yet terrified of the answer.

'Does Julia know about this?' he asked. She might take pity on him – tell Stephanie to get off his case. On the other hand, she had high standards and Hugo had fallen short – he wouldn't be her blue-eyed boy now.

The metal detector screeched in censure as Hugo walked through the arch. He produced an ill assortment of coins and paper clips, but the alarm still objected to his presence. Stephanie stood with pursed lips as he was forced to remove his cufflinks.

'Does Julia know?' he repeated, once he'd eventually been allowed through.

'Yes, obviously she does – she's in an absolute panic over it, trying to sort it all out.'

Hugo swallowed.

'Does she appreciate that it may have been my fault?'

'May have been! What do you mean may have been? It is your fault! And the answer to your question is obvious – no she doesn't, otherwise you wouldn't be coming with us on this trip.'

'So are you going to tell her?'

'No, I'm not going to tell her – why let her know we employ cretins?'

'So where does she believe the leak came from?'

'As matters have turned out, you've got the luck of the devil, Hugo.'

Stephanie scowled at him as though he might be the devil. Meanwhile, Hugo didn't feel lucky at all.

'Julia's convinced the leak came from Bioinvestments, their private equity investor – they've a seat on the board and so have been privy to all the negotiations with BEP. She believes they leaked it to give their own investors confidence. Needless to say, they've denied it, but they would, wouldn't they?'

'It might have been them, of course,' said Hugo, brightening.

Stephanie slapped him down immediately.

'Don't you dare try to wriggle out of it, Hugo – we both know the truth. However,' she added, 'as matters stand, dragging you into it won't serve any purpose.'

'It won't?' It was hard to accept she was passing up an opportunity to shaft him. 'Surely, if it is my fault, shouldn't we disclose the breach of confidentiality to the client? The firm's risk management manual says...'

He was loath to talk himself into a problem, but Stephanie was a stickler for that manual – not least because she'd written half of it. She cut Hugo off in mid analysis.

'You,' she said, 'are in no position to lecture me about risk management, Hugo.'

Hugo let it go. Stephanie was keeping quiet to save face, but the outcome was the same.

'Do you mean I'm officially off the hook?'

'That's one way of putting it, yes,' said Stephanie.

'And unofficially?'

'Don't push your luck, Hugo. I'd still brush up your CV if I were you. And one more step out of line...'

The threat hung there, unspoken. But at least Hugo now had a hold over Stephanie – she'd flouted the firm's procedures, and he knew it. Although whether it could ever be used against her, except in a kamikaze scenario, was debatable.

Julia arrived with messed-up hair and a pink flush to her cheeks.

'I'm sorry I'm so late,' she gushed. 'I've been stuck on the phone to the broker and it took an age to get through security. And just when the deal was panning out so well.'

Hugo felt a twinge of guilt.

'How's it all coming along since we spoke earlier?' asked Stephanie.

Julia put her bag on the seat next to Stephanie.

'Well, we've expressed our displeasure to Bioinvestments. As expected, they've denied all knowledge,' said Julia, 'But we can't imagine who else might have done it. No point in asking the *Globe*. They'll never reveal their sources.'

Stephanie and Hugo exchanged a conspiratorial glance. Like it or not, they were manacled together by their shared secret. Julia produced a piece of paper.

'Here's what I hope is the final draft of the announcement to the market – it hasn't changed much since we went through it, but would you mind having a quick peek?'

Hugo marvelled at the hubbub of activity which had taken place so early in the day.

'I'd be glad to,' said Stephanie.

She held the paper a long way from her eyes as she read – too vain to use reading glasses.

'Preliminary discussions,' said Stephanie, nodding. 'Very nice – a low-key disclosure.'

'Yes,' agreed Julia, 'it sets the right tone. Naturally, it would have been preferable to announce once the agreement was in the bag. Still, every cloud has a silver lining. The shares opened up fifteen percent this morning.'

Still well below BEP's indicative price – still a tidy profit to be had. If only it was legal for Hugo to trade the shares, he would solve his financial problems at a stroke.

He took in the impressive array of wines and spirits on the business lounge bar. All that free booze, and neither Stephanie nor Julia showed the slightest interest. So he mustn't either. He poured himself a coffee and one for the two women, for once pre-empting Stephanie's request.

'Biscuit?' he asked, directing the question to Julia – Stephanie seldom ate much at all.

Julia took a piece of shortbread and Hugo helped himself to two chocolate chip cookies and a large slice of fruitcake.

'I don't know where you put all the food you eat,' said Stephanie with some irritation. The remark was a sideswipe at Julia, although ostensibly addressed to Hugo.

'I expect Hugo works out,' Julia replied.

'Never,' said Hugo, with a snort, his mouth full of cake. 'Exercise is for old people.'

Too late he remembered that Stephanie went to the gym three times a week.

'Oh gosh,' said Julia, rescuing Hugo from his gaffe. 'They're calling our flight already. We must go.' Hugo was forced to jettison most of his food as the two women set off at a furious pace.

As the runway disappeared beneath him, Hugo's anger at Claudia morphed into relief. The worst had happened and he'd survived. His promotion was lost, but he suspected it had never really been a runner. Now, if he kept his nose clean, he wouldn't be fired and he could put all his efforts into finding another job.

Sitting behind Stephanie and Julia on the plane, he'd knocked back the welcoming glass of champagne unobserved. Once airborne, he was offered another drink. 'Vodka and tonic,' he whispered – not his favourite, but identical in appearance to the miserable mineral water Stephanie drank. He settled back to enjoy the rest of the flight, leaving some plausible-looking work papers in front of him as a smokescreen. There would be a nice lunch with wine to come, followed by a brandy or two if Stephanie wasn't watching. Best of all, none of it was denting his finances.

As the vodka kicked in, he even began to kid himself that everything had been for the best. Much better to have found Claudia out early, and to be spurred on into hunting for a more suitable job. And if he put in a sterling performance on this trip, his promotion might even be resurrected. In fact, whatever happened, he would easily get his life back on track.

Claudia knew she'd behaved badly. She'd publicly humiliated Hugo – and why? Jealousy. Hugo's concern for Julia was irritating, but her response had been well over the top.

And what had she achieved? Less than nothing – she'd alienated Hugo precisely when he'd be in Julia's company for the best part of a week. How unintelligent was that? To cap it all, she now saw clearly that Hugo's witch of a boss had whipped up the whole confrontation out of a vacuum. She hadn't believed she could be any more miserable, but further horror rapidly unfolded – she gasped when she saw the piece in Monday's *Globe*.

Hugo would never accept that she hadn't been involved – they couldn't kiss and make up after this. Not that she understood why she even wanted to kiss and make up – it defied rational analysis.

But if it wasn't her who'd leaked the takeover to Sam Turner, the *Globe*'s business editor – who was it?

'Why are you asking?'

'Well, it may link in with my loucura story,' said Claudia vaguely.

'I doubt if it does, but it was a broker,' said Sam.

'Name?'

'I can't tell you sweetie – the guy's career is on the line if anyone finds out.'

'Why did he give you the tip off?'

'Quite possibly to cover up insider trading – the FSA has a hell of a job securing a conviction if there are rumours buzzing around. Anyhow, it's been doing the rounds on internet chat rooms as well for the last couple of days.'

'Oh, go on, please tell me who it was.'

'Certainly not. And what's the real reason you're asking?'

Claudia hesitated – it might be unwise to tell Sam she'd already been aware of the deal.

'Sorry,' she said. 'If you can't tell me where the leak came from, I can't tell you why I'm interested it.'

'Your loss, not mine,' said Sam. 'By the way, how's your loucura story going? Would have thought Miss Holier Than Thou Julia Fraser would drop BEP like a shot if it's true.'

Claudia winced at the mention of Julia's name.

'It's been crap, if you must know. And Bill's been less than supportive as well.'

'No surprise there,' said Sam.

'What do you mean?'

'I'm not telling you that either,' he said. 'Bill would kill me.'

'Forget it then,' said Claudia, baffled by the meaning of Sam's cryptic comment.

She logged into her e-mail – Rodrigues had replied, but it wasn't what she'd hoped for. He never did telephone interviews – too much potential for misunderstanding. This was a definite brush-off – he was counting on a face-to-face being impossible. And he was right on the money there – hell would freeze over before Bill signed off on a trip to Rio.

The Brazilian angle was dead. And now she'd blown it with Hugo, he was hardly likely to speak to Morrison either. Claudia had run out of leads and although all her instincts screamed out that this story was a corker, without proof, she'd have to let it lie. Perhaps it was time to capitulate and agree with Bill. And maybe it was safer that way.

Inexplicably, her mind kept returning to Hugo. He must be in big, big trouble – fired, or at least kicked off the US trip. He couldn't afford to lose his promotion, let alone his job. Despite her anxiety, Claudia was disinclined to call him – he'd probably hang up on her anyway. Surely he hadn't been fired – not on her account? It was all too terrible to contemplate.

She tried to tidy these disturbing images away, but they kept bursting out again. And all the while she couldn't help but wonder – why did she even care about the jerk?

31

As the aeroplane descended into Newark, anxiety got the better of Hugo. The breath mints he'd been sucking did nothing to disguise his problem, let alone solve it. He'd seriously overindulged in the British Airways complimentary bar.

He swayed slightly as he stood up to disembark, and prayed that no one had noticed. But as he picked up his laptop case, disaster struck and all the contents fell out onto the floor in a jumbled heap.

As Stephanie bent forwards to help him throw the motley collection of items back in the bag, she caught a whiff of his breath.

'Hugo – have you been drinking?'

Only Stephanie could ask such a silly question. Julia looked on, smiling beatifically.

'Um – er – a couple of glasses of wine,' he said.

It was not a real lie – 'a couple of glasses' was an elastic description which stretched to cover most situations short of lying in a gutter. Thankfully Stephanie let the subject drop – she wouldn't be nasty to him in front of Julia, after all. As long as he didn't fall over, he might yet get away with it.

'You don't half keep a lot of junk in here,' she remarked, handing Hugo some bank statements and a dog-eared *Accountancy* magazine. Her eyes lingered on the copy of Morrison's paper Claudia had given him before they'd fallen out, but she made no comment.

'There,' she said, with a rictal smile. 'I think that's all.

Why on earth didn't you sort through all this before you set off?'

Stephanie was a person who sorted through bags – Hugo was not. This polarity between them lay at the very root of their problems. Hugo almost told her so, but wisely refrained.

By dinnertime, a now sober Hugo contemplated the unbearable prospect of Stephanie and Julia's polite small talk. He was relieved when they were joined by a group of BEP executives, including Edgar Morrison.

The sight of Morrison jolted Hugo – a painful reminder of the mess Claudia had landed him in. Yet despite this, he felt an urgent and irrational impulse to speak to her, which he repressed.

Hugo studied the dapper little head of R & D with interest. Although Morrison must have been at least twenty years older than Julia, this didn't prevent him from turning the charm on. Julia responded warmly without overtly flirting – but despite the superficial affability, Hugo picked up on some tension between the two of them, and wondered about its source.

Could he envisage Morrison skewing the results of a drug trial? Without a doubt – he came across as a man who took care of his own interests. Could he imagine him killing someone, or ordering someone killed? Frankly – no.

Once or twice, he caught Morrison's eye. Was Morrison watching Hugo, or watching Hugo watching him? He wasn't sure. Meanwhile Brad Hillman, BEP's CEO, scrutinised the whole table with hawk-like precision. What was he on the look out for, Hugo wondered?

The chat mainly revolved around industry gossip. Frustration at being unable to dominate the conversation bubbled away under Stephanie's polite facade. For his own part, Hugo was content to sit quietly, adding occasional platitudes as and when required. Not much wine was flowing, but after his assault on the British Airways free bar he had no desire for alcohol. Instead, he gulped down at least five glasses of iced water.

During a lull in the chatting, Morrison turned towards Hugo. Hugo panicked – what could he say to this suspected villain? Yet he was anxious not to waste the opportunity – he was now even more determined than ever to prove that Claudia's story was a hoax.

'I believe we have a mutual acquaintance in common,' he began, 'or rather we did.'

The words had tumbled out automatically – there was no going back. He glanced uneasily at Stephanie, who was debating the merits of International Financial Reporting Standards versus US Generally Accepted Accounting Principles with the BEP chief financial officer. Julia was deep in discussion with an owlish man from the BEP's in-house legal department. He was safe – no one was listening.

'Who's that?' asked Morrison, without much interest.

'George Hubbard.'

Morrison's features clouded over for an instant – but he recovered his composure at once. Brad Hillman's eyes flickered as he listened to Morrison's response.

'Yes, we worked together for a while.'

'I heard he died recently.'

'Yes, I heard that as well – shame. What's your connection?'

'The Hubbards are old friends of the family,' Hugo said.

He was suddenly aware of Hillman's eyes boring into him – he knew Hugo was lying. The deception would be exposed in an instant if Morrison chose to develop the dialogue.

But Morrison merely murmured about it being a small world, and moved swiftly on to speak to Julia. For a while,

Brad looked poised to take up the baton, but changed his mind. Hugo unclenched his knuckles, thankful to have escaped detection.

He went directly to his room after dinner, fatigued by a combination of jet lag and alcohol. He debated whether to call Claudia, but she'd made her position plain. She'd be bound to hang up on him, and Hugo wasn't minded to set himself up for rejection. Even if she was prepared to speak to him, what would he say? Morrison's fleeting reaction didn't prove anything – and it was perfectly possible he'd imagined it. After smoking a sneaky cigarette out of the window, he flopped onto the bed. Before long, he'd dozed off.

The shrill sound of his bedside telephone jarred him awake. He grabbed the receiver on autopilot – Julia – what the...?

'Hugo,' she said. 'I hope I haven't woken you.'

'No, no – just catching up on some work.' He hoped to God he didn't sound as groggy as he felt. 'What can I do for you? Did you have a question about the meeting tomorrow?'

He fervently hoped not.

'Nothing like that – I thought you might fancy a quick nightcap. My body clock's on UK waking up time right now, and I can't help but feel a small nip of alcohol might ease the transition.'

'Where are you?'

Hugo's heart skipped a beat – was she about to ask him to her room?

'Why, in the bar downstairs.'

Deflated, and cursing himself for allowing his imagination to run riot, Hugo replied, 'I'll be right down.'

Julia was alone, perched seductively on a bar stool.

'Stephanie called it a day?' he asked.

She nodded and handed him the drinks menu.

'Now, what do you fancy?'

Hugo skimmed through the long list of elaborate cocktails – none of them appealed.

'Vodka and orange please.'

'Very pure and simple,' Julia pronounced. 'Should chase off the remnants of your hangover beautifully.' She ordered a cognac for herself.

Hugo was about to protest that he didn't have a hangover, but this would have been a lie.

'I hardly drink at all usually,' she told him, without waiting for a response, 'but I'm not going to get a wink of sleep if I don't have something to knock me out.'

She wore tight jeans, a pale blue batwing top the colour of her eyes, and grey peep-toe shoes. Her hair, usually styled in an elegant chignon, was loose. The successful business woman of earlier in the day had transformed herself into a hot babe.

'So, Hugo,' she said once the bartender had taken the order. 'How are you?'

It was an extremely open-ended question, which initially Hugo felt reluctant to answer.

'Why do you ask?'

'Ah well, you did seem to be laying into the booze on the aeroplane.'

'Not that much,' said Hugo, aggrieved. Honestly, all he'd done was accept a few free drinks – it wasn't as if he was a real soak.

She laughed.

'You're too defensive – don't be. You're young, you embrace life – what's wrong with that?'

'Everything, according to Stephanie.'

Julia tossed back her hair.

'Stephanie's jealous of you, in my opinion. Also, I couldn't help noticing, I think she may find you attractive.'

'No,' said Hugo, practically choking on his drink. 'She's

nearly as old as my mother, and treats me worse than a disobedient puppy.'

Hugo had not intended to bad-mouth Stephanie, but Julia seemed to have a way of coaxing out whatever popped into his head, however inappropriate. He should be more careful – for all he knew Stephanie might have asked Julia to spy on him.

'Well, she's certainly not very happy with you right now,' Julia agreed. 'Have you any idea why? Or is it pure jealousy of your carefree youth and good looks?'

Bruised by his latest encounter with Claudia, Hugo greedily lapped up Julia's flattery.

'We've had a bit of a run-in,' Hugo confessed, 'though I shan't bore you with the details.'

In fact, he couldn't bore her with the details without mentioning the press leak – and he wasn't going there. But Julia didn't ask.

The conversation flowed spontaneously. Julia instinctively understood Hugo's emotions, and Hugo unburdened himself. Throwing caution to the wind, he poured out all his insecurities – his job, his finances, the whole shebang.

Julia sympathised without patronising. These were temporary difficulties which might afflict anyone, she told him. Someone of Hugo's capabilities would rise above them and would be all the stronger for having been tested. As Hugo's self-esteem soared, he opened up even more. Much later, he would reflect on how little Julia had revealed about herself, but for now he was entranced.

They finished their drinks, and Julia suggested another.

'I'm still wide awake,' she said. 'Perhaps a second cognac might do the trick.'

Hugo ordered the same as before – the first one had slipped down so pleasantly.

It had also emboldened him. Morrison's reaction at his mention of George Hubbard still worried him. Who was more conversant with the technicalities than Julia, an expert in the field? It was now or never, while Stephanie wasn't around.

'I was thinking. Wouldn't it be wonderful if IDD's technology was used to create a miracle cure for some dread disease, like cancer for instance?'

Julia ran her hands through her hair – she wore three rings on her fingers, Hugo noticed.

'Well, yes, it would be nice, but it's not at all likely.'

'Why not?'

She sipped delicately at her drink.

'Cancer is a multifaceted disease, Hugo, and currently the emphasis is on therapies for specific tumours. It's highly improbable that there's a silver bullet, a magic cancer-killing drug.'

'Suppose there is,' Hugo persisted, 'and it's already been discovered?'

'I'm not with you, Hugo.' Julia furrowed her brow, as if perplexed by the question.

'Well, if you surf the internet, there are lots of stories about cancer remedies being censored by the drugs industry.'

'And that's what they are, Hugo – stories. Why do you think the big pharmaceutical companies would hold back a sensational cancer cure?'

'Money,' said Hugo.

'I think you're over-simplifying. An all-singing-all-dancing cancer cure is the holy grail – whoever found it would be immortal, in scientific terms. What researcher would pass up on the opportunity? And what drug company wouldn't covet it for their blockbuster list?'

'Ah,' said Hugo. 'That's exactly the thrust of my argument – if it came from a plant, it couldn't be patented...'

Julia choked him off.

'Leaving aside the scientific implausibility of what you propose, there would have to be a massive conspiracy.

Somebody would be bound to break ranks and tell it straight.'

'Not necessarily. Not if they all had a strong motivation to keep quiet. So suppose BEP had found a natural cancer drug. If they buy IDD, they can manufacture a synthetic version, patent it and make an absolute packet – it totally changes the dynamics of the transaction. You might be selling out too cheap.'

As Julia roared with laughter, Hugo saw how ridiculous the notion must seem to her and he laughed as well. Perhaps Morrison's reaction had after all been a product of his imagination.

'I'm sorry – I shouldn't laugh,' said Julia, unable to stop herself. 'The concept is absurd, but I do understand where you're coming from. In economic terms, you're asking whether IDD has a value to BEP which we don't know about.'

'Yes, exactly,' said Hugo, relieved that she'd managed to perceive some sense in his deliberations.

'Now there's a more serious question,' said Julia, treating it as such. 'I guess it's entirely possible that BEP may use our technology in some groundbreaking innovation. That's the nature of scientific research – you can never be sure what applications your work may have down the line.'

'So wouldn't it be more prudent to sell the company when you are sure? I mean, you told me yourself last week that the commercial uses for the software weren't all apparent yet.'

'It's sweet of you to consider of our interests,' said Julia, resting her hand on his for a few seconds. 'But we debated long and hard about the right time to exit. Yes, we're aware the technology has yet to realise its full potential and we analysed the pros and cons of raising more money on the market to develop it further. But ultimately we chose to sell out, taking into account all that we knew.'

'Surely the point is you didn't know everything,' said Hugo.

'We took that into account as well,' she said, effectively closing the door on the debate.

Julia took another sip of her cognac – she was drinking much less quickly than Hugo and he tried to slow his pace.

'Totally changing the subject, Hugo, tell me a bit more about yourself. Do you have a girlfriend, or are you footloose and fancy free?'

Hugo wavered – why was she asking this? And how, in all the circumstances, could he give a straightforward answer?

'I was sort of seeing someone,' he replied, 'but we had a big bust-up before we'd even really properly got together.'

He sounded like a psycho, he knew. And to blame Claudia would only further raise Julia's suspicions.

'Oh dear – can you make it up with her?'

'I don't think so,' Hugo said. 'She was hard work – I'm well out of it.'

This mature, emotionally stable woman was poles apart from Claudia. She understood him even before he spoke, she hung onto his every word, and she wasn't hypersensitive.

'In my experience,' said Julia, 'a relationship that's hard work is doomed. It's so important to be with someone who totally gets you, isn't it Hugo?'

She smiled at him – her charming, unaffected, honest smile.

'Yes, yes,' agreed Hugo, lost in the moment. 'So important.'

'How did you meet her?'

'By chance, at a speed-dating event – not my normal sort of evening out, but I'd gone for a bet with my friend Charlie.'

He felt a compulsion to disclose all this, but hoped she wouldn't probe further – if he wasn't careful, he could easily come across as some sort of sexual predator.

'Is she an accountant as well?'

'No,' said Hugo, tensing and hoping that his monosyllabic answer would end this worrying line of enquiry. If he told her Claudia was a journalist, it was all too obvious which way the discussion would go.

'I suppose she wouldn't be, if you met at the speed dating. So what does she do?'

Despite his misgivings, Hugo blurted out the truth before he could stop himself.

'She's a journalist,' he said.

Now he was sunk, but amazingly Julia seemed to veer off in a different direction.

'Chance encounters are so unpredictable,' she said. 'so random and yet – doesn't everything happen for a reason?'

'Definitely so,' Hugo gazed deep into her eyes.

'Do you honestly believe it was chance that you met this journalist when your work is so confidential? I mean, mightn't she have been fishing round for some information?'

Hugo's heart raced. She'd approached the subject somewhat more obliquely than he'd expected, but had nevertheless made the connection he'd feared. Still, unless he confessed all, she couldn't be sure.

'Never,' said Hugo. 'You can hardly get more random than speed dating, can you?'

'I guess not.'

Hugo's pulse returned to normal.

'And,' Julia went on, 'it must be totally random you were selected to work on Project Acorn...'

'No it wasn't – it was because I'm bloody fantastic at my job!'

This was an outright fib, and Julia almost certainly knew it, but she didn't care.

'Yet,' she said, 'I wouldn't be sitting here with you if you were someone else, now would I?'

'Wouldn't you?'

A shiver of anticipation shot through Hugo as Julia's hand brushed his – her sparkling blue eyes probing deep into his soul. And when he asked her to come back to his room, he had no fear of rejection – he already knew her answer would be yes. It was inevitable, pre-ordained even, that they should make love.

Electricity crackled between them on the long elevator ride to the eighth floor. They fell on each other as soon as Hugo closed the door to his room.

There was nothing safe about this sex. It was like being swept out to sea by a huge breaker then, at the point of drowning, being hauled back to shore. Hugo had never known an experience so intense – maybe he never would again.

They sank back into the pillows afterwards, half laughing, half crying.

'I love you,' said Hugo, the words spilling involuntarily from his lips.

Julia leant forward and kissed him.

'Oh Hugo,' she said. 'You're so sweet.'

Afterwards, they said nothing – what words could capture the perfection of the moment? They lay in each other's arms and soon fell asleep.

Hugo woke before 5 a.m., ravenous. Julia had vanished. Only her perfume lingering on the bedclothes convinced him he hadn't awoken from a crazy dream. Yet for all its air of unreality, the experience had been so genuine, so right – he and Julia were perfect for each other. He composed a text to her, but stopped on the brink of sending it, as though he might somehow break the spell.

Food was the priority now – his stomach wouldn't wait until breakfast. He surveyed the mini-bar. Ignoring for once the rows of brandy miniatures, he grabbed a jar of cashew nuts, some Pringles, and a Hershey's chocolate bar – nowhere near enough to fill the void, but better than nothing.

He noticed he'd missed a call on his mobile – number withheld. It might be the office, but there was no message. Surely it wasn't Claudia? He was damned if he was going to humiliate himself by ringing and asking her whether she'd called – she'd have to take the initiative. Last night he'd have been glad to talk to her, but events had moved on dramatically since.

'Everything happens for a reason,' Julia had said.

What if she was right? Suppose it was more than a strange fluke that he should bump into a journalist running a story on BEP – suppose the *Globe* had already found out about the offer for IDD. Hugo ignored these half-formed ruminations. Right now, Claudia merely tainted his memories of Julia.

32

On Tuesday morning, Claudia at last succumbed to the urge to contact Hugo. She had now spent more than two days in bitter regret, desperate for him to realise that she hadn't sold him down the river.

Realistically, she knew he wouldn't even speak to her. But what use is logic in the face of powerful emotion? She'd fallen for the idiot, and the more she told herself it was ridiculous, the stronger her feelings became. Using what modest capacity for rational thought remained, she called from the anonymous office landline – at least he might pick up if he didn't see it was her.

He didn't pick up but the phone rang strangely, so that meant he was abroad – he hadn't been fired. She consulted her watch; it was 4 a.m. in New Jersey – hardly surprising there was no answer. Claudia sat on her hands for an hour before surrendering to the compulsion to call again.

This time, he answered on the first ring.

'It's me, Claudia.'

He heaved a sigh.

'Who else would be bonkers enough to call me in the middle of the night?'

'You can't have been asleep – you answered straight away.'

'Goodbye Claudia,' he said, in weary tones.

'Wait, wait – please don't hang up on me. There's something I must say.'

Amazingly, he stayed on the line.

'If you're calling to apologise – don't bother.'

'I never apologise,' Claudia reminded him, although she was sorely tempted to on this occasion.

'So why are you calling?'

'To explain about the article in the *Globe*.'

'What's to explain? You've been a total bitch.'

'I promise I didn't say a word to the paper.'

'You're asking me to swallow that? Oh, come on.'

Hugo was as cynical as she'd anticipated. But at least he was still speaking to her.

'It happens to be true.'

'You must think I'm dense.'

'Why deny it if I'd done it?'

'Christ knows – why do you do any of the crazy things you do?'

'Don't you believe me?'

There was a long silence – painfully long.

'No, I don't.'

'They must be satisfied that the leak wasn't via you – you're still in a job.'

'Barely – and no thanks to you.'

'Honestly, I had no part in it.'

'You know what,' said Hugo. 'I don't trust you at all. And I'm beginning to suspect that everything else you've told me is a pack of lies.'

'Such as what?'

Claudia wasn't prepared for this – what could he possibly mean? Apart from the small matter of snooping through his bag – and she'd owned up even to that – she'd been completely honest with him.

'Don't play the innocent – it doesn't suit you. It wasn't by chance I ended up opposite you at the speed dating, was it?'

'Oh, come on – you know it was.'

'I don't know anything, but I suspect the *Globe* set all this up. There's been nothing but trouble ever since we met.'

'I don't understand what you're talking about.'

'I'll give you this,' said Hugo. 'You're damned good, but the game's over now.'

'What do you think my game is?'

'I've no idea, but why have you been so eager for me to buy into this loucura nonsense of yours? What's the hidden agenda?'

'Hugo, there is no hidden agenda.'

'Well, you're aware that I'm trying to close out Project Acorn. And you know the transaction's dead if what Hubbard says is true. Perhaps you're trying to destroy the deal? Or maybe destroy me, my promotion, my life? Who's paying you to do this?'

This was a crazy, paranoid rant – where had it come from? In any event, Hugo was doing a more than adequate job of ruining his own life without her assistance.

'Hugo, are you drunk?'

'No, I'm stone cold sober – it's five o'clock in the morning here.'

'OK, you're sober. So you tell me – how did I orchestrate you leaving your bag behind so I'd learn about the takeover?'

'You didn't – you already knew about Project Acorn, before we ever met.'

It still didn't make sense, any of it.

'What exactly would I gain from screwing up the deal?'

'I can't imagine.'

'So why accuse me?'

'I just don't trust you any more – ever since I met you, I feel as if I'm a pawn in someone else's game. Well I'm not playing any more, Claudia. Why did you call me after you said you never wanted to see me again?'

'I wondered how you were doing.'

And I'm in love with you, but you're too moronic even to work that out.

'No, you planned to keep me dangling. Well, no more.

This is finished – we're finished – forever. And by the way, I've been reliably informed that a simple cure for cancer is a scientific impossibility. So that story you're working on, if you are really working on it, is the biggest pile of crap ever.'

Now it all fell into place – Julia was behind Hugo's sudden paranoia. Why hadn't she seen it before? How easy it must have been for her to get Hugo to open up and play on his suspicion about the leak. With a few well-aimed poisoned verbal darts, Claudia had been comprehensively discredited.

It was useless even trying to reason with him – his mind was made up. Their chat was going nowhere, their relationship likewise.

'I can't force you to trust me, Hugo. When you've had time to mull it over...'

'I've no intention of mulling it over.'

'Well, can we catch up over a drink when you get back?'

There was an exceptionally long pause this time.

'That won't be happening,' he said.

Both women were already in the dining room when Hugo strolled in. Stephanie was immaculate, in her eighties Pan Am stewardess style, and Julia looked effortlessly appropriate, as always. She betrayed no outward sign of what had happened, and Hugo hugged the delicious secret to himself. Then, to his surprise, Julia winked at him conspiratorially. Taking care to avoid Stephanie's eagle eye, Hugo winked back.

'Morning Hugo,' Julia said. 'I trust we're suitably clear-headed today?'

Stephanie scowled at Hugo, although he wasn't sure why. He ignored her ill temper and helped himself to some coffee and a piece of toast. Why wouldn't he be clear-headed?

'Well, I don't know about you ladies, but I'm feeling razor sharp.'

'Excellent,' said Julia.

Hugo longed to reach out and touch her, to prove she was real. Resisting the temptation, he flagged down the waiter.

'I'll have eggs Benedict, with a side order of bacon, and some more toast please – with marmalade if you have it,' he said.

'Delicious,' said Julia. 'I'll have the same. What about you, Stephanie?'

'Oh, a bowl of fruit salad for me.'

It struck Hugo that Julia was being rather cruel in flaunting her ability to eat normally in front of food-phobic Stephanie – such behaviour wasn't at all worthy of such a lovely creature. But he swiftly pushed the critical thought away – he would forgive Julia anything this morning, and Stephanie deserved to be ridiculed.

The strained atmosphere contrasted starkly with the delightfully uncomplicated intimacy of the night before. There was palpable tension between the two women, but it was Stephanie's presence which cast the pall of gloom. Had she somehow found out about him and Julia? Perhaps there'd been some subtle shift in his body language. He wouldn't know – he wasn't used to this kind of deception. Under close scrutiny, the slightest movement, word or gesture might give him away. He strained every sinew trying not to stare at Julia, even though his eyes were drawn inexorably towards her.

Despite this, Hugo dived into his breakfast with enthusiasm, grateful for any distraction. Stephanie watched him enviously as he ate, while she ran through the day's agenda. Calm, unflappable Julia made judicious comments, but Hugo's mind was elsewhere.

Was it a one-off or something more? With Claudia, he'd

been mildly curious to know, but the same uncertainty about Julia ate him up. His thoughts wandered off to an alternative reality, where he and Julia were blissfully happy together, content with each other's company and each other's bodies. Then he crashed back to earth with a jolt, the possibility that this might not be on her agenda too painful to contemplate. He found his gaze drawn to her again – an involuntary action he couldn't control. She rapidly averted her eyes.

'Good heavens – is that the time?' she said with a theatrical flourish, looking at her watch.

'We must go and get ready,' agreed Stephanie. 'Let's meet in reception in half an hour. Hugo, can you order a cab please?' Hugo trotted off, using all his willpower to tear himself away.

The line at the concierge desk was frustratingly long, and everyone in front of him asked complicated questions. He was on the verge of returning to his room to telephone for a taxi when a guy about the same age as himself joined the queue behind him. Hugo identified him instantly as a fellow bag carrier.

'Terrible, isn't it?' said the newcomer, 'I'm only trying to order a cab – you'd think in a place as plush as this you'd snap your fingers and it's done.'

'Yes, definitely,' Hugo agreed.

'I saw you in the dining room earlier. Those two women – are they your bosses?'

'One's my boss – the other's a client. You here on your own?'

'No, my boss is here too – he's having his shoes shined over there.' He gestured to a bald, fat, pompous looking man across the lobby. 'How long are you staying?'

'Depends how long it takes to wrap the discussions up. How about you?'

'Similar,' he said. 'Look, only a suggestion, but how about

a drink this evening if you're free? It's a bit claustrophobic, if you get what I mean.' He rolled his eyes in the direction of his boss.

'Possibly,' said Hugo, 'but I might be busy tonight.'

Nothing could be allowed to get in the way of spending more time with Julia.

'Well, if you're free, I'm Tom – room 605. I have to go out for dinner, but I'll be back by ten latest – call me.'

Hugo extended his hand to finish the introductions.

'Hugo,' he said. 'Room 819. Maybe see you later.'

He very much hoped he wouldn't need to take Tom up on his offer.

33

Hugo struggled to keep focused. His future career with Pearson Malone dangled by a thread, and for the moment his survival depended only on producing a coherent set of notes. But Julia's presence made the task nigh on impossible.

Each time she moved, he caught a whiff of her perfume, transporting him back to the ecstasy of the night before. When she spoke, he subjected every word to meticulous analysis in case she was transmitting a message in code. However hard he tried to turn his gaze away, his eyes locked onto her.

In truth, she'd shown no sign of what had passed between them since her wink at breakfast; and moreover, she'd neatly sidestepped all Hugo's efforts to snatch a few seconds alone with her. This worried him.

At morning coffee break, he'd tried to manoeuvre himself next to her. Immediately, but not too obviously, she buttonholed one of the lawyers. At lunch, she intentionally positioned herself at the opposite end of the table. In the afternoon she left the room – probably to go to the Ladies. Hugo followed her out after a judiciously timed interval, only to find she'd mysteriously disappeared. If she'd been trying to taunt him, she couldn't have done better. And all the while, Stephanie spoke to him only when strictly necessary, and watched him intently, as if waiting for him to slip up.

By the end of the day, most of the finer details sailed over Hugo's head. Indeed, as the negotiations stepped up in pace, Hugo's notes became sparser. When they were all done for the day, Hugo heard Morrison ask Julia out for dinner on her own – ostensibly to go into the integration of the R & D functions post-deal. Hugo suspected there was more to the invitation than met the eye and a jealous nausea welled up in him as he heard her graciously agree to go. He craved Julia's company again, so badly he would have gone to any lengths to engineer a couple of minutes alone together. Why wasn't she prepared to do the same? In his heart of hearts, Hugo knew the answer to this question.

He was running out of time. At the end of the week they'd all go home with the agreement in the bag. After that, he'd have little professional reason to contact Julia. Of course, there would be nothing to stop him from calling her up and asking her out, but unaccountably he shrank from this, just as he'd decided not to text her that morning. Last night, he'd been certain she was crazy about him – now doubt began to creep into his heart and mind.

Dinner without Julia was a torture. When IDD's lawyers joined them in the hotel restaurant, Hugo hoped this would rescue him from a ghastly dinner à deux with Stephanie, but he'd underestimated the dullness of the company. There were two of them – the partner, a rotund man with pasty white skin and a loud voice, and his sidekick, a girl about Hugo's age with lank mousy hair. She wore a cheap navy suit and a white blouse, grubby-looking even by Hugo's uncritical standards.

Stephanie watched Hugo suspiciously as he toyed with his food – unusually, the gnawing anxiety about Julia had utterly killed his appetite. The small amount of wine available did nothing to anaesthetise his pain, and the unhurried way the others sipped at their glasses ensured a second bottle would not be ordered.

Stephanie chatted up the law firm partner – in a purely

professional sense – which left Hugo to try his best to converse with Alexandra, the girl.

'Weren't you at the record-breaking speed-dating event the Friday before last?' he asked her. Certainly, she wouldn't have been out of place there.

To Hugo's chagrin, she interpreted this remark as some kind of come-on, and expounded at length about her fiancé Ralph and his PhD in mediaeval architecture. What a senseless subject for anyone sane to study, thought Hugo. Most of it had been demolished and it wasn't as if anyone would build any more.

As soon as he could decently escape, Hugo sidled off outside for a cigarette and then into the bar. It would be a while before Julia returned from her dinner, and he had seldom felt such an acute craving for a strong drink. Tom, the bloke from the hotel lobby, sat on one of the over-stuffed sofas with a large cognac in front of him. He saw Hugo and waved him over.

'Hi there, Hugo, how are you? I was about to call you.'

'I was going to call you as well,' lied Hugo, who'd forgotten all about him. 'Dinner ran on a bit – you know.'

'Oh, yes,' agreed Tom. 'Boy don't I know it. I am sick of the sound of my boss's voice, and he's on my back twenty-four-seven – do this, don't do that...'

'Like my boss,' said Hugo, sensing an instant rapport.

'Your boss is one gorgeous babe.'

'She's my client. The clapped-out air stewardess is my boss.'

'Ah – she might be harder work,' Tom conceded. 'Anyway, I guess you could use a drink – what can I get you?'

Hugo eyed the cognac. Waiting for Julia would be more bearable in Tom's company and with a drink in his hand.

'Well, one of those would be great.'

'Rémy Martin?'

'Excellent.'

'So what do you do, Hugo?' asked Tom after he'd given the order to the waiter.

'I'm in corporate finance,' he said. 'How about you?'

'I'm in sales.' He handed over a card.

Hugo scarcely registered the name of the company, focusing more on the fancy job title – Assistant Vice President. He hadn't imagined Tom to be so very important. Then again, these Yanks hyped everything up, so Tom might be the American equivalent of Assistant Manager for all Hugo knew. Hugo dug out one of his own dog-eared cards.

So far as Hugo recollected, that was the only time they even touched on the subject of work during the evening. They watched a baseball game on the widescreen, and chatted about sport and girls. Hugo exaggerated his brief fling with Claudia. Tom told him he wouldn't have minded giving Julia one. In my dreams, Hugo told him. They knocked back a few more cognacs and played cards. Hugo won, and retired to bed.

Back in his room Hugo checked his mobile and landline for messages – there were none, and it was five past midnight. It was hard to hide from harsh reality now.

Hugo brought up Julia's number on his mobile, but chickened out of calling. Their relationship seemed oddly asymmetrical – she made the running and he followed. Besides, by leaving it to Julia to initiate contact, he could delude himself that she'd been held up somewhere, or didn't care to disturb him so late – anything but confront a painful rejection.

Dejected, Hugo climbed into bed, but sleep eluded him. He lay in the darkness, praying to a God he didn't believe in. If Julia wanted him as much he desired her, he would never make another demand again. But it was no use and intellectually Hugo knew the score, even if his heart tried to deny the truth.

34

The next morning, something was afoot.

Outside the meeting room, Morrison asked Stephanie for a word in private. He glared pointedly at Hugo.

Stephanie raised her eyebrows – so did Julia – but Morrison insisted. Hugo was thrilled to be left in the reception area with Julia.

'How was your dinner last night?' he asked.

'Very productive, Hugo – thank you for asking.'

'Did it go on very late?'

'Good Lord, no – I was absolutely exhausted. I expect it was the jet lag catching up with me at last.'

She offered no other explanation for not contacting him – made no reference to the events of their night together. She was polite enough, but firmly back into her client mode, even though they were alone.

'Jet lag can be deceptive,' said Hugo, playing along with the fiction. 'It can sneak up on you in a nasty way after a couple of days.'

He could in theory have easily steered the conversation to more intimate matters, but again his perception of the inequality between them held him back. Julia alone had the power to determine what happened.

'I wonder what Edgar's after from Stephanie,' she said.

Hugo noted the first name terms. He'd been wondering as well. After a couple of minutes, Stephanie's head appeared round the door.

'Please can you join us, Julia,' she said.

Hugo stood up too, but Stephanie indicated for him to

sit back down. She glared at him even more than usual. Hugo leafed through the *New York Times,* and five minutes later Stephanie summoned him as well.

It was only as they all sat there, poker-faced, that Hugo belatedly grasped they'd been talking about him. A wild panic seized him. Had Julia claimed he'd harassed her – or worse? Stephanie asked Morrison, Julia and another man, whom Hugo did not recognise, to leave while she spoke to Hugo alone. Hugo tried, in vain, to establish eye contact with Julia.

'Is there a problem?' he asked inanely.

'The problem,' said Stephanie, white-lipped with anger, 'is you.'

'Me?'

'I suppose you gambled on not being caught – you thought you'd found an easy way to make a quick buck to pay off those damned credit cards of yours.'

He was doubtless being accused of a serious offence, but he had no idea what it might be. And how did Stephanie even know about his freaking credit cards?

Stephanie laid out a photograph on the table in front of Hugo. The quality was poor, but it unmistakeably showed him and Tom in the bar the previous evening, their neckties loosened and looking a little the worse for wear.

'How could you?' said Stephanie. 'After everything that's happened?'

This puritanical witch hunt was too much. Hugo resolved to start his job search the minute he got back to London.

'I may have had a drink or two,' he conceded.

Who had taken the picture and how did Stephanie come to have it? Had she been spying on him?

'I can't see it's a big issue,' he went on. 'I mean, I'm here this morning, I've done all you've asked of me – so what's your problem?'

155

'This is the most embarrassing episode in my career.'

Hugo still didn't get it. They had to be talking at cross purposes – this couldn't be about him getting a bit tiddly in a hotel bar on a business trip. Yet, apart from Julia, there was nothing else.

'We didn't do any damage did we?'

He was unable to recall so much as breaking a glass, let alone any misbehaviour which might warrant a response at this level. The reference to his credit cards was still puzzling, though.

'Damage!' Stephanie shrieked. 'How can you stand there and ask me if you've done any damage? Or maybe you don't remember...'

'I simply don't understand what you're on about,' said Hugo.

Stephanie pointed at the photograph.

'Who's this man?'

'It's a bloke called Tom – I met him yesterday.'

'He works for SP, Hugo, one of BEP's competitors. Don't bother to deny it, because BEP's security has positively identified him.'

'I've no intention of denying it,' said Hugo. 'I know who he is. He gave me his card.'

Now Hugo reflected on it, he saw why BEP might be unhappy at him speaking to one of their rivals – he'd found out a lot about BEP while working on Project Acorn. But there was no law against having a few drinks with a guy – it wasn't even as though they'd discussed business. And why had BEP's security team been sniffing round in the first place?

'I'm guessing you are going to deny giving him confidential information on Project Acorn?'

Hugo's chest tightened as he fought for breath.

'Absolutely. I do deny it,' he said when he'd recovered his composure. 'We didn't talk about work at all.'

156

'Well, BEP have evidence that you disclosed price, timetable, post-merger integration strategy – the works.'

She appeared triumphant, as though she'd caught him out in a huge lie.

'This is ludicrous! Look!' Hugo picked up the photograph and stuck it under Stephanie's nose. 'We're only playing cards, can't you see?'

'Hugo, you were overheard. It's useless to deny it.'

'That's ridiculous,' said Hugo. 'I can't have been overheard saying things I didn't say.'

'You were overheard,' she repeated.

'But surely...'

Stephanie cut him off before he'd even begun.

'How could you stoop so low as to sell confidential information?' she asked, her face screwed up in fury.

Now at least he understood the allusion to his finances, but these accusations were as grave as they were un-founded.

'I didn't – I wouldn't. This doesn't stack up.'

'Hugo, stop lying and turn out your pockets.'

'I don't see why...'

'Just do it,' she snapped.

He produced the usual Hugo-esque assortment of scruffy bits of paper, old receipts and an empty cigarette packet, but there was a new item he hadn't seen before – an envelope full of $100 bills.

Stephanie snatched the envelope and regarded Hugo with contempt as she counted the money.

'You creep. You sold out for a lousy ten thousand – not even pounds, but dollars. Every time I think I've plumbed the depths, you disgust me even more. And don't tell me you won the money at cards – I'm not dim-witted.'

The money from the card game – a tiny fraction of the amount in the envelope – was safely in Hugo's wallet.

'I can't imagine how the money got there,' he protested.

'But the conversation didn't touch on anything to do with work, I promise you.'

His heart sank as reality dawned on him.

'I suppose BEP have evidence of me taking the money as well.'

'Why, yes.'

She produced another picture.

'But that was the money from the card game! Look – it's not in an envelope.'

The notes themselves were visible, but their denomination was unclear. The lack of envelope did nothing to alter Stephanie's perception.

'It's no use telling lies, Hugo.'

'I'm not telling lies – we were playing cards! You can see on the other picture.'

But Stephanie's mind was made up.

'Hugo,' she said. 'I'm not prepared to discuss it any further. You plainly became so drunk you yielded to temptation, and now you don't remember anything that happened.'

'I remember it all! We didn't talk about Project Acorn – I'm certain of it. And I don't have the faintest where the money in the envelope came from.'

'Oh, come on Hugo. Look at you in the picture – you're half-cut. You were seen to consume at least five large cognacs, on top of the wine you had with dinner. Nobody could keep track of what they did or said after drinking so much.'

The suggestion that the thimblefuls of wine at dinner might have made a jot of difference to his sobriety would have been laughable if he hadn't been in such a bad place.

'We were playing cards!'

'What a gift you were to SP,' Stephanie continued, ignoring Hugo's protestations of innocence. 'It's obvious they planted this Tom in the hotel on purpose to extract information from you. I'll bet they were rubbing their hands with glee when you turned out to be such a soft touch.'

'I'm sure I didn't do anything,' Hugo repeated, but with less conviction this time. Doubt was beginning to creep into his mind. What if he had accidentally let some information slip and Tom had thrust the money into his pocket when he wasn't watching? He restrained himself – this way lay madness – he must hang on to his certainty, no matter how hard they tried to shake him.

Slowly, Hugo's panic settled as he began to use his wits. Odd that BEP's security people should happen to be in the bar at the critical time, conveniently armed with a camera. How robust was this evidence really?

'Is there a recording of the conversation?' he asked. This would at least establish the alleged facts one way or another.

'No, there isn't a recording – do you really think BEP's in-house security go around bugging people?'

'Well they go round loitering in bars, listening in to conversations and taking photographs. What's the difference? And why were they in the bar last night anyway? I don't suppose you even thought to ask.'

'As a matter of fact, I did ask. BEP were watching Tom. They've suspected SP for some while of using social engineering techniques to spy on them, and Tom was one of their main weapons – young, well-spoken, friendly, easy company. And you,' she said, jabbing at his chest to underline her argument, 'were foolish enough to fall for it.'

'So basically, it's my word against theirs?' said Hugo, more hopeful now.

'It is,' Stephanie agreed. 'But why would they lie about it?'

'Why would I lie about it?'

'Hugo, the evidence is damning.'

She waved the wodge of banknotes in front of Hugo's face.

'In other words, you've chosen to accept their version of events?'

'In view of the evidence, yes.'

The hope died.

'But the evidence is false,' said Hugo. 'I've been set up. Don't you think I would have had the intelligence to hide the money if it wasn't a plant?'

Stephanie shook her head, apparently more in sorrow than in anger.

'It won't wash Hugo. And let's be realistic – your track record on confidentiality hasn't been impressive recently. I cut you some slack on Monday, but this time you've gone too far.'

'Has anyone asked Tom?'

Hugo still clung to a forlorn hope this was all some bizarre misunderstanding – perhaps they'd mixed him up with someone else. Tom had seemed a decent enough bloke – surely he would help. Hugo extracted Tom's card from his wallet and dialled his direct line from his mobile.

'I'm sorry,' said the voicemail. 'I can't take your call right now, but I'll get back to you as soon as possible. Will you please leave a message after the tone, or if you require further assistance...'

He dialled the other number – at last, a human being.

'I'm sorry, but Tom is no longer with the company.'

He dialled Tom's cell phone – voicemail again. He left a message, but he wouldn't hold his breath waiting for a call back.

'God, you're naive,' Stephanie said with contempt. 'What the hell did you expect?'

Hugo was defeated, overwhelmed and completely alone in a nightmare world. Weary acceptance took over from shock, incredulity and anger.

160

'What happens now?' he asked.

'You are on a flight out of here ASAP. I've spoken to Christian already – the others insisted. I hardly need tell you how disturbed he is about all this. Assuming you can get back in time, he'll see you at three o'clock tomorrow. If you're lucky, he'll demand your resignation.'

'What if I'm unlucky?'

'I wouldn't ask if I were you, Hugo.'

Hugo's heart flipped as his thoughts turned to Julia. He would never be able to speak to her again, not even to say goodbye, unless he called her privately – which didn't seem a great plan in his present predicament.

'I don't care what it takes – but I will prove I'm innocent,' he said resolutely.

But Stephanie was having none of it.

'Hugo, it's over – you can't wriggle your way out this time. On a personal note, I must say how saddened I am, after I've fought your corner, not only now, but time and time again.'

If this was an example of Stephanie fighting his corner, he wondered what on earth she would have done if she'd set out to destroy him.

Two broad-shouldered security guards appeared from nowhere to escort Hugo from the building. As he walked past Julia, he caught her eye for a nanosecond – there was some emotion there, he was sure. But this glimmer of hope did nothing to improve an otherwise forlorn situation. He'd been stitched up like a kipper, and there was damn all he could do about it.

Brad and Wayne met in the usual diner. To the casual observer, they looked like nothing more than two regular guys enjoying a steak and a beer, nattering about the baseball game.

'This business sure isn't doing my waistline any favours,' Brad complained. 'Jill definitely suspects something's going on.'

'You make it sound as if you're cheating on her,' said Wayne.

'Maybe she'd be happier if I did,' Brad replied. 'At least I'd burn up some calories.'

Both men laughed and clinked their glasses.

'Brad, I'll level with you. This business with that Fleming character was not a smart move.'

'Morrison wanted him out.'

'Not a smart move for Morrison, either. Think about it – Fleming gets back home and he starts asking questions. There was a reason he mentioned Hubbard's name.'

'What?'

'Fleming's screwing the journalist who was talking to Hubbard – he told Tom all about it.'

'All the more reason to get Fleming out of the way,' said Brad.

'I don't agree. He would have never gotten anywhere with Morrison, but now he's certain he's onto something. Why bother to frame him otherwise?'

Brad had no answer to that. 'Tom was one of yours, wasn't he?' he asked instead.

'Yes, he was.'

'I heard he was fired from SP – I hope he's being taken care of.'

'Right now, he's sitting on a pile of money,' replied Wayne, 'enough to keep him going for a while. His number was up in any case – these double agents only have a short useful life. This tied off all the loose ends and he never blew his cover.'

'Very neat,' said Brad.

'But not so neat to have Fleming and the journalist both poking around,' Wayne reminded him, returning to the central issue.

'I told you,' said Brad. 'We've nothing to hide.'

'Morrison has – he's mad keen to do this deal. Aren't you curious to know why?'

'Shoot.'

'This may be crap,' said Wayne, 'and I'm sure you'll tell me if it is. I guess you understand why you're buying IDD?'

Brad was vaguely uneasy – he'd not over-involved himself in the detail of this comparatively small acquisition and had only showed up at the dinner because Morrison told him it would help the negotiations along.

'Technology,' he replied.

'What does the technology do?'

'It analyses the effects of different molecules on different parts of the body.'

'What are you planning to use it for?'

'To reposition some of our blockbusters.' Brad took a swig of his beer.

'Can you see where I'm going with this?'

'In a word, no,' said Brad. 'Seems a reasonable business rationale to me. And these questions have already been asked and answered, surely?'

But Wayne knew exactly where he was going.

'This technology – what else does it do?'

'Lots, in principle, although the other uses are a bit speculative as of now.'

'So what are they?'

'Well, potentially, the technology can be used to screen naturally occurring molecules and produce more effective synthetic versions.'

'Spot on,' said Wayne.

'But we won't be going there. I mean, biological products research is so over.'

'Not for Morrison, it isn't.'

Brad held his forkful of steak in mid air as he latched on to what Wayne was telling him.

'No,' he said, 'it's not possible. It's not even scientifically possible.'

'Who says?'

'Everyone. Cancer isn't one disease, you know – it's a whole complex range of diseases with multiple causes. A simple across-the-board treatment simply wouldn't be feasible.'

'Cut the crap, Brad. You don't have to sing from the party hymn sheet for me. Suppose loucura is a quick fix for cancer. You can't patent it, so you won't make money from it – and the cash flow from your existing cancer drugs is screwed. Now you tell me – would you necessarily be keen to have loucura out there?'

'I can see all that,' said Brad irritably. 'You haven't told me anything new. But whatever we wanted wouldn't make a blind bit of difference. If there was a phenomenal cancer cure, no way on God's earth could it be squashed.'

'Verse two from the party hymn sheet. Now if this IDD technology can develop a synthetic substitute, you can patent it and...'

'If, if, if...' Brad said shaking his head. 'There's a hell of a lot of supposition here.'

'Stick with me a while longer. Suppose Morrison did fix the loucuramine study, but now he's planning on retiring in a blaze of glory – saviour of mankind.'

'You mean Morrison's intending to trial a loucura substitute?'

'Yep.'

'You're joking. To begin with, there wouldn't be time before he retires.'

'FDA fast track process?'

'Even so.'

'He could announce it?'

'No, he couldn't. Morrison can't pursue his own agenda and to hell with the rest of us – not in an organisation of this size. His line of enquiry would have to be sanctioned at the highest level. It would have to be... And this is only hypothetical, isn't it? We already agreed a simple remedy for cancer was impossible.'

'I believe we did. And you've also agreed that you're not ecstatic about this hypothetical situation – why, look at all the money BEP earns from the useless cancer drugs you're selling now. You can't charge nearly so much for a one-off solution.'

'I pay you to sort out problems, not create them,' said Brad.

'I was paid to unearth what Morrison was up to, and I'm telling you,' came Wayne's retort. 'You can't blame me just because you don't like it.'

'You were right about one thing – this is crap.'

'Maybe,' said Wayne. 'But let me finish. Fact: at least two people believed in loucura – Hubbard and Morrison.'

'Morrison doesn't, I tell you.'

'I say he does. Now, I don't have to enlighten you on bio-piracy.'

'Bio-prospecting, we prefer to call it,' said Brad.

'So to synthesise loucura, Morrison would require access to the original plant, right?'

'Right,' Brad agreed, reluctantly.

'And he'd have to cut a deal with the Brazilian authorities?'

'I guess so, but...'

'No buts. Remember those calls to Brazil?'

Brad stared at him, open-mouthed, as realisation dawned.

'Ministry of the Environment – remember?'

'You sure?'

'Certain,' said Wayne. 'Now, is this still hypothetical?'

'If it is, my head of R & D has lost his marbles.'

'And if it isn't?'

Neither scenario was appealing. Brad laid down his knife and fork. Suddenly he wasn't hungry any more.

35

'You screwed up, Morrison. And that's putting it politely.'

'It was for the best – Fleming would have jeopardised your plans.'

'No, he wouldn't.'

'The situation was out of control.'

'Believe me, it was all in hand – much more than you knew.'

Morrison strove to justify his position, but his efforts were futile – he'd acted in haste and upset the one person he should have kept on side.

'Fleming had split with the journalist. He wasn't taking this any further.'

'So why did he ask about Hubbard?'

'Who knows – curiosity? But you can bet your bottom dollar he's curious now he realises you've set him up. He's not going to let this go. And I have to pick up the pieces, as per usual.'

'How will you do that?'

Hubbard's death and the question of who was responsible still loomed large in Morrison's mind. He feared for himself as much as Hugo. Living to regret his actions might now be a best case scenario.

'Why should I tell you? You've already proved your incompetence.'

With that, the caller hung up, leaving Morrison to sweat.

36

Hugo boarded the evening flight to Heathrow.

He planned to make the most of this final business class journey at Pearson Malone's expense. What would they do if he rolled up drunk for his meeting – fire him? He had nothing to lose.

Hugo's head buzzed – and not only from the booze. A confusing medley of emotions jockeyed for pole position – anger that no one had faith in him, heartache for Julia, and above all a deep and crushing sense of humiliation.

The cabin lights dimmed and Hugo lay in the darkness with his misery. Why did everyone immediately assume he'd do something silly? Where had he gone wrong? He knew he was better than people imagined – so why could he never prove this when it counted? Charlie always accused Hugo of being lazy, but laziness was a symptom, not the disease – it was pointless to expend any energy when nothing seemed worthwhile.

Amid this turmoil of self-flagellation, a calmer and more reasonable internal voice began to clamour for attention. Why, the voice demanded, had this happened? Why had BEP set him up?

There were three possibilities. One – he'd mentioned Hubbard's name in front of Hillman and Morrison and this had spooked them. Two – BEP had detected his connection to Claudia after all he had told Tom about her. Three – they'd sussed out Claudia was using him to wreck Project Acorn.

All these options only raised further questions. Why try

to kill a deal with a story which didn't stack up? And why was anyone so agitated about loucura if it was as useless as they all claimed?

Hugo tied his brain in knots – none of it stood up to analysis, unless...

There was another explanation, in many respects much simpler. Julia was wrong and Hubbard's story was true.

In this case, it was only natural for BEP to be concerned about his links with Claudia. In fact, their actions strongly suggested that there was some mileage in the story after all. Why bother to get rid of him otherwise?

But however well this hung together logically, proving it was a different matter. Yet this is exactly what he'd have to do if there was to be any hope for his reputation, his career and his heart.

Which brought him back to Claudia. Two heads were undoubtedly better than one, especially when one of them belonged to a nosy journalist. And as Claudia was working the story he was trying to substantiate, she was a useful resource. In the interests of expediency, Hugo would put aside her possible betrayal, although it went without saying that any sort of relationship was out of the question. But like it or not – and on the whole he did not – Hugo's best plan was to work with Claudia. That's if she'd let him, of course.

To Marcus's immense displeasure, Richard had drawn a blank on the secret shareholder in IDD.

'I know this is only a two percent holding,' said Marcus, 'but it may be the tip of the iceberg, with more connected holdings in different names. Is there really no way you can discover who's behind them?'

'Nominee companies ensure secrecy – as you're well aware. They've been set up by the same company formation agent, and that's all I can say.'

Marcus had predicted this response, but still he'd hoped Richard would pull a rabbit out of a hat.

'Couldn't you get someone inside the formation agents?'

'I tried – but security's as tight as a drum.'

'Pity,' said Marcus.

'For what it's worth, I'm not convinced these people are out to thwart your proposals – it's much more likely to be a plain vanilla insider dealing ring,' said Richard.

'Hmm,' Marcus growled. 'Most people are trying to ruin my plans – why should these people be any different?'

Richard was right, though – there were countless reasons why people hid their shareholdings. Yet Marcus had an instinct on this, and his instincts were usually right on the money.

'Anyway,' Richard went on. 'They'd need a much bigger holding than this.'

'Than what?' said Marcus. 'As I said, there may be more we don't know about.'

Richard leafed through the shareholder register.

'The timing of the share acquisitions we do have details on is interesting. Some of them were bought before yours even.'

That was going some – Marcus had been pretty quick off the mark thanks to his contact at BEP. Who could have beaten him to it?

'Then, they bought more at the beginning of this week, precisely when the rumour appeared in the press.'

'Now that is interesting,' said Marcus, perking up. 'Possibly it is insider trading after all.'

Though he didn't really believe it.

37

Claudia was about to bite into a prawn baguette when her mobile rang.

Hugo – bloody typical. She'd spent the last two days trying to forget him, and now when sanity had at long last prevailed, here he was to torment her again.

She put aside her sandwich and let the phone ring five times before answering.

'You were right,' he said, before she could even say hello.

No apology for his paranoid ravings the other night, only this terse statement, its meaning unclear. He sounded drunk, too. She loathed him drunk – come to think of it, she didn't even much care for him sober. Yet despite that, on hearing his voice a crazy passion surged through her body like electricity.

'Right about what?'

'There is something in this loucura business.'

'But weren't you reliably informed that loucura was a scientific impossibility?' Just because her hormones were jumping didn't mean she had to give him an easy time.

'Yes, well, I've changed my mind.'

'So you decided it wasn't some evil plot cooked up by me to kill off your project, and ruin your life?'

'Maybe not, no.'

'Well, it's big of you to say so. You don't need me to help you screw up your life – you're doing a fine job of it already.'

'Will you shut up and listen for a minute? I'm about to lose my job because of you.'

'What, you mean the leak?'

'The one you denied – no, that's history, let's not even go there. This is much more serious.'

'What then?'

'I asked Morrison about Hubbard, to see if there was a reaction.'

'So why do that if I'd made it all up?'

'Right,' said Hugo. 'If you don't stop this, I'm going to hang up and never talk to you again.'

His plain speaking stopped Claudia in her tracks. This was silly – the other day she'd been desperate to cosy back up with him, and he'd been totally obnoxious. Now he was speaking to her sensibly again, and she was being vile to him.

'No, don't,' she said. 'I'm only mad at you because you acted like a total arsehole the other day.'

'I felt you deserved it. Now I'm not so sure.'

He spoke in grave tones – and he'd said he was about to lose his job.

'Hugo, what's happened?'

'I've been set up.'

'Set up?'

'They believe I've been selling information on Project Acorn to one of BEP's competitors. BEP planted ten grand in my pocket and said they'd heard me discussing it in the bar. That's why I'm getting fired.'

There was a certain irony in the situation. Hugo had escaped the consequences of one confidentiality breach, only to be framed for another.

'Why would they do that?'

'Because they didn't appreciate me asking about Hubbard.'

'Is that all?'

'It's all I can think of – I let them know I was on to them.'

'What did you say exactly?'

Hugo told her. It sounded trivial – he hadn't accused them or even said much at all. If Hugo was telling the truth, they'd hugely overreacted, and you had to wonder why.

'Are PM really going to fire you?'

'It's a cert,' said Hugo. 'It might be dressed up as a face-saving resignation, but then again it might not.'

'And you're sure you didn't do it?'

She hated to ask – but he was hideously short of money and at first sight logic suggested guilt rather than innocence.

'Oh, don't be so daft Claudia.'

'Then why can't you prove you're innocent?'

'Because it comes down to their word against mine, and Stephanie chose to accept their story.'

'Well, no surprise there,' said Claudia. 'The bust-up we had last Saturday was all due to that toffee-nosed bitch.'

'And not due to you?'

Claudia ignored this.

'So, I've been thinking,' said Hugo. 'The only reason they'd bother with all this is if Hubbard's story is true.'

'It would be silly even so – by attacking you they'd only be flagging up the fact they had something to hide.'

Claudia had written off the loucura story now, practically lost interest. There had to be another explanation for Hugo's downfall. And even if he had been set up, it didn't make the story any easier to prove.

'So we must get together,' said Hugo, 'ASAP. I'm damned if I'm going to be scapegoated for nothing. The only way I can prove I'm not to blame is by showing Hubbard's story is true. We should work together on this.'

Hugo's utterly self-centred view of events depressed her, and the prospect of a joint effort with him left her cold. What more could they do, in any case? But the anticipation of seeing him again sent her pulse racing.

She didn't intend to let Hugo know that, though.

'Suppose I don't want to? You can't pick people up and put them down when it suits you.'

'You're a fine one to talk – you were the one who walked out on me at The Dorchester and called me up a couple of days later. If you won't get together, that's fine – I'll work solo. Though it'll be easier if we pool our resources.'

'Easier for you, no doubt.'

'And for you as well,' said Hugo. 'I'm trying to help you.'

'Maybe I don't need your help.'

'Don't need or don't want?'

Claudia didn't answer.

'Look, I'll meet if you insist,' she said at last. 'The Avalon at nine – but this purely work-related, OK? And I'm not even saying I'm prepared to work with you, I'm only agreeing to discuss it with you.'

It was well-known that men lusted after what they couldn't have – playing hard to get was the way to go.

'Fine with me.'

Claudia felt a pang of dissatisfaction at this, but she was sure she'd played it right – Hugo's emotions were unmistakeably elsewhere. She knew, without him saying so, that proving a point to Julia was high on his agenda.

'Great – I'll see you later. I hope you don't get fired.'

'Thanks,' said Hugo. 'Pray for a miracle.'

Hugo's group head, Christian Temple, had been at Oxford with Hugo's father. He was also a personal friend of the master of Hugo's old Oxford college. Apart from the revelation that Hugo's degree in PPE was the worst 2.1 in a poor year, these connections had worked to Hugo's advantage in the past. Now they were an embarrassment to both parties.

'I must say, Hugo,' he began, 'I was most surprised to

hear what had happened. What on earth went through your mind?'

'You must believe me, please,' said Hugo. 'I honestly didn't chat about Project Acorn with this chap.'

'I'm afraid there can be little doubt you did,' said Christian. 'Perhaps you might have forgotten – my understanding is you may have been slightly under the influence.'

Hugo had sobered up after his final binge courtesy of British Airways, but was conscious that his breath might be less than fragrant. He tried hard not to breathe on Christian – on reflection, the last thing he needed was hints dropped to his father that he might be an alcoholic.

'I may have been a bit drunk,' Hugo confessed, 'but not enough to sell information for money. In fact, I'd never do that.'

'Stephanie feels you may be in, er – to put it delicately – some financial difficulties.'

It really pissed Hugo off that all these people knew about his problems – how, for God's sake?

'It's only a small cash flow issue,' Hugo defended himself. 'However hard up I was, I would never, ever ... you do realise that, don't you?'

'Is it gambling?' asked Christian, deftly avoiding giving an answer. 'Gambling can drive a chap to desperate deeds.'

Hugo was appalled that Temple might mark him down as a gambler – what if he mentioned this to his father? Hugo squirmed at the idea. He was sick, so sick, of people assuming the worst of him.

'God no! The money in the picture was the money I won playing cards – about ninety dollars, but I haven't got a gambling problem. And I honestly haven't a clue how the other money got into my pocket.'

'I'm inclined to accept your word about the money,' Christian said, twiddling his fountain pen around in his fingers, 'but the breach of confidentiality is a different matter. Understandably, it's terribly easy to get carried away after a few drinks...'

Hugo stiffened, convinced that Temple was now about to suggest he was an alcoholic – perhaps he had caught a sniff of his breath after all. But in fact Temple was offering him a way out.

'I don't remember talking to this chap about Project Acorn,' said Hugo, playing along.

'But you probably don't recall everything you said by a long chalk.'

'Possibly not.'

'So let's attribute this to a drunken indiscretion.'

'Well, I suppose it might have been...' Hugo curbed the urge to proclaim his innocence.

'Not that this in any way exonerates you. You've behaved extremely foolishly and this is a very serious breach of the firm's rules. Stephanie tells me this is the second time in a week there's been an issue with confidentiality, although she didn't go into details about the first one.'

Well she wouldn't, would she – not when she'd failed to follow the correct procedures herself. But there was nothing to be gained at this stage by grassing Stephanie up.

Temple stood and walked towards the window.

'So Hugo, we have a blatant contravention of the firm's policies. As such, we would be perfectly entitled to invoke formal disciplinary procedures against you. I must tell you this was Stephanie's preferred solution.'

'It would be,' said Hugo, no longer caring what he said.

'However,' Temple went on, 'that process would probably end up with you being summarily dismissed. This would be rather messy for all of us, and it would be a shame for your career to be ruined because of one drunken mistake.'

For one deluded moment, Hugo believed he might be reprieved, but his hopes were soon crushed.

'So as an alternative, I'm asking you to resign with immediate effect. You'll get the standard reference, so it shouldn't affect your employability.'

'I'm not sure I should resign,' said Hugo. 'What if I hang on and make every effort to prove I didn't do it?'

'I wouldn't if I were you,' Temple advised, shaking his head. 'Take the offer on the table.'

In practical terms, Hugo had no choice.

'Fine – I'll take the face-saver, but I must say something first.'

'Go ahead,' said Temple.

'I was set up because I have some dirt on BEP which they're desperate to keep hidden. They aren't the ethically sound organisation they're cracked up to be.'

Temple nodded.

'Twenty years ago, BEP held back a cure for cancer because there was no money in it for them.'

'Stephanie told me about this notion of yours,' said Temple wearily.

'Personally, I believe we should have raised the matter with Julia Fraser – there's no way she would sell out to a corrupt organisation. But Stephanie refused.'

Temple sighed.

'I understood this was a rumour which emanated from the somewhat feisty young lady you brought to the party last weekend. We can't advise our clients to pull out of deals on the strength of rumours, Hugo – surely you must see that.'

'The rumour is true. That's why they had to get me out of the way.'

'Can you prove what you're saying?'

'No, not yet.'

'Then it's still a rumour.'

'I will prove it. I will.'

'Hugo, do you really believe that a reputable company like BEP would get involved in this kind of shenanigans?'

'Yes,' said Hugo. 'I do.'

Temple peered at him over the top of his glasses.

'Hugo, can I offer you two pieces of advice?'

'Well, yes – please do.'

'First, you should concentrate your efforts on finding a new job – and stop trying to prove this mad conspiracy theory.'

Hugo was about to say he hadn't even started on the conspiracy theory yet, but checked himself.

'And secondly?'

'Moderation in all things, Hugo, that's always been my motto. You enjoy yourself to excess, and your weaknesses set you up as an easy target. Do you understand what I'm saying?'

Hugo understood all too well – he was, as he was rapidly coming to appreciate, his own worst enemy.

Temple handed him a ready-prepared resignation letter – short and functional. He told Hugo he'd be paid up to the end of the month. A bizarre euphoria swept over Hugo as he signed his own death warrant.

'Sounds odd,' he said, 'but I feel this may be for the best.'

God knows he'd tried over the last four years, but it had been a strain. Now freedom beckoned, and he had never felt happier.

'In a sense, yes,' agreed Temple. 'Though your father will be very disappointed.'

'If you don't mind, I'd prefer to break the news to him myself,' said Hugo.

'Yes, yes – I wouldn't dream of saying a word.'

Temple stood up to shake Hugo's hand.

'Our paths will cross again, Hugo. The professional services world is surprisingly incestuous, even in a big place like the City. I do hope you'll mull over your experiences and learn from them. Underneath it all, you're a bright boy with a lot of positive qualities – I'm sure you'll find your niche.'

Hugo took the hand proffered.

'I do hope so,' he said.

An HR officer supervised Hugo as he sifted through the detritus of his failed career. There was little worth keeping – a fountain pen with a scratchy nib, a box of Alka-Seltzer and a pair of cheap cufflinks. His hideous emergency spare tie went straight in the bin. All in all, it was not much to show for four years in one of the world's most prestigious professional services firms.

On the way out, he caught sight of Stephanie. She tried to avoid him, but he called out to her. She turned – he knew she wouldn't blank him in front of HR.

He was free to say absolutely anything now. She was a mean bullying bitch concerned solely with her own advancement. She lacked any human warmth. A style makeover might not go amiss. The temptation to tell her all these home truths was almost too much. But no – there was only one comment worth making now.

'I'm certain there's something funny going on with BEP, and I will get to the bottom of it.'

He looked her straight in the eye – she didn't even blink.

'Hugo,' she said levelly, 'you've undoubtedly learnt nothing from the events of the last few days. I do hope you improve in the future. Goodbye.' She turned away and strutted down the corridor in her lilac stilettos.

As Hugo left the office, a beggar outside held out his hat. Hugo chucked in some coins. He wondered why – with no debts, the beggar's net worth must be considerably higher than his own.

38

That evening, Claudia saw a more driven side to Hugo. Yes, he was tired and melancholy, but full of a gritty determination to pull himself up from the abyss. Here at last was some evidence that he might not be a total idiot after all.

A light drizzle fell in the garden of the Avalon and the sunshades now served as giant umbrellas. Hugo lit his second cigarette in fifteen minutes as he catalogued his demise in minute detail.

'I'm sorry you lost your job,' said Claudia, resisting the temptation to comment on his chain-smoking. They were wary of each other – both painfully aware of the fragility of their tentative alliance.

'At least technically I wasn't fired – it could be worse.'

'Any idea what you're going to do next?'

'Job-wise, not a clue.'

'Otherwise?'

'I must prove I'm innocent,' said Hugo. 'And to do that I have to prove Hubbard's story is true.'

Hugo's logic was badly flawed. If Hubbard's story was true, BEP had cause to frame Hugo, but it wouldn't prove they had. How could she tell him this tactfully? And how would she break it to him that she'd pretty much given up on the loucura story?

'What makes you think I can help?' she asked. 'It's not as if I've got anywhere myself.'

'You've explored several avenues, haven't you?'

'They were all dead ends. Rodrigues will only speak to

me if I go to Brazil, and the others won't speak to me at all. Oh, and I called Morrison pretending to be writing an obituary on George Hubbard – he hung up on me.'

'No wonder he was so jumpy when I mentioned Hubbard as well.'

'I've run up against the buffers – nowhere else to go.'

'I don't agree. What's stopping you from doing the face-to-face with Rodrigues?'

God – Hugo was so naive.

'The fact he's in Brazil?'

'Surely the *Globe*...?'

'Get real, Hugo – I plucked up the courage to ask Bill about a trip to Rio, and he told me to go and do something physically impossible.'

'So this is it – you're quitting?'

'I'm sorry Hugo, but I don't see what else I can do – I'm getting nowhere, and Bill's so negative I'm starting to think he's a shareholder in BEP. What can I do?'

'If you went to Rio, what would you get out of it?'

'Weren't you listening? I can't go to Rio.'

'What if you could?'

'I'd go and eyeball those dudes. They must know the real story behind loucura. I bet I'd get at least one of them to crack.'

'Right,' said Hugo, with his new found decisiveness. 'Let's do it. Come on.'

He knocked back the remains of his lager.

'Where are we going?'

'Back to mine – see if we can book a last-minute weekend in Rio.'

'Oh Hugo, don't be a prat. Who's going to pay for it?'

'If you find what you're looking for, I'm sure the *Globe* will cough up later.'

'And if not?'

'I'm paying,' said Hugo.

He couldn't be drunk on two pints – the balance of his mind must be affected in some other way.

'You're nuts, Hugo. You're skint, you've lost your job and you're talking about flying out to Rio for the weekend.'

'Yep.'

'I bet it isn't even possible.'

'Well, I suggest we find out.'

'But Hugo...'

'You saying you don't want to go?'

'I never said that – I said you were nuts.'

'Fine – let's do it all the same.'

It was hard to argue against such resolve, and frankly Claudia had no desire to try.

Charlie nearly choked on his cup of tea when Hugo broke the news of his upcoming trip. His girlfriend, Marianne, now returned from San Francisco, rolled her eyes in despair.

'Rio – for the weekend?' said Charlie. 'You've been involved in some mad schemes in your day, Hugo old chum, but this takes the biscuit – you must be off your rocker.'

Marianne looked up from painting her nails. 'Personally,' she said, 'in your position I would be putting one hundred percent into finding a new job.'

Marianne never took any action which might derail her perfect life. It was all mapped out in advance – partnership in her law firm by thirty, marry Charlie, before throwing herself into full-time motherhood. When boredom kicked in, she'd set up a 'little business'. Meanwhile poor old Charlie would be on the treadmill for life, a partner in Pearson Malone, a slave to Marianne's lifestyle aspirations.

Charlie's life was ostensibly more successful than Hugo's, but in reality he had no autonomy at all. Whereas Hugo was a free agent.

'Marianne,' said Hugo. 'You don't understand. I have to clear my name.'

She regarded him with bemusement. She was pretty enough – blue eyes, regular features and expensive blonde hair – superficially attractive, but spiritually empty.

'I don't see why – you're getting the standard reference from PM. If anyone asks you why you resigned, you can give them some waffle about not seeing eye to eye with your boss – that's perfectly true, after all.'

'I don't see how a trip to Rio will help,' Charlie added. 'Looks mighty suspicious from where I'm sitting. Why go chasing off halfway across the world, unless you're guilty as charged?'

'You two don't have any confidence in me, do you? You think I had too much to drink and shot my mouth off.'

'Well it's not entirely unknown, is it?' said Charlie.

Charlie and Marianne exchanged a knowing glance. It was quite evident what they thought.

'For example, that gala performance you gave while I was away.' Marianne had finished her nails now, and waved them around in the air as they dried.

Charlie's disloyalty stabbed at Hugo – time was when Charlie would have kept his mouth shut instead of blabbing to Marianne.

'I don't care what you two think,' he said. This was only half true – he didn't care about Marianne's views, but still placed some value on Charlie's opinion. 'I've been set up – end of discussion.'

'You can't simply jet off to Rio this evening.'

'Oh yes I can – I've booked it all online.'

'Don't you need a visa?' Trust Charlie to focus on practicalities.

'Nope – I checked. The flight leaves Heathrow at six fifteen tonight – Claudia and I get to Rio on Saturday morning.'

'I might have known she'd be involved in this lunatic caper,' said Charlie. 'Hugo, you've lost the plot big style since you got involved with that crazy Jamaican bitch.'

This was, of course, precisely the moment Claudia chose to walk into the kitchen.

'Which crazy bitch is that you're talking about?' she said, calmly. She eyed Marianne with disdain.

'We've not been introduced,' she said. 'I'm Claudia, Hugo's girlfriend. Are you a permanent fixture or a one-night stand?'

Marianne bridled at Claudia's direct style.

'I'm Charlie's fiancé,' she retorted, wrinkling her nose as she took in Claudia's outfit.

To Hugo's knowledge, Charlie hadn't yet popped the question – but he hadn't disagreed with Marianne either. Mind you, Claudia was taking equal liberties in describing herself as his girlfriend. Although despite his firm intentions they'd ended up spending the night together, he preferred to regard this as a one-off lapse.

'I'm sorry,' said Charlie to Claudia. 'I didn't realise you were here.'

'So it's all right to slag me off behind my back?'

'Yes, well.' Charlie dissembled. 'I said I'm sorry.'

Claudia helped herself to a large bowl of Cheerios.

'You will be sorry if you do it again.'

She turned to Marianne.

'You a lawyer?' she asked.

'Well yes – how did you guess? Did Hugo tell you?'

'Hugo told me nothing,' said Claudia. 'Surprisingly, you don't feature much in his conversation. You look like a lawyer, that's all.'

'Do you know many lawyers?'

'Mainly criminal ones,' said Claudia, responding to the put-down with a wicked smile. She waltzed out of the room, carrying her bowl of cereal.

Marianne flounced off, slamming the door behind her.

'Sorry. Marianne expects to be the queen bee.'

'Looks as if Claudia does as well.'

'I'm worried about you Hugo,' said Charlie, now they were alone. 'I mean, jetting off to Rio, just like that – it's insane. Apart from anything else, how much is this costing?'

'About a grand each.'

'Where did you get the money from, if you don't mind my asking?' Charlie understood enough about Hugo's financial situation to grasp that £2,000 could not be summoned up in a jiffy.

'I do mind, actually.'

Charlie shrugged.

'Well, it's your money, your life. I only hope you find what you're searching for.'

Which might be easier, Hugo reflected, if he knew what that was.

39

Hugo carped non-stop on the flight. He bemoaned the lack of airport lounge, the inadequate leg room in economy class, the hopeless drinks service, and the plastic cutlery provided to attack the plastic food. There was no escape – Hugo refused to sleep and kept Claudia awake with his whining. Already, she regretted coming with him.

He was only silenced by the stunning view as they descended into Rio de Janeiro International Airport at dawn. Beaches, blue sea, mountains and the tall buildings of downtown appeared beneath them as they both craned towards the window.

'Well,' said Claudia, 'of all the places to come seeking answers, this one takes some beating.'

Inside the terminal, Hugo scoffed at the glacial slowness of the single line for non-Brazilians – it wasn't even as if the official was examining the paperwork properly. But with no baggage to collect they still picked up their hire car within an hour of landing – and it was only 7.30 a.m.

Brazilian driving was exhilarating. Before they'd even left the airport, Hugo was carved up in spectacular style by a silver Mercedes, its driver gesticulating madly and sounding his horn. Stop lights were purely optional, as Hugo learnt to his cost when the car was nearly rammed from behind. By dint of extreme self-control, Claudia held her tongue as he cursed and moaned all the way to their hotel in Copacabana.

There they ditched the car and set off on foot in search of breakfast.

'What on earth is that?' asked Hugo pointing to the huge iconic statue on the top of Corcovado mountain.

'It's Christ the Redeemer.'

'How did you know?'

'The benefits of a state education,' Claudia replied sarcastically.

'I hope Rodrigues isn't on holiday,' said Hugo, rapidly changing the subject as he drained his cup of coffee.

'A bit late to bring that up now – anyway, I checked. I've got the addresses for two other members of the research team, but I vote we begin with Rodrigues, straight away – we've a better chance of catching him in if we go early.'

Tempers frayed again on the drive to Rodrigues' house, but before too long they drew up in front of an elegant villa in an affluent suburb.

Rodrigues' wife answered the doorbell – a timid little mouse with dark rings under her eyes, although she was no more than thirty. Small children squealed in the background as she called her husband.

A small, intense man appeared at the door, his face deeply lined by years of heavy smoking. When Claudia disclosed who they were, he didn't seem surprised to see them, but equally he wasn't overjoyed. She held her breath – surely he wouldn't shut the door on them when they'd come all this way?

'Outside, please,' he said. 'We have a smoke. My wife will prepare some coffee.'

He gestured to some chairs on the veranda.

Hugo accepted a cigarette from Rodrigues, seemingly oblivious to the irony of the chain-smoking cancer researcher.

'I am most surprised to see you here,' he said, dragging on his cigarette as though his life depended on it. 'I hoped perhaps you might arrange an appointment.'

Yet he'd acted as though he'd been expecting them.

'Or more likely you hoped I wouldn't come at all,' said Claudia. 'But thanks for seeing us.'

'You have travelled for such a long time – how could I refuse?' he said with a nervous smile. 'Now what was it you wished to talk about?'

'About your work on loucura,' Claudia began. 'Is that OK?'

The apprehension in his eyes intimated that it wasn't OK at all.

'Yes, for sure, but there is not too much to discuss, I think.'

She produced her copy of Rodrigues' paper.

'I don't do Portuguese – but I'd say this work proves loucura eliminates cancer.'

'It proves nothing,' said Rodrigues, exhaling a long jet of blue smoke.

'The results were amazing, though – all those patients still alive months after they should have died.'

'If you have come here to find the miracle cancer therapy, I'm afraid your journey has been wasted.'

In that one sentence, Rodrigues had deflated all Claudia's hopes – but still she persevered. She hadn't come all this way to turn tail at the slightest setback. And people didn't always say what they meant straight away.

'Surely it can't have been a coincidence that all those patients suddenly improved?'

Rodrigues' wife appeared with a tray of coffee and cakes. Hugo took two cakes, even though they'd finished breakfast barely an hour earlier. He'd be fat long before he reached middle age – although Claudia severely doubted she'd be still around to see it happen.

'At the time,' Rodrigues said, 'we also believed the results were remarkable. A significant proportion of patients who took the extract from the loucura bark appeared to improve. However, unfortunately the methods of our study were seriously flawed.'

'You mean according to Morrison and his team.'

'Ah yes – Morrison.'

Rodrigues looked nostalgic at the mention of Morrison's name – he apparently bore no ill will towards the man who had discredited his work. Claudia pounced on this anomaly.

'So how do you feel about Morrison invalidating your results?' she asked. Open questions – exactly as Bill had taught her.

Rodrigues shook his head.

'It is not correct to say our results were invalidated. Our results were what they were. The mistakes we made were in the conclusions we drew from our work. The improvement in the patients could not be properly attributed to loucura.'

'But as I said, it couldn't be a fluke...'

Rodrigues cut her off before she even finished her sentence.

'You must understand. Nothing we did proved that any improvements in the patients were due to loucura. It is the proof which is important, you see.'

Claudia did see – and the proof which she sought also remained as elusive as ever.

'Why not?'

'Because many of these people were undergoing chemotherapy already, because we did not undertake proper double blind trials. Also, we should have properly measured the strength of the loucura extract. Yet these mistakes were trivial compared to our worst error.'

'Which was what?'

'Ah!' He lifted his forefinger, as though to caution these two young people about similar folly. 'The big mistake was to become excited, excited at the prospect of eradicating cancer, at glory for ourselves, at saving many lives. Excitement is dangerous, you see, contagious even – and it blinds our judgement. I was a young man – not much older than you.'

His eyes darted suspiciously towards Hugo – the silent visitor who had done nothing since he arrived apart from smoking his cigarettes and munching his cakes.

'We all make mistakes when we're young, you see, we're too impatient. Perhaps,' he suggested, 'you have also made a mistake in coming here.'

Privately, Claudia was inclined to agree with him.

'No,' she said, 'it's important to establish the truth. Now, to summarise, in your opinion loucura does not kill cancer.'

'Certainly not – I am sorry if something caused you to suppose otherwise.'

Yet there was an insincerity about Rodrigues' certainty, and his eyes flitted nervously from side to side as he spoke.

'You can't say for sure it isn't effective, only that your work didn't prove it – from a logical point of view, they're different.'

Hugo had spoken up for the first time – and he'd been surprisingly incisive.

'Indeed they are different,' agreed Rodrigues. 'You are more intelligent than you appear.'

'And Morrison's work was different from your study, wasn't it?' Claudia added, homing in on the second key issue. 'His study dealt with loucuramine, a chemical derived from loucura.'

'That is correct.'

Claudia now saw her route clear to the punchline.

'So why didn't you redo your study with loucura, to eliminate the flaws which Morrison identified in the first study?'

'What would be the use? Morrison's team established that the active chemical in loucura was toxic to rats.'

'Who's to say loucuramine is the active component in loucura? Maybe it has to be combined with the other components in loucura. Or in humans not rats...?'

'Miss Knight,' said Rodrigues. 'Do you have a scientific background?'

189

'No,' admitted Claudia.

Rodrigues threw back his head.

'Ha – I thought not. If you did, you would understand why such a phenomenon would be impossible.'

So, Rodrigues agreed with Julia – but was it a cop-out? The cloak of 'scientific impossibility' had once more shrouded the matter in impenetrable confusion. And if she asked him why it was impossible, he would surely spew out a barrage of incomprehensible jargon.

'Even so,' she said, persisting with her line of questioning, 'it seems you gave up on your loucura research very quickly. Was there any other reason?'

'Is this not reason enough?'

'Yes, but were there other factors at work?'

All she required was an admission that BEP had squashed Rodrigues' research, and she was in business.

'Indeed there were.'

Claudia's hopes soared.

'If we had continued, the whole developed world would have ridiculed us. At this time, we were not prepared to take that risk...'

He paused, as though unsure whether to continue.

'Why not?' Claudia prompted him, thrilled as she closed in on the very crux of the matter.

'Our country was entering into some key commercial alliances with the US. A new hospital was built here as the result of one of those partnerships. We could not have our credibility called into question by continuing with these researches.'

Rodrigues had now pretty much admitted he'd capitulated when big bucks were at stake. He'd been leaned on, but by who? That was the killer question.

'So did the big drug companies stop your work on loucura by threatening to pull out of these alliances?'

'No, no!' said Rodrigues, snorting at the absurdity of

the idea. 'It was quite the other way around. We chose to terminate these unscientific enquiries ourselves because it would have been embarrassing to continue.'

'Surely the point is, if you'd redone the trials properly, they wouldn't have been unscientific, or embarrassing,' said Claudia, zeroing in relentlessly on the logical flaw in Rodrigues' argument.

'Do you not understand?' said Rodrigues. 'I have already stated that a simple antidote to cancer is impossible – it was only in our naivety that we felt differently. Even if such a remedy existed, it could not have been kept hidden as you suggest without a worldwide collusion of doctors. And we are all human – which of us would not revel in the glory of such a marvellous breakthrough?'

Claudia's spirits sank. Irrespective of what had really happened, Rodrigues had no intention of playing ball. He was merely repeating what Julia had told Hugo – perhaps because it was true. Then again...

'Why shouldn't there be a global collusion, when everyone stands to gain?'

She took in the swanky villa in its extensive grounds. If there was a wall of silence around loucura, Rodrigues himself had not done too badly out of it.

'Why is everybody so fascinated by this loucura these days anyway?' asked Rodrigues, avoiding the question. 'Journalists, hedge funds – everyone?'

Claudia's ears pricked up.

'A hedge fund did you say? Which one?'

'This is none of your business,' snapped Rodrigues, apparently annoyed with himself for letting slip a snippet which he should have kept to himself. 'Just tell me – why are you so interested?'

Claudia wavered, before deciding to confess all. If she opened up a bit more, she might get more out of Rodrigues.

'Someone told me Morrison was instructed to discredit

191

loucura, and that loucura is a cancer cure. What's more, the guy I was talking to said he had proof.'

'This is nonsense, of course,' said Rodrigues with a nervous laugh. 'But why speak to me? This other man has the proof – maybe you should ask him.'

'He was killed in a hit-and-run, and his death wasn't accidental. Now how do you account for that?'

'I cannot account for any of this,' said Rodrigues. 'If someone considered these allegations were worth this poor man's life, then he has died in vain. I am very sorry to hear this.'

'So why would anyone invent the story?'

'I cannot say.'

Claudia lunched into a final attempt to break Rodrigues.

'Suppose loucura does work,' she said. 'Natural molecules can't be patented, so no drug company would touch it. Even if it was patentable, the industry would still lose money because the market for all their rubbish cancer therapies would dry up overnight. Wouldn't they have a good reason to keep loucura secret? After all, drug companies often sell dangerous drugs to earn a profit – so why not hold back a drug which wouldn't make any money for them?'

Rodrigues guffawed at this.

'Oh dear, I fear you have been reading up too many conspiracy theories – next you will tell me that the food industry sells us the food which causes the cancers so the drug companies can sell the drugs to treat them, and that they are in collusion together. Your suggestion is equally as crazy. I'm sorry,' he said, lighting up another cigarette. 'I hope you are able to see a little of our charming city while you are here, so your journey will not be entirely wasted. Now, if you will excuse me, I have to take my daughter to her swimming class – otherwise I would love to show you around.'

* * *

192

'So what do you think?' Claudia asked Hugo as they left the Rodrigues' residence. 'You sat there very quietly, apart from that one stunning insight you contributed.'

'It was your interview,' said Hugo. 'Better to let you get on with it.'

'But you must have an opinion.'

'You were brill – awesome.'

'Not about me, silly,' she said. 'About what he said?'

Hugo's brow was furrowed as he analysed the conversation.

'Well, he didn't completely stonewall us.'

'No.'

'I suspect he lied, though. He knows damned well that loucura works. Twenty years ago, he went with the flow and did well out of it. But there's no way he's going to admit now that he held back a cancer cure out of pure self-interest.'

It was a cogent, if depressing, summary of the position.

'So I still have zero basis for my story.'

'Never mind,' said Hugo gamely. 'We still have the other two researchers to talk to.'

But there their luck had run out. According to his neighbours, one of them was out of town – the other slammed the door in their faces.

Soon afterwards, Hugo casually mentioned that they were being followed.

'You sure? Which car is it?'

'That white Golf.'

'Where? I can't see it.'

'They've dropped back a bit now – it's not so obvious. Hang on, I'll see if I can lose them.'

Hugo swung abruptly round a right turn, all but tipping the car over.

'Careful,' said Claudia, clinging onto the grab handle.

Now she saw that Hugo was right – there was indeed a white car behind them.

193

'They're still on our tail,' said Hugo. 'Hold on tight.'

The car rocked as he took another corner, and another. Then he saw his chance, and cut left across a stream of rapidly approaching traffic. It was a manoeuvre outrageous even by Brazilian driving standards and horns blared in unison – but it did the trick.

'The good news is we've lost the tail,' said Hugo. 'The bad news is we're now totally lost ourselves. Where are we on the map?'

It was impossible to say. They could attempt to retrace their route, but it was doubtful whether Hugo would successfully backtrack on all the twists and turns they'd taken. The area looked dodgy enough that they might get shot at if they stopped.

'Where the hell are we?' moaned Hugo.

As if in response to his plea, a sign for Copacabana appeared – they were back on track. And although they kept their eyes peeled, there was no sign of the Volkswagen.

'This whole trip has been a complete waste of time,' Claudia pronounced when they at long last arrived back at the hotel, utterly shattered.

'If so, why was someone following us?'

'I'm not convinced they were – was it really the same car all the time? There must be thousands of white VWs in Rio.'

Hugo didn't reply, but pulled Claudia towards him and kissed her hard. Once again, against all reason, she surrendered to the moment.

40

When Hugo woke, the sun was already low in the sky, although his watch told him it was only five. Next to him, Claudia was still deep in slumber. Hugo lay motionless, trying not to disturb her as he straightened out his tangled emotions.

Without even meaning to, they'd had sex again – but Claudia had been on such delightful form he'd been powerless to resist her earthy allure. Yet for all that, Hugo struggled to undo the spell which Julia had cast on him. Here he was, stuck in the real world, while Julia co-existed in a parallel universe. This shouldn't have been an issue, except that she'd uncorked a bottle of complex feelings which too easily spilled over from one reality to another. How could he put the stopper back in the bottle now?

Hugo leapt out of bed and glugged down a litre of water. He couldn't go on like this, pining for a woman he could never have. He would have to force himself to let Julia go, exactly as he would have to accept his abject failure to establish the truth about loucura, and to prove he'd been framed. Now it was time to put all his illusions behind him and move on – but to where?

Claudia woke with a jerk as Hugo switched on the TV and rubbed her eyes as if disbelieving the gathering dusk.

'God, we're only here till tomorrow and we've wasted a whole afternoon and probably most of the evening – we should have been out sightseeing.'

'It's only quarter past five,' said Hugo. 'And anyway, we

didn't come as tourists. This was a business trip, remember. I'm always visiting different places and not seeing anything.'

'And do you always sleep with the girls?' There was a caustic edge to Claudia's voice, incongruent with her seductive smile.

'None of them are a patch on you,' he replied.

Ignoring him, Claudia picked up some leaflets from the dressing table.

'See here,' she said. 'If you're right about the time, we can go on an early evening tour to Sugarloaf Mountain – you can get to the top in a cable car. Afterwards, we can go for a slap-up dinner on the *Globe*.'

She pulled her clothes on hurriedly, as if there was not a second to lose.

'Will Bill sign off on dinner?'

'He'll think it money well spent, if I back off the story.'

Hugo tried his damnedest to feign cheeriness as they took in the dramatic views from the mountain. He smiled, held Claudia's hand and made all the right noises, but beneath the facade lurked a mind in chaos. Something Rodrigues said had sparked an inspiration, but the spark had been extinguished in the excitement of the car chase. If only he remembered what it was, he might be able to re-ignite the spark. But for the time being, he was stuck.

They ate at a barbecue house along the promenade – fixed price, stay as long as you like, eat as much as you can, live samba dancing. Hugo would normally have whooped with joy at the prospect of unlimited free food, but failed to do the buffet table any justice at all.

'Don't you like the food?' asked Claudia.

'It's delicious – just not very hungry, that's all.'

He knew what she was thinking, but she had it all wrong.

After copious amounts of Brazilian beer, he began to unwind. Then something of a miracle occurred. A question sprang unbidden into his mind – what about the hedge fund? Yes, he remembered now. Rodrigues had mentioned a hedge fund was enquiring about loucura. What on earth did it mean?

He opened his mouth to explain to Claudia what had been bugging him, but thought better of it. He simply wasn't sure what it meant yet.

After he'd forced down far more food than was wise, Hugo proposed a walk along the beach to burn off some calories. Who knew – it might also clear his head. Claudia decisively vetoed the suggestion.

'You must be crazy – even the guidebook says it isn't safe.'

So they walked along the promenade, arm in arm, in the refreshing cool of the night.

'What are you thinking about?' Claudia asked.

'Nothing,' said Hugo hurriedly. It would almost have been easier to pretend he was thinking about Julia, since this was evidently what she was expecting. How could he begin to explain that he was pondering on a passing comment about a hedge fund, without having the slightest inkling of why it might be important?

It was a classic distraction robbery – simultaneously brutal and polite in its execution. While Hugo was deep in contemplation, a local man asked him for the time. In the minute it took Hugo to tell him, his accomplice cut Claudia's bag from her shoulder. She shrieked like a banshee, but too late – the muggers had melted inconspicuously into the crowds.

They stood – paralysed with disbelief.

'You OK?'

'I guess so.'

'What's in the bag?'

'My phone, some cash – about one hundred pounds. Oh yes, and my research notes.'

No real harm done then.

'Good job you left the passports in the hotel safe.'

Claudia's face crumpled.

'Oh Hugo, I forgot, what with falling asleep. They were still in my bag.'

An unfamiliar surge of emotion welled up in Hugo – pure rage.

'You stupid bloody cow,' he said, his lips moving before his brain.

It was a snap response he'd quickly regret.

'You don't give a monkey's about me, do you?'

'You said you were all right.'

'Well I'm fucking not all right.'

She was shouting, her eyes full of tears. Hugo opened his mouth to apologise – he hadn't meant what he'd said, it was the shock, he couldn't explain what came over him.

Claudia shoved him away.

'Piss off Hugo – don't even try to say you're sorry.'

'I won't then – I'll take a leaf out of your book.'

'The trip has been a disaster from start to finish.'

'Well, that's the last time I spend two grand on you.'

'Don't pretend you did it for me, Hugo. You came here for you, to exonerate yourself, to impress Julia Fraser.'

'I've hardly mentioned Julia since I got back from New Jersey.'

'You don't have to – it's written all over your face. It's always about you and her – always has been. Well, I pity Julia – she's yet to learn just how selfish you are. At least the scales have fallen from my eyes.'

'There's nothing between me and Julia – nothing.'

'Do you think I'm so dumb I haven't noticed you've been here in body but not in spirit?'

'That wasn't because of Julia!'

Hugo's denials sounded half-hearted, even to him.

'Don't lie to me, you worthless turd. At least be man

enough to be honest about it – don't treat me as if I'm some Julia-substitute whore you've bought for the price of a trip to Rio.'

Hugo's fury bubbled up again.

'What if I have done it for me? I've lost my job because all you care about is your lousy story. That's the bottom line. You fly off the handle because you're jealous, jealous of me, jealous of Julia – it's all about you, not me.'

Passers-by backed away nervously – no one cared to intervene.

'Ha – so it's my fault you lost your job. Did I force you to get drunk with some dude in the hotel bar? No, no one has to force you to get drunk – you're an alcoholic. Why don't you go into rehab with all the other bratty rich kids?'

'And why don't you treat me as a real person instead of some kind of joke?'

'Because you are a joke. And I don't need this aggro!'

Tears coursed down Claudia's cheeks – she wiped them away angrily with her sleeve.

Hugo's anger subsided as quickly as it had flared up. A deep sensation of shame stabbed at his solar plexus. Claudia was a tough nut, but it wasn't the muggers who'd made her cry – it was him.

He took her in his arms. She pushed him away, but Hugo was stronger.

'Look, I'm sorry, so sorry – I lost my rag.'

She hiccoughed as she tried to stifle the sobs.

'And I lost mine – again. I...'

She broke off. Hugo had the strangest intuition that she'd been on the verge of apologising – surely not? Either that, or she'd been about to say she loved him.

'Please be honest with me, Hugo. It's Julia you want, isn't it?'

The lid finally blew off the jumble of emotion Hugo had

been barely holding at bay. He sobbed bitterly – his anger had been directed at himself as much as Claudia.

'I don't know, Claudia – I'm lost, my life is a mess.'

It was the most honest statement he'd ever made – the most honest, yet the most pathetic. They stumbled back to the hotel in silence, as stunned by the strength of their emotions as by the attack.

'We should file a police report and contact the British Embassy to get replacement papers,' said Hugo once they were safely back in their room. How much easier it was to sort out practicalities than feelings, he reflected.

'There's no way we'll be able to fly back tomorrow, what with it being Sunday. And Bill is going to murder me if I'm not back at work Monday afternoon.'

But Hugo had a brilliant idea. He pulled out his phone.

'What are you doing?' she asked.

'I'm phoning my father,' he said, basking in his role as knight in shining armour. 'We're going through diplomatic channels.'

They lay rigidly in the dark, not touching, not sleeping, not speaking.

Hugo's diplomatic connections had cut an impressive swathe through bureaucracy, and they'd been promised emergency travel papers the next day. Yet while Claudia was glad to see a speedy resolution of the problem, she resented Hugo using his privileged position to pull strings, and didn't mince any words in telling him so. She'd stood back and waited for the inevitable explosion, but he'd retreated unexpectedly into a gloomy silence. Who knew what dark thoughts played on his mind?

Why had she blown up at Hugo yet again? Yes, he'd been an insensitive jerk, but once more she'd overreacted. And even when he'd been trying to help she'd laid into him again. Their relationship was doomed – each time they built up a rapport, she destroyed it and sent them right back to square one. Something was wrong – the hormones worked, she was in love, so why was she so hell-bent on wrecking everything? After all, Hugo couldn't help who he was any more than she could.

41

'The journalist from London – she visited my house this morning,' Rodrigues said.

There was a pause on the line before the caller responded. 'Did she bring her friend, Hugo?'

'Yes, they came together, but he did not say too much.'

'So what did you tell them?'

'As we agreed – the usual story.'

'Do they accept it?'

'Maybe not, but as you say, what can they do?'

'Did you mention about the hedge fund?'

'Yes – yes I told them about this, as you instructed, although I did not understand why.'

'There's no need for you to understand why.'

Rodrigues flinched at this sudden rebuke, fearing a second bout of criticism. But it never came.

'How goes it with official channels?'

'Very smoothly – we should have the approval soon.'

'Excellent work. You see – everything is fine.'

'I hope so,' said Rodrigues. He feigned enthusiasm, although he wasn't sure.

42

People say knowledge is power – Morrison thought differently. Knowledge was dangerous. He wrestled against acceptance of what he'd found out, frantic for it not to be true. Were they aware that he knew? This was the crucial question. If so, he was a dead man.

He drove home that evening in a state of hyper-vigilance. A motorcyclist left the BEP parking lot as he did and followed him to the interstate. Was this a trained assassin on a mission to kill or another employee on his way home? Morrison relaxed as his pursuer peeled off to take the highway north.

As he joined the carriageway south, two cars crowded him on the ramp. He tensed again. Was this the end – was this how he would die? No – only a couple of impatient jerks keen to get on their way.

Beads of sweat formed at Morrison's temples, and ran in rivulets down his cheeks. This terrified state was not sustainable – sooner or later he'd have to let up his guard. Even if he remained on red alert, was there any realistic hope of forestalling a professional hit man? Could Hubbard have avoided his death if he'd known the risk? Somehow, Morrison didn't think so.

Morrison put on a CD of calming Mozart. He breathed deeply and slowly and tried to let the music wash over him as his fears receded.

A dark green Lexus appeared from nowhere in his rear-view mirror, zigzagged across the lanes and tucked into the flow of traffic several cars behind him. Morrison watched it with curiosity – most likely nothing to worry about. The guy had probably pulled over to be in position for one of the many exits coming up. The exits came and went, but the Lexus stayed stubbornly in place. Paranoia gripped at Morrison once more. One way or another, he had to be certain.

He stamped on the gas and pulled across to the left-hand lane. A reassuring gap opened up between him and the Lexus – he'd been wrong again. He lightened up, told himself not to be silly. All this adrenaline was a sure fire way to a coronary – if he went on like this they wouldn't need an assassin.

A couple of miles on, he noticed that the Lexus had slotted back in unobtrusively behind him. He speeded up – so too did the Lexus. He stepped on the gas some more, weaving around the lines of traffic – the Lexus mirrored his snake-like course and removed all doubt. They were on his tail and closing in fast.

In his wing mirror, Morrison saw that the passenger brandished a gun, apparently oblivious to the hordes of New Jersey commuters on the road. The Lexus swung out left as if to overtake. Drastic action was called for.

At the last possible moment, Morrison swerved across to an exit without signalling. A bullet shattered the window on the passenger side, missing his head by inches. As he reeled from the shock, the Lexus disappeared along the freeway. Morrison had been reprieved, at least for the moment.

In the shocked aftermath of the attack, Morrison didn't notice the queue of stationary traffic at the top of the exit ramp until far too late.

Ironically, as he slammed on the brakes in a futile attempt to avert disaster, the terror which had dogged him all day dissipated in an instant.

43

The Oxfordshire countryside flashed past Hugo as he made his final pilgrimage to IDD. Ever since Rio, he had been brooding. His hunch about the hedge fund hadn't really developed and now he was forced to accept he'd reached a dead end. But before he put this whole episode behind him, he felt compelled to confront Julia with the evidence.

Hubbard had been killed, Claudia burgled, he'd been framed, and they'd both been followed and robbed in Rio. He was certain Claudia's research notes had been the target of the attack, although she didn't agree. Whatever – if the loucura story had no basis, it seemed extraordinary that someone would go to all this effort to prevent it from seeing the light of day. Julia had a right to be aware of the facts before she sold out to BEP.

His logic had been plausible enough, but only now did he acknowledge his true motivation. Every sinew in his body and every part of his mind ached to be with Julia. Yet, despite the visceral reaction the idea of seeing her had evoked, he hoped that this last trip would enable him to exorcise her from his mind.

He had no idea whether she'd even be there; this in itself was a sign of his lunacy. But if Julia wasn't around, he would take it as an omen that they weren't meant to meet again.

As he signed in at IDD's reception, Hugo anxiously scanned the visitors' book. The prospect of bumping into Stephanie still unnerved him, even though she had no hold over him now. Thankfully, there was no indication of her presence today.

No, Julia wasn't expecting him, Hugo said smoothly. He was passing through and hoped to catch her for five minutes. He sweated as the receptionist phoned Julia's secretary. Would she be too busy to see him? Or have him forcibly ejected from the premises? A muscular security guard stood menacingly in the corner, a dead ringer for Bluto in the Popeye cartoons.

'Please take a seat, Hugo. Someone will be along in a minute.'

Hugo sunk into the sofa, overwhelmed by relief.

Julia stood gazing out of the window, but turned when she heard Hugo come in. He reined in the impulse to throw himself at her, to beg her for another night, for a kiss even. She was dressed as immaculately as ever, in the understated style she had mastered to perfection – tailored black trousers, striped top, hair in a loose French pleat. Hugo swooned as she smiled in greeting.

'Hugo,' she said. 'What a lovely surprise. How are you?'

She made no move to embrace him, or even shake his hand. Significantly, she chose to sit behind her desk, rather than on the comfy chairs in the corner of the room. Message received loud and clear – as far as Julia was concerned, their brief fling was in the past and would not be revived. Underneath all the elegance and charm was a hard woman, possibly harder at her core than even Stephanie.

'I'm well, thanks,' Hugo replied. 'How are you?'

'I'm also well.'

There was no offer of a cup of tea. That was fine with Hugo – now she had quashed his romantic hopes, his job was merely to impart the necessary information. He wouldn't need long.

'You must be wondering why I'm here,' he said, nervous and sweaty despite the coolness of the room.

'Yes, Hugo, I was. I guess you didn't drop by merely to say hello.'

Hugo took a deep breath. She was bound to ridicule him again, but he was prepared for that.

'I'm here to give you some vital information.'

'You'll have to be quick – ten minutes max, OK?'

Hugo nodded.

'Well, first of all, I swear I never said a word about Project Acorn to the bloke in the bar.'

'I know,' she said immediately.

'What?'

'Seems to me you were caught up in a nasty little corporate espionage scheme.'

Her faith in his innocence encouraged Hugo, even if her explanation for events differed from his own.

'So why didn't you speak up for me?'

'Because I couldn't be absolutely sure you hadn't done it. Sorry Hugo, but having a few drinks and being a bit indiscreet … it didn't seem impossible.'

In other words, when push came to shove, she'd made the same assumption as all the others. How depressing.

'You might have asked me about it.'

'Oh Hugo,' she said. 'I hardly had the chance. For what it's worth, I did complain to Brad Hillman about the ethics of them spying on you, but I got nowhere. There wasn't much else I could do – I'm extremely keen for this transaction to go through and can't afford to rock the boat. I'm sure you understand.'

Hugo understood only too well – the deal was far more important than some toy boy who'd pleasured her in a hotel bedroom on a business trip.

'You're right – I was set up,' Hugo went on, ignoring his feelings of inadequacy, 'but the real reason has nothing to do with corporate espionage.'

'I'm listening,' said Julia, tapping at her computer.

'You remember we discussed what might happen if your technology was used to synthesise a plant-based remedy for cancer?'

She sighed.

'Oh Hugo – we went through all this before.'

'Yes, but I wasn't making a hypothetical point. It's real.'

Julia wrinkled her brow as his suspicions poured out in one breathless torrent.

'What are you trying to say? That I'm selling out to some unscrupulous people who're ripping me off?'

'Seems that way to me.'

Julia held up her hands.

'Hugo, I'm sorry, but this is absolute pie in the sky.'

'Why – why is it pie in the sky?'

'I don't know where to begin.'

'A man has died because of this, doesn't that disturb you?'

'Hugo,' said Julia gravely. 'This nonsense wouldn't be coming from your journalist friend by any chance?'

Hugo ducked the question.

'Suppose it's not nonsense.'

'I did try to warn you about the journalist the other evening, now didn't I?'

'Yes, but you were wrong.'

'We never did establish where the press leak came from, did we Hugo?'

Hugo swallowed as he detected a note of menace in her voice.

'So according to you,' he said. 'I've been caught up in some sort of espionage caper with BEP and also the target of some sort of press scam. I mean, do I look like a victim to you?'

'No, of course not. Let's just say you're slightly gullible.'

Gullible! That was rich coming from her, selling her company for a pittance to a bunch of crooks.

'So will you act on what I've told you?'

'No, I won't.'

'You're not going to even raise this with BEP?'

'Hugo, I can't begin to understand why someone's got at you and your pal to sabotage this transaction, but there's no way they'll succeed. I'm actually quite insulted that anyone would expect me to leap into action based on such a ridiculous rumour.'

Hugo did his best to speak calmly – inwardly he was beginning to seethe.

'I understand what you're saying. Believe me, I was suspicious of Claudia as well, for a while. Now I'm convinced she's on the level – no one's pulling her strings.'

'It really doesn't matter either way,' said Julia, shrugging. 'I'm not letting some rubbishy tittle-tattle stop me from doing this deal.'

'Why don't you ask Morrison about loucura?' said Hugo. 'See how he reacts?'

Julia shot him a strange glance.

'That won't be possible.' She paused. 'Morrison was killed in a road accident last night on his way home from work.'

Hugo's head spun as he processed this latest news.

'Are they certain it was an accident?'

'You see,' she said, 'there you go again. Even if it wasn't an accident, wouldn't it go against your theory of this grand conspiracy? Who would murder the main conspirator? Or have you formulated a new theory, in the light of this?'

She was mocking him now, and it hurt.

'I don't know,' Hugo admitted.

But if the loucura story had no foundation, this was yet another coincidence to explain away. And if it did – well, as Julia said, to kill Morrison made no sense at all.

'Now,' Julia said firmly, consulting her watch, 'if you've said what you came to say, I must let you go.'

'I was only trying to help.'

'I'm sure you meant well, Hugo.'

There was a patronising edge to her voice which he'd never noticed before.

'One more question,' said Hugo. 'What about...?'

He'd been on the verge of saying 'what about us?', but it struck him there was no us, at least not as far as Julia was concerned.

He tried again.

'I enjoyed...' But he couldn't get the words out.

'Hugo, it was lovely and we had fun, but the other night was all there was. I do hope I didn't lead you to think otherwise.'

'No, definitely not,' he said, wishing the maturity of his emotions matched his adult words.

'Goodbye Hugo, and all the best for the future.'

She stood up as they shook hands. Hugo moved forward to kiss her on the cheek – his last chance to touch her. She didn't resist. As his lips brushed her cheek her scent evoked a flashback of their fleeting passion, the image fading as he pulled away.

'All the best to you as well.'

He closed the door behind him without looking back.

44

Claudia's ability to spring back into Hugo's life after a bust-up was usually as annoying as it was perplexing. But this time, he was pleased when her name popped up on the caller ID during his otherwise dispiriting journey back from Oxford. No apology – but at least he knew by now not to expect one.

'I'm surprised you're still speaking to me after Rio,' he said.

They had exchanged barely a couple of words on the flight back.

'Oh well, you didn't behave that badly, really. And you did pay for me to go.'

Yes, and God only knew how he was going to pay back his father, who had financed the wild goose chase.

'I was wondering if you fancied a drink tonight?'

Strangely enough, Hugo did. The sooner he expunged the memory of Julia, the better.

'As long as it's not the Avalon again.'

'Fine, we'll go up to town – I'll pay. How about somewhere in Covent Garden?'

'Sounds like a plan. Actually, it's funny you should ring because I was thinking of calling you.'

'You were?' she said. 'So did the physical exertion of pressing the buttons on your phone prove too much for you?'

Hugo ignored the sarcasm.

'I need to bounce some ideas off you.'

Hugo had been deliberating ever since he'd left Julia.

211

The news of Morrison's death had been puzzling, but had served to revive Hugo's flagging interest in the mystery. Seeing Julia had helped spawn an embryonic theory about the hedge fund as well. He was now ready to hear Claudia's views.

Two hours later, they sat on a terrace in Covent Garden drinking cold Sancerre. Claudia wore bright red harem pants with a military jacket – exotically conspicuous as ever among the tourists and grey-suited clientele of the bar.

'Have you totally given up on loucura?' he asked her.

'After Rio, I've pretty much had to – Bill's relieved, at any rate.'

'You may have thrown in the towel too soon,' said Hugo.

His comment failed to generate the excitement it would have done a week earlier, but he hadn't reached the punchline yet. Claudia grabbed a handful of cashew nuts from the bowl on the table.

'What do you mean?'

'Something I found out today.'

'What?'

'Morrison died in a road accident on the way home from work last night.'

'Oh well.' Curiously indifferent to the news, she threw the nuts into her mouth and took a large slug of her wine to chase them down. She didn't even ask how he'd found out.

'So if he's been killed,' said Hugo, 'it looks as if it wasn't BEP behind all this other stuff.'

'Your point being?'

She really had lost interest – much now depended on whether Hugo could revive it.

'We may have this all the wrong way round,' he said. 'We're assuming this is about what happened twenty years ago – suppose it's not.'

'What else could it be about?'

'Project Acorn?'

She put down her glass – he'd semi caught her attention now.

'How so?'

'Simple. If someone can prove BEP really did discredit loucura, then the takeover's off.'

Julia would still pull out of the deal if hard evidence came to light – she would have to, or forfeit her halo.

'Yes,' said Claudia doubtfully.

'So who stands to benefit from the deal?'

'BEP.'

'OK, but Morrison's been killed and that doesn't fit. So who else?'

'I can't think of anyone else,' Claudia said sulkily, plainly resenting him raking over the ashes of a dead story.

'Well I can,' said Hugo. 'Did you notice – everywhere we've been, someone else has got there ahead of us? Someone snatched Hubbard's briefcase. And the woman at the journal said you were the second person to ask for Rodrigues' paper.'

'That might have been BEP, or the other journalist.'

'And someone got to Rodrigues before we did. Who?'

'What, twenty years ago?'

'No, recently. Do you remember he mentioned a hedge fund?'

'Yes, though he choked me off when I tried to ask him about it.'

'Because he let it slip accidentally. What if the most important information he gave us was the one comment he never meant to make?'

'So what about the hedge fund?'

'That's exactly what I've been asking myself, and now I've remembered.'

'What?'

'This might be a bit off the wall, but there's a hedge

fund with quite a chunky shareholding in IDD – Umbra Capital Partners. And the shareholding they've declared is probably only half the story, knowing these hedgies. They would lose out big time if the takeover didn't go through.'

'Would they really go to all that trouble for Project Acorn?' asked Claudia.

'Maybe not, but Project Acorn's the thin end of the wedge. IDD has the technology to synthesise loucura, right?'

'Right.'

'Imagine the impact synthetic loucura would have on the whole pharmaceutical sector.'

'So?' She was still not convinced.

'Did you know that at a conservative estimate the cancer industry is worth $300 to $400 billion every year in the US alone?'

'No I didn't, but you've obviously been doing your homework.'

'Companies would lose massive revenue streams, but the lucky company who scooped the jackpot would be laughing.'

'You mean BEP?'

'Yes.'

'So doesn't that take us back to them? I still don't understand.'

'I've researched these Umbra people – they're serious players in pharmaceutical stocks. Suppose they found proof that loucura worked – imagine the positions they could take armed with that secret data. Then when it comes out into the open, they would make a fortune. So you see, they'd have a huge financial interest in getting hold of Hubbard's proof.'

Claudia screwed up her nose.

'OK, OK,' said Hugo. 'I can see you're still doubtful. And I don't blame you. I mean, for starters, how would Umbra know Hubbard was talking to the press?'

214

He knew this was a serious flaw in his otherwise brilliant theory.

'I would be doubtful, except...'

'What?'

'The name Umbra rings a bell.'

Claudia suddenly clicked her fingers.

'Umbra knew about the press because Hubbard told them,' she said, her eyes shining with a new-found enthusiasm. 'It all fits together now!'

'Now I'm confused,' Hugo admitted.

'When I went to Hubbard's house, there was a big Rolodex cardholder on his desk. It was open at a card for Umbra.'

Hugo livened up at this.

'Are you certain?'

'Yes – one hundred percent. And why would the Rolodex be open at the Umbra card?'

'Because that's who Hubbard was meeting – he must have recently called them. Ah, but...' Just as Claudia had begun to buy into the concept, Hugo zoomed in on another big snag. 'Umbra wouldn't have been aware of Project Acorn – it hadn't been announced.'

Claudia impatiently swept his objections aside.

'Oh, I wouldn't be too sure about that. I still have no idea how our business editor got wind of it – it wasn't through me.'

Hugo gave her a sceptical glance – he still had some residual doubts on that front.

'And these hedge fund types are always ferreting out restricted information – that's how they generate their profits,' she gushed, picking up on his reservations.

'But I wonder how Umbra got onto Hubbard in the first place?'

She slapped her thigh at yet another unhelpful comment from Hugo.

'Oh come on, Hugo, don't be so freaking negative. You've found a new angle and you've got me fired up again, and you're trying to knock it down before we've begun. Right now this is the only lead we have. We have to follow it up.'

'So you're back on the case?'

'You bet. Though I'd like to ask – why are you still so fixated on this?'

She eyed Hugo uncertainly.

Oh no, thought Hugo, here we go again.

'I told you before – I need to prove my innocence.'

'The real reason wouldn't be the sainted Ms Fraser by any chance?'

'No,' said Hugo. 'It certainly wouldn't. I really don't understand why you've got such a bee in your bonnet about Julia – it's not as though I'm ever going to see her again. I'm here with you – you're the one I want, are you so blind you can't see that?'

Claudia seemed to sense the sea change in Hugo, and for the first time to buy his denials. Her eyes lit up with excitement. Not only were they potentially back on course as a couple, but they had a new loucura angle to follow as well.

'Besides,' Hugo added. 'There's a moral dimension to all this. If loucura works, millions of people around the world have had their lives cut short in the financial interests of big pharma. And that's wrong – it deserves to be exposed.'

'Hugo,' said Claudia, unable to hide her surprise. 'You do actually care about other people after all. Perhaps you're too nice to be in corporate finance.'

Funnily enough, nobody had said this before – they'd told him repeatedly he was weak, indecisive, uncommercial and generally pathetic. Too nice? Never. Yet now he felt a glimmer of recognition – maybe this had been his problem all along.

45

'Umbra Capital Partners,' said Bill, peering over Claudia's shoulder. 'What's all that about?'

Damn – he had somehow managed to sneak up behind her, and she wasn't ready to share this with him quite yet. Still, honesty was the best policy.

'I've found a new lead on the pharma story.'

Bill sighed.

'Surely you got all that out of your system in Rio? After all, the bloke who was shafted won't talk about it and you can't get hold of any documents – haven't you run out of road? And what've these Umbra people got to do with it anyway?'

Claudia described her latest thinking on the subject, but Bill was not impressed. Even though he was twitchy, on his way out to have a fag, he insisted on giving her the benefit of his wisdom.

'Look Goldilocks, I admire your tenacity, but in this business it's just as important to know when to quit as when to persevere. I've given you free rein on this and you've drawn a blank. I let you have the time off to go to Rio, and nothing came out of it. Now you've embarked on yet another bout of pure speculation. Don't you think it's time to move on?'

One advantage of being black was no one could see you blush. By all rational standards Bill was right, but she was seized with such a strong instinct on this story that the flimsiest excuse seemed enough to justify continuing to chase it.

'I'm trying to prove the story and these Umbra people might have the evidence,' she said lamely.

'And are you expecting them to simply hand it over? I don't think so, babes – if you're right, they've been to considerable pains to keep this under wraps.'

'Well yes,' Claudia agreed, 'that may be a problem.'

Bill sat on the edge of her desk. He reeked of cigarettes and last night's whisky chasers.

'Claudia – this is a dead duck. For your own good, I forbid you to do any more.'

'Why?' asked Claudia. 'So far we have two mysterious deaths, two robberies and one sabotaged career. Doesn't that strike you as fishy?'

'OK,' said Bill. 'Now let me cut your list down to size. First, while you've been gallivanting round South America with Hooray Henry, it may have escaped your notice that the police have arrested the kids who were driving the car which killed George Hubbard.'

'So what? How difficult would it be for someone to put some poor kids in the frame if they had a mind to?'

'Then let's take these robberies. You said yourself your housemates are always leaving the front door off the latch and – well – Rio's a notorious spot for muggings if ever there was one.'

'And the sabotaged career?'

'Champagne Charlie shoots his mouth off in a bar – no surprise there. Amazed he lasted for so long in a proper job.'

Bill had never met Hugo, but that didn't stop him from acting as judge, jury and executioner.

'Which leaves Morrison's unfortunate death,' Bill went on, without giving Claudia chance to respond. 'When you check it out I'm sure you'll find all the evidence points to an accident. So basically, that leaves you with diddly squat.'

'Except a string of coincidences,' said Claudia. 'Including the fact that the Umbra people knew George Hubbard.'

'So what? That doesn't prove a thing.'

Claudia's temper was stirring now.

'That's just it. I'm trying to find the proof. I don't get why you're being so negative about all this.'

'I'm negative because there is no story,' said Bill. 'It's as simple as that. These drug companies have big pockets – they'll sue the pants off us all unless we have rock solid evidence. So far what you've dug up is about as robust as a piece of wet toilet paper. Working on a story you can't prove is not an effective use of your time. Do you understand?'

It was futile to argue. She nodded, but only to show she had heard what he was saying – there was no going back now. Besides, who was Bill to lecture her about effective use of time, with his countless cigarette breaks and extended sessions in the pub?

'Look, why don't you to write up any of these which look decent if you're short of something to do.' He handed her a wodge of press releases.

'Back to the daily grind of churning out crap,' said Claudia in a stage whisper, as Bill disappeared in pursuit of his nicotine hit.

Barely had she got stuck in before her e-mail pinged. Joe Doyle – the old hand who sat opposite her. Intriguingly it was headed 'The Reason Why'. Claudia clicked it open.

The reason why Bill is sweaty about this story can be found in the archives. Suggest you kick off with the 6 July 1985 edition – word search on BEP may be helpful. Then look at 15 January 1987.
    Rgds Joe

Ten minutes later Claudia had her answer. In 1985, Bill had written an article on BEP fixing the results of drug trials – not loucura, but an arthritis drug. Eighteen months

219

later the *Globe* had shelled out a record-breaking amount in libel damages.

This was reassuring on a number of levels. She gave a thumbs-up sign to Joe before returning to the Umbra website.

Umbra was owned by a Marcus Cunningham. The name seemed familiar – possibly from the card? In common with many hedge fund managers, Marcus kept a low profile – but there was plenty of information about his funds. As Hugo had already identified, Umbra specialised in pharmaceutical and technology stocks – they aimed for stellar returns to investors, irrespective of whether the stock market rose or fell.

The straightforward way in was to set up an interview with Marcus. But Sam Turner had already warned her that the guy was publicity-phobic. In any case, Marcus could hardly be expected to bare his soul in a press interview. More imaginative tactics were required.

The problem seemed intractable, yet halfway through the afternoon, long after she'd turned her thoughts elsewhere, Claudia remembered something she'd seen on the Umbra website. She flicked back to remind herself. Yes, of course – all that had been required was a touch of creative thinking. Here was a solution of pleasing ingenuity. Unable to contain her excitement, she picked up the phone to Hugo.

46

'So, Hugo,' said Marcus, 'why would you like to work with us at Umbra?'

Hugo had already passed the first test with flying colours – he'd spotted the job Marcus had put on the website specifically to reel him in. If nothing else, this demonstrated some rudimentary deductive powers.

Since he'd uncovered the link with the journalist girl, Marcus had been keeping close tabs on Hugo. It was time now to bring him under Umbra's control – as a loose cannon, he was far too dangerous.

Hugo knew none of this, of course – he was pleasantly surprised to even get to interview stage.

'At this point in my career, I would benefit from a fresh challenge, and the opportunity to use my unique skills and attributes in a stimulating environment.'

Marcus listened patiently. These clichés and trite phrases in no way cut the mustard, but what did it matter? He was buying Hugo off, not evaluating him as a long-term proposition. He would chew him up and spit him out, as he'd done with many others.

Yet even judged by these criteria, Hugo's performance was lacklustre. Apart from his stilted interview technique, he was less smartly presented than Marcus had anticipated – his tired shirt, slightly crumpled suit and dull shoes betraying a deep ennui. On the plus side, though, he was pleasingly bland, with no particular moral axe to grind, and desperately short of money.

'So what are these unique skills and attributes of yours?'

He would have to go through the motions – Hugo might smell a rat if he made it too easy.

'I'm bright, I'm personable, ambitious.'

Marcus stifled a yawn.

'Trust me, those qualities do not make you unique. We've had one hundred and twenty-three applicants for this job – they're all bright, personable and ambitious. Now tell me – how are you different from the others?'

'I've got a cutting edge,' said Hugo.

'Sorry pal – they all have that as well.'

Hugo floundered now – he stared at Marcus with incomprehension.

'Whatever you're looking for, I'm sure I'd be ideal,' he said feebly.

It was time to bring the charade to a close. Since Hugo insisted on failing to clear this undemanding hurdle, a more radical strategy was required.

'OK. Let's talk turkey,' said Marcus. 'Fortunately for you, I already appreciate what sets you apart from the herd. Would it help if I reminded you what it is?'

Hugo nodded inanely.

'The fact is, Hugo, our interests are already indissolubly aligned. If I say loucura to you, you understand what I'm talking about.'

He was curious to see how Hugo would react. Would he deny all knowledge, back off? Or would he freak out, like a frightened ferret?

In fact, Hugo merely shifted slightly in his seat, as though he'd sniffed danger, and it didn't smell sweet.

'I might do,' he said, without blinking.

'Hugo, let's cut the crap. Your girlfriend's a journalist with the *Daily Globe* and she's trying to run a story on loucura, the miracle answer to cancer. You've already lost your job at Pearson Malone trying to help her.'

Hugo's discomfort only enhanced Marcus's pleasure as

he twisted the screws further. His aim was to see what the lad was made of and so far, he'd hardly begun.

'By the way, how was your trip to Rio? Rather a dangerous place by all accounts – you were lucky not to be injured when you were mugged.'

'Very lucky,' Hugo agreed, growing more uneasy by the second.

'Luckier than poor George Hubbard,' said Marcus, going for the jugular.

Hugo dithered. Would he keep fighting or buckle under? Marcus had to know. Hugo stood up and walked towards the door – he'd bottled it. That suited Marcus perfectly – a coward was always easier to manipulate than a courageous man.

'Look,' Hugo began, his hand already on the doorknob. 'Maybe we ought to forget about this job business – I've got a feeling it wouldn't work out too well.'

'Oh, I'm not sure I agree,' Marcus replied. 'We seem to have a lot in common. In any case, if I murdered Hubbard, I'm hardly likely to let you go so easily, now am I?'

Hugo gulped, like a goldfish out of water. Marcus merely chuckled.

47

They sat in a discreet restaurant tucked away in a little mews road.

'Much safer to talk away from the office,' said Marcus. 'I pay a fortune to have it swept for bugs, but you can't be too careful these days. We should be all right in here, though.'

Hugo breathed easier now. Half of him knew it was silly to have let Marcus rattle him so much; the other half still couldn't quite accept he was safe. It was only when Marcus offered Hugo lunch before murdering him that he'd finally twigged he'd been the victim of a cruel joke. Still, given the circumstances, wasn't it understandable if he'd overreacted a tad?

'You don't really believe I'm a murderer, do you?' said Marcus, craning round to ensure no one overheard.

'Probably not, but you can't blame me for wondering.'

'Why? Do I look that sort of a man?'

Hugo evaluated Marcus – handkerchief in the breast pocket, pinstripe slightly too wide, patent shoes, his features set in a permanently supercilious expression. He was spivvy – a wheeler-dealer. Would he kill to do the deal? Who could say.

'You look like a man who's used to getting what he wants,' said Hugo tactfully.

'I am, Hugo, I am – and that's precisely the point. Why bother to have Hubbard killed? He'd offered me his papers, after all.'

'Ah, so it was you he was meeting the day he died?'

'Why deny it? I've nothing to hide.'

'You didn't come forward,' said Hugo.

'So? I prefer to keep a low profile.'

'Isn't that the same as hiding?' asked Hugo.

'No, no,' Marcus replied, appalled by the suggestion. 'Not the same at all.'

'You might have had him killed to stop him spilling the beans to anyone else.'

'True, but do credit me with some intelligence – in that case I would have made sure to get my hands on the papers first.'

This knocked Hugo back.

'What? You mean you haven't got them?'

'Certainly not – I wouldn't be hiring you if I did.'

'So you're offering me the job?'

'Yes, I'm going to make you an offer. Eighty grand per year, plus an immediate signing-on fee of ten grand – net of tax naturally. With a bonus of a hundred grand if you get me those papers.'

Hugo gasped at these mind-boggling numbers. Marcus had offered nearly £30,000 a year more than if he'd been promoted at Pearson Malone, with a bonus he could only have dreamt of there. Even the signing-on fee would solve his immediate problems. He could repay his father the money he'd borrowed to go to Brazil, for a start. Hugo's self-esteem instantly rocketed – he couldn't be a useless tosser if he'd landed a prestigious job such as this.

'What's my job title?' he asked, recovering his poise.

'Junior Analyst,' said Marcus.

Never mind about the poxy title – all that money! But reality abruptly intruded – there had to be a catch.

'The offer is subject to two conditions,' Marcus said, as though reading Hugo's mind.

'What?'

Surely the conditions would not be so onerous that he'd

have to refuse the offer – he was anxious to avoid this at all costs.

'First, confidentiality is crucial in this game,' Marcus went on. 'You don't tell a soul what you're working on, which especially includes your rather colourful girlfriend. Now, I'm aware you've had issues with confidentiality before…'

Creepy stuff – how did this man have so much dirt on him? How did he know so much about Claudia? Had he bugged Pearson Malone's offices? Been following him?

'No, I completely understand about confidentiality,' Hugo reassured him. 'The other matter was a misunderstanding.'

'Of course it was,' agreed Marcus, with a reptilian smile.

Hugo had a sudden intuition that Marcus may have somehow orchestrated his fall from grace at Pearson Malone, but that was impossible, wasn't it?

'If I get so much of a whisper that anything has leaked out – and believe me, I'll know – your employment terminates forthwith. Do you have a problem with that?'

In simple terms, Marcus was making him an offer to cut Claudia out. And he couldn't afford to say no.

'No problem at all,' he replied briskly.

Actually, it was an enormous problem – Claudia would go loopy if she found out.

'What's the second condition?'

'You buy a new suit before you set foot in my offices again.'

Hugo did some quick calculations – this would be tricky if not impossible until his signing-on fee had cleared the bank.

'I do have smarter suits than this, you know,' he said.

Marcus frowned, no doubt wondering why he hadn't worn one of them.

'Buy a new one,' he repeated.

'Fine – I will.'

'So are you going to accept?'

'I'd like to think about it,' said Hugo.

'We shake on it now, or the offer lapses.'

'We haven't even ordered the food yet. And besides, I do have some other irons in the fire.'

Marcus treated this revelation with the contempt it deserved.

'I fear they may take rather too long to heat up,' he said, 'in view of your financial situation.'

Hugo was flabbergasted. Was the whole world in on his debt problem? Had he inadvertently posted details on Facebook? Yet Marcus knew too much about everything for his comfort.

'I haven't much choice,' said Hugo, 'as you already seem to know. But tell me this – how did you dig up all the info on my finances, my girlfriend, my trip to Rio and all the other stuff?'

Marcus tapped his nose.

'Due diligence, Hugo, due diligence. Never underestimate the value of it.'

'Well, perhaps I should do some more due diligence on you.'

'Shake on the deal and I'll tell you everything.'

Hugo doubted that, but put out his hand nonetheless. He prayed Marcus wouldn't ask him to do anything illegal.

'Excellent,' said Marcus, beaming. 'Let's drink to a successful collaboration.'

He clinked his glass against Hugo's and sipped at the Puligny-Montrachet he had ordered. Hugo took a large slurp from his own glass. It was smooth and expensive – a taste of the life to which Hugo had now been offered an entrée.

'Cheers,' said Hugo.

'Cheers. And now down to the real business.'

Hugo hadn't signed any agreement. Theoretically, he was free to walk away and tell Claudia all that Marcus was about to share with him. But they both knew he wouldn't.

'Hubbard was killed before we met – run over right in front of my eyes.'

Marcus shuddered at the memory.

'He had his briefcase with him, but it disappeared.'

'Who took it?'

'Search me – it wasn't returned to his widow. I'm assuming whoever had him killed took the papers, but I may be wrong.'

'No copies, I suppose?'

Hugo already knew all this from Claudia, but it didn't harm to ask again.

'Not that we're aware of.'

'I must say, I assumed you'd got hold of what you wanted from Rodrigues. You did go to see him, didn't you?' asked Hugo.

Marcus topped up Hugo's glass.

'Yes, but he was as tight as a clam. He'd been nobbled and no mistake. We tried a straight bribe, followed by an obscenely large donation to the children's hospital fund. No use at all. So now we're back to square one. It's vital we get hold of those documents, Hugo.'

'Am I allowed to ask what you'll do with the information if you get it?'

'What do you think we'll do?'

'Well, there's your stake in IDD. That's where I set off with all this – I imagined you might be scared for Hubbard's story to get out. Julia Fraser would call off the transaction and you would lose...'

Marcus fell about at the mere suggestion that he might actually end up out of pocket.

'We would lose absolutely nothing. You've a lot to learn, sonny – let me enlighten you.'

Hugo was about to say that he wasn't that naive when

the waiter approached. Marcus turned his attention to the food order.

'The fish here is superb, Hugo. I recommend the grilled Dover sole, and I never have a starter. It's important not to overeat, you know.'

'Fine with me,' said Hugo, although he would have preferred a much heartier meal. Funny how Marcus had this way of choking off all dissent without being overbearing.

'Now, where was I?'

'You were saying how you'd avoid making a loss if the deal was pulled.'

'Ah yes – have you heard of a company called Bioinvestments?'

Hugo helped himself to a miniature roll from the bread basket in an attempt to take the edge off his appetite.

'Yes, they own twenty percent of IDD.'

'What do you know about them?'

Hugo racked his brains. They were a private equity firm, had a seat on the board and – yes, he remembered now – they were up against a serious deadline to realise their investment in IDD.

'They were in a hurry to sell out,' said Hugo.

'Indeed they are. You might say they're in a forced sale scenario. But they can't dump the shares on the market – the price will plummet.'

'So you mean they had an interest in getting rid of George?' asked Hugo. Now that was much more logical. After all, Umbra could afford to sit back and wait for another bidder. Bioinvestments didn't have the same luxury.

Marcus was shaking his head.

'I can tell you now, it's not them,' he said. 'When we found out the bind they were in, I made a side agreement with them. If the BEP acquisition stalls, they can offload their shareholding to us at a small discount to the price they would have sold to BEP. As a quid pro quo, we'd insist on the same rights on the board as they have so we'd be in a position to drive a sale to a higher bidder.'

'Neat,' said Hugo, getting into the flow, 'and there'd be no shortage of bidders for the company with the patentable magic cancer blaster.'

'You got it,' said Marcus. 'Even if it was only the big boys paying to ensure synthetic loucura never saw the light of day.'

'Surely they couldn't do that?' said Hugo. 'Not if the public knew the facts.'

'Couldn't they?' asked Marcus. 'You underestimate the inventiveness of the industry. They'd cook up some bogus safety issue in the clinical trials at the drop of a hat.'

The depth of the man's cynicism shocked Hugo.

'So you would rather the deal was pulled?'

'To tell you the truth, I'm tolerably relaxed – IDD's small beer in all this. When you have two billion pounds of funds under management as we do, it takes a lot more than a stake in IDD to make a difference.'

The waiter arrived with the fish, and miniscule portions of vegetables. Marcus ordered another bottle of wine – his iron-willed control evidently didn't extend to alcohol consumption.

'So what else?'

'This is your job interview – you should be doing the work,' said Marcus.

'But you've already offered me the job.'

'Don't get clever with me, young man. Now tell me – what would you do in my shoes?'

Hugo sucked in his cheeks as he pretended to think.

'At a conservative estimate, the cancer industry is worth about $300 to $400 billion annually in the US alone,' he said, hoping to impress Marcus with his grasp of the facts. 'If loucura is a runner, all that revenue comes to an end. And even if the big boys squashed loucura again, the mere possibility of a cancer cure would send shock waves through the pharmaceutical sector.'

'So?'

'So, I'd take massive short positions in the pharmaceutical companies most dependent upon cancer therapies, leak the news, and cash in big style when all the share prices crashed.'

'Spot on,' said Marcus, clapping his hands. 'We'll make something of you yet.'

'But you can't do any of this without Hubbard's papers?'

'No – and that's where you come in.'

'What happens if you get the papers, but they don't prove the case?'

Marcus shrugged.

'C'est la vie,' he said. 'We move on and capitalise on the next idea – there's always money to be made, Hugo, if only you look in the right place.'

'Talking of where to look, who do you think has Hubbard's documents?' he asked, returning to the central question. 'Is it BEP?'

'No, they're still hunting for them.'

'How do you know?'

'By asking the right questions,' said Marcus enigmatically. 'Besides, why would they have fixed you in New Jersey if they'd already taken control of the proof?'

Hugo didn't even bother to ask how Marcus knew about New Jersey.

'Because they'd be embarrassed about the story getting out – they decided to warn me off.'

'I really don't think so,' said Marcus. 'These drug companies have thick skins and their PR teams would smooth over any adverse publicity. No – the far bigger danger for them is the financial consequences of a quick and easy cancer treatment that actually works. And my guts tell me that the Brazilians did do further work on it, whatever that little shitbag Rodrigues says.'

'He is a little shitbag, isn't he? And a lying shitbag to boot – his reasons for quitting the research simply didn't ring true.'

They had quickly polished off the baby-sized main courses, which had barely blunted Hugo's appetite.

'You won't bother with dessert, will you Hugo?' Marcus said, crushing Hugo's already slender expectations of another course. 'Such a bore having to eat out all the time.'

The waiter returned to the table.

'Just two coffees, please, once we've finished the wine,' Marcus instructed him.

Hugo found Marcus's easy manipulation of him both disturbing and annoying. He hoped he would have more autonomy once he began work properly.

'I don't mind admitting,' said Hugo, 'that I haven't a clue where to begin looking.'

'Well, fortunately I do.' Marcus drew up his chair to the table. 'And we'll discuss it when you roll up on Monday morning and you've signed on the dotted line.'

It didn't surprise Hugo that Marcus was unwilling to share all his ideas on the strength of a handshake. No problem – he could wait till Monday.

'By the way,' said Marcus. 'In the interests of total honesty, I have a confession. And it's not about Hubbard.'

'Yes?'

'We followed you in Rio.'

'And snatched Claudia's bag?'

'Yes, I'm sorry – I know it was terrible, but we had to be sure you guys didn't have the proof yourselves. I can easily arrange for the bag and its contents to be returned, if you like.'

'Might be better to leave it,' said Hugo. The mysterious return of Claudia's bag could only complicate matters at this stage.

'Another confession – in case you hadn't worked it out,

I only advertised the job to get you on board. I predicted you'd apply.'

That didn't quite stack up, and Hugo challenged him. 'How did you guess I was on to Umbra?'

Marcus couldn't have known that Rodrigues had mentioned the hedge fund to him, still less that he'd figure out it was Umbra.

'Ah well,' said Marcus, 'let's say it's a trade secret.'

Hugo left the restaurant with his head spinning. His pride swelled at having landed a plum job so soon after his ignominious exit from Pearson Malone. At the same time, there were some downsides – in particular, he didn't appreciate being stage-managed by Marcus, nor having the intimate details of his life laid bare. And then there was the vexed question of how to handle Claudia, which was never easy at the best of times.

But what worried him most now – hot on the heels of his scare with Marcus – was his safety. Two men had died – was he putting his head over the parapet to be the third victim? Perhaps his main asset to Marcus was his expendability – the excellent pay no more than danger money in disguise. Hugo shivered as he crossed the road to the Underground.

48

'Wayne, I don't like loose ends,' Brad began, 'and I know you don't either. This loucura business…'

They met in the car park of a shopping mall after Morrison's funeral.

'Hell, Brad, it's over. Morrison's dead – you only this minute buried him, for heaven's sake.'

Brad was still wearing his sombre suit and black tie. Wayne's gaze was drawn to the straining seams of his jacket – some weight gain – no wonder Brad's wife was concerned to control his eating.

'I'm not even sure what loose ends you mean.'

'Hubbard's documents – you never did find them, did you?'

In reality, Wayne had called off the search.

'No, we didn't.'

'Well, that's a loose end, wouldn't you say?'

'No, I wouldn't say. If someone was planning to use them, they would have done it by now. Why are you so worried?'

'Morrison believed loucura worked.'

'Yeah, I know – but you told me you thought he was crazy.'

'I'm not sure. But I'd like to find out.'

'I'll see what I can do, Brad.' He wasn't enthusiastic, though, and didn't plan to bust a gut trying.

'Did you look in Brazil?'

'We did – we turned over Rodrigues' place while they were out and found nothing. He's a smart cookie.'

'What about Fleming and the journalist?'

'The journalist's quit working on the story.'

'And Fleming?'

'He was fired and then hired by someone else pretty quick.'

'So he won't have much time to brood on what happened.'

'You got it,' said Wayne.

He was loath to say more, but there'd be hell to pay if Brad found out from another source. 'There's one weird little detail, though.'

'What?'

'Fleming was hired by Umbra Capital Partners, a Brit hedge fund.'

'What's strange about that?'

'According to the widow, someone from Umbra was after Hubbard's papers.'

'Really?'

'Really. And you want to know what's even weirder?'

'I've a feeling you're going to tell me anyway.'

'Umbra owns a tranche of shares in IDD.'

Brad pursed his lips.

'It sounds,' he said, 'as if Hugo Fleming might just be a loose end you should take care of as well.'

49

Claudia and Hugo sat on a moored boat restaurant on the Thames, soaking up the early evening sunshine. Their celebratory meal would have been idyllic if Claudia hadn't been giving him the Spanish Inquisition.

'What exactly will you be doing at Umbra?'

'I'm going to be a Junior Analyst.'

'What does that mean?'

'Doing research and stuff.'

'Research into what?'

'Companies that Umbra might invest in, of course.'

Hugo was evasive, but how else could he play it? He'd been sworn to secrecy by Marcus, and Claudia was inquisitive – talk about being between a rock and a hard place.

'So what about the documents?'

'Claudia, I'm convinced Marcus has nothing whatsoever to do with Hubbard or loucura.'

Hugo realised immediately the words were out that he'd made a major tactical error – much more plausible to have said that, unsurprisingly, the subject hadn't come up at the interview. As he'd feared, Claudia homed in ruthlessly on his blunder.

'How can you be so sure? Did you cover the topic in depth?'

'Leave it, Claudia,' he snapped. Another mistake – only someone hiding something would become so angry.

'You're not even intending to try, are you?'

'I didn't say that.'

Yet he couldn't say he was going to look for the papers.

'Why can't you enjoy the meal and be happy that I've got a fantastic job?'

And, she was, for a while – until she launched a second attack.

'So tell me what you'll be working on with Umbra.'

'I'm afraid I can't,' Hugo replied. 'It's secret.'

'You bullshitting me? I mean, your past performance on confidentiality is the pits.'

'All the more reason to be ultra careful in the new job.'

'You sound as if you're actually planning to stay at this job and do it properly.'

'Why wouldn't I? It's a fantastic opportunity. I'll never get a better one.'

Claudia threw down her napkin in disgust.

'But surely we agreed – you're only going in there to have a sniff around.'

In truth, neither of them had actually considered in detail what would happen if Marcus hired him – it hadn't seemed at all likely. And Hugo felt it inappropriate to tell her it had been a foregone conclusion that he'd be recruited – for obvious reasons.

'Well, I've been doing some digging,' said Claudia. 'Your new boss is an out-and-out crook – it's well-known in the City that he's dodgy. Why, we'd be able to run a whole story on him and his machinations if we had a mind to.'

'Not with information from me you won't,' said Hugo. 'And you were the one who encouraged me to apply to Umbra. Look – can't you be glad I've landed on my feet?'

'I am glad. But can't you tell me in general terms what you'll be working on?'

'We're evaluating potential investment opportunities,' said Hugo.

'Name one investment opportunity you'll be evaluating,' she challenged him.

'That is not general terms. As I said, it's all highly confidential. I simply can't talk to you about it.'

'I'll tell you what I think,' said Claudia. 'You did mention loucura at the interview, and Marcus is still working on proving the story. He's hired you to help him and told you to keep it quiet.'

Hugo was no poker player and he knew it – even so, he couldn't fathom how Claudia had rumbled him so quickly.

'Are you calling me a liar?'

'Yes I am. You've sold out to Marcus.'

'That's not true.'

'Don't lie, Hugo – you're crap at it. Why can't you be honest with me?'

Because he would be fired.

'You're so freaking weak,' said Claudia, continuing with her tirade. 'Coming from your pampered, privileged background, you've never had to stand up for yourself or your convictions. I was nearly taken in the other night by all your ethical claptrap. But when someone dangles the pound notes in front of your eyes all your moral fibre crumbles to dust.'

'You suggested I go for this job,' Hugo shouted, 'and now I've got it you're all resentful.'

'I resent you. You're a pampered lazy white rich kid, who's slithered from one elitist institution to another. You've never had to work for what you've achieved – can't even see the point in it. Even now, you're laughing. The old boys' network comes up trumps again.'

'What are you on about? You told me yourself Marcus hadn't really been to Eton.'

'What difference does it make? You're all as bad as each other. You glide through life with no particular purpose, all rallying round and propping each other up. Come on, admit it, you've been seduced by this new job and the money and that's all there is to it.'

Hugo stood up.

'I don't have to take this,' he said. 'Before you go off on one and storm out and say we're through, I'll get in first. I was idiotic to imagine it was ever going to work between us, because you know what? You have this huge chip on your shoulder and nothing, nothing I can say or do will change your mind.'

Hugo walked away. By being so obnoxious, Claudia had provided him with the perfect excuse to escape from her clutches. He'd miss the sex, but not all the aggro that went with it – the relationship would never have succeeded long term. Nevertheless, a pang of self-disgust pricked him. She'd been right – he had sold out to Marcus. He hoped that later he would be able to put the situation right.

Neither Claudia nor Hugo had noticed the unremarkable man sitting in the corner – but they weren't supposed to. When Hugo left, the man followed a short distance behind.

50

Hugo arrived at Umbra's offices promptly at 7.30 – Marcus insisted all his people came in before the markets opened at 8.00. Hugo didn't much care for early mornings, but the mega money would do much to ease the pain.

He'd had his best suit cleaned – Marcus would never realise it wasn't new. But he needn't have bothered – today Marcus was preoccupied with much weightier matters. He sat in one of the meeting rooms, in a heated discussion with a geeky dude in tortoiseshell framed glasses.

When Marcus spotted Hugo at the entrance, the conversation abruptly died.

'Welcome to Umbra, Hugo,' said Marcus, offering his hand and exhibiting all the bonhomie he could muster.

'Glad to be here.'

Hugo found it strange no longer being part of Pearson Malone – in many respects this had all the feel of a short-term secondment. And yet he was here for the duration; he would have to figure out how to work with these guys, how to steer clear of the errors he'd made with Stephanie.

'This is Richard, one of my chief researchers.'

Hugo looked Richard up and down. His general demeanour was one of awesome intelligence – well out of Hugo's league.

'Hi Hugo,' said the geek. 'Pleased to have you on board.'

'Well, let's get down to business.' Marcus lit one of his cigars – Richard frowned as he wafted away a cloud of smoke.

'The room has literally just been swept by our security consultants, so we should be secure here for once.'

Hugo couldn't make up his mind whether all this talk of sweeping rooms was for real or to impress him. As he'd already spotted, Marcus had a tendency to hype himself up.

'Someone has been amassing a secret stake in IDD,' said Marcus, without any preamble.

'How do you know?' Hugo asked, immediately fearing he'd asked a daft question.

'We've studied the shareholder register. They bought some shares, gradually over the last couple of months and then a load more in the week after Hubbard's death.'

'How can it be a secret if it's on the shareholder register?' Another potentially stupid question.

'The stake's spread across different nominee companies,' said Richard. 'If you do a search on them, they all have the same directors and shareholders – all connected with the same company formation agent. There the trail ends.'

Hugo strained to recall fragments of the company law he'd studied in his exams.

'Can't the company issue a notice to get the nominee companies to own up to who is behind them?' he said.

'If they knew about it and if they cared, yes,' Richard explained. 'But this isn't so very conspicuous and the combined stake was only around one percent before Hubbard died and two percent after.'

'Why would you care?' asked Hugo, not unreasonably.

'I'm coming to that,' said Marcus somewhat irritably.

'And I don't quite get relevance of Hubbard's death.'

'You don't? You surprise me. You used the same logic yourself when you suspected that I was behind Hubbard's murder.'

He gave a little laugh.

'I did?'

'Yes, and the logic was sound even if the conclusion was false,' Marcus went on. 'Someone who had a lot to lose if

IDD doesn't sell out to BEP might well have cause to get Hubbard and his story out of the way.'

'This is where we disagree,' explained Richard, grimacing. 'We are looking at a comparatively small shareholding, after all. Killing someone seems rather OTT in the circumstances.' He looked to Hugo for support.

'Yes, you did say IDD was small beer for Umbra,' Hugo reminded Marcus.

Marcus sighed, impatient at having to contend with these imbeciles.

'For Umbra, yes. But for someone else, maybe not. And we have the flurry of transactions in the week following Hubbard's death. Once Hubbard's out of the way, they can see their way to buying more shares.'

'I disagree there as well,' said Richard. 'The second tranche of share purchases is more obviously linked with the rumours in the media.'

'I don't understand that either,' said Hugo, now bewildered by the entire conversation.

'It's classic ploy to avoid being caught for insider dealing,' Richard explained. 'Spread gossip and you can always argue you were trading on a rumour – the FSA can't touch you then.'

'Unless they can prove you spread the rumour in the first place,' said Hugo.

'Quite,' Marcus agreed, moving hurriedly on. 'Although you might try asking your girl at the *Globe* where the leak came from.'

'No chance,' Hugo replied sharply. 'We've split up – strangely enough, she didn't warm to your confidentiality policy.'

'No surprise there.'

Marcus looked smug, and well he might – his gamble to buy Hugo had paid off.

'I still say this is a good old-fashioned insider dealing

ring,' said Richard. 'Now, given our own holding in IDD, it might be sensible to identify who's behind it. But this link with Hubbard...'

Marcus cut him off.

'Richard, what you forget is I've got an instinct, like a sixth sense, for when something crooked is in the air. And take it from me, this involves Hubbard's evidence.'

Privately, Hugo agreed with Richard, but was reluctant to blot his copy book quite so early on.

'So what exactly is your theory?' he asked Marcus instead.

'Whoever killed Hubbard was trying to keep the story quiet. They'd got wind of the deal and bought shares, but they absolutely depended on the IDD sale going through. And when they heard on the grapevine a big scandal with BEP was about to hit the media, they knew it would jeopardise the takeover.'

'Surely after they read the documents and saw what the scandal was they would realise that there was a much bigger opportunity for IDD. Like you, they wouldn't care if the takeover went ahead or not.'

Hugo wasn't sure whether he'd overstepped the mark in saying this, but Richard was nodding approvingly. In the long term, it might be wiser to keep Richard on side than brown-nose Marcus. Encouraged, Hugo went on.

'A two percent stake would be about two million pounds on the sale, or a shade over a million profit based on the share price at the time. Would somebody have Hubbard killed for a mere million?'

'This is exactly what I've been saying,' said Richard, manifestly relieved that Hugo was supporting rather than undermining him.

'Why not?' argued Marcus. 'People have been killed for much less.'

'Well OK,' said Hugo doubtfully. 'Even taking that as read, how would these people have known about BEP?'

'Another excellent point,' said Richard, visibly warming to Hugo by the minute.

Marcus threw his hands up in horror. 'I give up!' he said. 'I suspect the question may be easier to answer when we discover who they are – which is your job, Hugo. I need you to expose who's behind this secret stake.'

Hugo had been keen to exert his independence of mind, but decided he'd challenged Marcus enough for the first morning.

'No problem,' he said breezily. 'I can do that.'

The remit was unambiguous. Right now, he wasn't being asked to prove the connection with Hubbard – for strangely Marcus was already convinced of that – only to find who was behind those companies.

'That's what I appreciate,' said Marcus, clapping his hands, 'a positive attitude – not giving me a hundred and one reasons why what I've asked for is impossible.' He stared coldly at Richard.

Richard cleared his throat.

'In fairness to Hugo, I should disclose that despite strenuous efforts I've utterly failed to identify the people behind the companies.'

'Don't discourage the boy. Hugo will try harder,' said Marcus. 'Won't you, Hugo?'

'Well, I'll certainly do my best,' he replied, beginning to worry.

'Good – I recommend you get started right away. I must check the markets.'

He strode out of the room, leaving Richard to brief Hugo on the work done so far.

'I'm sorry about that,' said Richard, once Marcus was out of the way. 'It can be quite challenging working for Marcus – he makes these snap judgements and there's no budging him. Goodness knows where he came by this theory about the insider trading being linked with Hubbard, but I'm afraid we're stuck with it for the time being. He also has a tendency to demand the impossible.'

'Such as finding out who's behind those companies?'

'Quite.'

'What can I do?' asked Hugo. 'If you guys can't find the answer, how does he expect me to?'

'Don't worry,' Richard smiled. 'He actually knows it's impossible. It's all a test to see how you react. Will you try to bullshit him? Inadvisable, by the way, in case you hadn't worked it out. Will you admit defeat too soon or waste too much time on it? Are you prepared to be creative in trying to solve the problem? Trust me, if you play this right, in about a week you'll be able to give up gracefully. I will offer you one piece of advice, though.'

'What?'

'Once you've drawn a blank on these nominee companies, as you surely will, you'd better have some other ideas on how to move forward on finding Hubbard's documents or else you'll be dead meat on the slab.'

Hugo swallowed hard.

'Thanks.'

Richard escorted Hugo to his office, showed him around and passed him the work he'd done so far.

'Well, he hand-picked you for this job,' said Richard, picking up on Hugo's anxiety. 'So you start with an immense advantage.'

'He seems to know a lot about me.'

'Oh, he enjoys flaunting his knowledge – keeps you on your toes.'

'How the hell did he guess I'd apply for the job?'

This had been worrying Hugo ever since the interview.

'I haven't a clue, but Marcus has his finger in a lot of pies – wouldn't surprise me if he had a spy in Globe Media. Anyway, must get on – if you want anything, I'm down the corridor. Best of luck, Hugo.'

'Thanks,' said Hugo. 'I think I'll need it.'

Alone in his office, Hugo put his head in his hands. This was a living nightmare. Even the bitch Stephanie had never asked him to attempt something she knew to be impossible. Hugo cast around him, as if hoping for inspiration from the blandly furnished office. Where on earth should he begin?

51

Claudia seethed – it was plain that Hugo had cut her out of the loop on the loucura project. And he'd even had the cheek to bawl her out when she'd challenged him. Honestly, he failed to stick to anything for long. First it was Julia, then it was some moral crusade – and in the end he'd been bowled over by Umbra's money. Fact was, Hugo had all the self-discipline of a defecating elephant.

She was angry with herself too. She'd tried so hard to have faith in Hugo, but he repeatedly fell short of her expectations. Well, no more – from now on Claudia would be ruled by her head and not her hormones. The infatuation was over – forever.

The story was a different matter, though. Bugger Hugo, and bugger Bill – Claudia was determined to find the answer first. It was just a question of where to begin.

What was Hugo working on? It was fair to assume Umbra didn't have the papers, otherwise why hire Hugo. That meant they'd also drawn a blank with Rodrigues. Yet Rodrigues must nevertheless have all the answers, and this was where she must start.

She googled Rodrigues and followed whatever came up. There was no shortage of material – he was a high flyer on the Latin American medical scene, a member of numerous committees and on the board of a dozen or so companies. Could the answer lie in Rodrigues' business interests?

This was a time-consuming line of enquiry, but that didn't mean it was useless – first, the directorships.

Claudia found a link to the Brazilian company registry

via the UK Companies House website – she was even able to hit a 'translate' button to get an English version. Unfortunately, there was no facility to do a search on directors. Damn – she was stuck already, and she'd hardly got off the ground. She called Sam Turner, hoping he wouldn't tell Bill.

'Do you know any way to do a search on Brazilian company directors?'

'The Brazilian Company Registry?'

'Tried that – no dice.'

'What are you after exactly?'

'A list of all the directorships for a certain person.'

'There's a US website – I'll send you the link.'

He didn't ask her why she needed it. He'd probably prefer not to know now practically everyone in the office including the cleaning lady was aware that Bill had vetoed the loucura story.

Ten minutes later, Claudia had downloaded a list of all Rodrigues' directorships, printed it out and stuffed it into a folder. And in the nick of time, too – Bill was marching resolutely towards her.

Hugo lay wakeful and apprehensive as he contemplated the quandary he was in. He'd made zero progress on day one and already had an uneasy sense of living on borrowed time. What should he do next?

Richard had said that Marcus knew the task was impossible. Should Hugo even believe this? After all, Richard must have his own agenda, having failed to resolve the problem himself. On the other hand, if Hugo acted on the assumption that the puzzle was soluble and it was not, he was merely setting himself up for disappointment. But suppose that not only was there a solution, but that Marcus already knew what it was?

Hugo agonised for hours over the various possibilities of bluff or double bluff before ultimately concluding that his strategy should be the same whether Richard was bullshitting him or not.

In fact, he should follow Richard's advice and look for innovative ways in which the problem might be solved. If a solution existed, then these ideas might actually lead him to it; if they did not, he could still score points for the originality of his approach. And if Marcus truly believed the task to be hopeless, then all the better. His initiatives could be judged entirely on their own merits, unimpeded by the issue of whether they had actually led anywhere. He had a brain, and an imagination. For this assignment, that was enough.

His brain had been churning so long that sleep was impossible, but at least he had some clarity on the way forward. He arrived at the office at 7.53 with a spring in his step and an iron determination to succeed. The awareness that Claudia would be back on the case and trying to beat him to it only spurred him on. She had a free rein and wouldn't have to waste time on these ridiculous nominee companies. There was not a moment to be lost.

There were thirty-four transactions in all, across thirteen different companies. As Richard had found, the trail ended there. Hugo called the company agents on a pretext – no luck – their security arrangements were impenetrable. So far, Hugo was conscious that he was merely retracing Richard's footsteps, but the illusion of activity boosted his morale and gave his subconscious time to yield up some more novel ideas. He grabbed another coffee – his third of the morning. He had hoped that the caffeine would galvanise his brain into action, but before the machine had even ejected his frothy cappuccino, an inspiration hit him.

Perhaps the key lay in the timing of the transactions. Hugo wasn't particularly familiar with insider trading, but he did know that people couldn't keep their mouths shut. They would whisper to someone in the strictest of confidence, who would whisper to someone else, and so it went on. Before long, the whole world would be in the know. So perhaps there might be other people on the shareholder register who were connected in some way with the insiders. And they might not be anonymous.

His hopes were frustrated to begin with – there were few transactions at the time the nominee companies had bought their first tranche of shares. But coincident with the second wave of acquisitions, nine other small holdings had been acquired in a flurry of activity, all with a similar number of shares. Were these connected? Maybe – three of them had Oxfordshire postcodes.

Hugo knew IDD shares were less illiquid than many of those on the AIM market, but even so, what were the chances? Four of the other shareholders were based in London, the remaining two in Harrogate and Aberdeen.

Hugo googled the names of the Oxfordshire three. The name which generated by far the most relevant hits was Toby Miller – he owned a software company called TM Technology. With dogged determination, Hugo continued his painstaking research. By lunchtime, he was rewarded with definite connections between Miller and seven of the nine shareholders. He called Marcus on his mobile to give him an update.

'Terrific work,' said Marcus. 'Let's touch base this afternoon.'

Hugo stood in front of Marcus, outlining what he'd turned up. He marvelled at how much his situation had improved in the last few days. Whatever hostility he might feel from time to time towards Claudia, it was entirely due to her he'd ended up in a shiny new job with his financial problems solved at a stroke. His life could be very much worse.

'The connection,' Hugo announced proudly, 'is a man called Toby Miller. He owns a company called TM Technology Limited based in Abingdon. Two of the other shareholders are based in Oxfordshire. One is a non-executive director of TM and the other is a governor at Toby's son's school. The two shareholders in Harrogate and Aberdeen are Toby's sisters. And according to Friends Reunited, one of the guys from London was at school with Toby. The seventh shareholder is a partner in the law firm which advises TM. I don't know about the other two, but I'm sure if I dug deep enough I'd unearth some link.'

'This TM,' said Richard, apparently unperturbed by Hugo's success. 'Are we to take it they're involved in the same kind of technology as IDD?'

'No,' Hugo replied. 'I thought so too to begin with, but they're into web-based document management solutions, so there's no obvious link.'

'No matter,' said Marcus, 'you've done tremendously well.'

'Thank you.'

'By the way,' Marcus added almost as an afterthought, 'any joy with those nominee companies I asked you to look at?'

Hugo's ego swiftly deflated.

'Untraceable,' he replied as confidently as possible. 'Though I wouldn't be surprised if Toby knows who's behind them.'

There was no rational basis for this contention, but why should Marcus have the monopoly on gut instinct?

'So how do we move forward from here?' asked Marcus.

It was an obvious question to which Hugo had already prepared an answer.

'I suggest we should pay Mr Miller a visit on a pretext.'

'What pretext did you have in mind? Surely you're not considering applying for another job quite so soon, especially as you're doing so well here?'

Hugo ignored Marcus's heavy-handed humour, and outlined his scheme.

'Well, I've studied the company's accounts and various press releases about planned expansion of the business. I haven't enough information to make detailed calculations, but it's fairly clear the company isn't in a position to finance all the proposed developments. One of Umbra's niches is technology companies. Now if we were to suggest an investment...'

'Nice work,' said Marcus, managing to imply that Hugo had merely caught up with his own, infinitely faster, mental processes. 'Go and meet him, and report back on what you uncover.'

'Hang on a mo,' said Hugo, suddenly vulnerable. 'I can't go on my own. It's my first week here. I haven't a clue how you would conduct a potential investment meeting.'

'It's only a subterfuge,' said Marcus.

'He'll see through the subterfuge in the first five minutes and we'll never get anywhere.'

'Point taken. Richard will go with you,' he said, avoiding volunteering to get his own hands dirty.

'I'd be glad to, but I can't be in two places at the same time. You asked me to go to Switzerland.'

'Oh, all right,' said Marcus, irritably. 'I'll go with Hugo. Let me give Miller a bell this morning – see if he bites. Nice work, Hugo. You've got off to a flying start.'

52

Toby Miller fully lived up to Hugo's image of a computer software entrepreneur. He had a faraway look resulting from a combination of too much time on the computer and a fondness for powerful narcotics. His Hawaiian shirt, torn jeans and glasses nicely completed the geek-chic aura.

Toby greeted Hugo and Marcus effusively, while regarding their sharp suits with distrust. Nevertheless, he described the company's situation with engaging candour, apparently unconcerned about how the information he divulged might be used.

Hugo took copious notes and waited for Marcus to turn the discussion around to IDD. But even as they stood up to go, there'd been no mention of the subject.

Toby insisted on giving them a conducted tour of the building before they left. TM's premises were unremarkable, and the workforce consisted of identikits of Toby, all tapping away at their computers. The one exception was a man in a grey suit, hunched over a desk with his back to them.

'That's Peter Dick, our finance director,' he said.

Another bean counter, thought Hugo, with all the conceit of a high-rolling hedge fund executive.

'Well,' Marcus said to Toby, 'we've been most impressed with what we've seen today and we're keen to take matters further. Naturally, we'll wish to conduct full financial and commercial due diligence.'

The penny finally dropped – this was only the warm-up. Marcus planned to sniff around in an attempt to dig up some dirt on the company. Then he'd use whatever he discovered as a bargaining chip to get Toby to open up about IDD – neat.

'Well done, Hugo,' said Marcus as they climbed into his chauffeur-driven Bentley. 'He doesn't suspect a thing.'

'Well, he had no reason to, did he? You acted exactly as if you were looking to make an investment.'

'As indeed we might,' said Marcus. 'Stranger things have happened. And who knows – when we do our due diligence, we may even find the money for the IDD shares has been "borrowed" from the company.'

Ah, thought Hugo, so that was the game.

'Now – back to the office, and please write up those notes by close of play today.'

'I'll do the notes, but I have to go early tonight, if that's OK.'

'Surely you've finished with your little black girl? Don't tell me you've found another young lady already. I don't know – you young chaps.'

It crossed Hugo's mind that Claudia would have a fit at being referred to in such patronising tones. He would have loved to see her lay into Marcus in the same way as she'd done to him at the speed-dating event.

'No, it's not that – it's my leaving drinks at Pearson Malone.'

'What – you have leaving drinks even when you've been fired?'

'I wasn't fired – I resigned,' said Hugo, annoyed. 'I can hold my head up, however much those bastards would prefer me to slink off with my tail between my legs. I've walked straight into a plum job, and I intend to show them what's what.'

Marcus smiled at this outburst – he'd only been joshing.

'You can tell them you're doing very well, too. Yes, of course you can go off a bit early – it wouldn't do at all to miss your own leaving drinks. I should say it would be a major faux pas.'

'Yes,' agreed Hugo. 'It would.'

'Now, take it easy won't you,' cautioned Marcus. 'I need you in bright and early in the morning.'

Hugo had no intention of going overboard. For the first time in several years, he looked forward to coming into work in the morning. Why undo his early success by acting the goat?

It struck him now that the very same attributes which had led to his downfall in Pearson Malone were highly cherished outside the stuffy confines of the Big Four accountancy firm. An enquiring mind, independence of spirit and an ingenious approach to problem-solving had all been regarded with suspicion in an environment where preordained procedures reigned supreme. At Umbra there were no such constraints, so Hugo shone. And the icing on the cake was a salary he could live on with ease.

He stretched out in the comfortable limousine as Marcus produced a Scotch from the in-car drinks cabinet.

'Don't worry,' he said. 'I'm sure you'll find another girl soon.'

'I'll drink to that,' said Hugo.

As they clinked glasses, Hugo realised he hadn't thought about Julia all day. He was definitely on the mend.

Two-thirds of the way through the Rodrigues list, Claudia ground to a halt. The public companies were easy – plenty of information online. But Rodrigues was also a director of several small private companies, or *limitadas*. There was much less data available about these, but even so, Claudia managed to piece together the salient facts for most of them.

But when it came to a company called Perpetua, she

had only found an embryonic website – little more than a blank page, no press commentary, no advertising. In fact, she found no clue anywhere online to what this company was about.

Frustrated, she went back onto the website where she'd found the director search. A company profile report would cost £395. Claudia winced – under the *Globe*'s expenses policies this was well above her limit to authorise. And she didn't fancy getting Bill's agreement.

She stewed for a while, before whipping out her credit card – Hugo would have been proud of her. Claudia had an intuition about Rodrigues, and she would to follow it through to the bitter end, even if it involved spending a hefty chunk of her own money.

53

Hugo strolled into Belushi's in Covent Garden a few minutes after six, more than satisfied with the day's work. Charlie was already propping up the bar with a few of his nerdy tax colleagues, and had opened up a tab in Hugo's name. Hugo handed his credit card to the barman in exchange for Charlie's – a simple act in his new-found prosperity.

Over the next hour fifty or sixty people drifted in, including – to his astonishment – Stephanie, her blonde hair bouffed up to within an inch of its life.

'I didn't expect to see you here,' he said.

'You shouldn't have invited me then.'

Hugo didn't think he had.

'I'm surprised you came – you never liked me.'

'Well, I felt I should give you a bit of a send-off all the same, show there's no hard feelings.'

She made no attempt to deny her dislike, though.

'No hard feelings on my part either – you'll have heard I got a new job already.'

'Yes, congrats – how's it going?'

Not that she cared.

'Great so far – loads more autonomy than working for you, and a lot less red tape.'

'Good,' she said, with a brittle smile. 'I hoped you'd find a position more suited to your talents.'

Bollocks. She'd hoped he would end up selling the *Big Issue* outside Blackfriars station. Still, what did any of it matter now? He could afford to be magnanimous. He'd progressed to greater things while Stephanie was still in the same place.

'Let me get you a drink,' he said, and ordered himself another pint as well – his fourth.

'I must circulate,' he said, handing Stephanie her glass of wine. 'See you later.'

'Of course,' she said, not wishing to prolong the discussion any more than he did.

He moved across the room to Christian Temple, who was considerably more effusive in his greetings.

'Tremendously glad you found yourself another job so quickly. I knew it would all fall into place for you. Your father will be delighted.'

Guiltily, Hugo remembered he hadn't kept his father abreast of recent developments. They'd last been in contact when he'd asked the old man to help him escape from Brazil, and even then he'd been less than forthright. He really should get in touch with him now, if only to pay back the money his dad had lent him for the Rio trip. Still, all that could wait until the morning.

Hugo finished his pint and excused himself to go the loo. He swaggered past his former colleagues. Since joining Umbra, he'd undergone somewhat of a transformation in their eyes. No longer could they classify him as a loser – he was a man of substance, a hedge fund yuppie.

He was also quite drunk. He should pace himself out if he was going to keep his word to Marcus. Still, it was early yet, and one more pint wouldn't hurt.

As he emerged from the Gents, someone rammed him sharply from behind. His arm was twisted in a vice-like grip – a prank by Charlie and his friends, obviously.

'Now look here lads...'

They rammed his face up against the wall.

'What the...?'

They grasped his hand tight and he found himself unable

to move it when he tried. The back of his hand smarted for a second, like a bee sting – then they released him.

He spun round, but his attackers had disappeared, lost in the heaving crowd by the bar. There were plenty in the room Hugo hadn't seen before. Too bad all these freeloaders had crashed his party... If a chap couldn't even go for a pee without being molested...

Instinctively, he reached for his wallet. Relief washed over him as he found it still there. Perhaps they'd been interrupted while trying to rob him. Ah well – no harm done. He dusted himself down and sauntered back to the bar.

'Anyone for another drink?' he cried.

The relief morphed into something else – a euphoria which swept over his whole body, setting it on fire as a tidal wave roared in his ears.

'Are you OK, Hugo?' someone shouted, but they were far, far away on the shoreline. His heartbeat pounded in his head ... so loud... The beer – my God – so strong, stronger than me ... out of control ... room spinning ... out of control ... oh bugger...

An uncontrollable tide of vomit spewed onto the bar, as he lunged towards it for support. But too late – the floor rushed towards him, swallowing him up. And then, oblivion...

54

Across town, Claudia hung out with friends in a bar where the building pulsated to the loud music. She'd come out tonight in an effort to forget about Hugo, and so far she'd succeeded, if only because the noise made all meaningful thought impossible. Then her mobile vibrated in her pocket.

She checked the caller display, hoping it wasn't Bill.

Hugo! She shouldn't answer – mustn't answer. On the other hand... Unable to resist the urge, she rushed outside.

'Hi Hugo,' she said breathlessly. 'What? What – I can hardly hear you...'

Even outside, the music precluded a normal conversation, but she quickly gathered it was Charlie calling from Hugo's phone.

'He's what? What did you say?'

She walked along the street to a quieter place.

'In hospital,' Charlie told her. 'It's serious – touch and go whether he makes it. I know you two have split up, but I had to call you.'

Panic rose.

'What the fuck's happened to him?'

'Do you have any idea what he might have taken?' Charlie was frantic.

'What do you mean?'

'He's overdosed.'

Oh Christ, no. It was all her fault.

'Drugs – what drugs does he do?' said Charlie, on the verge of hysteria.

'I've never seen him take any drugs. Anyway, why ask me – you've known him forever, haven't you?'

In normal circumstances, Claudia might have taken umbrage at the insinuation that Hugo had acquired some terrible drug habit under her influence. But Claudia's world had just suffered a seismic shift – for once, she had more to worry about than being insulted.

'I don't know, it was only an idea. I'm sorry.'

'Don't hang up,' said Claudia, desperate to learn more.

She struggled to visualise Hugo hovering on the cusp between life and death. A few days earlier they'd been sitting in the sun drinking wine – both of them with decades of life stretching before them. Now Hugo's life might be ebbing away.

'Honestly, if I knew, I'd tell you. I never saw Hugo do any drugs,' Claudia repeated.

'Well, it was only a long shot – he might have taken up some different habits since he met you. They say it might be cocaine, and well, all people in the media do coke, don't they?'

Claudia was so shaken she let that jibe go as well.

'He's going to be all right, isn't he?' she said. 'Isn't he?'

'I don't know,' said Charlie, a sob in his voice.

'Which hospital are you at?'

'I'm not sure – I came with him in the ambulance.'

She heard him ask someone.

'St Thomas'.'

'I'll be right over.'

'There's no need.'

'I said I'll be right over.'

She rang off.

Stupid bloody Hugo.

Claudia fervently wished she could turn the clock back – if only they hadn't had that last silly argument. She would have let him off, told him she loved him, if she'd been

261

able to predict this. But that wasn't how the world worked – if they hadn't rowed, it wouldn't have happened. This was all her fault.

So what if he was after the loucura papers for money – what was wrong with that? He'd spent a load of cash he didn't have in taking her to Rio, and hadn't grumbled when the trip proved to be fruitless. Now she might never have the chance to make it up to him.

She stuck her chest out and practically threw herself in front of the first cab which came by, to the immense annoyance of people who'd been waiting longer.

'This is an emergency,' she said, in tones which brooked no argument. 'St Thomas' hospital, please.'

Halfway there a shocking thought hit her. If Hugo was still after the loucura papers, then chances were this was no accidental overdose.

55

'He had to go, he was on to you – you said so yourself. It was only a matter of time. '

'Yes but, I didn't think...'

'You help me and I help you, right? That's what we agreed.'

'He will survive, won't he? You've only knocked him out for a while – teach him a lesson?'

'There was enough cocaine in that shot to take out an elephant. But why should you care? You didn't even like him.'

'Yes, but he's a human being. I'm sure it would have been possible to reach a settlement with him.'

'Maybe, but would you be prepared to take the risk? This way you don't have to worry about that. You don't have to worry about anything. Goodnight.'

56

The doctors were still trying to stabilise Hugo when Claudia arrived at the hospital. Charlie stood outside the building, smoking a cigarette. His jacket was spattered with vomit and his face streaked with tears.

'I didn't know you smoked,' she said.

'Only in extremis. I took them out of Hugo's pocket.'

He offered one to Claudia, who shook her head.

'What happened?' she asked. A livid scratch ran across Charlie's cheek.

Apparently, Hugo had been fine – well-oiled in a Hugo-esque kind of way, but in much better shape than he'd often been. Then, without any warning, he'd gone berserk – vomiting, howling like a dog, clutching at his chest, before collapsing and going into seizure. When Charlie had tried to help him, he'd lashed out wildly.

'Jeez – have they found out what it is yet?'

'A massive cocaine overdose – confirmed. They're giving him a sedative to bring down his pulse rate, but he already had two cardiac arrests in the ambulance – it was scary, but they managed to pull him back from the edge. The paramedics found the syringe in the toilets.'

'Hugo – mainlining cocaine?'

'I know, I know. It's hard to understand,' Charlie agreed. 'Could those people at Umbra have led him into bad ways?'

'I doubt it – he hasn't even been there a week.'

'Well, whatever – he's been really silly this time.'

It shocked Claudia that Charlie was so quick to judge Hugo harshly – she felt both sad and angry that Hugo's

264

closest friendship appeared to be so shallowly rooted.

'I wish I'd been a more caring friend to him,' Charlie went on, oblivious to the offence he'd caused. 'I should never have let it come to this. You know, Marianne had even persuaded me to ask him to move out. Mind you, I never guessed he'd sink so low as drug addiction.'

'Where is Marianne, by the way – will she be coming over soon?'

'No, she has a big meeting on tomorrow – needs a good night's rest.'

Marianne's indifference towards Hugo came as no surprise, but the reluctance to support her fiancé ought to have given Charlie pause for thought. If she was this self-centred before they'd even married... Still, it was none of Claudia's business.

'There's another explanation for what's happened to Hugo,' she said.

'I can't imagine what,' said Charlie with a sigh.

'Obviously not.'

Her acid tone surprised Charlie.

'You sound as if you're annoyed with me.'

'Do I?'

'Why yes, but I don't understand – it wasn't as though I encouraged Hugo to take those drugs.'

'You seem so sure Hugo did the drugs on purpose – why can't you give him the benefit of the doubt?'

'So what's your theory?'

'Attempted murder,' said Claudia.

'Oh, that's ridiculous. Look, I can see you're anxious to believe the best of poor old Hugo, but really. I mean, who would want to do away with him?'

'How much has Hugo told you about loucura?'

'More than enough – he's been obsessed with it ever since he was fired from PM. I should have seen there was something looming then, he was getting ridiculously paranoid – told me two people had died over it. Must have been the drugs all along.'

'Suppose it wasn't paranoia.'

'Surely you've not bought into all that nonsense as well?'

'Actually, I have,' said Claudia. 'And I hope to God Hugo isn't the third man to die.'

As she spoke, she came to understand Charlie's scepticism. Her talk of murder sounded melodramatic even to her own ears.

'Loucura was your story in the first place and you're still a picture of health,' he pointed out reasonably. 'How do you account for that?'

'Possibly because I haven't got anywhere near proving it. But maybe Hugo's had more luck. Look, has he said anything about what he's doing at Umbra?'

'Not much, no – he waffles on about evaluating investment opportunities and how it's all mega confidential. Frankly, I think whatever he's doing is deadly boring and all this mystique is to glam it up a bit. Why do you ask?'

'I reckon he's been trying to prove the loucura story.'

'For Umbra – why?'

'They're a hedge fund, you dork – with information on a cancer cure they can rake in a shedload of money.'

Charlie was not used to being called a dork, and it showed.

'Even so, I can't believe someone would want to kill Hugo. Besides, whoever did it would have to have been at the party – and that's impossible.'

'Did you know everyone who was at the bar?'

'Well, no – there were a lot of people there I didn't recognise. You can never tell who half these madcap corporate finance people are at the best of times. Even so, you have to admit, it's far more likely Hugo took the drugs himself.'

Poor Hugo – it didn't matter what happened to him,

everyone always assumed the worst. Charlie took Claudia's hand as her eyes filled with tears.

'Hugo's strong,' he reassured her. 'He'll pull through. He must have the constitution of an ox to have survived some of the drinking sessions he's been on.'

True – but they hadn't led to cardiac arrests.

'Have you told his parents?'

'Yes, all done – less unpleasant coming from me than the hospital. Though as it happened Hugo's old group head had beat me to it. He's a friend of Hugo's dad, you know.'

'Really,' said Claudia. The old boys' network had struck again.

'They're stationed in Madrid at present,' continued Charlie, 'but they'll be on the first flight back in the morning.'

Claudia hoped it wouldn't be too late.

They sat waiting in silence, watching the second hand on the clock – one minute, and another, and another, and another – five minutes, another five – half an hour – an hour – another hour... After what seemed an eternity, the consultant appeared.

'You're with Mr Fleming, aren't you?' he asked. He looked as though he'd had a rough night as well.

'Yes,' said Charlie. 'How's he doing?'

'Well he's not in great shape, but we've managed to stabilise him for the time being.'

Thank God.

'Can we see him?' asked Claudia.

'I'm afraid not. He's in intensive care, and unconscious – under sedation.'

'Is he going to be all right?'

'Too early to say. There may have been some bleeding on his brain, but we can't be sure until we run the tests. Renal failure is also a possibility. He's on a ventilator at present. On the positive side his heartbeat has settled nicely, and we've managed to lower his temperature. He's a strong healthy young man so his chances are better than they might be otherwise. It's simply a question of waiting I'm afraid – no short cuts.'

'I see,' said Claudia, choking back the tears. 'How long will he be unconscious?'

'We don't know. All the alcohol he's drunk hasn't helped – cocaine and alcohol are a pretty toxic combination. And if he gets through this, it'll be vital to focus on the longer term future. Frankly, the prognosis isn't hopeful unless he kicks the cocaine habit.'

'Hugo doesn't take cocaine,' said Claudia firmly. 'I'm sure somebody tried to kill him.'

'It's very loyal of you to stick up for your friend, but terribly misguided.' The doctor peered at Charlie sternly. 'In fact, for future reference you should bear in mind it's most unhelpful if you don't tell us what your friend has taken. We're not here to judge, you know.'

'But, but...' Charlie spluttered, but before he could say any more, the doctor had wandered off to deal with the next patient. To him, Hugo was merely another bratty rich kid with a destructive drug habit.

57

Claudia was loath to tear herself away from the hospital, but realistically there was nothing she could do to help Hugo. And skipping work would only provoke Bill's wrath.

'Well, look what the cat's dragged in,' he said as she rolled up five minutes late for the morning editorial meeting. 'Love the outfit, though.' He let out a wolf whistle.

Claudia had forgotten she was still wearing the gold leggings and shocking pink ra-ra skirt from the night before. Even by her own standards the outfit was outlandish.

'I can't handle this now, Bill,' she snapped. 'I've been at the hospital all night with a friend.'

No more was said, and Claudia more or less managed to hold herself together during the meeting, although she contributed nothing to the discussion. She put her mobile on vibrate mode in case there was any news, but it remained inert.

'It's Hugo, isn't it?' said Bill afterwards. She nodded, her eyes welling up with tears. Seeing how upset she was, Bill let it go at that and held back on his usual caustic anti-Hugo tirade. She didn't dare tell him what was wrong with Hugo – like everyone else, Bill would quickly draw the inevitable conclusion. But Claudia was now certain this was no Hooray Henry drugs overdose. Hugo had paid the price for his curiosity. And now she hoped to ascertain exactly what he knew that had put his survival in jeopardy.

She called Charlie on his mobile. He too had left the hospital.

'Any news?'

'No change last I heard – could be a while.'

'By the way, did you call Hugo's work to say he wouldn't be in?'

'Oh no – I forgot what with everything else. I'm not sure what the number is, but I can find out.'

'Shall I call them for you?'

'Oh, um yes, if you wouldn't mind.'

She cut Charlie off and dialled the main switchboard for Umbra.

'Can I speak to Marcus Cunningham, please?'

'Who's calling?'

'I'm Claudia Knight, a friend of Hugo Fleming's. I must speak to Mr Cunningham urgently.'

Marcus took the call straight away.

'Miss Knight. If you're calling to say that Hugo has a hangover and won't be in, I'm absolutely not impressed. He's only been working here for four days, and we're on quite an urgent deadline. For heaven's sake – what kind of a state must he be in if he can't call me himself?'

'He's in hospital in a coma,' she replied.

This silenced Marcus for a moment.

'My God – some hangover. What was he drinking? Tequila slammers?'

'It's not a hangover,' said Claudia.

'Road accident?'

'Not that either. Look – it would be easier to talk this through in person.'

'Why?'

'Because it's a very sensitive matter.' Claudia chose her words with care.

'I do have a very busy diary.'

'Yes, and so do I, but this is important.'

'I understood that you and Hugo were finished.'

How the freaking hell did he know that? It was hard to see Hugo dissecting his love life with his boss of four days.

'That's irrelevant. I simply must speak to you.'

Curiosity got the upper hand and Marcus arranged to see Claudia at the Audley at twelve-thirty. She'd be gone for at least two hours and Bill would go mental, but she would worry about that later. She certainly didn't intend to ask permission in advance.

'I guess I'll have no difficulty in recognising you,' said Marcus.

Presumably, that meant he knew she was black. She wondered how.

'I guess not.'

The line went dead.

If Marcus was behind all the killings, she might be walking into a trap. And after Hugo's experiences, she couldn't even conclude that she'd be safe in a crowded bar. No matter – she'd have to take the risk.

She was on the verge of leaving when her e-mail pinged – the Brazilian company profile had arrived. She printed it out and stuffed it into her bag, before grabbing her jacket.

Unfortunately, there was no way to leave without walking past Bill.

'Where do you think you're going young lady?'

'I'm going to meet a contact.'

She smiled sweetly and scuttled off towards the exit before he could ask any questions.

Marcus waited on one of the U-shaped leather benches by the window. He spotted her as soon as she came in, wearing what looked like fancy dress. In the civilised ambience of the Audley, she resembled an extra who'd walked onto the wrong film set. Was she trying to make him a laughing stock?

Hoping to God he didn't run into anyone he knew, he

waved at her to come over – there was no way she'd be able to pick him out from the other grey suits in the bar. As it was, some of them gave him shocked glances as Claudia sat next to him. He dreaded to imagine what they thought.

The girl's figure-hugging outfit left little to the imagination, and when she smiled she flashed a row of perfect white teeth – she certainly knew how to draw attention to herself. Hugo was handsome, but didn't have much pizzazz – how on earth had he managed to land such a stunner?

Marcus steeled himself – it would be all too easy for this siren to throw him off his guard. Journalists were dangerous, and exotically glamorous ones doubly so – he mustn't loosen up for a second.

'So, Miss Knight, to what do I owe the pleasure?'

He would disarm her with his politeness, the same tactics he'd employed with Julia Fraser in Geneva.

'Please – call me Claudia,' she said. 'Can we talk about Hugo?'

'Ah yes – poor hungover Hugo. How's he doing?'

'He's not hungover,' said Claudia. 'Besides, I didn't think you cared.'

Marcus was used to respect – he winced at the sharpness of her rebuke.

'Of course I care. I was shocked by the news, that's all. Can I get you a drink?'

'I'd prefer to go for a walk, if you don't mind.'

Marcus groaned inwardly. Really – this girl was impossible. It was embarrassing enough being seen with her in the pub, let alone having to walk down the street with her.

'I do mind,' he said. 'We're staying here – it's unlikely anyone has bugged this booth. Now, what will you have to drink?'

He'd started off decisively enough – all he had to do was continue in the same vein.

Marcus returned from the bar with Claudia's Coke – a little girl's drink – and a Scotch for himself.

'So – what's so urgent? And what's up with Hugo if it's not a hangover?'

'Hugo's suffering from a massive overdose of cocaine.'

Ah – that figured. Hugo had a drug problem which Marcus, for all his due diligence, hadn't managed to uncover.

'I'd never have credited it. He looks a clean living young man to me – partial to a drink, but who am I to talk?'

He slurped at his Scotch, as though to reinforce his point.

'Hugo doesn't do drugs,' said Claudia. 'Someone gave him the overdose – someone tried to kill him.'

'What? Are you sure? Were you there?'

He tried hard not to sound alarmed, but even so his voice quavered.

'I wasn't there, but we're not talking a quick snort of a line or two – the paramedics found a syringe on the floor. Hugo was injected deliberately.'

'He might have injected himself,' said Marcus – any explanation more palatable than attempted murder.

'He could have, but I'm certain he didn't.'

'I'm not sure what this has to do with me. If you believe he's been attacked, surely it's a matter for the police...'

'I think this has a lot to do with you,' said Claudia. 'Or, at least, a lot to do with what you two are working on.'

'Hugo's work is confidential,' said Marcus, 'especially where journalists are concerned.'

'It's about loucura, isn't it?'

So Hugo had broken his promise. Marcus had never been entirely comfortable about his commitment to confidentiality, but to go blabbing to this girl quite so soon was beyond the pale – not to mention the lies he'd told about splitting up with her.

'Hugo's work is confidential,' he repeated. 'I had hoped he'd respect that.'

'Oh, he did. He didn't say a word – that's why we split up. But I'm smart – I worked it out.'

He looked at Claudia – she met his gaze, straight as a die. Though perhaps this merely showed the depths of her cunning.

'Oh, did you?' he said. He didn't know what to believe now.

'Suppose he got a bit too close to the truth,' Claudia suggested. 'Now, if you would tell me a little about the line of enquiry you two are pursuing…'

Marcus noticed a modest flutter of the eyelashes. He was ninety-nine percent sure this was a set-up. Hugo must have told her more than he should, and now he was laid up with a humdinger of a hangover this opportunist minx was trying to scare him into giving her information with some cock-and-bull story about a murder attempt. And she'd had the nerve to tell him he didn't care about Hugo.

'Then lo and behold, the next day it's all over the front page of the *Globe*. Do you think I'm dim-witted?'

'I'm beginning to wonder,' said Claudia. 'Either you're thick or a murderer. At least two people have died because of loucura. Doesn't that worry you at all?'

Marcus had never been called stupid before – even the infant school teacher who'd whacked him over the back of his legs with a ruler had respected his intellect.

'There's no way you will get one iota of information from me about Hugo's work.'

'Well, in that case,' Claudia went on, 'we can let this play out very differently.' She folded her arms and stuck her chin out defiantly. Marcus reminded himself she was only a little girl with silly clothes and ridiculous hair – nothing to be scared of. And yet his palms were sweaty.

'Meaning what exactly?'

'Meaning an in-depth exposé about insider trading in a hedge fund.'

She had no dirt on him – this was yet another tactic to scare him into spilling the beans.

'Are you threatening me?'

'Only if you choose to interpret it that way.'

Marcus shrugged.

'I'm not worried – if you print lies about me, you'll find yourself on the wrong end of a lawsuit, young lady.'

'So can I quote you as denying that Umbra has been involved in insider dealing?'

'You may not quote me on anything, Miss Knight. I don't care for either your tactics or your tone and I shall be complaining to your editor. How dare you try to get information out of me on such a shabby pretext? Now, if you'll excuse me, I'm meeting someone for lunch, and I'm hoping you'll be out of here by the time he arrives.'

Claudia's eyes blazed with anger.

'There is no pretext. Hugo is in a coma – seriously ill. It doesn't appear to bother you someone may have tried to kill him because of what he was doing for you. I mean – what happens if he dies?'

'Well, I'll have to manage without him in that case, won't I?' he said in his most deadpan voice.

'God – you're so heartless and cynical. I hope they murder you as well.'

She rushed out of the pub without saying another word, leaving Marcus more bruised by the encounter than he cared to admit.

A residual anxiety gnawed away at him. It would be an easy matter to verify whether Hugo was in the hospital, and what was wrong with him. But what if the girl's story was genuine? What was the likelihood of Hugo injecting himself with cocaine? He didn't seem the type. Was there a chance he and Hugo were closer to the answer than they'd envisaged?

Right now, Claudia's threat to expose Umbra worried

him more than his physical safety. Bodyguards were parasites, feeding on rich men's paranoia, and he could afford them if he deemed it necessary. But there was no protection from the hogwash journalists manufactured. These days, even business journalists did no more than whip up public hysteria. All the little people were baying for the blood of anyone who earned a decent living, tarring them with the brush of greed. But which of those people would have the balls to go out and take risks to create money for themselves? None – they all demanded risk-free returns.

It was little people who were greedy, buying flat screen televisions on credit and trying to rise above their little lives. Little people clogged up the roads – little people caused wars and recessions. The one redeeming feature of little people was that their existence enabled big people like Marcus to profit from their greed.

Marcus drained his Scotch and went to the bar for another.

58

Claudia boiled over with rage. The man was a creepy slimeball. Bill play-acted, Hugo moved in restricted social circles, but Marcus made her flesh crawl with his sickening combination of desire and revulsion. Clearly, her blackness automatically made her an object of suspicion in his eyes and he would never accept that she wasn't trying to hoodwink him. But that didn't mean that he'd won. She owed it to Hugo to determine if and why someone had tried to kill him, and now she knew exactly where to start the search, especially as Marcus's prejudices seemed to justify a less than ethical approach to the problem.

The snooty receptionist at Umbra greeted her with frosty disdain, but Claudia wasn't fazed.

'Hi,' she said, with supreme confidence. 'I'm Claudia Knight. We spoke earlier on the telephone.'

The girl's icy facade thawed instantly.

'Ah yes,' she said, 'Hugo's friend. How is he?'

She might be suspect, but Hugo melted the hardest heart.

'He's in a bad way.'

'Oh, what a shame. We were all so sorry to hear the news. He's only worked here for a few days, but he's already a big hit with all the girls.'

I bet he is, thought Claudia sourly.

'Actually, we're having a small collection to send him some flowers. I don't suppose you know which hospital he's in?'

'I do,' said Claudia and told her.

'Am I allowed to ask what's wrong with him?'

'They're not quite sure,' Claudia lied. 'They're doing a load of tests.'

'Oh dear, and he looked so healthy as well. I do hope he's on the mend soon.'

Taking advantage of the rapport they'd built, Claudia moved swiftly on to her real purpose.

'Hugo asked me to pick up some work for him and take it to the hospital.'

The woman was hesitant now, astute enough to realise that she shouldn't let just anyone poke around the office.

'Mr Cunningham said it would be OK,' Claudia went on. 'He said he wasn't having Hugo slacking off because he was in hospital, and asked me to come and pick up the stuff.'

Claudia easily pictured the callous Marcus saying exactly this, and evidently so did the receptionist.

'If Mr Cunningham has requested it, then it's fine. I didn't realise. He isn't in at the moment, unfortunately.'

'Pity – I'd have loved to have said hi to Hugo's new boss,' said Claudia, adding a neat little final touch to her deception.

She prayed the woman wouldn't call Marcus on his mobile to confirm, but she needn't have worried – her story had been swallowed without question.

'I'll buzz Hugo's secretary to show you where to go.'

Hugo's secretary was a hard-bitten redhead of indeterminate age. She had much more on her mind than questioning Claudia's motivations.

'Here's the key to his drawer – leave it on the top of the desk when you're done.'

'Thanks,' said Claudia, amazed at how effortlessly she'd gained access to Hugo's confidential papers.

Knowing Hugo's slipshod ways, she was surprised to find the desk drawer locked. Perhaps that meant there was something of value in it. She scooped up Hugo's notebook, some lists and a memory stick. She vacillated over the laptop – it was unlikely she'd be able to hack into it, but if Hugo had been asking for his things, it would seem odd not to take the computer. She waved cheerily to both the secretary and the receptionist on her way out – fingers crossed they wouldn't get into too much trouble.

How much time would she have before the theft was detected? Marcus would be at least an hour at lunch, but it was too much to hope that no one would mention her visit once he returned. Marcus would do his nut, and get straight on the blower to Bill, who would also go berserk. In the circumstances, it wasn't wise to go back to the office.

She called in and told one of the secretaries she was ill, then headed towards the nearest Tube station to go home.

The trains were running late and there was quite a crowd on the platform. People tutted as Claudia pushed to the front. Too bad – she didn't have the time to wait her turn patiently.

She'd successfully thrust her way up to the yellow line when a violent shove from behind threw her off balance. For a split second she teetered on the platform edge, confident she would conquer this unstable equilibrium. By the time she'd figured out she couldn't, she was lying on her back in a pit between the tracks. The crowd let out a collective gasp then fell into a stunned silence. Claudia glanced upwards to a sea of horrified faces peering over the edge of the platform.

The world stood still – until she detected a rumbling noise, faint and distant at first, then gradually louder. The tracks rattled. Only one word went through her semi-paralysed mind – oh shit, shit, shit!

'Sound the alarm,' someone shouted. 'There's a girl on the tracks!'

'Grab my hands – grab my hands,' came another voice from the platform.

'No – stay put, or you'll fry,' said someone else. 'We're going to turn the power off.'

Claudia couldn't have moved in any case – she was frozen with fear.

The rattle in the tracks faded, then died as the train glided to a halt, coming to rest about six feet from Claudia. A man appeared beside her.

'Are you hurt – can you get up?'

It was a good question. With some help, Claudia pulled herself to her feet. Her ankle hurt when she put pressure on it – was it broken? No, only a slight sprain. A pair of hefty arms pulled her back onto the platform, where she stood, shaken by the brutal jar of the attack. A warm liquid trickled down her temple. She wiped it away with her hand – blood, lots of it. There were some tissues in her bag – oh my God, the bag! Incredibly, it was still over her shoulder, with contents intact. A woman held a handkerchief to her head, and led her to a seat. She plonked herself onto in it, her whole body trembling.

'Somebody tried to kill me,' she said.

The witnesses were agreed – Claudia had brought it on herself. After all, she'd been seen forcing her way across the crowded platform to the front.

'Let this be a lesson to you,' said an officious London Underground man with a walrus moustache, who peered at her over the top of his glasses. 'Next time you might not be so lucky.'

Physically, the damage wasn't too severe – the ankle was bruised but functional and the bleeding out of all proportion to the insignificance of the cut on her head. Mentally, the damage was harder to assess. But whatever they were saying,

Claudia knew this had been no accident – and whoever was after her was unlikely to quit trying. She wouldn't be safe until she'd exposed the truth.

Meanwhile, where should she go? They knew where she lived and she still had sound reasons for staying away from the office. The answer was some anonymous hotel where she could lie low, but she couldn't check in resembling a bag lady.

She remembered she still had the keys to Hugo's flat. She wouldn't be safe there for long either, but she'd be able to have a quick wash and smarten herself up.

'Are you sure you're fit to continue with your journey?' asked the transport official, interrupting her train of thought.

'Yes – yes, I'm fine thanks.'

A train was approaching – she didn't even care where it was headed. By now, she was desperate to escape from the claustrophobic gloom of the Tube station and the curious stares of the people around her. On her own, in the fresh air, she'd be fine. She staggered on board and clung onto a pole for dear life, dazed and clammy.

After a shower, Claudia's state was much improved. She rubbed the dust off her leggings and pulled on one of Hugo's T-shirts – not exactly glamorous, but less sinister than a bloodstained, grimy top.

Next, she called the hospital, and just about collapsed with relief as they told her Hugo was out of the woods. They wouldn't know for sure until he regained consciousness, but the early signs were promising. Reassured, she turned her mind to the papers she'd taken from his office.

Hugo's organisational skills were woeful – it was the devil's own job to decipher his handwriting, let alone attribute any meaning to the words. Bill would have hauled him over the coals for such sloppy research.

For starters, the insider dealing TM Technology connection had her flummoxed. How could Hugo seriously suggest some tie-in with Hubbard? Either it was a leap of logic too far for her, or total drivel – she suspected the latter. But it wouldn't do to dismiss the theory out of hand – there'd been an attempt on both their lives after all.

The nominee companies were a bugger too. Unwittingly, she followed in Hugo and Richard's footsteps – nothing doing. Finally, she turned to Hugo's typed notes on TM.

At first sight, Hugo's jargon-laden business waffle seemed irrelevant. But as she skim read, a name jumped out at her – Peter Dick. She knew Peter Dick and so did Hugo, but he probably didn't realise it yet.

At least the mystery of the insider dealing had been solved.

59

'This is serious, Wayne.'

Brad had once more grown tired of his enforced starvation and they revisited the diner. But the news of the attack on Hugo distracted him from his food.

'There must be a reason why someone tried to kill this Fleming character,' Brad said.

'The guy's a total pain in the ass – isn't that reason enough? And you said yourself he was a loose end.'

Wayne had already identified Hugo as one of those people who habitually left a trail of devastation in his wake and consequently had little sympathy for him.

'Didn't you think that Hugo was working on something different from IDD?'

He had, but now the reports of Hugo's near demise appeared to contradict this.

'It seems like there's more of a connection than we envisaged.'

'How so?'

'Far as we could tell,' said Wayne, 'they had an idea that these people at TM were trading IDD shares on inside information.'

'Who are these TM people again?' asked Brad. He tentatively took a mouthful of steak. 'Do we know them?'

'No – they've no connection with the drug industry. But somebody there has the inside track on Project Acorn and a whole bunch of people have piled into IDD shares.'

'So what?' said Brad. 'What's that got to do with loucura?'

Relaxing now, he took a forkful of fried onion rings and a swig of beer.

'There's a connection somewhere, but we're not seeing it yet.'

'Are you sure this dumb ass didn't overdose?'

'I'm not sure of anything, but you know I don't believe in coincidences...'

'What about the girl, the journalist? You been keeping tabs on her as well?'

'We're working on that angle,' said Wayne. Annoyingly, the cunning vixen had given them the slip, but he wasn't going to mention that to Brad.

'I have to find out if Fleming was getting close to those papers,' said Brad. 'Then maybe we can grab them for ourselves.'

'My team are doing their best,' said Wayne.

'Well, their best evidently isn't up to scratch. Any chance of you taking a trip across the pond?'

Wayne was unenthusiastic. The mission was pointless – even, and particularly, if the documents did hold some earth-shattering facts, they must have been copied by now. So Brad would never be able to hide them away. Still, there was no use in arguing – Brad was a man who insisted on getting his own way, particularly when he was paying for it.

'OK, I'll go.'

'Great stuff,' said Brad. 'And if you can't get the documents, don't bother coming back.'

And people told Wayne he was brutal.

60

Peter Dick hadn't attended Hugo's meeting at TM Technology, so chances were Hugo hadn't made the connection yet.

Claudia only knew by chance – when she'd chatted to him at The Dorchester, she'd asked what 'Pod' was short for.

'It's my initials,' he'd said.

'Isn't Stephanie's surname Clark? Or is she one of these feminist women who kept her own name on marriage?'

'Actually, she worried that she'd be ridiculed – how would you like to be called Dick in the macho world of corporate finance?'

Claudia had smiled and agreed she wouldn't.

So the innocuous looking Pod was the missing link. But would the sweaty little nerd have the bottle for insider trading, let alone murder? And while Stephanie was a cold-hearted bitch, Claudia couldn't see her as a killer either. And then there was Hugo's cock-eyed logic – where did this all fit with Hubbard? There were too many unanswered questions for Claudia's liking.

Claudia's mobile rang – Bill. Not picking up would only aggravate matters. She sincerely hoped Marcus Cunningham hadn't been in touch.

'Where the hell have you been? We've been running round like headless chickens without you.' Bill was as irate as Claudia had ever heard him. 'First of all you go swanning off without warning and then I get a message you're taking the rest of the afternoon off. What's going on? Something to do with Hugo, at a guess.'

Despite Bill's fury, Claudia relaxed a little. If Marcus had been in contact, he'd have mentioned it by now.

'I left a message – I'm not well,' said Claudia. If it hadn't been true when she'd left the message, at least it was semi-true now.

'Don't lie to me,' said Bill.

'Seriously, I feel crap. I was up all night because of Hugo and this afternoon I fell over and cut my head.'

'You drunk?'

'Oh please – do I sound as if I'm drunk?'

'No – you sound as if you're skiving. Now I want you in here tomorrow morning without fail.'

'Not my turn to work Saturday.'

'Let's call it payback for this afternoon,' was Bill's sharp rejoinder.

Claudia returned to the puzzle of the insider traders. Why should there be any connection with Hubbard's death? Was it the same reasoning again – that Hubbard's killer was someone who stood to lose if the IDD takeover failed? Or was there a more sinister explanation – was Marcus leading Hugo down a blind alley for some mysterious purpose of his own?

For Claudia's money, the answer still lay in Brazil. But if Hugo had been on the wrong lines, why had someone tried to kill him? And why had someone tried to kill her for following in his tracks? None of it added up.

Right now, she didn't have the luxury of hanging around to work it out. It was only a question of time before they ran her to ground. She caught sight of Hugo's car keys on the kitchen counter – a car might be useful, particularly with her sore ankle. She picked up the keys and bundled all her belongings, including Hugo's papers, into her bag.

Charlie walked in the door as she was leaving.

'What are you doing here?'

'Needed somewhere to go – I'm off now.'

He eyed the Elastoplast on her head with suspicion.
'What happened?'

'Oh, nothing – I fell over, that's all.' She jangled the car
keys in front of Charlie. 'Is it all right if I borrow Hugo's
car? It's an emergency.'

'Where are you going?'

'After the loucura story – where else?'

'Isn't that rather dangerous if your theory about Hugo
is correct? Wouldn't it be more sensible to call the police?'

Even without knowing about the incident on the
Underground, Charlie was right. He was always right about
everything – that's why Hugo found him so irritating. But
contacting the police was out of the question. Technically
she'd just committed an act of theft from Hugo's office,
which Marcus might well have reported.

'So it's OK if I borrow the car?'

'I'd prefer it if you didn't...' Charlie said.

But it was too late for objections – she was already out
of the door. Plan of action – buy some overnight gear and
check herself into somewhere they'd never think to look.

The keys sported a BMW logo. Claudia walked along
the street blipping the remote control, until the lights
blinked on a red 3 Series. Predictably, Hugo's car was top
of the range, with leather seats, satnav and lots of other
bells and whistles – an emblem of his mindless materialism.
No wonder he was broke.

The tyres screeched as Claudia blasted off, leaving a
protesting Charlie waving vainly in the distance.

61

Hugo gazed around him in blurry-eyed bewilderment. This was the worst hangover ever.

Something stuck in his throat made him gag.

'For heaven's sake,' someone said, 'call the doctor. He's coming round.'

The voice reminded him of his mother. As his vision cleared, he saw it was his mother, red-eyed from crying, his father beside her.

Someone removed the gag from Hugo's throat. He focused with alarm on the whole panoply of medical equipment beside him. God – this must be serious.

'What happened?' he croaked. His larynx felt as though someone had run a cheese grater over it.

His mother rushed forward to take his hand and soothe his brow.

'Now you mustn't worry, Hugo,' she said. 'Everything's fine.'

Nothing was fine. First, he had this real corker of a hangover. Second, he was in a hospital. Third, his parents had flown across Europe to be by his bedside. And fourth, he had no idea how he'd come to this sorry state.

'Water,' he cried feebly. 'Water.'

'We'll ask the doctor when he comes,' said his mother. 'You might not be allowed to have any.'

Not allowed water – how weird was that? He attempted to sit up, but failed to even lift his head off the pillow. A consultant appeared and shone a light into Hugo's eyes.

'How are you, Hugo?'

'Terrible – utterly dreadful. Can I have some water please?'

Hugo drank three glasses in succession – water was the traditional enemy of hangovers, after all.

'Do you know why you're here?'

'Here? You mean in hospital?'

'Yes, here, in hospital.'

'No I, um, don't know. I must have had way too much to drink.'

In front of his parents he'd normally claim he'd had two pints of beer, which had gone to his head, but such a story wasn't credible now. He had never landed up in hospital before.

'Hugo,' said the consultant, 'you've overdosed massively on cocaine.' Hugo's eyes flitted from the doctor to his parents. There was a sadness in their eyes he'd never seen before.

'Cocaine? I never took cocaine in my life.'

'I'm afraid the blood tests told a different story,' said the doctor, 'although we didn't find any evidence that you habitually inject yourself.'

'I injected myself?'

'The syringe was found by the paramedics.'

'I hate needles – I couldn't have...'

'Hugo, it would be better to own up,' said his father with weary resignation. 'We're only trying to help you.'

Jeez – was it really possible he'd become a raving drug addict overnight?

A tsunami of panic washed over him, as a half-buried memory emerged into the daylight. He clutched the doctor's arm.

'They tried to kill me,' he said. 'They did.'

His parents looked at each other and then towards the doctor for reassurance.

'Episodes of paranoia are a common by-product of cocaine

poisoning,' the consultant pronounced, carefully extricating his arm from Hugo's grip. 'It doesn't necessarily mean there will be ongoing mental health issues.'

He wasn't mad, he wasn't – no matter what they said.

'No, no – trust me. I'm not making it up.'

'Of course not,' agreed his mother. But her fearful little glance at his father betrayed her disbelief.

Charlie would have the facts at his fingertips.

'Where's my phone?'

'It's with your wallet and other things,' said his mother.

'You can't use it in here,' said the doctor. 'Sorry.'

Hugo's father's watch said 8.00 a.m. – sure Hugo felt incredibly rough, but not so much groggier than a nasty hangover. All in all, he wasn't sure why the hospital had encouraged his parents to fly over, or even why he'd been brought into hospital in the first place. A couple of Alka-Seltzers would fix him up and he'd be able to drag himself into work. Marcus would never know about this ridiculous cocaine business. But something bothered him – his parents had arrived very quickly from Madrid.

'How long have I been asleep?' he asked.

'Since Thursday night,' said the doctor.

'What day is it today?'

'Saturday, dear,' said his mother.

Hugo sat bolt upright with shock, before the weakness reclaimed him and he sank back into the pillows.

'I've been asleep for a more than a whole day!'

'Unconscious, in a coma, would be a more accurate description,' said the consultant, as he continued his examination. 'I'm afraid you've been in a very bad way. You're lucky to be alive – a majority of cocaine overdoses of this magnitude prove to be fatal, especially combined with so much alcohol.'

'Fatal?' echoed Hugo, in alarm.

'Don't worry – you're going to be fine. We're going to

run a few more tests, but chances are you've sustained no lasting damage – this time, at any rate. You're a very lucky young man.'

He swept out of the room, leaving Hugo still trying to understand what had become of him. He didn't feel lucky – quite the reverse. Fragments of memories came back to him – leaving drinks, Stephanie, going to the Gents, panic, and then a blank. And somewhere within his incomplete recall, there was the chilling certainty that someone had tried to kill him – and they hadn't finished the job.

'They did try to kill me – they did,' was all he could say, over and over.

'I know, how dreadful,' his mother said, putting her hand on his forehead. 'Don't worry, darling – you're safe now.'

She humoured him as if he was a three-year-old frightened of monsters under the bed – but these monsters were real.

'No, no I'm not safe,' he said. 'I'm so not safe.'

'Look, why don't I get the doctor back,' she said. 'He can give you a pill to make you sleep.'

'I've been asleep for too long already,' said Hugo irascibly.

He wished his parents would stop exchanging their stealthy looks.

'Please get some rest, Hugo,' said his father. 'When you're a bit stronger, we can consider rehab – there are some first-rate places...'

'Dad – I know you won't listen, but I do not need to go into rehab.'

'That's what they all say in the beginning,' his father replied. 'But trust me, son, it's best to face up to your problems.'

Hugo was too enervated to argue, and what was the point? His parents had already written him off as a druggie.

'We'll leave you in peace now,' said his mother. 'We'll be back later on this afternoon.'

Hugo watched his parents leave, his father's arm

protectively over his mother's shoulders. Then, despite having recently woken from a long, long slumber, he drifted off once more, the memories of bogeymen receding as he slipped back into unconsciousness.

In the afternoon he woke again and forced down a light lunch. Afterwards, he remembered he'd been planning to call Charlie, and sweet-talked one of the nurses into letting him use his mobile.

Marcus had left a voicemail message on Friday afternoon. It was brutal and succinct, informing Hugo that he was fired forthwith and he'd be hearing from Umbra's lawyers about the return of the £10,000 signing-on fee. It was a bit over the top for missing one day of work, but not really surprising – Marcus wasn't a man to take prisoners. So, to add to all his other problems, he was unemployed again.

Charlie was delighted to hear from him, though.

'Your mum called earlier and told me you'd come round,' he said. 'How are you?'

'Pretty crap, since you ask,' Hugo admitted.

'Do you remember what happened?' asked Charlie.

'Don't you know? I mean you were there, weren't you? It was my leaving do.'

'So you don't remember?'

'No, nothing – though I have this awful feeling someone tried to kill me. But no one believes me.'

There was an ominous silence at the other end of the line.

'They said you must have been shooting up in the toilets – they found the syringe,' said Charlie in the end, his voice without emotion.

Charlie's lack of confidence in him totally deflated Hugo. First his parents – now his best friend. What hope was there for him if those closest to him had no faith?

'Oh Charlie, please – not you as well. You know I don't do drugs.'

'Well, I've been trying to stick up for you with your parents and the doctors and everyone,' Charlie said defensively. 'But it's hard to argue against the evidence. Anyway, it doesn't matter now – you're on the mend and that's what's important.'

'How can you say it doesn't matter that someone tried to murder me? It matters to me.'

'But who would want to kill you?'

'Those bastards at BEP, that's who. They've already killed at least two people.'

Even as he said it, Hugo couldn't help thinking how much this must resemble the paranoia of a cocaine comedown.

'Oh Hugo, no – please don't talk this rubbish.'

'Why will no one listen to me?' said Hugo in despair.

'Actually, there is someone who agrees with you.'

'Who?'

'Why Claudia – who else?' said Charlie.

'You spoke to her?'

'Only to ask her if she knew what you might have taken. But she was so sweet – she came to the hospital and stayed all night, even though you've split up.'

Claudia was a kind person in many ways, Hugo thought sadly. If she could shake off her appalling attitude, the pair of them might have stood a chance.

'That's nice,' said Hugo. 'I'll call her – tell her I'm fine.'

'I'm not too sure where she is,' said Charlie. 'I got her mobile number from her work this morning, but they haven't seen her since yesterday – her boss is spitting fire. Apparently she was supposed to be in the office this morning. She's not answering her landline, either.'

'When did you last see her?' asked Hugo, suddenly apprehensive.

'Yesterday evening, when I got back from work – she was round the flat. She borrowed your car and set off God knows where, said she was going to nail this loucura story.'

Claudia wasn't insured to drive his BMW, but this was neither here nor there.

'So she hasn't come back?'

'Not that I've seen. Look, I did my best to stop her – it was very inconvenient because I was planning to borrow the car myself to ferry your parents around. I've had to get taxis everywhere and it cost...'

Hugo cut Charlie off – he hadn't the slightest interest in these trivialities.

'Has she been in touch?'

'No.'

'Did she say where she was going?'

'No – not a word. Except that she was after the loucura story.'

'Why didn't you ask her?'

'Look – I'm not responsible for the actions of your girlfriends and ex-girlfriends.'

'No, but all the same...'

'Well, I'm sorry,' said Charlie. 'At the time, I obviously didn't realise it was important – but I did warn her it might be dangerous. Anyhow, she's been away for less than a day – there's no cause to get alarmed.'

'Oh isn't there? Honestly Charlie, you're completely useless as a friend.'

Hugo rang off, seething with rage at Charlie – for not believing him, for failing to look after his car, and worse, for failing to look after his friend. Charlie had changed since Marianne had stuck her claws into him, and it wasn't an improvement.

Hugo tried to call Claudia himself, praying that she would answer. The phone went to voicemail. He texted her – no response. As a last resort, he dialled her landline at the *Globe*.

'Claudia Knight's phone,' was the terse response.

'Could I speak to Claudia, please?'

'Who's calling?'

'It's Hugo.'

There was a sharp and audible intake of breath, then silence, followed by a rapid stream of abuse.

'You've got a bloody nerve calling here. And you can tell your girlfriend if she doesn't get her arse in here in the next hour, she is fired.'

'Who are you?' asked Hugo, although he had a pretty good idea.

'Bill Gordon – her boss.'

'Ah yes – sorry to bother you. I only wondered if you knew where Claudia was.'

'Oh you did, did you? You called on the off chance that she might have found a few minutes to drop into work in between ministering to your complicated life? I take it you've recovered from whatever tragic affliction laid you low.'

'Well, I thought...'

'Don't think – it's a dangerous activity for a moron like you. She flounces off yesterday afternoon, leaving us all in the lurch big style. And what does she do with her unauthorised afternoon off? Only a spot of breaking and entering – into your office. So I've had your boss breathing down my neck and threatening to report me to the Press Complaints Commission.'

'That's hardly my fault,' said Hugo, managing to squeeze in a few words. 'I was unconscious.'

It did however shed some light on why Marcus was so mad at him.

'I don't care whose fault it is – it's a mess, and you can tell your girlfriend she has terminally screwed up. I can't imagine you're going to be too popular at work either.'

'I would tell her, but I don't know where she is.'

'The hell you don't,' said Bill before slamming down the phone.

It took Hugo a few moments to recover from Bill's invective. What was it he'd said about Claudia breaking into Umbra's offices? Fearing the worst, he called Marcus on his mobile.

'Which part of my message did you not understand?' said Marcus. 'You are fired.'

It sounded pretty final, but an effort at conciliation had to be worth a shot.

'Look, I'm sorry I missed yesterday – I was rushed into hospital on Thursday night and I was unconscious until...'

'Don't give me that crap,' said Marcus. 'Credit me with a bit of intelligence at least. The reason why you're fired is not because you had a hangover or a drug problem – hell, we're all human. It's because that sneaky little journalist girl of yours bluffed her way into the office and took all the stuff you've been working on. You promised me you wouldn't say a word to her – promised me. How can I work with a man whose word means so little? Confidentiality, Hugo, is the bedrock of our business. I hoped you'd learnt your lesson after what happened at Pearson Malone. Well, more fool me. You are terminated, fired and I'll be suing you for your signing-on payment, unless I receive a cheque by return.'

Without further ado, Marcus rang off.

Hugo flopped back onto his bed, drained and dispirited. None of this augured well. Someone had tried to kill him, Claudia had stolen his notes, and now she'd disappeared too. And the worst of it was that Hugo had no idea why any of this had happened.

62

Claudia came to with a start on a bed in a darkened room. Her head throbbed viciously, as if after a lively party. She winced as she tentatively probed a sinister lump at the epicentre of the pain. What the hell had happened? She remembered nothing since setting off for a stroll after dinner at the Heathrow hotel she'd checked into. How long had passed since then?

She hauled herself up and staggered around, bumping into random items of furniture as she blindly searched for the light switch. Once she found it, she screwed up her eyes against the unaccustomed glare.

Slowly, she took in her surroundings. To judge from the windows high up on the wall, this was a basement in somebody's house. There were two doors – one firmly locked, the other leading to a small shower room with a toilet. The sheer joy of emptying her overstretched bladder momentarily buoyed Claudia's spirits. Then reality kicked in.

The bathroom mirror reflected the shocking image of a face caked with dried blood. The cut from her fall on the Underground had opened up again and possibly the lump had bled too – her hair was too matted to tell. Clearly, she'd been knocked out, but had they meant to kill her or not? Common sense suggested not, or they'd have finished the job.

Claudia looked round for escape routes. Apart from the locked door, sturdy metal bars – designed, ironically, to keep burglars out – blocked the window. No doubt about it – she was trapped. They didn't mean to starve her, though – when she opened the door of a small fridge in the corner, she found it well-stocked with basic food and bottles of mineral water, suggesting that they planned to keep her alive, at least for a while. She cried out, her voice resonating in the sparsely furnished room, but nobody came.

The thought of food nauseated her, but she gulped down a whole bottle of water. Why were they keeping her here, she wondered. Why hadn't they gone right ahead and killed her as they'd tried to do on the Underground? Was it even the same people behind this?

All Claudia could do now was wait, but with no clue to what she was waiting for, terror gripped her. They're not going to kill you, they're not going to kill you, she repeated to herself like a mantra – but she wasn't convinced. She switched on the TV as a distraction, but only one channel worked, showing back-to-back reruns of an old sitcom. She found out it was 11 p.m., still Friday evening – useful information – but the feeble humour did nothing to drown out the scary voices crowding into her head.

Rescue looked unlikely, mainly because no one yet knew she was missing. Bill would be livid if she didn't show up in the morning – but only on Monday would fury turn to worry. The hotel might query why she hadn't checked out, but not until Sunday. Her parents might become concerned on Wednesday or Thursday if she hadn't called. And her friends? Well, who could say? And anyway, how would any of them have a clue where to look?

Then there was Hugo – in a coma. And even if he came round he wouldn't be able to figure it out. He was still sniffing round the false trail of insider dealing. Besides, there was no reason for him to even bother. He'd made it quite plain he didn't give a damn about her now.

There was no hiding from reality – Claudia's situation was hopeless. Utterly dejected, she sat down on the bed and sobbed.

63

Hugo woke on Sunday morning feeling considerably brighter, and with a strong compulsion to find Claudia.

As he tucked into breakfast with the beginnings of his normal enthusiasm, an inspired and useful idea popped into his mind. His car was fitted with a tracker – its exact location could be pinpointed at any time. All he had to do was call the tracker company.

But his first priority was to get out of hospital.

'Not a chance,' the consultant told him. 'You're still very weak, and we still have a few more tests to run, including the psychological evaluation.'

'Don't you need the bed for someone more deserving?'

'Sorry, young man, but we can't let you go yet.'

'I must leave – it's extremely urgent.'

'You should have thought of that before you went on a major drugs binge.'

'For the last time!' Hugo suppressed the urge to shout. 'I am not a drug addict. Someone tried to kill me.'

'Which is why we would encourage you to have a chat with the psychologist, Hugo. Your continuing paranoia is concerning. Now, try to get some rest and I'll be back to see you tomorrow.'

Hugo lay back, exasperated by the Kafkaesque situation in which he found himself. There was nothing else for it – he would have to escape.

Hugo mapped out his departure with military precision.

He concealed the clothing he'd found in his bedside cabinet underneath his gown, and when the nursing staff were changing shifts he moved to implement his plan.

Theoretically, getting up should have been easy, now he'd been disconnected from all the drips and monitors. In practice, it was virtually impossible – his first attempt to stand in nearly three days left him clutching helplessly at the bed for support. Slowly, though, the dizziness abated and he was able to stagger across the ward before inching stiffly along the corridor to the bathroom. This was hardly the slick getaway he'd envisaged. And at any time, some well-meaning busybody might offer to help him, discover his hidden clothes and raise the alarm.

With some difficulty, he managed to dress – there was little trace of the successful hedge fund executive in his appearance now. His suit reeked of vomit and much of his shirt had been cut away by the paramedics. He examined his wallet – thirty pounds in cash, enough for a taxi home. Hopefully, it would be some time before anyone noticed his absence.

Wayne called Brad from his cell phone.

'Fleming's on the move. He's just left the hospital.'

'Checked out already?'

'No way – looks real furtive to me, as if he's on the run. Looks sick as well.'

'What about the girl?'

They'd lost track of Claudia a couple of days earlier and still hadn't picked up the trail. Never mind – Fleming was key now. It was Fleming who'd almost been killed because he'd got to the nub of the matter, and Fleming who was now back in the game. With luck, he would lead them straight to what they were searching for, and Brad would never be any the wiser.

'Fleming's our priority right now,' said Wayne, evading the question. 'He's in a taxi, and we're right behind him.'

'Good – now you guys mustn't let him out of your sight, understood?'

'Crystal clear.'

Wayne hoped, without any real conviction, that the next contact with Brad would be to report he'd found the documents. But Hugo looked rough – rough enough that he might collapse before he'd led them to their destination. He crossed his fingers as he swung out of the hospital car park on Hugo's trail.

64

'Your car is parked in Balham Grove, SW12.'

'No, no,' snapped Hugo. 'That's my address – I'm asking where the car is.'

'In your road, Mr Fleming,' the tracker man replied, implying that Hugo was a prize idiot without saying so directly.

'I was told the car had been taken.'

'Obviously not very far.'

A peek out of the window proved the point – his BMW was parked a short distance down the street. How had he not noticed it himself?

'Is there anything else I can help you with today?' The man's voice was laden with sarcasm.

'No, that's fine thanks,' said Hugo. He grabbed his spare keys and tottered towards the car.

His BMW was unlocked and undamaged, with the other set of keys in the glove compartment. Who said London was a hotbed of crime? He glanced at the petrol gauge – almost full. Then he switched on the navigation system.

Unsurprisingly, the most recent destination was Balham Grove, but the one previous was a Willow Farm, near Abingdon. Hugo felt a buzz of excitement. Yes, yes – it all fitted together. TM Technology was based in Abingdon – she'd stolen his notes and picked up where he left off. Though it was odd, because he didn't recognise Willow Farm as being one of the shareholders' addresses. And odder, she'd apparently returned safely.

Hugo called Charlie, who was staying over at Marianne's.

'Hugo, where are you? Your ma and pa are going berserk.'

'I'm at home,' said Hugo, 'but I'm off out later. And do not tell my mother. By the way, you might have told me that Claudia had brought the car back.'

'I wasn't aware that she had,' said Charlie. 'All well?'

'Amazingly, yes.'

'Well, perhaps now we've got a happy ending, you'll have the decency to apologise for blowing up at me yesterday.'

'Charlie – we have not got a happy ending. Claudia is still missing. She hasn't been to work since Friday morning and you were the last person to see her. Why do you imagine I left the hospital when I still feel like death?'

'That's what we've all been asking,' said Charlie. 'Everyone's terribly concerned about you – mainly about your mental state. You really should go back, you know.'

Charlie did have a point, as he often did, but Hugo was going to ignore his advice, as ever. Whatever anyone else said, Hugo knew his mind was working fine – it was the condition of his body which worried him.

He sent a text message to his mother.

'Sorry had 2 go – speak soon x'

It was as unilluminating as it was concise, and would hardly allay her fears.

The next step was clear – Willow Farm beckoned. Claudia had seemingly made it back to base, but by following her footsteps he might be able to deduce where she'd gone next. Yet even as he settled on this course of action, Hugo wondered whether it was perhaps just too obvious – was he walking into a trap? It might at least be sensible to see who lived at Willow Farm before setting off. Impressed by his own ingenuity, Hugo logged in on Charlie's desktop and laid out £3.25 for an online electoral roll search.

The result shocked him to the core.

65

Hugo sat, unable to move, dumbfounded by what he'd dug up. It was scarcely credible that Stephanie, the great stickler for rules, would risk her hard-won status and professional reputation for the sake of a million quid. Yet what other explanation was there?

And if Marcus's theory was correct, this meant Stephanie and Pod were also behind Hubbard's death. Much as he disliked Stephanie, Hugo couldn't see her as a killer, still less the ineffectual Pod. And much as Stephanie disliked Hugo, would she really resort to murder?

Yet, on reflection, these improbable scenarios tied up some loose ends. It had always puzzled Hugo how Hubbard's killer had got wind of his plans to go to the press. Easy – Stephanie knew because Hugo had told her. And naturally Stephanie had known where he'd be for his leaving do. But he still struggled to accept this analysis, especially when Claudia had evidently escaped unscathed from Willow Farm.

One quick call might clear this up, and he still had Stephanie's mobile on speed dial. After five rings it went to voicemail – how Hugo loathed that smug recorded message. He rang off, the task of phrasing a tactful enquiry beyond him in his enfeebled state. Fatigued, he lay on the bed and dozed off.

Within half an hour later, he was woken by his own mobile ringing. Still worryingly woozy, he hit the answer button.

'Hello Hugo – it's Julia here.'

Hugo nearly dropped the phone – was it really her, or was he dreaming? Immediately, he perked up.

'Julia, gosh – I didn't expect to hear from you ever again.'

'I had to call you Hugo. I'm sorry if I was a bit off with you when we last met.'

'No, I'm sorry – I shouldn't have barged in on you unannounced. You've nothing to apologise for.'

'Ah, but I do. The thing is, you were right about loucura. After you came to see me, I did some more research. I was as sceptical as anyone to begin with, but I do understand now there's a special feature in the molecular structure of loucura which could mean it has the ability to shrink tumours. So what you told me about George Hubbard seemed more feasible, and I dug around a bit.'

'What did you find?'

'Among other things, that BEP did lean on Morrison to produce the right results. And as you said, I couldn't possibly do business with such an unethical company.'

'So Project Acorn's off.'

'You bet.'

'And what else did you find?'

'Oh Hugo – you'll never believe who's behind everything, including Hubbard's murder.'

'Try me.'

'Stephanie and her husband.'

So it was true, after all.

'I, er, sort of thought it might be but...'

'Shocking, isn't it?'

Beyond shocking.

'She tried to kill me too,' he said, contemplating the scale of Stephanie's wickedness as he spoke.

'Yes, Hugo – I know. Are you OK now?'

'Not completely, but I had to leave the hospital – Claudia is missing.'

'That's the other reason I'm calling, Hugo – Claudia is safe. She's here with me. She's a bit shaken, but otherwise fine.'

'Thank God. That's fantastic news. What happened to her?'

'Stephanie was holding her hostage – I rescued her.'

'Really? Can I speak to her?'

'Yes – certainly.'

Claudia came on the line. Understandably enough she sounded less than ebullient.

'Hi Hugo – how are you doing?'

'I've been really sick, but I'm all the better for hearing your voice. How are you doing?'

'Fine, since Julia saved me.'

'What happened to you?'

'It's your bitch ex-boss, Stephanie – she took me prisoner, but Julia rescued me.'

'Thank God. I'm coming right over to fetch you.'

'It'll be fab to see you, Hugo. I hope you got your car back – I'm sorry I borrowed it.'

'Oh, that's no problem,' said Hugo. 'I'm pleased you're OK.'

'I'm apologising. I'm really, really sorry.'

'I said it's fine. Look, I'll see you soon, but can I have another quick word with Julia?'

He could sense Claudia's reluctance, but there were questions to be asked which seemed more important than her feelings.

'How did you find out?' he asked Julia when she came back on the line.

'I figured out that Stephanie and her husband had been trading in IDD shares. And naturally they were desperate for Project Acorn to go through because of all the money they had tied up in it. Then I found that you'd spoken with Stephanie about loucura and Hubbard.'

How, Hugo wondered fleetingly.

'But surely they wouldn't be desperate enough to kill?'

'I wasn't convinced either, but this morning I went over to Stephanie's house to confront her about the share dealing. She did a runner, but I found Claudia locked in the basement. She'd been there since Friday, poor girl – but so plucky, so brave. And then I knew for sure.'

'I wonder where Stephanie and Pod found the money to buy the shares,' said Hugo. 'They must have cost the best part of a million quid.'

'An excellent question,' said Julia. 'I went to see Toby Miller today, to address the matter of his insider trading. He was surprisingly forthcoming when I threatened to report him to the FSA. Pod apparently "borrowed" the money from the company. He might have got away with it, but once Hubbard was out of the way, they became greedy and bought more shares, and Miller found out the money was missing. So Pod confessed all and Miller, being a bit of a wide boy, said he'd let it go as long as he got his money back and Pod let him in on the trade.'

'Which accounts for the timing of Miller's share acquisitions.'

'Exactly,' said Julia. 'In fact, it was Miller's dealings which led me to Stephanie and her husband – otherwise I'd never have figured out who was hiding behind those nominee companies.'

How gratifying that he'd applied exactly the same logic as the intelligent Julia. Only one detail puzzled him.

'But Claudia came back from Willow Farm – my car...'

'No, she didn't. According to Claudia, Stephanie arranged to have the car brought back to you, so you'd spot the address in the satnav and immediately set off on the trail. Then she planned to get rid of both you and Claudia in one fell swoop.'

'She surely didn't think I'd be dumb enough to fall for

that?' said Hugo, mortified at how narrowly he'd avoided being duped.

'I'm afraid she did,' said Julia. 'She never had a high opinion of your intelligence. Of course, I never saw you being taken in by such a simple ruse.'

Ah, lovely Julia – she'd always believed the best of him.

'Shouldn't we tell the police?' he asked.

'Already done – I imagine they'll want to speak to you as well in due course.'

'I'm coming over right now,' said Hugo. 'What's the address?'

He scribbled down the location of Julia's Cotswolds cottage.

'OK. I'll be there in about two hours.'

'Excellent,' she said. 'Oh, and Hugo – the police have asked for all this to be kept quiet while they're after Stephanie and Pod. I shouldn't even have told you...'

What an honour to have been taken into her confidence.

'Oh, don't worry – I won't breathe a word to a soul.'

'Well done,' Julia said to Claudia. 'You could have been on the stage if you hadn't gone into journalism.'

Claudia didn't bother to reply. Who wouldn't have turned in a bravura performance with a loaded gun against their head?

Two thickset goons flanked Julia – Claudia recognised one from the Tube station. Quite why they felt they required three people to restrain a 110-lb girl was a mystery – she didn't have much fight left in her anyway.

'So Hugo's coming to see you,' said Julia. 'Isn't it nice?'

It wasn't nice at all. Hugo had fallen hook, line and sinker for Julia's spiel, as she'd known he would. There was no one as brainless as a man with a hard-on.

'Why can't you let me go?' pleaded Claudia. 'I promise

I'll keep quiet and I'm sure Hugo doesn't even realise – why involve him?'

'I can't afford to take the risk. What I intend to do will have huge benefits for mankind. I can't let two people ruin it for the world.'

Two lives to be sacrificed for many – in Julia's mind the moral equation had only one solution.

'Oh, don't worry,' said Julia, seeing Claudia's apprehension. 'You won't suffer – I'm no sadist. You'll drift into a deep, deep sleep and never wake up – a tragic drugs overdose. With Hugo's track record no one will suspect a thing.'

She flounced out of the room with her flunkies.

Despite Julia's assurances, Claudia was suffering now. The knowledge that this was probably her last day on earth consumed her whole being. Yet she still clung pathetically on to the one remaining shred of hope. In their short conversation she'd apologised twice to Hugo for taking his car. Hugo should therefore be able to deduce she was acting under duress. But would the clue be too subtle for Hugo in his present delirium? Whatever – for now, Claudia preferred to believe in miracles.

66

Bill's response to Claudia's disappearance followed a predictable path. On Saturday morning, he'd cursed her, tried to call her, and ranted and raved in the office before concluding that she'd thrown a strop and pulled a sickie. By God, there'd be hell for her to pay on Monday morning – there was no room for prima donnas at Globe Media.

Hugo's call on Saturday afternoon had rattled him, though. He had a hunch Claudia was still working on the loucura story behind his back. No one had been more dismissive than him of her suggestions of murder and skulduggery, but now he began to doubt his own judgement.

It would be overkill to report her absence to the police, but clearly some action was called for. He asked the IT department for access to her internet usage and e-mails. They dithered, then told him his request must be authorised at a higher level. He told them to hurry up, but wasn't optimistic about the outcome. Meanwhile, he pursued other lines of enquiry.

Having drawn a blank with her parents and housemates, his thoughts turned to Umbra. Marcus Cunningham's obnoxious blustering had got right up Bill's nose. Plus, Marcus must have been one of the last people to see Claudia before she'd vanished and as such was a prime suspect.

Information on Cunningham was sparse. Apart from a brief article about secretive hedge fund managers, all Bill had managed to find online was a mention of his recent attendance at a hedge fund convention in Geneva.

He asked Sam Turner, the business editor, if he knew anything.

'I've known Marcus for years,' said Sam. 'We've had some useful tip-offs from him in the past.'

'I had the impression he doesn't care for journalists.'

'No, but he likes me because I've given him some hot tips as well.'

'So you're friends with him?'

'Marcus doesn't have friends – his whole life is Umbra. He has useful acquaintances.'

'But he's useful to you as well?'

'To be honest with you Bill, I'm hacked off with Marcus. It's getting more and more one-sided with him – he's after all the latest gossip, but keeps the rumours he hears under his hat. Why are you asking, anyway?'

Bill filled him in on Claudia's disappearance, the Press Complaints Commission and the loucura story.

'Oh, loucura,' said Sam, rolling his eyes.

'You don't believe there's anything in it?'

'I shouldn't have thought so, but for Claudia's sake I did ask Cunningham, seeing as how it's his industry sector.'

'And?'

'He said he'd never heard so much as a whisper about it.'

'When was this?'

'The weekend we got the heads up on IDD and BEP.'

'Funny – according to Claudia, one of his people was in Rio right then talking to the main man on the loucura research team.'

'So he was lying to me?'

'Seems so, yes. In which case, isn't there a chance he knows more about Hubbard's death than he's letting on?'

Sam shook his head.

'You're wrong there. Marcus may be a liar, but he's not a killer.'

'Well, how about this?'

Bill produced a grainy photograph of a man and a woman sitting at a table in an unmistakeably intimate pose.

'Apologies for the quality – there are zillions of pictures of the European Hedge Fund Convention but only one with Marcus Cunningham in the background. I had to blow it up. Any idea who the woman is?'

'Oh yes,' said Sam. 'That's Julia Fraser – IDD.'

'That's what I thought. They look very cosy, don't they?'

'Well, they would wouldn't they? They're having an affair.'

'What! Are you sure?'

If Sam was right, this might explain a lot.

'Certain. You remember the night the stuff on the IDD takeover came through?'

Bill nodded.

'I went over to meet Marcus, see if he could authenticate. After much stonewalling, he kicked me out, said he had company coming round – female company. He wasn't at all anxious for me to acquaint myself with the lady concerned. So I figured, well fine, she's high profile – or even married to someone high profile. So being the nosy bugger that I am, I hung around to watch who went into his apartment building. It was Julia. Now you try telling me Cunningham wasn't aware of the takeover. And from what you say now, chances are he knew about loucura as well.'

'Where did the IDD tip-off come from?'

'A broker, but I don't see what it's got to do with loucura.'

'Claudia believed there might be a connection. Umbra is a shareholder in IDD.'

'I'd get into her e-mail if I were you,' advised Sam. 'Find out exactly what she was working on.'

Bill grimaced.

'I'm trying to, but IT are being obstructive.'

'Bet you we can get her password,' said Sam.

'How?'

313

'She has it written on a piece of paper in her drawer.'

'How on earth do you know that?'

'I saw it the other day when I was standing by her desk.'

They rushed over to Claudia's workstation to find the drawer locked.

'Facilities have spare keys.'

'They'll most likely be as anal as IT,' said Bill grumpily.

He was wrong, and five minutes later, Bill was scrolling down Claudia's inbox. An e-mail from Brazil jumped out at him from the crap. There had been many times over the years when he'd cursed the march of progress, but for now technology was his friend. He opened up the attachment.

'She's been after some info on a company called Perpetua.' He turned to Sam in amazement as he skim-read the attachment. 'You'll never guess who's a director of this company.'

'Marcus?'

'No – Julia Fraser.'

'Interesting,' said Sam peering at the screen. 'And who's this other director, Rodrigues?'

Bill clicked on a few more of Claudia's e-mails.

'Ah – she's been delving into his background too. Looks as if he's one of the team who did the research on loucura all those years ago. Now the question is this – why would Julia set up a company with Rodrigues?'

'No idea – but my money says Marcus has to be behind it.'

An inspiration zipped through Bill's mind.

'Could they be trying to do something with loucura?'

'If they are,' said Sam, 'they'd have to get access rights agreed by the Ministry of the Environment. Brazil is incredibly picky about research into natural products – bio-piracy and all that.'

'Is there any way we can dig deeper?'

'Through official channels – no.'

'Unofficially?'

'Leave it with me – I've got a contact. I'll see what I can do.'

Less than two hours later, when Sam reappeared with the news that Perpetua had indeed applied for access rights to research into loucura, neither of them was surprised.

'That bastard Cunningham must be involved in this,' said Bill.

'His name isn't on any of the paperwork.'

'He might be hiding his interests.'

'Why hide behind someone as high profile as Julia Fraser?'

'Perhaps he's using her name without her permission.'

'I suggest we confront Cunningham with the evidence.'

'He's a secretive bugger at the best of times,' said Sam. 'He'll shut up like a clam.'

'Call him.'

'No – I've got a better idea.' Sam checked his watch. 'Best to take him by surprise and watch his reaction. Marcus is a creature of habit, if nothing else – I'm ninety percent sure I know where he'll be this time on a Saturday evening, if he's not with Julia.'

'OK,' said Bill, 'but there's something I must do first.'

The latest revelations had done nothing to assuage Bill's concern about Claudia – he knew he'd never forgive himself if something awful had happened. Forcing her to go behind his back on a story she felt passionately about was poor management of the worst type. With a heavy heart, he rang her parents and then the police.

67

Sitting in the Audley at a discreet distance from their boss, Marcus's newly appointed bodyguards tensed as Bill and Sam approached.

'Good evening, Marcus. Not with your lady friend tonight then?'

'What are you doing here?' Marcus asked Sam, while eying Bill suspiciously.

'Just enjoying a quiet sociable drink with my colleague Bill. I believe you two have spoken on the phone.'

'Now look here – if you're trying to persuade me to withdraw my submission to the Press Complaints Commission, you can forget it. That little bitch's behaviour was disgraceful.'

What a cheek, to barge into his local pub on a Saturday evening and attempt to bully him into backing down.

'Yes, I'm sorry about that,' said Bill. 'She shouldn't have done it.'

'Sorry isn't enough. I'm entitled to protest.'

'Of course you are,' said Sam soothingly. 'That's not why we're here.'

'Then why have you come? I'm assuming this quiet sociable drink is a cover story.'

'Surely you're not going to refuse a drink if I buy you one?'

'Maybe not,' said Marcus, intrigued by the purpose of their visit, but at the same time still wary. 'Although, I wouldn't care to undermine my case with the PCC.'

'Oh, come on man – this is nothing to do with the PCC. We've been pals for years.'

'OK, a Scotch then – make it a large one.'

While Sam was at the bar, Marcus said to Bill: 'I hope you've torn a strip off that girl for what she did.'

'That's been a little tricky,' said Bill, 'seeing as how she disappeared right after visiting your offices.'

A chill ran through Marcus. He'd already confirmed Hugo's story – Claudia hadn't been lying after all – hence the bodyguards. And now this.

'You're joking.'

'I wish we were,' said Bill.

Sam returned from the bar with the drinks.

'Surely you don't suspect that I was implicated in her disappearance?'

From where Marcus was sitting, that was certainly the way it sounded.

'Why no, how could you think that?' said Sam.

'Although, something nasty has happened to Hugo, her boyfriend, as well,' said Bill pointedly. 'Were you aware?'

'He was my employee.'

'Was? He's not dead, is he?'

'No – I fired him.'

Marcus knew now he had acted in haste as far as Hugo was concerned. Along with all the new worries which now assailed him, guilt pricked at his conscience.

'The point is,' said Bill, 'we'd be interested to know what you and Hugo were working on.'

'I bet you would,' said Marcus. 'That's what that girl of yours was after. You're vultures, the whole bloody lot of you.'

'Whatever it was,' said Sam, 'it was plainly dangerous stuff – wouldn't it help you to share it?'

Marcus weighed up the merits of full disclosure versus non-cooperation, and remained silent.

'You met Hubbard on the day he died,' Sam went on.

Another veiled accusation, thought Marcus. Yet on

reflection, he had been rather too close for his own comfort to all these events. And looked at objectively, the evidence might be regarded as damning.

'Can I get you another drink while you're contemplating?' Bill suggested. Marcus had drained the first one in short order, as he'd reeled at the unexpected news about Claudia. Marcus nodded.

'Strictly between us,' he said to Sam while Bill was out of the way. 'Hubbard approached me with the information he had on loucura and we were due to meet, but he was killed before we had the chance. Ever since, I've been trying to get hold of the evidence and Hugo was helping me.'

There, he'd got it off his chest now, and the world was still turning on its axis.

'Where were you looking?'

'Well, it appeared that some people who'd been doing a spot of insider trading in IDD shares might have the evidence.'

'What made you think that?'

Marcus hesitated.

'Because obviously the existence of loucura would have a real impact on the value of the shares.'

Sam furrowed his brow – like everyone else, he clearly had reservations about Marcus's logic.

'Who are these people?'

'We don't know for sure,' said Marcus, 'but we'd tracked a lot of activity back to a company called TM Technology.'

Bill had by now returned from the bar with the drinks, and had overheard Marcus's last comment.

'I can tell you now, that wasn't the line of enquiry Claudia was pursuing,' he said.

'In the interests of mutual cooperation,' said Marcus, 'am I allowed to ask what was?'

'Well, let's kick off with this.'

With a flourish, Sam produced the photograph of Marcus and Julia.

'This is you and your lady friend Julia Fraser, looking very intimate together at the European Hedge Fund Convention.'

'Claudia got hold of this?'

Marcus was amazed – the photographers at the convention had only been interested in the big dicks. How had he been caught on camera?

'No – I did,' said Bill. 'But it's pertinent to her enquiry.'

Marcus didn't feel too comfortable with the way this was going. There was no reason why he and Julia couldn't be out publicly as a couple once the IDD deal was done and dusted – but until then, it was all a bit tricky. Ironically enough, at the point the picture had been taken there was nothing to hide anyway, since Marcus hadn't lured Julia to his room until the following evening.

'You told me you had no idea about the BEP offer for IDD. Tut, tut, Marcus – holding out on an old friend.'

'I swear to you, Julia did not say a word about the takeover,' he said, carefully avoiding a lie. 'Look, what is this? That girl said she was going to run a story about Umbra's insider dealing. Is that what this is about?'

'No,' said Sam. 'It's not. From what I know of Julia, I'd be amazed if she said a word to you about the BEP offer.'

Marcus relaxed. Sam at least was not out to get him. Even so, he was still apprehensive.

'Too damned right, she didn't. I was quite cross with her about it. I mean, we met in the first place because she'd asked to see me about our holding in IDD. And I was entirely straight with her about our intentions.'

Well, not quite entirely straight, but Sam would never be able to prove otherwise.

'I must say, in the photo you both seem very cosy for a friendly business discussion,' Bill observed.

'And I did spot her coming into your apartment block that Saturday night I came over,' Sam added.

'OK, OK,' said Marcus, holding up his hands. Honesty, or at least apparent honesty, was the best policy. 'We are having a sort of relationship – it's not serious. It only took off in Geneva – after that photo was taken, if you must know.'

'Only a fuck buddy,' said Sam, reiterating what Marcus had told him that night.

'Well, yes – exactly. Julia understands that my work comes first and I haven't much energy left for relationships. She's in the same position – we have fun together, that's all. I'm done with women who demand any more than that.'

Marcus asked himself why he had felt the need to disclose all this personal information to these two scavengers. He wondered whether maybe he was trying to convince himself that Julia wasn't after more from him.

'Did you mention Hubbard and loucura to her by any chance?' asked Bill.

'Why yes. I'm completely ignorant about biochemistry. I simply sounded her out, as someone in the business, about whether a simple cancer drug would be possible.'

'What did she say?' asked Sam.

Marcus was again seized with anxiety. Sam had a predatory look about him, as though he was moving in for the kill. Where, exactly, was all this leading?

'Now look here. I'm not answering any more of these damned intrusive questions, until you tell me where you're going with this. You were supposed to be explaining what your reporter was working on – so why's this become an interrogation?'

Bill and Sam looked at each other, as if exchanging some secret sign between them.

'How well do you know Julia?' asked Bill.

'Is this relevant? As far as I'm aware, relationships between consenting adults are not illegal, either here or in Switzerland.'

Enough was enough. He stood up to go, but Sam restrained him with a hand on his shoulder. The bodyguards stiffened again, ready to pounce.

'Do you trust her?' he asked Marcus.

'Of course I trust her – she's one of the most honest people I've ever met.'

But there must be some reason for Sam to ask the question. And some reason for the sliver of doubt which had suddenly penetrated his soul.

'I need another drink,' he said, sitting down again.

Bill went to fetch it, leaving Sam to continue the cross-questioning.

'Let's go back to loucura – what did she think about the concept?'

Marcus could now see that he'd overreacted. On balance, there was little harm in answering the question.

'She said it was absurd, but I told her I would prove it. If it was true, she was sitting on a gold mine – her IDD shares would be worth a fortune.'

'Yet you weren't aware of the IDD sale at the time?' said Sam, quick as a flash.

'Irrespective of the takeover,' snapped Marcus.

'And she'd never heard of loucura before?'

'No – I'm sure of it.'

'Let's say I can prove Julia lied to you, that she already knew all about loucura before you spoke to her.'

'Really?'

It didn't seem credible – what reason would Julia have to be untruthful? And yet...

'Yes. She was negotiating with the authorities in Brazil for the rights to loucura, under the bio-prospecting laws. And she'd set up a new company in Brazil – ninety percent hers and ten percent the original loucura team.'

Sam produced the profile of Perpetua. Marcus saw that its business was described as pharmaceutical research and product development – and that one of the directors was Julia.

'No,' said Marcus. 'It's impossible.'

It was perfectly possible – reluctant as he was to believe it. It was clear now who had reached Rodrigues first.

'A contact of mine in the Ministry of the Environment in Brazil just confirmed the negotiations,' said Sam.

'So what does it mean?'

'That she had her own plans for loucura? Maybe to create a synthetic version?' suggested Bill.

On reflection, it occurred to Marcus that perhaps this was not as disturbing as the other two seemed to believe.

'So she kept a new business venture under wraps – it's hardly the end of the world, is it? I don't tell her all about my business dealings – far from it.'

Marcus took up his Scotch and swiftly put it away. It was his fourth drink that evening, but he'd yet to take the edge off his sobriety.

'She must have been pretty sure about loucura to set up a new venture,' said Sam.

'Whereas she told you it was an impossibility,' Bill chimed in.

A fair observation – she hadn't merely concealed, she'd actively misled him.

'Tell us again why you believe the insider traders had the papers?' asked Sam.

Marcus faltered – this was the question everyone kept asking and now as he reiterated his logic once again he privately acknowledged that it didn't begin to hang together. The connection had been Julia's idea – and it had been Julia who'd recommended he hire Hugo. But why encourage him to search in the wrong place for information she already possessed?

'Julia's been feeding me a line,' said Marcus, suddenly seeing the light. 'While I've been scrabbling after these insider traders, she's been...'

He paused. What exactly had she been doing?

'Listen,' said Marcus at last. 'Everyone's always presumed that if Julia knew about what BEP did with loucura, she would walk away from the offer. Hell – I did. I was trying to get the proof in part so the transaction would be aborted. What if the assumption's wrong? What if I've got it totally arse about face?'

Both the newsmen regarded Marcus expectantly. He clicked his fingers.

'I've got it! She's planning to use the money from the deal to finance the new venture with loucura in Brazil. So it's essential that the takeover goes ahead.'

'Why bother?' asked Sam. 'If the transaction aborts, IDD could raise money on the market to develop synthetic loucura – she doesn't have to sell the company.'

'Julia prefers to be in charge,' said Marcus. 'She hates having to answer to shareholders and analysts. She gets off on this image of herself as a saviour of mankind. Already it frustrates her that she's had to give up the reins since IDD's flotation. This way she can be in complete control. It's perfectly logical that if loucura works she'd choose to plough her own furrow.'

'So you think it's all right, what she's done?' Bill suggested.

'No, I bloody well don't,' said Marcus, as the enormity of Julia's deception began to sink in. 'It's a fraud on the IDD shareholders, of which I'm one.'

'I don't see how it would work anyway,' said Sam. 'The software rights will go to BEP, along with the rest of the company. How can she develop the product without the software?'

'Do you really think she'd get hung up on such a minor detail?' said Marcus, irritated by Sam's naivety. 'If BEP sues, she threatens to expose what they did twenty years ago.'

'So would Julia have a motive to get rid of Hubbard?' asked Bill, now knowing the answer.

'Yes, I suppose she would,' said Marcus. 'If it became public what BEP did, she'd have to call the deal off or lose credibility. And since the money was key to her plans... Although, I still can't picture Julia as a killer – if she is behind Hubbard's death, she must be in this with someone else.'

'Yes,' said Bill, in a deadpan tone. 'We'd wondered if it was you.'

Marcus was so preoccupied with the question of Julia's guilt that he let Bill's insinuation wash over him. Julia – a killer? He defended her in public, but in his own mind he wasn't so sure. He saw now that only a person utterly devoid of feelings could have manipulated him with such brutal efficiency – a psychopath, perhaps. And in retrospect, he'd never been altogether sure of her – she'd simply been far too good to be true.

'Well, all this is very interesting,' said Sam, breaking the silence, 'but it doesn't take us any further forward in finding Claudia.'

'So I guess we have to leave it up to the police,' said Bill.

Marcus braced himself.

'No reason to mention any of this stuff to them,' he said.

'Naturally not,' Sam agreed, although Bill remained silent.

Where was Julia, Marcus wondered. She'd cancelled him at short notice the previous day and he'd had no word since. Not that he was particularly keen to confront her. This conversation had unsettled him. Once again, his instincts were working overtime, and he didn't much care for what they were telling him.

Yet murder aside, he harboured a grudging respect for Julia. She'd been very, very clever. If she succeeded with her designs, she'd be shafting not only the IDD shareholders, but the whole of the pharmaceutical industry.

On the other hand, Marcus didn't appreciate being shafted by people who were very, very clever, particularly people of the female gender.

It was time to hedge his bets.

68

So it was over, Hugo thought. Whether or not Stephanie had Hubbard's proof now seemed strangely irrelevant. Perhaps even Claudia would no longer be so eager to nail the story. Julia was truly amazing, though – who else would have been intelligent enough to get to the bottom of the whole dirty business so quickly?

Hugo had found it tough going away from the safe confines of the hospital ward. But after Julia's call he rallied, buoyed up by a raft of unrealistic hopes for the future. He easily rationalised away his vague guilt about Claudia – they were finished and he had no ties. Why shouldn't he look forward to seeing Julia? And besides, he was doing Claudia a big favour by picking her up.

He jumped into his car with a renewed energy and programmed the Cotswolds address into his satnav. In two more hours his life would be back to normal. True, he had some pretty serious issues to resolve, such as finding a new job and sorting out his debts, including Marcus's menacing demands for £10,000. But Hugo managed to put these depressing thoughts aside – he was alive and about to be reunited with the only woman he'd ever truly loved. Why, surely they'd be able to pick up where they'd left off...

At a discreet distance, Wayne and his burly sidekick Jeff followed Hugo. They'd tapped into Hugo's mobile and had listened with mounting incredulity at how easily he'd been duped.

'The idiot's walking into a trap,' said Jeff. 'Are we going to let him do it?'

'None of our business,' said Wayne. 'Our instructions are precise, and they don't include saving that moron from his own craziness.'

They had the loucura papers, but they weren't done yet. When Jeff had cracked the safe in Julia's Chelsea town house he'd found a whole lot of other stuff as well – paperwork on Perpetua, applications for access to loucura.

They'd scarcely left the house before Wayne hit the speed dial to Brad. Brad's response was short and sweet.

'Holy cow,' he said. 'We've been had.'

Hubbard's papers were now the least of their troubles. Julia Fraser had to be stopped.

Hugo had no inkling that he was being followed. Even if Wayne and Jeff had been rank amateurs he would have been oblivious to their presence. He was wholly consumed by the delicious anticipation of seeing Julia again.

The Sunday afternoon traffic was light leaving London and Hugo sped along the M40, slowing only to pay lip service to the speed cameras. He sang along to songs with corny lyrics on the radio – seldom had he felt in such high spirits. At precisely four-thirty he rang the doorbell of Julia's cottage.

She had never looked so radiant. She wore white linen trousers and a black sweater, with a string of black and white pearls. Her hair was tied back in a bandanna. Hugo became weak and giddy again at the very sight of her.

'Why Hugo! How lovely to see you – do come in. You would never know you'd been ill. You're a picture of health.'

Hugo doubted that.

'And you're more stunning than ever,' he replied.

She touched his arm with an immaculately manicured hand, her nails polished blood-red. Hugo leant forward – electricity surged through him as their lips touched.

'Oh Hugo – maybe later,' she breathed.

'Is this your place?' Hugo asked, looking around him.

'One of them, yes,' she replied.

It flashed through Hugo's mind that she was lying. He couldn't visualise Julia living here, with its fussy, tired furniture and mismatched ornaments. A vague unease pierced his elation.

'Shall we set off?' she said.

'Set off where? Isn't Claudia here?' His disquiet grew.

'No – she's at another cottage nearby. Stephanie will drive you.'

Stephanie had appeared behind Julia – holding a revolver pointed straight at him.

The unease instantly crystallised into fear.

'I don't understand. What the...?'

'Oh Hugo,' said Julia. 'You are really an incredibly imperceptive boy – sweet-natured and lovely to look at but so, so dumb.' At a stroke, the empathy and warmth had evaporated – her features were blank and calculating. For the first time, Hugo glimpsed the real Julia Fraser.

'But I thought...'

'Oh no Hugo, you didn't think – you never do.'

A clammy nausea took hold.

'You said...'

'That's your whole problem Hugo – you're so trusting. You always swallow what people tell you. Now shut up and get in the car.'

Hugo had often wondered why people allowed themselves to be corralled into cars at gunpoint. Why didn't they kick and scream and try to escape? Now he knew. He was a dead man, but prolonging life by an extra few minutes or hours still seemed a smart move. He went meekly, like a lamb.

'They're on the move again.'

Wayne watched through binoculars from their vantage spot along the road.

'They've got the poor bugger at gunpoint,' said Jeff. 'He looks scared stiff. Can't we do something to help him?'

'No way – we have to see where they're taking him.'

'Poor bugger,' said Jeff again. 'He's stupid, but he didn't deserve this.'

69

Hugo sat in the front of the car as Stephanie drove. Julia sat behind, poking the gun into the back of his neck.

'Don't try any tricks,' she said.

Hugo had relaxed now Julia had possession of the gun – she wouldn't shoot him, for sure. But Stephanie's features were set in a steely mask. Hugo had seen this look on her many times before, but now there was a worrying difference in intensity.

'It was bad luck you stumbled into all this,' Stephanie said.

All what, wondered Hugo. His mind was racing, yet he still couldn't fit together all the latest developments.

'Tell me – why risk your reputation for a million quid?' he asked Stephanie quietly. He waited for her to tell him to shut up, but she didn't.

'Why do you think?'

The answer should have been obvious all along, but he'd been so miserable at Pearson Malone himself, he'd never noticed the signs in Stephanie. Behind the ruthless, professional facade was a woman disillusioned with life, heartbroken by how little she saw her husband and kids.

'Because you hated the job so much.'

'You're more perceptive than I realised, Hugo. It must be all those drugs you take.'

She allowed herself a wry smile – Hugo smiled half-heartedly back. If she hadn't already tried to have him killed, he might almost have sympathised with Stephanie.

A couple of miles along the road, they turned off into

a quiet lane and stopped at another cottage, more imposing than the first.

'Nice place,' Hugo observed, as he walked with the two women towards the front door. 'This one of yours as well?'

'Shut up and walk,' said Julia. 'Your girlfriend is waiting for you.'

Hugo was once more aware of the gun – this time in the small of his back. Julia wouldn't shoot him, but now Stephanie was in charge again and she was a completely different proposition. He endeavoured to keep calm – panicking wouldn't help at all.

How do you escape when being escorted downstairs with a gun stuck in your back? Simple answer – you don't. Stephanie unlocked the basement door and shoved Hugo into the room, relocking the door behind him.

'I'll be back soon,' she shouted through the door. 'And don't worry – we won't kill you.'

Claudia sat on the bed, in the same defiant pose as at the speed dating.

'You useless piece of shit,' she said.

70

Claudia didn't hold back – her last illusions had been shattered, the embers of her hopes doused. To imagine she'd actually fallen in love with Hugo – she must have been insane. Now her frustration gushed out like soda from a shaken-up bottle.

Hugo sat still and took it, enraging her further.

'You should have made yourself clearer,' he said lamely, when the deluge of insults had dwindled to a trickle.

'Made myself clearer? I apologised for taking the car – you know I never apologise, anyone with the intellect of a retarded orang-utan should have picked up on that. But oh no – not you.'

'I was relieved you were safe. How was I supposed to guess that I should subject everything you'd said to a detailed textual analysis? Anyway, since you've such a low opinion of my brain power, you should have said something a bit less subtle.'

'Such as what? That crazy bitch you're so infatuated with had a gun held to my head. Come on, Hugo – I gave you a big clue and you blew it. Now we're both going to die.'

'But Stephanie said...'

'Yeah, yeah, yeah – she may even buy it herself, but Julia has other plans.'

'Julia wouldn't kill us,' said Hugo.

'Poor deluded Hugo,' said Claudia, spitting with rage. 'When will you figure it out? Julia is the villain in all this. And not only did I give you a clue, she did as well!'

'What was that?'

'I heard her say that Stephanie knew all about Hubbard because you'd told her. But Stephanie wouldn't have mentioned it to Julia unless they were working in partnership together.'

'You know, I did think that was odd,' said Hugo, casting his mind back to the conversation.

'Which makes you even thicker than I thought.'

Hugo ignored her jibes – clear thinking, not blind rage, was called for.

'There must be a way out,' he said, vainly trying the door.

'If it was so easy, why have I stayed here for two days? Take it from me, there is no escape. The one way out was you and you've loused up. Unless you happened to contact the police and tell them where you were going.'

'Well, no – Julia said . . .'

'There's the whole problem,' said Claudia, slapping her forehead. 'Men think with their dicks, not their brains.'

Hugo sat next to her on the bed – she moved quickly away, reclaiming her personal space.

'I don't get it,' he said. 'Is Julia somehow involved in the insider dealing? She owns twenty-five percent of the company already, you know.'

'Hugo, you really are thick.'

'Well, what about you?' he said defensively. 'What did she lure you here with?'

'Nothing – I checked into a hotel near Heathrow. I didn't think anyone had followed me, but they must have done. I went for a walk to mull over what I'd found and they knocked me out – next thing I knew I was here. And before that they tried to push me off the platform on the Underground.'

'Why?'

'Because I found out what all this is really about, and it's nothing to do insider dealing. Stephanie's caught in the spider's web as much as you are.'

'So who's the spider?' asked Hugo.

Claudia regarded him with scorn.

'Why Julia – you prat,' she said.

Hugo listened quietly as Claudia told him what she knew about Perpetua.

'So you believe that Julia plans to make the synthetic loucura herself?' he said at last. 'Is that why she had Hubbard killed?'

'Yes, congratulations – finally you've figured it out.'

'Wouldn't it have been more logical for her to let Hubbard go ahead and then pull out of the sale to BEP? IDD could have developed the synthetic loucura.'

'You don't get it, do you Hugo – you've a total blind spot where Julia's concerned. The woman is a nutcase – she craves global domination, a place in the history books. She can't get all that personal glory in a public company.'

'I simply can't accept that Julia has been involved in killing anyone,' said Hugo, loyal even in the face of all the evidence to the contrary.

'Hugo, she is a psycho bitch – trust me.'

'Well, it takes one to know one – look at that rant you just went off on.'

'I went off on that rant because you're useless,' she replied.

Hugo's uselessness had defined his life, but until now he had always assumed he had plenty of time to rise above it.

'How did they get on to you?' he asked, allowing her statement to go unchallenged.

'I'm not sure – they may have seen that someone from the *Globe* had been on the Perpetua website, or maybe the company enquiry people contacted them. What does it matter now?'

'It doesn't, I suppose.'

Realistically, none of it mattered any more.

'Look,' said Hugo. 'Arguing won't get us anywhere. And

this time neither of us can walk off in a huff. So I'll accept that I've been pretty useless so far, but no more. I promise you I will get us out of here.'

This was said with such determination that Claudia came close to believing him.

'In fact,' he went on, 'I've already got an idea.'

'What?'

'Well, they have to come down here sooner or later and when we hear the footsteps on the stairs, one of us can hide behind where the door opens and then spring out and surprise them.'

'Great,' said Claudia. If that was the most imaginative scheme he could come up with, they were doomed. 'I vote it should be you.'

'I'm surprised you didn't think of it,' he added.

'Yes, well I didn't have a clue what was happening, did I? And Julia only came the once when she phoned you.'

'Ah, but she came again when she brought me – you could have done it then.'

'Hugo – only you would come up with an escape plan and criticise me for not having carried it out earlier. And I hate to pour cold water over your gem of an idea, but there are two big muscular dudes here as well.'

'How do you know?'

'Because I saw them – they were with Julia the first time.'

'But not the second time?' said Hugo, loath to jettison his brainchild.

'No, not the second time, but I didn't realise that beforehand. All in all, Hugo, I have to say I don't have much faith in your grand scheme.'

'So – do you have a better suggestion?'

Claudia had to admit she didn't and while the most likely outcome of Hugo's plan was at least one of them getting shot, this wasn't much of a downside in their present predicament.

'In that case shut up and leave it to me,' said Hugo, in response to her silence.

'So we're just going to sit tight and wait?'

'That's right.'

For all the lunatic simplicity of Hugo's scheme, there was something about his cockiness which boosted Claudia's morale. For the first time since she'd been taken Claudia allowed herself some real hope.

'Footsteps – only the one set,' whispered Claudia, a few minutes later. 'Stephanie or Julia?'

'Julia – I'd recognise Stephanie's footsteps anywhere.'

He armed himself with a water bottle and flattened himself against the wall.

'That's it,' said Wayne, after there had been no sign of activity for half an hour or so. 'We can't just sit here and wait for developments.'

'So what do we do then? Charge in there?'

Wayne shook his head.

'No way. We need a more low key intervention. Let's call the cops – they can take care of it.'

'You told us she had to be stopped,' Jeff protested.

'She will be, and the beauty is it won't have a damned thing to do with us. There's a payphone in the village – let's call from there.'

'Yes, sir.'

Jeff put his foot down and they sped off.

71

As the door opened, Claudia flew at Julia like a dervish. Before she had chance to react, Hugo leapt out from his hiding place.

He faltered – he was loath to hit a woman, especially Julia. She cocked her gun and took aim. Swallowing hard, Hugo cracked the bottle against Julia's skull with all his might. She lurched from the force of the blow but stayed on her feet. Then she fired.

Incredibly she missed, but Hugo could delude himself no longer – adrenaline coursed through his veins. There was no time to lose – she couldn't miss a second time. A brute strength sprang up from nowhere as Hugo rammed her up against the wall.

'You bitch,' he said, slamming her head back against the bricks. She stared at him piteously as she slumped unconscious to the ground. The gun slipped from her grasp, clattering against the floor.

'Right,' said Hugo, pleased with his newly discovered pluck. 'We're out of here.'

They locked Julia in and sprinted up the stairs and out of the back door. A new grogginess overcame Hugo, but it had never been more urgent to make a move. At any moment, Stephanie or the two goons might appear.

They were unlucky. As they tore across the garden towards the fields at the back, the Bluto lookalike from IDD appeared from round the side of the cottage brandishing a gun. With hindsight, it had been idiotic to leave Julia's revolver behind in the basement, but there was no going back now.

Hugo sweated profusely as he gasped for breath, his throat still smarting from where they'd intubated him in the hospital.

'Run Claudia – run faster!' he rasped.

As if propelled by some invisible force, they vaulted over the garden wall. A shot rang out, missing Hugo by inches. They had to press on – Bluto mustn't be allowed to close in.

They landed in a grassy meadow and scarcely pausing, ran on. Hugo willed his feeble legs not to surrender, but the uneven terrain slowed their progress. Hugo glanced back – Bluto was gaining on them.

Every fibre of the muscles in Hugo's legs screamed in agony. His lungs felt fit to explode, but the normal limits of physical endurance didn't apply now – they were running for their lives.

'My ankle's killing me,' said Claudia.

'Run through the pain,' Hugo told her.

A flowering crop filled the next field, tangled and obstructive and as tall as Hugo. Yellow flowers showered them with confetti as they picked their way through. The crop would provide safe cover if only they could get far enough into the field. Agonising as their progress was, they mustn't stop now.

Bluto had gained considerable ground. He stopped at the edge of the field, knowing it would be madness to dive in there. Shots whistled past Hugo and Claudia – terrified, they threw themselves to the floor. They were hidden now and Bluto was firing blind. Hugo panted for breath. How many shots did a gun fire before it had to be reloaded? Six? Couldn't be – he'd heard many more.

The gunfire stopped. They crawled forward, inch by inch. Could Bluto see the crop moving? Hugo had no idea, but staying still wasn't an option.

Once free of the tangled foliage they bolted again, praying

they were out of Bluto's sight, past some farm buildings and into a barn. There they threw themselves into a pile of hay. They were out of sight, but audibly panting for breath – if Bluto came in they were sunk. And it wouldn't take Einstein to work out they were holed up in one of the buildings.

Claudia sneezed loudly.

'For God's sake shut up,' hissed Hugo. 'Do you want to get us killed?'

'It's the hay – it's driving my nose mad.'

Claudia hiccoughed strangely as she tried to swallow the sneezes. Footsteps came – Bluto's steps. They froze at the sound – the footsteps stopped. There was no way of judging how close Bluto was, but he didn't intend to leave. What was he doing?

They were no happier when they found out. Metal jarred against the concrete floor close beside them. Hugo shuddered.

'You can come out now or get this pitchfork through you.'

Foolishly, they stayed put. A searing pain shot through Hugo's hand.

'Jesus Christ!'

Bluto pulled the pitchfork out of the hay and unceremoniously unskewered Hugo's hand. He squealed in agony, like a pig being slaughtered. Surrender was undoubtedly the sensible option. They burst out of the hay pile with their arms in the air.

'Put your hands on your head and walk outside,' said Bluto, a man of few words.

Would Bluto shoot them here? In cold blood? Hugo's injured hand throbbed as blood leaked steadily onto the tarmac.

A rabbit ran across the farmyard. It seemed incredible that their own lives were over, yet the world would go on without them.

72

Hugo stood, mesmerised by the gun pointing towards him, deciding whether to stay put or run. Cold sweat dripped from his brow. It didn't much matter – either way he'd had it.

Imminent death brought a stark mental clarity. He was unemployed, had maxed out his credit cards and been written off as a crazed drug addict. Yet all these trivial problems were soluble given time – unlike this new crisis. For Hugo, time had run out.

He cast around wildly for an escape – the car parked 50 yards away might as well have been on the other side of the world. Even if he reached it, the keys wouldn't be in the ignition.

Claudia caught his eye – an understanding flashed between them. One gun couldn't shoot in two places at the same time – if they fled in opposite directions, one of them might make it out of range.

Hugo had it badly wrong. Overcoming the weakness in his legs, he bolted, zigzagging to confuse their assailant. A volley of shots rang out, but Claudia stood still, screaming horribly – the last sound Hugo would ever hear.

He'd got that wrong as well. He heard the final gunshot. And as the thick black velvet enveloped him, he realised how pointless it had all been.

73

When Hugo came round, Claudia was at his bedside. His confusion on waking morphed into a sensation of déjà vu – not another hangover, surely?

No, it couldn't be – he'd been shot, hadn't he? Was he dead? Was it possible that being dead might feel exactly the same as being alive?

'I was shot,' said Hugo. He searched under the bedclothes for signs of a wound, but found none. His left hand was heavily bandaged. Then he remembered that too – the pitchfork.

'Where was I hit?'

'You passed out,' said Claudia, in her matter-of-fact way.

'But I heard a shot.'

'You did.'

'Did he miss?'

Claudia took his hand and paused, as though about to deliver bad news.

'What?' asked Hugo, alarmed by her reticence. 'What?'

'Someone else shot him before he could get you.'

'Julia!' said Hugo, unable to contain his excitement. 'I knew she wouldn't stand by and let me be killed.'

'Oh Hugo, please – do me a favour,' groaned Claudia.

'Who?'

'Stephanie.'

Instantly Hugo's world was upended. The woman he adored had tried to kill him, while Stephanie, his nemesis, had saved his life. It defied all understanding.

'I guess she's hoping we'll keep our mouths shut about

the share dealings,' he said, unwilling to accept that Stephanie might have acted out of pure kindness.

'She's not hoping anything – she's dead.'

'The other guy shot her?'

'No – after she shot Mr Muscles, she took the gun to herself.'

Now Hugo's eyes had focused properly, he saw Claudia's clothes were spattered with blood – Stephanie's blood.

The news kicked him hard in the stomach. On the whole, he'd detested the woman, but that was before he understood her motivations. Now he felt sick at the waste of a life.

'Why?'

'Before she did it, she said "I'm sorry – I can't live with this."'

'With killing the bloke, or the insider trading?'

'I'm not sure, she didn't say.'

He knew the answer, all the same. She couldn't live with the shame of what she was compared to what she ought to have been – a conflict all too familiar to Hugo.

'Very sad,' he said with a sigh.

'Yes – Stephanie was a victim in all this,' said Claudia. 'Julia manipulated her like she did everyone else.'

'You said that in the cottage – what do you mean exactly?'

'Julia found out about Stephanie's insider dealing and had her over a barrel, running round at her bidding. And although you didn't see Pod at TM, he saw you and concluded that the net was closing in.'

'What terrible luck I ended up at TM.'

'Luck didn't have anything to do with it. Bill told me Julia was having an affair with Marcus – did you know?'

Hugo detected an unmistakeable note of glee in Claudia's voice.

'No – I had no idea.'

Though it did account for Marcus's in-depth knowledge of him.

'What's that got to do with TM?'

'Julia led Marcus up the garden path, and told him it was the insider dealers who'd killed Hubbard.'

'Why did she do that?'

'Mainly to divert attention from what was really happening, but it also gave her another lever over Stephanie. Stephanie must have been getting panicky as you homed into her relationship with TM. Pod would have told her you'd been there.'

'Was it Stephanie after all – the cocaine?'

Claudia shook her head.

'I don't think so. Julia was behind it, although she may have pretended she'd done it for Stephanie.'

'But why? Especially when I was going down a dead end?'

'Mainly to keep Stephanie in line, I think.'

'Are you totally sure it wasn't Stephanie?'

In a way, he wished it had been her. She'd atoned for the crime, saved his life and was no longer alive – this simple sequence of events would have made it easy for Hugo to achieve closure and move on.

'Oh really, Hugo,' said Claudia. 'Why do you have such a hard time accepting that Julia's the villain?'

Mainly because it galled him to have been no more than a bit-part actor in Julia's theatre of world domination – but for obvious reasons he wasn't going to confess that to Claudia.

'How is Julia?'

He hardly dared ask – wasn't even sure what answer he wanted.

'Hugo, this is seriously pissing me off. You have to get that woman out of your head – she is evil.'

'I just need to know whether she's all right.'

'She came round – she's been arrested.'

'What for?'

'What for? You must be joking. Kidnap, false imprisonment – isn't that enough?'

'What about murder and attempted murder?'

'They can't pin that on her – yet. She says she never meant to kill us, she only planned to keep us out of the way until the IDD sale went through. You know how plausible she is. Why, she'll probably send you a get well card.'

Claudia was joking, but now he thought about it Hugo wouldn't have been surprised at all.

'Her line is that she had to ensure a loucura substitute was made available to the world, and all her actions were driven by that goal.'

'So she's not evil – she simply did evil things for the greater good.'

'And that justifies trying to kill you? Honestly, Hugo, you must still be besotted with her.'

But he wasn't – not any more. He now recognised that the Julia he adored had existed only in his own head. The real Julia was a merciless bitch who'd pulled a gun on him and fired.

'One thing was weird,' said Claudia. 'I ran back to the cottage to get help and the police were already there.'

'Had someone got round to reporting you missing?'

'Well yes, Bill had. And bless him, he was a long way towards figuring out that Julia was behind it all. Although there was no way they could have found me – both those cottages were rented in a phony name.

'Did you ask the police how they got on to you?'

'They said they had an anonymous tip-off.'

'Stephanie?'

'Male.'

'Pod?'

'American.'

'That is odd,' Hugo agreed. 'Who do you think it was?'

344

'Search me. I'm only a journalist. I ask the questions, but I don't always get answers.'

A nurse came round.

'Ah, I see you're awake now.'

She looked at Claudia severely.

'I hope you haven't been tiring him out.'

'I'm fine,' Hugo protested. 'I only passed out.'

'Not surprising – you've behaved like a lunatic.'

She rearranged the sheets where Hugo had dislodged them.

'Sometimes lunatic behaviour is the only sane course of action.'

The nurse gave Hugo a puzzled look, before putting a thermometer into his mouth. In due course, his temperature was pronounced to be normal.

'By the way, the police have been asking to speak to you. Do you feel up to it?'

Hugo considered this. All in all, he wasn't too bad – miles better than the hangover after the speed dating, for example.

'I think so,' he said.

'Well, I'll send them along.'

'I say,' he said to the nurse as she turned to leave, 'I'm totally ravenous. I don't suppose there's any chance of a bacon sandwich?'

The nurse smiled at him indulgently.

'I'll see what I can do.'

Hugo returned home the next morning, filled with profound joy. He had never before appreciated the elegance of his flat, the mouth-watering taste of even simple food, the miracle of television and the internet, the melodious singing of the birds in the sky. Ah yes – the blueness of the sky next to the luxuriant green of the trees! How magnificent the whole world was. He even viewed his adventures with

345

Claudia through a nostalgic haze. Life was all the sweeter for having nearly been snatched away.

His rapture might, of course, have been attributable to the powerful painkillers he'd been popping like sweeties, but this never occurred to him.

When Bill Gordon called, Hugo greeted him as if he was a long lost friend.

'I'm ringing to apologise,' Bill said. 'I was very rude to you the other day, and there was no call for it.'

'No apology required,' said Hugo airily. 'In fact, I'm glad you've rung. I'd like your advice about Claudia.'

'I'm not sure I'm the best person.'

'But you are – you work with her every day. You must understand what makes her tick.'

'I have some insight,' said Bill. 'Though she's a complicated person.'

'You can say that again. She's a chip on her shoulder the size of Mount Everest. I mean, I find her very sexy and all that, and she can be fun to be with, but we never seem to go very long without falling out.'

'And you'd like me to tell you why?'

'Well, yes, I would. Maybe if I understood I'd be able to manage her more effectively. First of all she told me I was a racist, but I know that's just a little game she likes to play. But she still has it in for me because I'm a public school boy – that's the root of the problem. I guess it must be her working class background.'

Bill hooted at the very idea.

'Working class background my arse. Her father's a deputy headmaster and her mother's a GP.'

This revelation knocked Hugo sideways – much of the abuse Claudia had heaped upon him about his privileged background no longer added up at all.

'But I thought...'

'Has she never told you what her parents do?'

'No – we've never discussed it.'

'So because she's black, went to state school and sounds as if she's grown up on a sink estate, you made assumptions.'

Hugo now realised that was exactly what he'd done – perhaps he was a racist after all.

'Well yes,' he said. 'That's terrible, isn't it?'

He waited for a sharp rebuke from this liberal-minded journalist, but it never came.

'Ah well, you're not alone. Claudia joined the *Globe* on the diversity programme, which is supposed to be for people from deprived backgrounds. I didn't uncover the facts until much later.'

'So for a bunch of journalists, you didn't check the details very thoroughly.'

'No – we didn't,' said Bill, perhaps a touch defensively, 'though to be fair she didn't tell any lies either.'

'So how does that tie in with her being such a cow to me?'

'You think about it. She's ambitious – it eats her up. Not a day goes by when she doesn't feel guilty about pulling the wool over our eyes. And she'll never know whether she'd have been accepted on the regular recruitment programme.'

'I get it.' Hugo suddenly understood. 'The old boys' network isn't in it – this diversity lark is much more of a con. She projects her own guilt on to me.'

'That's it – you've got it. Mind you,' he added darkly, 'even I had you pegged as a bit of a Hooray Henry at first.'

Hugo might ordinarily have been offended by this, but nothing could puncture his drug-induced elation. Now he understood where Claudia was coming from, their relationship would be fine. Julia had been a fantasy – even if she'd been real, Hugo would have never lived up to her impossible standards. Claudia was human, beautiful but flawed – the same as him.

74

Claudia was proud of the way she'd held herself together. She'd found a new physical courage as the dramatic events at the cottage had unfolded. She'd provided a calm and coherent account of events to the police, and had written up a cracking article for the *Globe*. When she spoke to her parents, she was able to assure them with all sincerity that she was fine. With the aid of some magic pills from the doctor, she'd even managed a decent night's sleep. All in all, she was one feisty babe.

In the morning, she wasn't feeling quite so perky. Her disgusting clothes lay on the floor, spattered with fragments of Stephanie's brain. Without inspecting them too closely, she bundled them into a carrier bag and dumped them in the dustbin outside.

Bill had told her not to come into the office for a few days. Last night she'd assumed he'd said this out of kindness, now paranoia took over. He was plainly cooking up a case to get her fired. So why postpone the evil moment? She would go into the office in the afternoon – get it over with.

But first she'd promised to go and see Hugo.

In cruel contrast to her own downbeat state, Hugo was dangerously ebullient. He had at last unburdened himself to his parents, and was now revelling in a post-confessional euphoria. Not only had the Flemings been supportive to their pampered only son, they'd offered to bail him out.

'My parents would never do that,' said Claudia, with contempt.

But Hugo was flying far too high to pick up on her negativity.

'Christian Temple's been in touch,' he continued. 'They're prepared to reinstate me at Pearson Malone with immediate effect, including the promotion to Manager. And you know what – Eric Bailey, the head of the UK firm, actually called me to commend me for my courage in standing up for myself.'

My God, thought Claudia – the whole world has gone mad.

'My father's delighted, of course,' said Hugo.

'But what do you want? Why go back when you hated it there?'

It was depressing to discover that Hugo had learnt so little from the events of the past few weeks. Hugo didn't reply, but merely continued with his exhilarated monologue.

'Umbra have offered me the job back there as well. Marcus apologised for being a bit hasty when he fired me. He said I was the most creative analyst he'd ever seen.'

Claudia wasn't at all sure that Marcus's sort of creativity was a virtue.

'Jeez – surely you're not going back to work for that reptile? Surely that would be even worse than Pearson Malone?'

'Actually, I may not go back to either job.'

'So what then?'

'I told Father I could do with some space – you know, to find myself,' he said with a wistful smile. 'So I'm thinking of travelling in South America for a year. Father said he'd pay.'

Further cross-questioning revealed that Hugo's concept of travelling consisted of moving round from one five-star hotel to another.

'Isn't it fab?' he said, oblivious to Claudia's growing discomfort. 'And, I'd like to ask you whether you'd come

349

with me – I mean, you and me, we're pretty good together aren't we?'

Claudia would have laughed if she hadn't been fighting back the tears. Was Hugo suffering from total amnesia?

'I'm not sure that's such a great idea,' she said.

She couldn't delude herself any longer. This was the real Hugo – spoilt, undisciplined and selfish. The glimpses she'd caught of someone different had been an aberration.

'Oh, if it's a question of the money…' said Hugo dismissively.

'It's not a question of the money – it's a question of you. It's never going to work between us.'

'Well, obviously we've had our ups and downs, but that's all in the past now – and now we've ironed out our differences, we should be fine.'

'What do you mean "ironed out our differences"? There's a yawning unbridgeable chasm between us.'

'No, you're equally as bad as me – worse even! So we're quits!'

He sounded triumphant.

'I don't understand.'

'Well now, come on – you go on to me about my privileged background, but you're not exactly from the bottom of the pile yourself. A little bird tells me mummy's a GP and daddy's a deputy headmaster.'

Claudia felt as if she'd been hit in the chest with a sledgehammer.

'Who told you?' she asked, although she knew the answer.

Hugo tapped his nose, in an unconscious reprise of Marcus.

'Due diligence,' he said. 'Never underestimate it.'

She didn't have to ask in what way she was worse than him – she knew damned well.

'This diversity lark,' he pronounced, as if on cue, 'is much more of a con than the old boys' network. It's the

350

pot calling the kettle black, if you ask me, and you know it.'

He cackled at what he evidently regarded as a hilariously funny joke.

'Fuck you Hugo – I've nothing to be ashamed of. I'm diverse – end of. There's no way you and I are the same. No way would my parents bail me out if I was idiotic enough to get into a financial mess. I've made my own way in life – you're just a useless tosser.'

'But I rescued you from the cottage.'

'Only after you'd been lured there by your own stupidity. You know, I kept on giving you the benefit of the doubt, but there's no doubt now – you're a total cretin.'

'Give me an example of me being a cretin!' cried Hugo.

He had no clue at all. Back at the cottage, she hoped at last she'd seen some backbone in Hugo, but he'd slotted right back into his happy-go-lucky existence. This was the real Hugo. She steeled herself against the irrational temptation she still felt to forgive him for all his failings.

'Do I really have to spell it out?'

'Is this about Julia?'

'No – Julia was a symptom of the disease.'

'I don't understand...'

'No Hugo, you don't and you never will. Goodbye and don't try to call me – whatever it was we had, we're through.'

Claudia rushed past Charlie and out into the street. She ran until she was out of sight and sat on a wall and howled.

That night Claudia drank vodka from the bottle to wash down her pills. But no cocktail of drugs could do more than smooth the jagged edges of her despair. Sleep was out of the question. She lay in the dark, crying, shaking and jumping at the lights cast on the ceiling by passing cars. She hated Hugo, for the way he'd sucked her in with his looks and failed her in all other respects – how could she have been dense enough to fall for him? She hated Bill for having told Hugo about the diversity scam. Most of all, she hated herself.

Slowly, the crying subsided and an eerie calm descended over her. She'd been too upset to go into the office after seeing Hugo, but the next day she would take the initiative and confront Bill. Once she had suffered for her sins, she would begin to rebuild her life.

'Hi Goldilocks,' Bill said as she walked in. 'Didn't I tell you to take a few days off? Oh well – as you're here, can we have a quiet word?'

He indicated an empty meeting room.

'Go on,' she said as soon as he'd closed the door, 'fire me – it's no more than I deserve.'

'What's brought this on?'

'Isn't it obvious? I conned my way in here on the diversity programme, and I've cocked up seriously. Fire me – get it over with.'

She waited for what seemed an eternity, before Bill finally said, 'I've no intention of firing you. You've made some mistakes – haven't we all – but when all's said and done you've got the makings of a bloody fine journalist. Your piece on all this was superb.'

Understandably enough, the article entitled 'Dying for a cancer cure?' contained no allegations against BEP, but there was enough material there even so, what with journalists being kidnapped, dramatic shoot-outs and insider trading.

Claudia took no credit for it – her fingers had moved and the words had appeared on the computer screen by a magical process disconnected from her brain.

'You're not just saying that to be nice?'

'Goldilocks, have you ever known me say anything to be nice?'

'No, I guess not.'

'Come to think of it, have you ever known me to actively follow the *Globe*'s policies?'

Even though Claudia strove to contain herself, her eyes watered up. She shook her head.

'So I have to confess, Goldilocks – I would have hired you, diversity or not.'

'Honestly?'

'Yes, honestly – but you've been too blinkered to see it.'

Tears streamed down Claudia's cheeks.

'But you're always poking fun at me about it – I knew you'd found me out.'

'Surely you understood it was all a little joke between us?'

'I guess I did – most of the time.'

'But not today?'

Claudia couldn't answer. When she tried to speak, all her vocal cords produced was a strange hiccoughing noise.

'Look, go home and rest up. You've been through one hell of an experience, you can't bounce back to normal in an instant. And no one else expects you to either. For now, will you be kind to yourself? And please patch it up with Hugo – he's a decent lad.'

'It's too late for that,' said Claudia, barely able to get the words out. 'I've given him his marching orders. He's the most useless dude I ever met.'

'He's a lost soul,' said Bill. 'Though I'm sure he could find himself with you.'

'Well, he's not going to get the chance.' She collapsed in a paroxysm of sobbing.

Like most men, Bill wasn't much use with crying women. He remained silent and waited for the sobs to die down. For there was evidently something Claudia was attempting to say. Eventually, she got the words out, although they nearly choked her.

'I'm sorry,' she said, and fled from the room without looking back.

Brad scoffed his plate of steak and fried onion rings with delight. It would be the last decent food he'd get for a while, and he was determined to enjoy it.

'So all's well that ends well,' he said. The loucura papers had been safely shredded and Julia Fraser was out of action for the foreseeable future, if not permanently.

Frankly, Wayne didn't give much for her chances. There was too much resting on this whole loucura business – too many interested parties. Someone would take her out before long, exactly as they'd done with Morrison.

'How do you view all the press coverage across the pond, Brad?'

'There's no mention of BEP, and not a word's hit the press over here.'

'No, but the suggestion that there's some miracle cancer treatment...'

'So what? There are thousands of myths out there – no one takes a blind bit of notice. But just to make sure, in six months' time our oncology research team will have completed a new study on loucura's effectiveness. We shouldn't prejudge it, of course...'

'Of course,' said Wayne. But they both knew what the answer would be.

Denise, Hugo's old secretary at Pearson Malone, opened the parcel with some trepidation. She wasn't expecting a package, let alone one by Special Delivery.

Inside were eight Pearson Malone pads, twenty branded pencils, and a stapler. Strange – who would be sending her company stationery through the post?

Her question was answered by the discovery of a scruffy handwritten note.

'Found these – had a guilty conscience and decided to return them. Hope you're well. Rgds Hugo.'

She smiled to herself on spotting that the cost of postage was £21.65 – more than the stuff was worth.

Still, Stephanie had always said Hugo was an idiot.

75

Three months later

Like a recovering alcoholic who inexplicably craves a glass of wine, Claudia dialled Hugo's mobile number on a whim. He answered on the first ring.

'Hi – I was wondering when you'd call me.'

When – not if – cheeky monkey.

'You didn't think of calling me then?'

'I considered it – but you blew me out, remember, so I wasn't prepared to grovel.'

Claudia took a deep breath.

'I'm sorry,' she said.

'Now let's get this straight – you're not trying to subtly tell me you've been abducted by aliens or anything?'

'No – I'm apologising.'

'What for?'

'For everything – for crashing into your life and getting you involved in all that mess, for believing the worst of you, for bawling you out all the time.'

'You were right, though – I was useless, and deep down I knew it. You know, the worst part about being on the verge of death was realising precisely how pointless my life had been.'

'I didn't pick up those vibes last time we met.'

'Well no – I was as high as a kite on those blasted painkillers they gave me at the hospital. Didn't you notice?'

The possibility hadn't even occurred to her, she'd been so wrapped up in her own misery.

'I wasn't making any sense even to myself. And when I'd come back from Planet Euphoria, I realised my life had to change. So don't apologise – you've been a catalyst. I'm happy now. For the first time in my life I have a purpose.'

'So where are you – halfway down the Amazon in a dug-out canoe?'

Hugo laughed.

'No – I'm in London. I didn't go to South America.'

'So did you go back to Pearson Malone or Umbra?'

'Neither – I'm working as treasurer for a cancer research charity.'

This came as such a shock; Claudia hardly knew what to say. But she was unable to resist asking the obvious question.

'How do you manage financially? Although, if your parents have paid off your debts...'

'But they didn't,' Hugo protested.

'What? I thought they'd agreed to bail you out.'

'They did, but I realised I should sort out my own problems. So I turned in my car, moved into a cheaper place and came to an arrangement with my creditors. All the interest was frozen and everyone will get their money back in about five years.'

Claudia was flabbergasted at what she was hearing. Was this Hugo speaking, or an actor imitating Hugo's voice?

'Why did you do that?'

'As I said, things had to change, so I changed. I cut loose from the vicious snare of the BMW and Armani suits to do something worthwhile. So that's me – how are you?'

'Oh, I got a promotion. Apart from that, much the same.'

She couldn't begin to compete with Hugo's astonishing transformation.

'But what happened to the girl who never, ever apologises?'

'OK, you're right. I guess I've changed too. When I was staring down the barrel of that gun it struck me that all the times I'd avoided being in a one-down position didn't matter a damn. I've been making a point of apologising to lots of people, and it feels fantastic. Why, I even apologised to Bill about conning my way in on the diversity programme.'

'He can't have minded too much about that if he promoted you.'

'No, he didn't,' Claudia agreed, eager to put the shameful episode behind her.

'By the way,' said Hugo, 'did you know the FSA are sniffing round Marcus for insider dealing?'

'How do you know?'

'He rang me in a bit of a funk last week, telling me to keep quiet if they asked me any questions or he'd sue me for the ten grand signing-on fee.'

'Oh no – not that again. What would they hope to gain by talking to you? You worked there for less than a week.'

'Marcus took massive short positions in IDD shares shortly before Julia's arrest made the news. Naturally, the share price crashed and he made an obscene amount of money.'

Amazing – even when he'd been facing up to his girlfriend being a killer, Marcus's first instinct had been how to profit from the situation. The man really was a moral vacuum.

'And did you know Julia denied having any hand in Morrison's death?' asked Claudia.

'No. But who else would have done it?'

'Who can say – perhaps it really was an accident. Some witnesses said that just before he crashed, someone pulled a gun on him, but the car was so badly wrecked it was impossible to tell, and the autopsy found no bullets in Morrison.'

Claudia had her own suspicions – it was far too convenient for BEP that Morrison was out of the way. And if it hadn't been them, there was no shortage of other suspects.

'So unless they can pin it on Julia, we'll never be any the wiser,' said Hugo.

Claudia had said her piece – and now she had been freed to move on. Hugo had different ideas, though.

'Um, I don't suppose you fancy a drink sometime, catch up properly?'

Claudia vacillated – she had no desire to be hurt again, but it was only a drink after all. And this time Hugo really did seem to have changed...

'When did you have in mind?'

'Well sometime – no urgency – but since you mention it, I'm free for lunch.'

'So am I.'

'How about twelve-thirty at the boat on the river?'

She looked at her watch – it was twelve-fifteen already.

'Make it twelve-forty-five – I don't have a teleportation device, you know.'

Claudia had tried to speak quietly, but since her promotion she sat closer to Bill and he'd heard every word.

'Where do you think you're going young lady?' he asked, grinning broadly.

Claudia beamed back at him.

'I'm going to meet a contact,' she said.